The Lilbury Murder

James Quentin

For mum who always said I could do it.

Chapter 1

Cold, dark, and damper than a go-go dancer's underwear after a busy night. That was my first impression of my new home. It was a freezing cold winter's day with fog that seemed to seep into your bones and give you a chill, sending shivers down your spine.

I was huddling under an awning of the estate agents on the high street of the tiny village I was soon to move into. Had I known what horrors awaited me there I probably would have just turned around and gone back home.

This tiny village was a veritable city compared to the even tinier village I was actually moving to. Well, a cottage in a field near the miniscule village, near the tiny village.

The fog seemed to be getting worse instead of rolling back as the morning drew on. I checked my watch and saw that I was now on time. My propensity to always be early was an annoyance that I never managed to shake. I would have loved to be reckless and be three, four, or heavens, even five minutes late. Unfortunately, my mind wasn't wired that way, so here I was. Now twenty minutes into standing in ball-shrivellingly cold weather on a freezing January day waiting for a fucking estate agent.

I was standing under the awning of Bliss Real Estate: *Family run and owned and serving Compney Parva and surrounds since 1987*. Compney Parva being that aforementioned veritable city. It had something along the lines of three thousand residents and a Tesco. My God, it was a metropolis.

Despite being a Monday morning there wasn't a fucking soul about. There were, however, rows of unopened businesses along the streets. Apparently, Dorset didn't believe in nine to five. The estate agent who was supposed to be greeting me was now seven minutes late. Seven. Unacceptable.

There were no parking spaces on the high street, the nearest being several streets over at the base of the small hill the town was built on, by its minute train station. I'd had to walk up here and face the cold.

I looked up and down the deserted high street again and saw nothing except my inability to make good life decisions. It wasn't too late; I could hop back on the motorway and go back to London. Except I didn't have anywhere to live in London. Well, I did, but that was a complicated topic.

So, I was here in the heart of Middle England (Tory-lite, Lib Dem swing seat, I was pleased to say).

A rather rotund woman in the café across the road from the estate agents opened her door and peered out into the cold, sniffed disparagingly, and turned back to the warmth of her kitchen. She saw me just before she turned and gave me a deeply unpleasant look.

Great, I'd made an enemy by making their Britain in Bloom high street look untidy. I tried to avoid her beady eye. She left the window and then came back a minute later – eating a croissant.

It was 9.08am.

Still no sign of the estate agent. I made a plan to ring her at ten past. I fumbled through the stack of papers I had and looked for her number. She was a different estate agent to the one I'd dealt with for the past several weeks over email.

My correspondence had all been with someone called Dhapinder, who emailed me and spoke on the phone in precise, exact language with a flat, bland accent. She was awful but efficient (the only bearable sort of estate agent). It was yesterday when I was told I would be greeted by Sonia instead. Sonia left me a voicemail that was pure West Country – she signed off by calling me "my lover" and her email confirming our meeting place had "xx" at the end.

I watched my phone go from 9.10am to 9.11am. Perfect. She was late and I was in the right. As I dialled Sonia's number, I heard a car careering down the tiny, narrow high street and the hoot of a horn.

"Hiya!"

A woman I assumed was Sonia opened the door to her sporty little car that she had stopped in the middle of the street. She was thirty-ish, blonde, with a short bob, and was wearing a Topshop-style black-and-white dress. She had a furry collar on her coat, and she sat in the driver's seat as she changed her Uggs to a pair of heels.

"I'm Sonia. You must be Arden," she said as she bounded over to see me. I grimaced. So loud, so trashy. So very much not what I wanted to present myself as. "Get in and we'll drive out to see the place!"

I awkwardly wedged myself in her car and we sped off, the Rotund Woman in the café still staring at us.

Compney Parva's urban sprawl lasted about twenty seconds from the estate agents and soon we were in foggy open country (or at least what I thought might be countryside – it could have been Mars for all I could see of it). Sonia kept up a flow of conversation as we drove the five minutes to the next village.

"You've been talking to Dhapinder? My sister-in-law."

"Yes, I wondered about the connection," I replied. I was happy to see that family-owned wasn't a lie. They all had the surname Bliss.

"Yeah, she married my brother Trevor. Now that Dad's semi-retired, the three of us all muddle along running the place with a few others. It's not London, there's no million-pound penthouses around here, you see. Trevor specialises in farms and commercial land. Dhaps – that's Dhapinder – leads us in the residential sector."

As soon as she'd finished this explanation, she reached for the radio dial and turned it up as loud as possible.

"Have you been here before?" she asked as we took a corner ten miles an hour too fast. Sonia's car was overflowing with detritus, most of which seemed to be shoes and McDonald's wrappers. I never understood how skinny people managed to eat so much junk food and not put on any weight. If I so much as looked at a burger I couldn't fit into my jeans.

We continued to speed through the countryside as we spoke. "I've been a few times, for breaks to hotels and the like. But I know several people from around here who said it was beautiful and quiet," and more importantly one of the last few bastions of Southern England where house prices weren't a cause for heart attacks, just a mild stroke. "I thought I'd give it a go and see what was on offer."

"But you've never been to this place specifically?" Sonia seemed shocked. Maybe she was worried I'd hate it. Her commission was disappearing before her eyes.

"I lived in the countryside when I was young," I assured her. "I'm no stranger to cows and sheep. And after all those years in London, I'm happy to escape to anywhere."

She took this at face value. "Well, I'm born and bred. I'd never left Dorset until I was about thirteen."

I grimaced but did my best to hide it.

We reached a T-junction. Sonia pointed right. "Here we are: Lilbury, a prettier village you will not find."

I girded my loins. Lilbury was a little more than ten streets. A pub, some shops, a church and a few other businesses lined the B-road that passed through it.

On the east side of the village was a loop of small streets with whimsical names where most of the village was situated, including the church and a tiny primary school. All the streets were filled with gorgeous houses. On the west side were a couple of lanes containing ramshackle cottages, and one cul-de-sac of fifties council houses.

The village comprised around eight hundred souls, most of whom seemed to be well-to-do, community-minded and prolific breeders.

We drove through at a reduced speed, with Sonia staring at me rather than the road.

"My brother comes jogging out this way three times a week, usually all the way to the pub and back. He could probably give you a better rundown than I could, to be honest, but I'll try. That's the Co-op. They're lucky to have one, I don't know how it turns a profit. That's the pub, the Fox and Lamprey. Won loads of awards. Good food. Run by a Black lady," Sonia added absent-mindedly. No malice was meant here, I surmised. But in Dorset, this was still unusual enough to be commented on; a hotbed of diversity Lilbury was not.

Oh yes, rural mindsets. Quite.

When I'd been doing my stalking – I mean research… no, let's be honest, stalking – I'd ended up on the forum of the local parish council's website. Local denizens adding their two pennies' worth about bake sales and tombolas. There seemed to be a fairly diverse list of surnames in all the lists. Several Polish names in there, one or two that could have been French, and a handful of Spanish and Italian. No Asian names appeared, but Compney Parva seemed to be well stocked with Kumars and Singhs according to its website's gallery of local faces, and I even saw a photo of someone called Kamara in the caption underneath, meaning the landlady of the Fox and Lamprey wasn't the only Black person in the whole district.

We continued through Lilbury. I was already in love. The houses were chocolate box cottages of stone, and French windows with creeping hedges and ivy. The streets were narrow lanes with patches of well-tended flowerbeds along them. The church was handsome and imposing, with a graveyard, while the shops were practical but a tad quaint. The pub looked great, the primary school was open, and there was even a tea shop, which didn't look too twee.

For the first time in months, I breathed easily.

Sonia was looking at me still. My reaction made her smile. "Nice, innit?"

We drove on about a mile south-east of the village, doubling back on ourselves a little towards Compney, but the hill we were driving up only had one road crossing it diagonally. The hill was lacking trees, and I couldn't see far back into the fields but could see rustic stone walls.

"Sheep," Sonia pointed out helpfully as we passed some white fluffs staring at us through a gate.

"Here we are," she said suddenly, and pulled off to the side of the road into what I thought was a ditch but turned out to be a short driveway.

The car drove onto gravel, and we progressed forward about twenty metres into what was a small, but new, parking space, surrounded by a stone wall. Ahead of us on the rise of the hill was the place we'd come to see – hopefully, my new home.

In front of us was a small bank of stone to create a brake for the cars, then a winding path took us up to a small stone shed with a slightly haphazard roof, before arriving at the main event: a cottage straight out of a fairy tale.

It was all grey stone with a huge chimney in the middle of its black slate roof, with windows at each end of the triangular roof, one facing north, one south. On the ground floor were a few small windows, and a porch around the doorway, which was a huge solid wooden door. Around it, the hues were of blues and greys, but through the winter light, they had somehow been tinted to almost lavender.

The grey stone was shiny from overnight rain. The surrounding grass wasn't muddy but moist and lush.

It all looked heavenly.

"Shall we go inside?" Sonia asked, changing shoes yet again.

I bought it that day.

Chapter 2

"Does this mean we're, like, the new Brighton or something?" Nigella Pettoni asked as she looked up from her iPhone at the bar.

"No, not Brighton, Hay-on-Wye," the barman serving her a glass of Prosecco corrected as he sat it down in front of her. Nigella tapped her debit card on the card reader and pulled a face.

"So, he's an author? Big whoop," she continued. "We don't need authors; we need a bloody petrol station and a new teacher."

Odette Douglas fixed her glasses. "I think it's wonderful, Nigella. Don't you, Cytrine?"

Cytrine Hughes, the landlady of the Fox and Lamprey, wiggled her eyebrows (she was half listening). "As long as he likes a drink, I'll have anyone. We need some fresh blood," she said, gesturing to the room, at the same faces she'd been serving since she and her husband had taken over the pub fifteen years earlier.

Odette's husband, Tommy, appeared to be offended by this, but no one really gave a shit what Tommy thought.

The door to the pub opened again and another wave of cold air wafted through to the corner where the regulars sat. Odette shivered. She could be cold in the middle of summer. Or overheating and sunburned. Odette was never comfortable. Nigella wrapped her fur around her a little tighter.

A man in his mid-thirties walked towards them and gave Cytrine a kiss on the cheek as he stood at the bar. He was in a navy shirt under a jumper, and wore a pair of blue chinos and riding boots.

"Guy, the very man," Nigella said, extending her hand to his. He took it briefly and leant in for a kiss on the cheek.

"*Mwah, mwah.*" Nigella nudged him. "Have you heard about our new resident?" she asked.

Guy's handsome face was blank.

"Surely your aunt has told you something about him?"

Guy thought for a moment. "Oh, the writer chappie who's bought Stone Cottage on the hill?" he said. "Yes, another London luvvie bore come to serenade us with tales of how dull we all are before hopping it back to the city in three months."

"So Lady Georgina is not a fan?" Odette asked.

"No, Aunt Georgie can't wait to meet him." Guy sounded pained. "That was my personal opinion."

"I think he sounds cool. At least that's what Sonia said when she was in here the other night," drawled a voice from behind Guy and Nigella. The Fox and Lamprey's barmaid Arabella was behind them, her thin frame pushed forward to accentuate her cleavage. She was twenty-two and posh, and "seeking direction" in her life. She was a distant cousin – and we mean distant – of Guy's, so she thought of him as family. He thought of her as annoying.

Cytrine glared. "Arabella, there are glasses on that table that've been there for twenty minutes," she gently reminded her. "Just waiting for you to clear them."

The door from the kitchen opened and a handsome young man with brown hair came out into the bar; he wore the chequered trousers and white shirt of a chef. “Sunday roast. Trimmings?” he asked in a lilting accent.

“Over here, Pawel,” said a Scottish voice from the corner. Pawel carried the plate and assorted accoutrements over to the corner of the enclosed snug of the bar, where a red-haired man was sitting in the shadows.

“Thanks,” he said, and tucked into his food.

“What do you make of him, Simon?” Odette asked. There was silence except for the sound of the chewing of a Yorkshire pudding. “He should be fine,” he said in an Aberdonian accent.

“I’m sure that place’ll be full of broken bits and bobs he’ll need fixing up,” Odette continued. “Bob Jeffries, bless him, was hardly a house-proud sort. I doubt there’s been a lick of paint since the seventies.” Everyone rolled their eyes. Of course, Odette had read the house’s listing on the Bliss website, as well as going so far as to buy Sonia a glass of rosé the other night to pump her for more info. That’s when she’d found out the new owner was a successful novelist from London.

“Loaded, he is,” Sonia had said. She had no idea how much novelists got for their work, but it must be shitloads. Like J. K. Rowling or that woman who wrote *Fifty Shades of Grey*. “He didn’t even hesitate, handed over the deposit just like that. Never had such an easy transfer.”

“What’s he actually written?” Arabella had asked at this new information.

“Can’t say,” Sonia had told her through a mouthful of wine and crisps. “Anonymity is very important in our line of work. But we googled. He’s written a series of novels, all of which have been bestsellers.”

“What kind?” Odette had asked, her eyes boring into Sonia, her eyes especially buggish in her spectacles.

“Um, sort of sci-fi, fantasy, I think.”

Everyone groaned in disappointment.

"You never found out what he wrote?" Guy asked, back in the present.

"Nope, Sonia wouldn't say, but I've done some digging," Odette said. Nigella rolled her eyes and downed her fizz.

Guy drank his ale and kept his thoughts to himself.

"Spill," said John, from the other corner. John was a farmer who owned the land across the way from Stone Cottage. He would be the novelist's nearest neighbour. He wiped beer froth off his moustache and leant forward as Odette began to explain.

"Well, over the last ten years there's obviously been an explosion of fantasy and sci-fi series on the bestsellers list. So, I counted it down to British men, from 2005 onwards—"

"Why from then onwards?" Nigella asked. "He could've written it in the seventies and still be living off the profits."

"Why British?" Simon asked.

"Why a man?" Arabella asked. "He could've used a woman's name when writing."

"Because," Odette answered, vexed, "Sonia assured me he was a man who lived in this country and was around thirty-ish."

"They're only teasing," said Cytrine's husband, Arnie, from where he stood at the bar. He winked at her. Odette was unimpressed.

"Lady Georgina and I—" Guy started.

"are planning on inviting him over to our book club as soon as he's settled in," Odette followed on. "I even suggested we have it here, so he can meet people. Whenever anyone moves here, they always do as Guy says and scuttle off back to London after a few months. We all need to make an effort to make him feel welcome."

"And the fact that he's a famous, rich writer has nothing to do with this plan?" Guy asked.

"Of course not," Odette said.
There was a collective tut.

Chapter 3

A few weeks later, I was zipping – yup, the only word for it, zipping – down Dorset's highways and byways on the way to my new life.

My car, however, didn't agree with zipping. It was a hunk of shit, to be frank. Having spent my entire adult life in London, I was so out of practice at driving that it was a wonder I hadn't killed anyone yet.

It was just as well the only car I could afford was this geriatric piece of clapped-out rubbish. It was the sort of car that a Soviet factory worker would've been insulted to receive free of charge.

I changed down a gear and had to wait several moments for it to kick in, at which point the overworked engine and hydraulics sounded offended at going about their business.

Yes, I could afford something better. But you know what? That'd make me a car person. One of those men. Didn't they know how much these things depreciated?

When I'd first got the hare-brained idea of ditching the city and decamping out to the sticks, a car had been a necessity. Unfortunately, my publisher, Verity, was withholding royalty cheques from me as she was currently in "talks" with my American publisher about my remuneration, through her negotiating prowess at my new deal to publish the books over there.

Long story short: Verity was sitting on my money until she got what she wanted, and until then all I got when I asked for my hard-fought cash was a "Hang the fuck on, I'm doing this for you, you know. You should be grateful. Why are you so ungrateful? This is why they always leave you."

We eventually settled for a much higher profit share than we were originally offered – Verity promptly passed on all my money and took me out for a slap-up meal on the South Bank, where she treated me as if I was a whore on the make. "Have some truffles, some champers, some cheese – it's French."

She attempted to order frogs legs, but in her Swansea accent the waiter couldn't understand a word and so she reverted to buying more wine instead.

"Why the fuck are you moving to Upper Lowerbummingtonshire?" she said after the main, reverting to her favourite topic, namely, me and my private life. "He's said he's sorry. Move back in and cut his balls off if he does it again."

"I'm doing this for me. It's not for anyone else," I argued back. "It's like when you bought that God-awful nude painting, and your husband hated it, but you kept it up."

"He soon learnt to love it," she said, sucking the chocolate off a strawberry.

"And you'll soon learn to love that I have dared to leave the hallowed streets of Southwark for the fields of Dorset."

"The fuck I will. You'll be impossible to reach, and you'll never get drunk any more either, cos you'll always have to be running for the train from Waterloo. Face it, this was your own slow form of suicide. You're going to do nothing out there but stare at the four walls of the bloody ugly cottage you spent all your money on and resent everyone and everything. The internet's rubbish out there as well. Once you've tried to rub one out on dial-up speed you'll be fleeing back to London."

I fumbled with my lobster and sighed. "Well, maybe you're right. But I've got to try. I can't do this anymore." I gestured out over London. "I am exhausted. I need a break. That ugly cottage is what I need."

I should've known.

Chapter 4

A few minutes later I pulled up outside my cottage just in time to see the removal truck coming up the road behind me. I quickly made my way towards and unlocked the door. The cottage was empty and clean – the debris of the late Mr Jeffries now gone.

The removal men were two plump gentlemen in their forties with bad backs and expanding waistlines. They were as efficient as they were attractive, so I ended up doing a lot of the work myself. I paid them as soon as the truck was empty and sent them on their way.

My zipping down here had been the best option. I was now present and correct. I put down the last of the boxes in the small hallway, leaned upwards and stretched. My back was killing me, and I was knackered. I hadn't been sleeping well for the past few weeks, but now I could relax.

All I owned – my entire worldly goods – was in this house. If I had a worldly belonging and it wasn't in this house, then I didn't care for it.

I looked at the sea of boxes and furniture and nearly cried. It wasn't even 11am, but I decided to give myself a break. I mean, I had been up since before dawn.

I took another turn around my house and touched everything. I couldn't believe it was mine. I owned the bricks and mortar. I owned every nook and cranny. The garden, the driveway, the grass, the sheds and outbuildings that clustered around the house. It was all mine (well, twenty per cent was mine, the rest was my bank's for another twenty-five years). The cottage was old and creaked. Wood and stone surrounded me. There were signs of how long it had been lived in all around: the blackened hearth in the living room, the ancient cooker (which I would have to replace), the walls, the temperamental bathroom taps, the ancient shower (oh God, the list of things I had to replace was bowel-looseningly long).

It all spoke of a dozen generations of happiness and homeliness within these four walls.

And at the end of the day, wasn't that what I wanted? I felt the familiar sense of dread and a knot in my stomach begin to form, and instead of letting it overtake me, as I had so often these last few months, I ignored it.

"Right," I said aloud to myself, feeling empowered, content, all the good emotions, basically. "I need food."

I picked up my car keys and made my way over to the small, battered green shell that vaguely resembled a car. Money had been so tight during the move that I hadn't really had the available readies to buy anything in preparation for it. Now my finances were all on track again, and I was back to having the most obscene amount of money, which no single man in their early thirties should have without some sort of physical graft to have earned it, but there you are. Life ain't fair. I worked for it and now it was mine. Although the black hole of financial despair I'd been looking at for the last few months was, admittedly, probably a sign that maybe I should have put off buying my first property for just a while longer. But what kind of sad sack listens to those emotions?

I hopped in my car, enjoying a surprisingly mild, sunny February day and drove down to my new home in the village. The Co-op and the small village shop were at opposite ends of the high street. I made a vow that I would pay the exorbitant prices in the village shop to support local businesses once I was more settled but right now I had an empty kitchen to stock. I'd do a proper shop in the half-decent-sized Tesco in Compney tomorrow, but the village would do for today.

There was a small lay-by in the road where parking spaces for four or five cars had been allowed outside of the very plain whitewashed brick building that housed the Co-op. It was a bright Monday morning, and the village was deserted. Surely there should be someone around?

I walked into the Co-op. Aside from the Asian man on the checkout, who didn't even look at me, I was the only person in the shop. I grabbed a basket from a stack of them. Above them was a local community noticeboard advertising singing lessons and firewood for sale. A piece of pink A4 announced that there were five kittens available free to a good home. The bottom of the sheet comprised serrated strips of paper with three strips left that hadn't been taken. I put out my hand to grab one – I'd always wanted a cat but had never had space for one having spent the past few years living in a fourth-floor flat. I thought better of it though – maybe leave it a few weeks, or at least until I actually had food. I set about buying lots of boil in the bag rice and anything else that could be kept until I eventually got a fridge. It was supposed to arrive today, but it was now looking like it would be several more days.

I wandered down one of the three aisles and began looking for milk powder and fizzy water – you know, healthy things one must have without refrigeration.

I could buy meat and a few other things, as I'd discovered an old chest freezer in the shed outside. Sonia had assured me it was totally usable and not at all likely to give me lead poisoning from being forty years old. "Mr Jeffries was a keen shooter, you see. No pheasant was safe."

I was pontificating about what I could live on until my fridge was delivered when I saw a face out of the corner of my eyes. Ah-ha! Another customer.

The face disappeared. It had been a low face, close to the ground. Hopefully a child, otherwise Lilbury had a terrible wasting disease epidemic. I made my way down to the end of the aisle and tentatively stepped out into the little corridor running along the back of the shop where the ready meals and frozen pizzas were stocked, which let's face it, was the part of the shop I was really after.

I saw a small child staring at me. "MUM!" it yelled all of a sudden.

"Jesus." I recoiled away from it and almost turned to run in case the little brat accused me of being a paedophile or something. It would not be a great start to my new life if from day one I was considered the new kiddy fiddler in town.

"Mother," the kid continued, in an annoying cut-glass accent. "Mother, do come, the man is here." The child had a patch over one eye, presumably to help cure a lazy eye, and was dressed in a cardigan and a floral dress with cute little socks and shoes. She had long brown hair with a butterfly clip in it.

It was all rather cute, but something about the child made me want to swat it with a rolled-up newspaper. I'm not normally like that; I have no problem with children usually, but this one looked like she was itching to piss me off.

A woman came scuttling down the aisle towards us. She stopped to arrange her handbag and glasses. "Oh, Tatiana, there you are." She pronounced the girl's name "Tuh-tahhhhn-yaaar".

"Good, you found him, how wonderful," she said, holding out a hand. "I'm Odette Douglas, and this is Tahtaaaanya."

I took her hand. "Arden."

"Aaardeen," she replied, saying my name as if it was magical. "Arden Forrest, I presume?"

"Yup, that's me."

"See." The little girl gripped her mother's ankle-length skirt. "See, I told you it was him. You were convinced it was George R. R. Martin."

"I'm sorry?" I asked as Odette blushed.

She took a second to collect herself and shushed the demon-child. "Oh, I must explain," she began. "We've all been very excited since lovely Sonia told us all we were going to have a novelist in our midst. I mean, I've tried my hand at writing a bit myself, you see. I was a feature writer for *Hound and Country* magazine in my twenties, before I settled down, but never a novelist" – she pronounced it noh-vahh-list - "and since I became a mother, all I do is chase after this rapscallion.

"We were all so excited, we may have researched you a little." She was suppressing a giggle as she said this. She waved her finger at me, as if I was being hard to find, as if I didn't have a fucking website that Verity insisted that I update and go on book tours where American housewives tried to tongue kiss me at airport bookshops. "We're so happy the old cottage will get a new owner. Especially someone so young and so famous."

I studied Odette. She was wearing glasses that made her eyes appear insect-like and a green suede cardigan over a white chunky knit turtleneck and a matching ankle-length skirt. She had court shoes under the skirt and was clutching a purse.

She'd called me young, but I had the distinct feeling our ages were separated by months not years.

"I'm a big fan of your novels. So vital and full of life."

“They’re sci-fi,” I corrected her. “That’s surprising, most of my readers are teenagers.”

“Oh, I’ve read them all,” Odette said. “I loved *Freya’s Cross to Bear*. The ending was so well done.”

“You mean the ending where she dies by throwing herself into a wormhole at the school prom to avoid the town being swallowed by an army of zombie aliens?” I didn’t believe she’d ever heard of my novels before two days ago and had definitely never read one.

“Brilliance. Such imagination. Such a searing account of how women in our society are always sacrificed for the greater good.”

“You know she comes back to life two books later, right?”

“Er, of course, masterfully done. You know, we often see that newcomers have trouble integrating into our village, especially if they haven’t got children to break the ice at school.” I noticed she was looking at my basket with its awful food in it. “We were all determined that you should be thrust into village life as soon as possible.”

Thrust?

“Lady Frobisher would love to hold a reading of one of your novels at our monthly book club,” Odette said. She seemed very excited.

“Lady Frobisher?”

“Lady Georgina Frobisher MBE. She lives at Honningtons. Last year her nephew moved back down from London where he was a stockbroker in Mayfair to take over running the place. She has a huge deal to do with the social events in the village.”

She hadn’t been on the parish council’s website when I’d done my stalking. Clearly not a digital eagle. “What’s her MBE for?”

Odette smiled. “Services to horticulture. Floral horticulture. The horticultural arts.”

Flower arranging, in other words.

I was determined to be nice. "Well, that sounds lovely. I'd be honoured." I even smiled down at Tatiana.

"Wonderful!" Odette clasped my arm and squealed at Tatiana. "Give me your mobile number, email, and Twitter handle, and we'll see it's arranged at the first opportunity. I was thinking Friday?"

"Um, sure, okay."

"Oh, wonderful," she said again. "That way you young folk can all pop over to the Fox and Lamprey for a quick pint afterwards. Oh, it's a lovely pub. My husband Tommy is always there. Incorrigible," she added in a faux-gruff tone.

If Thomas was ever allowed out of his wife's sights for longer than five minutes, I'd eat my Calvin Kleins.

Odette made her excuses, and together she and Tatiana bustled away like Victorian spinsters out of the shop and on their way.

I moved on to the ready meals.

Chapter 5

A few hours later, I was sitting there eating a huge sandwich overfilled with all the dry ingredients I could find in the shop when there was a knock at the door of my cottage. I swallowed my huge chunk of food, tried to brush the crumbs off my jumper, and made for the door.

At the front door was a tall, lanky man with black hair and a thick moustache, wearing a wax Barbour jacket and galoshes.

"How d'you do?" he said, holding out a hand the size of a frying pan. "John Parkinson. I own the farm that surrounds your cottage."

"Hello, wonderful to meet you." (Odette was having an effect on me).

"I popped in to see if there's anything we can get you while you sort the place out. My wife and I had to move out of our house last year on account of a fire, so we've had recent experience with the horrors of having only a campfire to cook food on and no television."

"Oh, yes, it's quite a challenge. I haven't got a fridge yet…"

John wasn't listening. From under his jacket he pulled out the biggest chunk of meat I'd ever seen. "Yeah, this is a welcome present for you. Fresh lamb. All raised and fed organically. Even a vegan couldn't fault the ethical treatment of this here sheep." He tapped the meat and thrust it into my arms. He slapped down a bit of paper on it as well. "That's our number – any problems, only happy to help." He looked at the cottage. "God knows you'll need it. Old Jeffries never really looked after the place, sadly."

The lamb seemed to be dripping. "Anyway, have a pleasant day. We'll see you on Friday at the book club. The wife's gone and downloaded all your books on her Kindle, so she's looking forward to it."

Well, if nothing, moving seemed to have done wonders for my sales. "Look forward to it," I said. "Did, err, Odette Douglas, tell you about it?"

"Course, she was all over the village Twitter about it earlier."

"Oh, um, okay. Listen, your land – is it all right if I walk across it from time to time? Now that I'm in the countryside, I'd like to actually experience it."

He nodded and turned to point. "All that," he said, gesturing to the field across the road, "is mine, all the way down to the back of the village, right until you get to the pond out the back of the Fox and Lamprey. A little path goes down the side of the pub and leads you straight on to the high road. We get loads of ramblers in the summer. Might be a bit muddy at the moment, but you're welcome to use it." With that, he waved goodbye and walked off down my path, whistling before crossing the road and vaulting the fence back into the fields and making his way over the grass to wherever his half-burnt down farmhouse was.

I deposited the dead sheep in the freezer and pinned the Parkinsons' number to my otherwise empty noticeboard before making tracks to find my phone. I'd been so good at ignoring it recently I half the time forgot where it was – to Verity's anger: TWEET, YOU COCKHEAD was an almost daily message from her. Social media presence = book sales, you twat. You know, that sort of thing.

I looked up my Twitter and found I had 117 notifications. As I'd checked it under forty-eight hours before, and frankly wasn't that popular on there, or anywhere else, this was above average. I clicked on the little bell and saw that @OdetteJDouglas86 had retweeted @LilburyVillageLife:

> @ArdenForrest is @LilburyVillageLife's newest resident! Come one, come all to Honningtons on Friday, 16 Feb @ 7pm for an exclusive reading of his latest novel just for his neighbours!

The tweet had been retweeted twenty-five times. There was a later addendum:

> Only for residents of @LilburyVillageLife, a refusal often offends so don't even try :) :) :).

"Fuck's sake." The Twitter feed then went on to Odette having an argument with a woman I recognised from a book signing who was based in Bristol, wondering why she couldn't attend too.

Odette quickly became shrill and terse on the thread and had blocked the woman.

Someone else called @GellaPettoniXO had been spamming Odette with LOLs! and @OdetteJDouglas86 is a numpty who couldn't organise a piss-up in a brewery.

I did my best for Verity's social media strategy and liked the two original messages pertaining to it being a locals-only meeting.

I had two missed calls and a voicemail. I ignored those and went back to my sandwich.

Chapter 6

The next day was a success story from start to finish, or at least to 11am, when the broadband engineer arrived and gave the gift of Wi-Fi. He stared at the cottage in horror. "There's never been an internet connection here before?" he asked.

"Not to my knowledge."

He got his drill out and held it menacingly. "Right, brace yourself. This could get messy."

An hour later, Colin and I were the best of buds, and after much swearing, crying and cajoling, I had a working internet connection that would be the envy of the neighbourhood.

"Sorry about the wall," he said as we shared a manly hug on his way back to his van.

"It's fine, I didn't need it anyway," I replied.

As he pulled away, a young guy in a much bigger van appeared, and in an almost comical West Country accent asked me if I was "the bloke what needed a fridge?"

Another hour later, both sweating with exertion, my newer new best friend, Wayne, left. I danced around the house at the joy of being amongst the world of the living once again. I opened my fridge and closed it again several times, taking in the majesty of modern technology. It had a light and a door. Truly, the wonders of human ingenuity knew no boundaries.

Now, if only there was food in it.

I grabbed my phone and car keys and set out in my pencil case of a car to Compney Parva, happily yelling out the words of songs on the radio as I went along. I drove the length of Hill Lane (my road) instead of heading back through Lilbury so I could explore the other end a little bit. It was more of the same, rolling green fields and painfully idyllic-looking villages. I got stuck behind two tractors and everything was wonderful. Sure, the bed I had was ancient, but I had a fridge and Netflix. I was happy as Larry. Sure, I hadn't slept a wink the previous night as the deep crushing sense of my own impending death and mortality weighed down on me, but I could do Verity's bidding on Twitter once more and answer email. Sure, the boiler was one frost away from packing up completely, but now I could research Freya's trip to the jungles of Borneo to save her boyfriend from having to become a slave to the cannibal Martian overlord.

First things first, I made it to Compney Parva and parked at the same car park on the bottom of the high street as I had when I met Sonia, before heading to Argos, where I bought, well, everything. Everything I had been put off buying for my entire twenties and the first portion of my thirties. Towels, a dish rack, a toaster, a kettle, knives, a chopping board, a blender, a telly the size of a small country, a DVD player (did people still have those? Don't care, I had a royalties cheque burning a hole in my bank account and I was going to power the British economy through to economic growth if it killed me).

More shopping continued. I hit every shop on the high street, buying sheets, bedding, clothes, candles, frying pans. I got quotes from the kitchen and bathroom shop on the corner. I walked past Bliss Real Estate and shuddered but kept smiling. It was around 3pm by the time I was done. The village was spent of every piece of retail stock it had. All mine. All weighing down my beloved green Beetle or winging its way to me over the next few days, with every deliveryman in the south-west of England currently plotting the GPS coordinates for Stone Cottage, Hill Lane, Lilbury.

I made my way back to my car, loaded down with consumerism, and drove around the town's tiny bypass system to Tesco on the other side. As I did, I sang along to the radio again. Some talentless twit was singing about love and heartbreak, but I didn't care, I was crooning out a song of unfiltered joy. It was a mild February day – some light clouds, soon spring would be springing, I had a perfect house to call my own, a successful career which kept me in international travel, and the ability to buy out an entire Argos without a second thought. Life was good.

At that moment my phone started ringing. I looked over. If it was someone worth answering, I'd pull over. I was only a hundred metres or so from the turn-off to the Tesco car park. I'd let it go to voicemail and ring Verity back. I didn't know if it was Verity, but no one else ever rang me.

I brushed my jacket off from where it was covering the name. The screen was vibrating with the name OLLIE written across it, the little profile picture for him smiling at me from under his name. And that's when I did something stupid.

As I said, I hadn't driven for so long I was still getting into the swing of it. There had been several stalls on the way to Lilbury the other day, I'd had trouble merging onto the motorway leaving London, and my ability with roundabouts was a solid six out of ten at best. I was hazy on the indicating rules.

However, even I know that looking at your phone and then swerving into oncoming traffic, before realising what you were doing and trying to brake, and then swerving back, was a no-no. Which is what I'd just done. Luckily, the road was clear, but the driver who'd been coming out of Tesco honked his horn at me. He was some rich prick in a Porsche. He wound down his window and a good-looking face yelled several obscenities at me.

"You idiot, you could've killed us both!"

"I-I'm very sorry," I stuttered.

I was burning up with shame and self-loathing, but not with a sufficient amount to not notice that the other driver was very handsome. He fired off a few more choice phrases at me – his plummy accent making "Fucking wanker" sound quite nice, to be honest – before screeching off. I started the car up again with shaking hands and slowly pulled into the car park, which mercifully was mostly empty, and sat in a spot farthest from the shop's entrance and rested my head on the wheel.

I was going to have a minute to quietly reflect (feel sorry for myself) but was interrupted by a noisy thumping.

I looked up and had to refrain from screaming in fright. Sonia was looking through the window grinning maniacally and waving so hard it looked as though her hand was about to come flying off. I wound down the window.

"Hello, my lover, just seen you almost have a to-do with a posh bloke in a nice car. Honestly, learn to drive, you!" She reached in and tugged on my cheek. Without any sort of invite, she opened my car door and bundled me out. "Come on, I'm skiving off work to get some posh things in for dinner. I'm cooking for my boyfriend tonight."

I was dragged into the shop like a petulant child. People in this part of the world don't understand a modern man's need for privacy while supermarket shopping. Sonia kept up a rapid-fire analysis of everything that had happened.

"He'll be some Hooray Henry down from London. We get loads of them around here. All over the show. Can't stand 'em myself, but they spend, so we don't mind 'em. London must be awful if that's who lives there." She looked to me for confirmation.

"Actually, London's so varied that posh people are a tiny proportion. Unless you're in Chelsea obviously, or somewhere like that, but I didn't used to live in Chelsea."

Sonia was squeezing a tomato. "Sounds nice. So how're you settling in?"

"Oh, everyone's being very nice."

Sonia looped her arm through mine. "*Prarrper* gent, you are," she carried on. We eviscerated the aisles, Sonia hoovering up each and every morsel of food. Her boyfriend, it turned out, was a new acquisition. "My Darren, he's lovely, he works at the gym."

"He's a personal trainer?"

Sonia nodded with glee and my loins quivered with jealousy. *Lucky sket*, I thought. She took her phone out to show me a picture. His Insta profile was handed to me. A tattooed Joey Essex lookalike stared gormlessly back at me. I swiped through his photos. In only one of them was he wearing a shirt. He appeared to be as thick as a rock, with two misspelt words in his bio caption. My loins returned to their normal state as they concluded that he was not my type. "What a charmer," I said, and returned Sonia's iPhone.

"We went to school together, but he never used to look like that," she explained. "He's hench now."

I thought about explaining how he'd got so hench – maybe the acne on his shoulders was a giveaway – but thought Sonia would figure it out on her own.

We made our way into a new aisle and bumped straight into a man. "I'm terribly sorry," I said.

"Oh, hi, Ade," Sonia said, and settled in for a chat.

"All right, Bliss," said the handsome man she addressed. He was about our age and wearing a police officer's uniform.

"Arden, this is PC Adebayo Oduwole, a friend of my brother's from school."

"Pleasure," he said, holding out a hand.

"Nice to meet you," I responded.

"Arden's a posh writer from London," Sonia told him. "He'll probably put you in a book or something seeing as you're one of the local coppers."

"Is that right?" Ade seemed fascinated, though more so by Sonia's low-cut top. "What kind of things do you write about?" he asked Sonia's left tit.

"Um, sci-fi, fantasy. I have a book out at the moment called *The Chimera*."

Ade shot me a look. "Wait. You're Arden… you're Arden Forrest? Holy shit, man! I love your books." His face lit up. "I pre-ordered *The Chimera* and read it in one day. Aw, man, I can't believe you killed off the only Black guy in your books in that one!"

"It was necessary for the plot!" I said, reddening.

"I'm just fucking with you," he said, grinning. "I love that your main character is a strong Black woman though. Even though it'd be totally Freya, I'd have a crack at it if I had the chance. Why is she still dating that emo loser?"

That emo loser was the easiest character for me to write and the one I loosely based on my own experiences. "Umm, oh, he'll get killed off soon enough!"

"Man, I'd love to buy you a pint sometime and pick your brains about the books. I'm a huge fan."

"Thanks. It means a lot to meet people who actually like them. And, yeah, I'd love to tell you all about them."

"Yeah, I'll message you on Twitter. I follow you on there already." And with that, Ade was gone, giving us a thumbs up as he went, his police helmet under the crook of his arm. Sonia watched him depart. "I hate to see him go, but God, I love to watch him leave," she said, and cocked her head.

My loins remained unstirred. I thought of Ollie. I looked down at my phone; it was flashing with yet another voicemail.

"I see you're doing a reading at the Lilbury Book Club on Friday?" Sonia asked as she pulled a baguette out of her trolley and started eating it.

"Yeah, you should come," I said without thinking, and remembered it was supposedly for Lilburians only.

Sonia's face showed her joy at being asked. "I've always wanted to go to that fancy book club. Ever since Dhapinder sold one of the houses in the village last year to this widow who moved down from Oxford. She joined and they all sat around getting pissed and eating cake. Sounded amazing."

"How did you know I was doing a reading?"

"I follow Lady Frobisher's nephew on Twitter. He's gorgeous. He retweeted it."

I shrugged. "Never met him."

"According to his retweets he'll be there. I can't wait to finally be introduced. He's the only fit bloke around here - apart from my Darren," she said remembering herself. "Sometimes you see him on the road with a bunch of his posh mates all riding horses."

"He sounds awful." He sounded like Ollie.

Sonia munched on her bread. "Dhapinder said he was once in Casa Roma, which is this nice Italian restaurant in Sittingston (a village about another four miles further on. Twice the size of Compney Parva. They had a Sainsbury's and a Waitrose.). It's really posh in there. I can't afford it, but it was Dhaps and Trevor's anniversary, so they were putting it on the credit card. Anyway, her nephew was at the next table with some big-titted blonde slag, and they were guffawing and having a great old time. The four of them all got talking for a bit too. Apparently, he's not nearly as much of a dick as Trevor thought he'd be."

I was now acutely worried I'd made a faux pas. Sonia seemed to be treating this as a way of climbing up the social ladder. One did not invite estate agents to ladies that lunch-style country sets. Fuck, she'd make a fool of herself, and I'd get the blame. Then again, she was the only person who'd made an effort to talk to me and it would be nice to rock up to Honningtons with a friend I'd made off my own back. Well, admittedly, one who'd handed over the keys to my house.

Later that night, I sat in my bedroom shivering under the blankets. I turned my phone over and over in my hand. I wanted to listen to the messages but couldn't bring myself to do it.

Ollie's voice was sitting there, electronically stored and waiting for me. His voice. His perfect enunciation. I pressed the button and began to listen to the messages. My hand drifted from where I rested it on my chest down to my sweatpants, but I chastised myself and yanked it back up. I rested my head under it. Both hands accounted for.

"Hi," Ollie's plummy vowels came through the phone, "it's me, again. I've heard through the grapevine that you've moved to Devon or Dorset, or somewhere. Why? What's happening with you? Please answer me. Please let me apologise. Come home, I miss you."

The real kicker was the next part: "We're all worried about you."

Chapter 7

The following day was a storm of deliveries as all my purchases began to make their way to me. I opened the door about ten times throughout the morning, in various states of undress, as it rang every time I attempted to get dressed or take a shower. After living off crisps and sandwiches for the past few months, I was not exactly feeling at my most body confident, so a grumpy delivery man catching me with just my jocks on was not a great start to the day.

It was late afternoon before I was even done with setting everything up and could think about starting on my day. I put away the vacuum cleaner I'd purchased, and washed and put away all my new plates, glasses, and cutlery. I had the essentials to live on now, but there was still so much to do – and most of it hideously expensive.

On that track, I sat down at my laptop and began to bash out a few pages of the latest Chimera novel. I took out my folder of notes and scribbles on plots, spread it out over the floor, and spent the next hour happily finalising the book's plotting. I kept on changing who was going to die in chapter thirteen when the aliens blew up the holiday resort the teenagers were living in with their families after their world was invaded. I was thinking that maybe my telepath's wayward younger brother would be good cannon fodder. She'd not had much to do in the last book, so a convenient plot device death should give me the leverage to a storyline where she seduces an alien leader for information.

I finished up and noticed it was pitch-black outside. I put a pizza in my ancient oven and ate it over my notes, debating whether the telepath needed to sleep with Freya's boyfriend too in her grief. The written word: the possibilities are endless.

Out of the pile of my notes and other debris was the *Guardian*'s review of my latest book. Two out of five they gave it. They also said it was "merely perfunctory. Forrest has perfected wringing the plot of all depth until it is a sallow corpse of storytelling, merely seeking to go forth and conquer the next chapter with no feeling or wants, except a zombie-esque need to fulfil a page count."

I mean… that is just rude. Accurate, but rude. I did feel like emailing the reviewer to tell her "actually, love, I did write a searing drama about man's quest for betterment and progress in a materialistic world, but after the fortieth rejection letter, I wrote this teenage dross instead, and guess what? It's sold a million copies. Now excuse me while I sop up my tears with twenty-pound notes."

Verity said I wasn't allowed to send it.

After I'd made an emergency trip to the toilet to combat the inability of my oven to completely cook a pepperoni pizza all the way through, I decided to go through with a goal I'd set myself the previous evening when I'd been reduced to watching *EastEnders*: I went down the pub.

I did my hair and changed out of sweatpants into jeans and hopped in the car. It wasn't far, but it was pitch-black, and I wanted an easy escape route. It was a mild night, which nagged at my guilt all the way through the village.

You're going to get fat if you keep driving everywhere like this, I told myself.

I parked up outside the Fox and Lamprey and looked at it. It seemed an okay-ish level of busy for a Wednesday in February.

I took a deep breath and stepped out. Around the side, where I presumed was the tradesmen's entrance, I could see the light from a cigarette as someone was having a smoking break. I got closer from where I'd parked, around to the door, and was within a metre or two of whoever it was. I hesitated. Going to a pub by myself? How desperate was I? What if everyone stopped and looked at me? What if no one did? Oh God. All of a sudden, *EastEnders* seemed okay.

The man a few metres away from me having a smoke got out his phone and made a call. It got my attention as he said something in Polish. He made more comments, in a few words I understood, before saying goodbye and putting his phone back in his pocket. The door at the back of the pub opened and there was a wash of light. Someone made a comment as they came out. I heard the rustle of a rubbish bag and the sound of bottles on the ground. A barmaid clattered around to the Polish bloke in her heels and said something quietly that I couldn't catch. He lit another cigarette for her, and she breathed in deeply. I was fascinated by this little interaction.

I couldn't really see either of them, just their legs through the trellis of rose bushes that separated the back of the pub from the path I'd walked up from the end of the car park. There was a small beer garden out the back that bordered a large pond that then went onto John's farm. I was separated from them by a five-foot-high brick wall with the alleyway where they were smoking.

I saw the girl's bare legs stand on tippy toes in front of the chequered trousers of the Polish guy. I presumed they were kissing. Nothing wrong with that. Couples work together everywhere. What happened next was a little more surprising. The chequered trousers dropped, and he was suddenly starkers from his white top (*a chef's jacket*, I thought) down, with the trousers around mid-thigh and his big old wang hanging out, which the girl in heels was now having a right old time with. She had it in both hands and sidled up beside him, so they were both facing the brick wall. I barely had time to register what was happening before the Polish chef gave a strangled cry and his massive willy shot out a wad of thick globular cum all over the brick wall and down the crazy paving.

He lifted his trousers back up and the light breeze carried one of the few distinct things I'd heard them say in the five minutes I'd been standing there: "Thanks, I needed that."

"Well, you seemed stressed," said the girl in a posh accent. My eyebrow went up.

They flicked their fags into the gutter and there was a clatter of the girl's heels as they both departed back inside.

Well, golly, I thought. I knew it had been far, far too long since another human had made any sort of efforts to have fun with my private parts, but even I had never got a handy in the car park. I had to admire her technique though; she managed to do it in record time. He must've been waiting there at full mast before she even arrived.

As my slight voyeuristic thrill abated (don't worry, I felt dirty), my own enforced celibacy came back with a miserable reminder. I sighed and tried to think of other things as I made my way to the entrance. Nothing proved enough to replace the sight of the man's shapely thighs and buckling knees as he orgasmed.

A few seconds later, I reached the pub door and pushed it open to reveal a warm and inviting space. There were maybe fifteen or twenty people inside, most of whom were couples sitting around tables eating. There was a small group of late-middle-aged men in the corner guffawing. A teenage boy was sitting morosely in the other corner, on his phone, one leg up on the seat, in that flexible way teenagers do that can't be at all comfortable.

Two older women were sitting at the table nearest the bar, gossiping over their Prosecco, and both were turned out in very nice clothes. One moved her Mulberry bag out of the way as I made my way past her. She flashed me a smile.

At the bar was a middle-aged Black lady. I presumed it was the landlady Sonia had mentioned. She wore a weave, which was styled with heavy blonde highlights, cut short in an altar-boy style. She was small with a massive chest covered in a tight black top, and wore a skirt and heavy black boots. Gold bangles and necklaces blinded me in the pub's dim light.

She greeted me in a heavy accent that I couldn't quite pinpoint but sounded French. "Hello, come in, make yourself at home." She asked after my drink of choice and, in a burst of originality, I looked for the nearest continental lager on tap and she handed it to me.

"Passing?" she asked, stopping to chat. The staff at the bar near Ollie's flat never did this. Then again, they would've charged three times for a pint of Peroni what she'd just asked me for.

"No, just moved into Hill Lane," I answered, knowing what would probably come next.

The landlady's face lit up (I was having a wonderful effect on these people). "Oh, you must be Mr Forrest? Lovely to meet you. I'm Cytrine Hughes."

She pronounced her name to almost sound like Citroen, the car, with a phlegmy intake of breath on the T.

"My husband and I won't be able to make it to your book reading on Friday, we'll be here obviously. But we're so hoping you'll pop by afterwards, and we can then get to know you a bit better."

"Thank you for the invite, I'd love to," I replied, while wondering if that were true.

The door to the pub opened and a man walked in. He came up to the bar not a metre or so from me and greeted Cytrine.

"Simon, this is Mr Forrest, who Odette was talking about." God, please tell me they weren't friends with the interminable @OdetteJDouglas86.

I looked over at the man. My age, probably a little older. Red hair, cut short, around five eleven, maybe six foot. A burly man. He took off his coat and revealed a T-shirt that was straining around biceps and pectorals. The sight of the chef's buckling knees came into my head again.

"Simon Anson," he said in a Scottish accent.

"Arden Forrest," I answered, my own voice sounding high and squeaky comparatively.

"Just moved here then?" he asked.

"On Monday."

He nodded and turned to face me. He was handsome, but not a pretty man. He had blue eyes and pale skin, with light ginger stubble and some chest hair popping out over the collar of the plain blue T-shirt he wore. He had freckle-covered tanned forearms and, sadly, stubby, thick hands.

He gave me a grin. "Aye, Odette's been quite excited about you coming to our party." His accent was like water over a rock in a stream. Mellow but with elements of something altogether edgier to it.

Ollie's Scottish accent had been drilled out of him at good schools and Durham University, by City lawyers and Clapham dinner parties. Only when he was well and truly plastered and had been awake for twenty-four hours straight did he start to sound like someone who'd been born in Dumfries.

"Simon's our local Mr Fix-It," Cytrine said to me, beaming like a proud mother. Simon gave a tiny flicker of an eye roll.

"Anything you need around the house needs fixing, Simon's your man."

I did a double take. "Really, cos I have a million things around my cottage that are either broken or about to break."

Cytrine laughed. "Not surprised there." The door behind her opened and a man came walking out holding a plate of wedges. "Potato wedges?" he asked her. He pronounced them "vedges".

Cytrine passed him a little basket with cutlery and condiments and pointed at the men in the corner.

"Evening, Pawel," Simon said.

"Hey, man, how was Scotland?" Pawel asked as he made his way around the bar. He came out to stand in the pub proper. He was wearing chequered trousers and the same black Converse trainers the man getting some wrist action outside had been.

"It gets colder every time," Simon answered.

Pawel was in his twenties, not an ugly guy but not handsome either. He obviously had a great muscular body under his chef's whites, but his chin was slightly weak and covered by a goatee. He had light brown hair. He wasn't a model, but you'd still do him if nothing else was on offer.

Simon and Pawel continued to chat for a moment before Pawel dropped off the food in the corner. On his way back he returned to us.

"Pavz, this is that writer we've all been hearing about," Cytrine said to him. We shook hands. He had a firm handshake. Big hands.

Pawel was clearly not much of a reader, and this meant little to him. He made a few pleasantries and made his way back to the kitchen. "Pawel's the best chef this place has ever had," Simon told me conspiratorially, though in earshot of Cytrine.

She slapped his arm. "Oi, do you know how hard it is to get good staff around here? Any that do make it last one year before they go off to work in one of Rick Stein's bloody restaurants or some vegan café in Bristol."

She turned to me. "We've had some terrible chefs. But Pawel's the best. He's a member of the family." I'm sure he felt like that too after the area voted Leave by two to one.

A middle-aged man came out from the back of the pub, tucking in his shirt. "This is my husband, Arnie," Cytrine told me, as the tall, rangy man came up behind her and put his arm around her shoulders. "Arnie, this is the writer that Odette was talking about." I tried to ignore the irritation that Odette seemed to be the one everyone associated me with. We shook hands.

"Arden writes sci-fi novels," Simon told him. I blushed. I was tempted to ask if he read them as well.

Pawel came out again holding another plate of *vedges*. "Here you are," he said, placing them between Simon and me. "Welcome to Lilbury."

I finished my pint and took a seat with my wedges. Simon offered to join me. We chatted amiably and I asked how long he'd been in the village. "About three years. Since I left the army."

"Army?" The handyman was an ex-squaddie. My thoughts on the military were enough for a book on their own. Not my cup of tea.

"Well, military intelligence." He gave me a very steady look.

"Oh," was my answer.

A young blonde barmaid wearing a tight grey dress came shimmying over to us and took our drinks. "Another, Si?" she asked in a croaky voice that drawled itself over the floor and took up residence in a comfy armchair by the fire. She was painfully posh; you could tell it by the large scarf she wore around her neck and her bird's nest of blonde locks that she continuously pushed back off her forehead. The sort of girls that moved to London after university en masse and I had done my best to avoid.

"Yah?" she said looking to us for confirmation; she gave Simon a cheeky grin. "I'll bring them over," she answered when he gave confirmation that we'd like another. She watched Cytrine at the bar and then turned back to us. "God, I need a fag," she said with a laugh. She dawdled off. It was then, as I watched her carry our pint glasses away, I clicked that her small hands were those that had been so deft around Pawel's cock half an hour earlier. *Quite the hotbed, the Fox and Lamprey*, I thought to myself.

"Posh girl doing her time in the trenches," Simon said by way of explanation. Though he hardly sounded like he came from a council estate himself, to be fair. Those of us who'd had free school dinners knew what we all looked like.

"She's a bimbo, but a harmless one."

I was dying to ask him more about being a spy, but I had a feeling he was merely sitting with me out of politeness, not any sort of desire to be my friend.

"Though Cytrine can't stand her," I added without thinking. Simon gave me a look, but I'd seen the evil glare the landlady had sent the girl when she'd come out to gather the empties.

Simon nodded in acquiescence. "Arabella's not exactly the most diligent member of staff. She only keeps her job because she's one of Lady Frobisher's goddaughters. Cytrine's no easy pushover, but even she knows when to pick her battles."

Arabella returned with our drinks and flirted with Simon some more. *Straight men*, I thought. Anything with a pair of tits and a tight skirt. I wondered exactly how many of the men who came in and out of this pub were getting the Arabella special.

Simon caught my expression. "Don't worry, Pawel won't mind if you have a crack. I think they're over. Or just not exclusive. Or on a break. I'm not quite sure. They're complicated."

"Her and Pawel?"

"Aye, they announced it by very publicly snogging each other's face off on Bonfire Night."

I pretended the thought of Arabella's lady garden interested me. Apparently, Cytrine was less than immersed in thoughts of it though – we all turned to hear a small scuffle. Arabella was receiving a telling off from Cytrine in hushed, furious whispers. Cytrine's finger was wagging in front of Arabella's face.

Arabella was doing the posh girl put-upon look of jaw stuck out and arms folded high, tiny, thin waist angled outwards. A louche air. Tears blinked back.

"This is your final warning," Cytrine whispered so loudly the entire pub heard. The women at the table next to us with the Prosecco and expensive handbags both stopped discussing their gardens to listen too. The teenage boy peered around the corner to get a look.

Arnie noticed it first. He stopped polishing a glass and made his way to the women. "Cy…" He gestured with a flick of an eyebrow that everyone was looking at her and Arabella.

Cytrine was clearly upset. "Oh, you're as bad," she said in a voice clogged with emotion, and fled into the back rooms. Arabella stood momentarily stunned, tears bubbling in the corner of her eyes. Arnie cajoled her into the back as well. "Go count the linen. Stay out of her way, eh?" He clearly looked uncomfortable.

He turned back to the customers as Arabella made a sulky exit to do her work. "Sorry about that, everyone."

I turned to Simon. "Is it always like that with them?"

Simon was staring at the doorway through which both Cytrine and Arabella had departed. As he did, Pawel came out of the kitchen and walked up to Arnie and the pair began their own conversation in a heated whisper. Arnie held up his hands at the chef and walked off, seemingly done with the conversation. Pawel remained standing in the same spot, his cheeks puffed out in frustration. He threw a tea towel on the bar and stormed back out to the kitchen, swinging the door violently behind him.

"Well, really," the woman with the Mulberry handbag said to her companion, "what a drama. This place used to be so much nicer before they let her take over the reins."

Simon turned to look at me and his response was a weary one. "There've been problems of late. Arabella's not the best at keeping her personal and work lives separate."

I briefly considered wondering if I should tell him about what I'd seen in the car park, but this is Britain and there are limits. Arabella made another appearance into the main pub and told Arnie she was going outside to collect the signs. He gave her a smile and a brief clap on the shoulder. Simon poured the rest of his pint down his gullet. "It's been nice chatting with you. See you on Friday." He held out a hand but didn't look at me. His eyes followed Arabella as she made her way through the pub, her blocked nose and blotchy eyes showing it was obvious she'd been crying.

I shook his hand and Simon departed after her, quicker than I thought was polite. I finished my own pint, gave a wave of thanks to Arnie and made my way out to the car park.

Arnie's actions made me wonder if he was the innocent father figure cum employer he appeared. He wouldn't be the first pub landlord to taste the goods. I passed the same spot where an hour earlier Arabella and Pawel had been having their lover's embrace – ahem – and saw it was empty. Across on the other side of the car park, I saw Simon leaning on a gate, having a cigarette with Arabella. She was crying. He pulled her close to him and embraced her. She sank into his arms. Oh. Simon was one of the men receiving the special too.

Chapter 8

The next morning, I slept late, and then had a champion's breakfast before embarking out to a bespoke carpentry shop in Salisbury that made bed frames to order. Googling things last night after coming home from the pub seemed a productive way to spend my evening rather than dwelling on the strange atmosphere I'd experienced.

They weren't cheap, but that morning Verity had announced we were being translated into the Slavic languages market. "Polish, Czech, Russian. All a go-go," she shrieked down the phone at 7am. I wondered if she was like this for all her clients. I know I was one of dozens. I didn't mind her lack of fidelity as I think I was the only one that made her any money.

"And you're doing an interview for a magazine in Canada on Tuesday next week, and I want you at a literary festival in Edinburgh in May." I groaned but added them to my calendar.

So, with the soon-to-be zlotys and roubles burning a hole in my pocket, I made my way twenty miles to the east and walked around the showroom until I found a suitably audacious bed frame that looked like it could take a whole rugby team sleeping on it without so much as a creak.

"Sturdy," said the salesman showing me around. "We'll deliver the version with your specifics in about six to eight weeks." I sighed. Bespoke took time, and I wanted my money to open doors for me. I just wanted it now.

I returned to Lilbury in the early afternoon, right on time to get stuck behind a platoon of horses, all striking beasts in their finery, with posh twats on top of them dressed up in livery with those little helmets on. I kept the green kitten purring several metres back and maintained my distance. We were approaching a tight corner, so I had no way of passing them without knowing what was coming, the left side of the road being overhung by thick foliage from a small copse. I held my speed as low as I could and rolled my eyes at the typical countryside scene.

The woman at the back of the little procession gave me a sanctimonious smile as I observed all legal road rules – as if I was just such a darling and this was her road but wasn't I just being a doll by not frightening the horses and sending her off into a ditch.

Every single person on the horses appeared to be blonde.

At that moment, I heard the roar of a motorcycle, and round the corner, at a truly dangerous speed, came a machine that took the bend in the road too close, and then had to over-correct to avoid the horses, who were on the inside.

The bike zoomed past and off down the road, but all the horses began to jump and buckle, their whinnies adding to the general mayhem. I watched with horror as the rider in front was thrown from her horse and landed with a thump on the tiny grass verge on the roadside.

"Holy shit." I stopped my car and whacked on the hazard lights. I grabbed my phone in case we needed an ambulance and made my way over to the mess of animal and woman.

She was surrounded by two other riders, while the remaining two members of their group tried to keep all five horses under control.

"Is she okay? Does she need an ambulance?" I called as I got closer.

"You fool!" said the woman who was aiding her companion. "Look what you've done!"

"Margo, shush, this was the driver. He didn't do anything wrong. It was the motorcyclist. This guy was keeping his distance and did exactly what he should've done!" her male fellow rider answered. "Yes, please ring an ambulance."

He flashed me a scared smile. "Stay with her please, I need to go help Henrietta and James." The man jumped up from where he held the fallen rider's hand to go help the other two (who I noticed now were both teenagers) to gather their horses under control.

The woman on the ground was breathing quickly and lying at an odd angle, and she had tears in her eyes. Frankly, to me, she looked like she was milking it a bit. But I'd never been thrown from a horse. There was a boy at my school who got kicked off his horse and then took a hoof to the head. He was permanently weird afterwards. So maybe she had a point.

"Stay still, Eleanor," Margo said.

I dialled 999 as I crouched down beside Eleanor.

"Hello… yes… ambulance."

The operator on the other end calmly asked for my location. I struggled and looked to Margo – another strike against me, not knowing my location. "St Candida's Lane, Lilbury, just outside Honningtons farm."

I relayed this down the phone. "A rider has been thrown from her horse," I explained when the operator asked for details.

"Don't move her; don't allow her to stand. It's very important she stays completely still," she told me. *Oh God,* I thought, *she's probably broken her neck.*

I passed this information on to Margo, who looked at me with such disdain my dick shrivelled up inside me. She was about fifty and looked like the sort of woman who'd been riding since she was in the womb. Of course, she knew what to do.

I looked to Eleanor; she was in her twenties, a very pretty girl, when not lying on the muddy ground with tears streaming down her face. She had large brown eyes and an awful lot of mascara on for a horse ride in the country. I took back my previous statement that all five were blonde. Eleanor had light brown hair.

The ambulance operator said they'd be there in six to eight minutes and repeated that Eleanor wasn't to move. The man who'd originally been with Eleanor had managed to wrangle all the horses, and the two teenagers were now keeping the five beasts under control and had taken them to the field across the road. There was a gate around twenty metres further down the lane where they had found a way into the field.

He jogged back to us. "Ellie, how're you?" he asked in yet another public school voice. Truly, the diversity of Lilbury's socio-economic backgrounds was startling.

"Don't talk," Margo scolded as Eleanor tried to say something. The man blushed at his silly mistake. He clapped me on the shoulder. "Thanks for helping out, mate. Really do appreciate it." He pronounced really as "rahhhllly".

The sound of an approaching car from the direction the motorcyclist had come from stopped any response. The man jumped up and waved his arms around to flag the driver down. The car, a Nissan Qashqai – housewife's vehicle of choice – came to a stop, and my least favourite person got out. Odette Douglas was aflutter at the sight before her and made no attempt to hide her horror. "Oh my God. Will she die?" she asked the man.

"No," he said with mild annoyance, as she clutched his arms and stared in fear at the scene.

"I was on my way to pick up Tatiana from school." She clocked me. "Oh, hello, Arden. Is this your doing?" She went all jolly and tucked a lock of hair behind her ear. As if Eleanor's possible paralysis was an awfully funny way of me making an introduction to village life.

"No, this chap's been terrific, pulled over and jumped straight into action," the man said of me. It was my turn to go bright red.

Odette put a hand to her heart. "Oh, Arden, you are fitting in nicely." She spun around to the man, who I was now staring at with open admiration – he'd practically called me a hero – "Guy, this is that writer chappie, Arden Forrest, the one you're having over tomorrow night. Arden, this is Guy Frobisher, Lady Georgina's nephew."

"Not really the place—" Guy snapped at Odette at the start of a reprimand, but gave in before he had started and instead leant forward to shake my hand. "Nice to meet you."

"Likewise."

"And I'm Margo Cadbury-Smythe," said Margo with an evil glint in her eye. Of course she was. Why wouldn't she be called that?

Before I could make any more remarks to get me in more trouble with Margo or reveal any other scrapes with death to give Odette a tingly feeling in her knickers, the sirens of the ambulance approached, and we all breathed a sigh of relief. The emergency vehicle pulled up and plodded along to Eleanor. A slightly overweight woman of about thirty-five and a zitty teenage boy who was clearly in the early stages of terminal homosexuality came to help her. Both spoke as if they, like Sonia, thought a day outside Dorset was an exotic voyage.

The male paramedic made absolutely no attempt to hide his appreciation of Guy. Guy didn't help by removing his helmet and sweeping back his blonde hair from his head. He wasn't exceptionally handsome, but neither was he anything to ignore. He had a sharp jawline and small mouth, with perfectly straight teeth and a stern, though very English face (i.e. forgettable). He was in his thirties and around six foot tall. Ten years ago, he'd have been devastatingly handsome, I reckon. Ten years from now, he'd be a middle-aged Tory.

He was sweating profusely and removed his jacket to show his shirt underneath. As the paramedics did their checks on Eleanor and moved her to a stretcher, he made moves to join her in the ambulance, but Margo insisted she go instead. "I'm practically her second mother!" she squawked. Eleanor was clearly hoping Guy would go with her. I stared at both of them before noticing that Guy's shirt was stuck to his chest with sweat. Oh. Oh, I can see why she wanted Guy to go with her. I didn't know abs could be that prominent through material that was only a little damp.

We watched as Margo lumbered up into the ambulance. The gay kid gave Guy another puppy dog glance and got in too and the ambulance drove off.

Odette was still in shock. "I should tweet about this… oh…" She whacked me playfully in the chest but caught me by surprise and nearly winded me. "Totes appreciate the retweet @ArdenForrest. The village account has gained forty new followers. All fans of yours."

"I'm sorry about that." My fans are a tad obsessive and don't like going outdoors, but Odette seemed happy. "Just makes tomorrow night all the more exclusive. Must go get Tatiana. She gets into a frightful strop if I'm late. Until then, ciao."

Guy made his leave too. He stuck his hand out to shake mine again as Odette drove her gas-guzzler past us.

"Thanks for the help, and I look forward to buying you a drink tomorrow."

"What about the motorcyclist?" I asked, coming back to reality.

"I'm sure the police will be in touch with Eleanor at the hospital. There's been a spate of these over the past year or so. Hopefully they catch the bastard. I know I'd like to get my hands on him."

Something about his voice seemed funny. "Do you know who it was?"

He looked at me very squarely. "Oh, yes. He's well known. And once I track him down his life won't be worth living."

And with that, he made to leave too and went off to the teens in the field to gather their horses.

I got back in my car and drove home. It was only 4pm but I was exhausted. Lilbury was seething, I tell you. Seething.

Chapter 9

I woke up on Friday and decided that, yeah, maybe I should sort my shit out for this bloody reading I was doing tonight.

For a start, I had to decide what to read. I had five published novels, all over three hundred pages long.

And all mostly dealing with alien invasions, magical spells, and unrequited teenage love. I tried to find two passages in the same book that gave the readers blood, guts and action (if that's what Odette wanted) or that gave them some more grounded emotional moments (in case she wanted me to be a bit more literary). At all previous readings, I usually did the guts one first, and then, if needed, the emotional bit after.

But most of my readings were for fans, not for the Lilbury Book Club.

I skimmed through and found the perfect two passages in my second novel. In one, my heroine Mariah escapes near-certain death at the hands of an invisible alien demigod in an A&E department with a madcap car chase scene afterwards. In the other, Mariah's best frenemy, Freya, laments her childhood crush being drained of life and turned into a zombie cannibal with some subtle emotional touches that *Sci-Fi Monthly* called "an immersive experience in the maelstrom of being sixteen and saving the world."

Verity rang. "You're doing your reading tonight, yes? Get pictures. Pose. Social media. Looks good, etc. And wear a clean shirt. Ironed, preferably."

"Thanks, I was going to." (The ironed part not so much.)

"How's it going down there, anyway?" I could hear her munching on her Pret a Manger chicken and falafel salad in the background.

I told her about the night in the Fox and Lamprey and then my heroics of the day before.

"Jesus, it's worse than *The Archers*."

I started to respond but was cut off. "Hang on, I'm googling Guy Frobisher. Phwoarr. Okay, I give my complete approval to ride his horse all night long, if ya know what I mean."

Verity was married to an investment banker and lived in a penthouse in Canary Wharf. Her husband was lovely, and they did ultramarathons together. Her views on *phwoar* were of no interest to me.

"Remember, you need to come up to London next week for a planning meeting for book number six. We're all very excited, yada yada," she said. Verity had never read anything I'd written since book number one. She had an intern for that.

"Don't worry. Progress is coming along nicely. It should be ready for publication by summer."

We rung off and I decided to put some truth to my statement on timeframes and spent the morning making a start. The book was planned so I had little room for manoeuvring, just write, write, write. The words came out easily, as they always did. The plot was so overconstructed that the sheer number of events I had to have characters react to meant that I was at page fifty before I'd even had a cup of tea. I scrolled back up through it and did my best to correct all the typos and grammatical errors. Sub-editors were a thing of the past, and Verity's intern was useless.

I was re-reading the scene where Freya is forced to undergo a healing process to vanquish the alien demon that had possessed her since her reincarnation in book four when my phone rang.

"Hi, Arden, Odette Douglas here." Her tone was breathy, as if she'd been sitting on the washing machine. I wondered what she actually did all day.

"I wanted to remind you that it's all kicking off around seven, so if you could get there for a quarter to, that would be wonderful. There'll be drinks and nibbles, and please choose a passage no longer than five minutes in total. Lady Frobisher struggles with her attention."

"Of course. Just one thing, where am I actually going?"

Odette laughed gaily down the phone as if something hilarious had happened. "You have no idea where to go, oh, how hilarious. Yes, Honningtons is at the far east side of the village. It's the Frobisher family's seat. Not a manor. Not a house. Somewhere in between. Just walk up the driveway and come to the main door. I'll be there at six to supervise Lady Frobisher's maid, Ewa."

Poor Ewa.

So, at six o'clock, I looked at myself in my newly purchased mirror. I was wearing a check shirt in dark blue, black trousers, black dress shoes and my black trench coat, a woolly scarf over it. I carried the book in one hand. I didn't want to drive as it seemed the undercurrent was that these things were booziness personified. I was clean-shaven, my shoes were polished, my hair was washed, my shirt was ironed, my teeth were flossed. I'd had a light dinner so I could nibble at the nibbles without having to stuff my face as the night wore on. I could have a few glasses of wine, eat one or two sausage rolls, and try not make a fool of myself by getting sloshed or eating like a pig in Lady Frobisher's refined presence.

I had a huge pile of my novels, so I didn't mind leaving this copy behind. My spare room upstairs was full of them. If only I could drop them off in random places and not have to schlep them around with me every time I moved to a new house.

I left with plenty of time to walk the mile and a half or so to get to Lady Frobisher's not mansion-mansion. The night was clear and mild for the time of year. Still, by the time I came down the hill to Lilbury I was cold and glad to be amongst the houses and, hopefully, nearly there. I had thought about walking down the path John had described, but decided it was best to stick to the road, lest I get lost in the dark, though his way seemed quicker. I turned past the pub and walked down "The Wedge", the main street westwards, and as I passed the largest of the houses, a tall, dark-haired woman in a fantastic fur coat walked out of the door and joined the footpath a few steps ahead of me.

It was obvious we were both heading to the same place, but I was far too awkward to introduce myself. So instead I fell back a few metres to quell any ideas she might have that I may be a rapist and followed her through the darker stretches of the village where the houses were more spaced out. Eventually we reached the imposing walls and gate of Honningtons. There was a sign: open for tours in the summer, apparently.

Honningtons was a Regency-era country house of red brick, with three tall rectangular windows on each side of its two main floors, with a large entranceway in the middle. Several attic windows shone out over the stone parapet that bordered its roof. The lights along the driveway were all twinkling as I began to walk up the noisy gravel.

"Who are you?" the woman I'd been following called back. She was about halfway up the drive, having not stopped to admire the house as I did.

“Me? I’m Arden Forrest.” I hurried up to her, holding out my hand.

“Our new writer in residence?” She sounded less than impressed. I got closer to her. She was around forty, maybe older, with luxurious black hair coming down in curls to her mid-forearm, bright red lipstick, and as previously mentioned, a magnificently decadent-looking fur coat on over a slinky black dress. She had walked up the country lane in heels. She regarded me for a second before she took my hand.

“Nigella Pettoni.”

Without another word, she turned and continued to walk on. I made to follow her. I struggled to think of something to say and eventually settled on asking her if she was a regular at the book club meetings, but before I could pose my question, the sound of a car behind pushed us to either side of the driveway.

I groaned as Sonia’s sporty little racer zoomed up the drive and parked outside the front of Lady Frobisher’s Grade II listed manse.

“Good God, what is that?” Nigella asked.

“Hiya!” Sonia called, stepping out. She was wearing high-heeled boots and a red wrap-style dress, with a dramatic black necklace of triangular glass shapes over her décolletage. I had the distinct feeling she’d had a fake tan and her highlights done.

I went forward and she kissed me on the cheek. I looked back to Nigella, but the older woman gave Sonia a disparaging look and moved inside. “Am I late?” Sonia asked, sounding unsure.

“No, early, I think.”

We bustled inside out of the cold and up to the door, where a maid – surely, Ewa – was taking Nigella’s voluminous furs. Underneath she was an hourglass-shaped woman who exuded confidence. Even with my predilections, I had to admit her voluptuous bosoms were quite something.

Ewa took my coat too, and in Polish-accented English, she (much older than I thought) invited us through to the room.

Odette greeted us with rapturous glee. She received a perfunctory *mwah mwah* from Nigella and then complete disdain. The black-haired diva dived on the Prosecco.

Odette turned to us, and her face fell. "You brought a friend?" She gave Sonia a not so subtle look.

"Yes, Sonia has been so helpful with helping me settle in I thought it only fair I bring her along to see what she's inflicted on you all." What I really wanted to say was, "Don't tempt me to walk out and go home, bitch. My sweatpants are ready and waiting."

I heard Nigella snort. She came over to Odette and gave her an evil grin. "Makes sense to me." Then she shovelled a mini quiche into her gob.

Odette glared at Nigella. The pair of them were not each other's biggest fans by the looks of things. In fact, I had the distinct feeling Nigella had arrived fifteen minutes early to rile Odette.

The doorbell rang again, and we heard Ewa greeting more guests. Odette munificently gestured for us to take a seat in what I presumed was some sort of drawing room – a large room at the front of the house with two tall windows, and a fireplace on the opposite wall (already lit and roaring, the whole room was boiling) and filled with chairs and sofas of all styles and ages, all encircling a lovely table filled with cakes and sweets. Another table off to the side was a coffee station cum bar. Booze was not in short supply.

Odette handed Sonia and I each a glass as we sat. The guest Ewa let in joined us.

"The Great Tommy Two Hands," Nigella called out. She beckoned him over and embraced him lovingly. I tried not to smirk as she purposely angled herself to emphasise that he was several inches shorter than her.

Odette pulled him away. "Arden, this is my husband, Thomas." She ignored Sonia.

Thomas was late thirties and highly respectable looking; a short, but good-looking man with a brown knit jumper on and light beige chinos with brown brogues. Thick, black-rimmed glasses framed his fashionably bearded face. If he'd been taller than five foot seven I'd have given Odette serious props for marrying a hottie. But as, when I stood to greet him, he came up to my nose, I felt less inclined. It's not as if I'm a giant; I'm five foot ten on a good day, and all the women so far tonight were wearing heels, so I was the second shortest person in the room. But I was taller than him. It's a dog-eat-dog world.

Thomas introduced himself. Another plummy accent.

"And what do you do?" I asked.

"I'm a GP in Sittingston," he said. He was receiving glares from Odette, who apparently was pleased by no one.

He excused himself and went over to his wife, who forgot to lower her voice as he neared. "You're late. Where have you been?"

"Trouble in paradise," Nigella said to Sonia and me, but more than loud enough for the Douglases to hear. Odette reddened. "The mind boggles what Tommy's been up to," Nigella continued, wagging a finger. "Naughty boy, Dr Tommy."

Nigella's voice was achingly luxurious. I doubt she had ever spent more than five minutes watching ITV in her life. She wouldn't even be aware of Channel 5's existence.

"And what do you do?" I asked Nigella. Apparently, this question was my new social crux, as I felt a little sorry for Odette, who was severely flustered.

"Me? Housewife extraordinaire. I have twins: Luca and Archie. They're my world."

"They're already away at prep school," Tommy said in acidic tones.

I didn't know how old children had to be to go to prep school – was it a posh primary school? Or high school? I went to a comprehensive.

"That Italian blood of their father's… they'll be shaving by Christmas," Tommy continued, as he poured himself a whisky. Nigella gave him a stare of death.

"Before I became a mother, I worked in politics doing PR," she continued, turning to me. "Then I was a director at a think tank. But before any of that, I was a producer at a TV production company. We specialised in only the goriest of police procedurals, and the tackiest of reality TV shows."

She got into the stride of telling her career trajectory. "But then I married an Italian pharmaceutical heir – his grandfather has the patent for Imodium or something – got knocked up accidentally after five rounds of IVF and decamped out here to where my aunt lived when I was a child. It had some special memories."

"Soho's loss was our gain," Odette said, back to being all smiles. The doorbell went again, and I saw Ewa crossing the foyer out the corner of my eye.

She greeted whoever it was warmly and took their coat. In walked Simon Anson. He, like Tommy, had gone for the jumper over a shirt and chinos look. His was green, with a blue shirt scruffily sticking out the bottom. He was wearing boots and looked painfully handsome as he stood in the doorway without any self-consciousness.

"Thank God," Nigella said, launching herself at him. "Come and have a drink with me, Anson. I need some intellectual stimulation."

Simon allowed himself to be walked over to the bar but stopped where Sonia and I sat and made his greetings. He apparently knew Sonia through her brother. "We played rugby together on our amateur squad a couple of years ago," he explained to both Nigella and me.

Ewa was already at the door again, and this time it was a big crowd. John Parkinson appeared at the door in a suit and tie, his hair freshly combed. "'Lo all." He waved a giant hand.

To my surprise, it was Nigella who greeted him warmest. She pulled him over to her, but he, like Simon, stopped and greeted me.

"And this is my life and strife, Rita," he said to me, gesturing to the small, round woman behind him. She was as squat as he was tall, as petite as he was oversized. She was a permanently smiling woman who came to sit with me and wanted to start talking books immediately. She had a rust-coloured frumpy cardigan on over a plain white blouse and stretchy trousers, which I could only guess came from the Tesco in Compney. She won me over by actually acknowledging Sonia, who I could feel becoming more and more embarrassed next to me, with a warm greeting.

Behind the Parkinsons was a group of guests who I think turned up at the same time out of coincidence, but who knows with Lilbury's complicated social groupings. Margo Cadbury-Smythe entered and looked completely unhappy with the room, with her fellow guests, with life, with her floral kerchief she had tied around her neck, with her blown-out blonde hairdo that she'd had since Sloane Rangers were a thing. After her came Eleanor, who everyone cooed over. She made a beeline for me, which was most flattering.

"Thank you so much for yesterday. I was so grateful."

"You're completely okay, Ellie?" Rita Parkinson asked.

Ellie gave a big smile. "Bruised to buggery all over, and utterly embarrassed. But no broken bones or anything to worry about. They kept me in overnight in case of a concussion, but I was let out this morning with a warning to hold on to my horse tighter next time."

"That is good news," said a new voice from the doorway. An older woman, who might've been sixty, or eighty (upper-class women age differently due to that whole not doing a day's work in their life thing). She opened her arms, and Ellie received a warm hug. "If my goddaughter was to end up in a wheelchair from one of my horses, I'd be devastated. And I know Guy would feel the same." Eleanor blushed at his very name.

Sonia looked at me, confused about all this horse business. "What have you been up to, eh?"

Before I could answer, Odette bustled over to drag me to Lady Frobisher's side and have me grovel at her feudal knee. "Lady F, this is Arden Forrest, our guest of honour."

Lady F literally shooed Odette away (something I'd never seen done before, but it was amazing to watch) and took my hand. "Welcome! I hope Lilbury will be a good home for you. We are really very pleased you've come to join us tonight." I felt a warm glow wash over me. If she was lying through her teeth, then she deserved an award for it.

"Now, as soon as my nephew and his friend get here, we shall make a start. Mr Forrest, you have a drink I see. Oh, you brought a friend… Hello dear, you are most welcome too. Now, is Arden your real name?"

"Unfortunately, yes. My mother thought it was funny. All my siblings have similar names," I lied.

"Your mother was quite the comedian." Actually, she was a barmaid at the Three Foxes, but I didn't say this.

"Why don't you sit in this chair here, so we can all see you? You have a book? Good. I know some have been reading up on you."

I took my seat and Lady F sat down beside me, with Eleanor at her side. The young girl was hovering.

We made polite conversation, and all the villagers took turns to ask me a slight variation on the same question of whether or not I was settling in well and what I made of the surrounds and wasn't it a change from 'that there' London, *haw haw*.

I smiled and laughed along with everyone else. I caught Nigella's eye as she looked to the ceiling and drained her glass.

Headlights from a car illuminated the room and the sound of laughter from outside wafted in. Ewa rushed to answer the door, and the laughter came inside. "Ewa, you're looking even more beautiful than this morning," said a voice drifting into the room.

Eleanor fixed her hair back. Odette put her shoulders back, Rita unbuttoned her cardie, Margo quickly checked her lippy in a mirror on the mantelpiece, even Nigella arranged her wavy hair in a more flattering angle.

"Hello all, sorry we're late!" said Guy as he entered. "Someone thought we had more time than we did," he said, addressing the person who walked into the room after him.

There was a collective *ooh* noise as Guy's companion followed him in. He was tall, dark, and fucking handsome. My jaw nearly hit the floor. One, because he was gorgeous. And two, because it was the man who'd screamed at me in the Tesco kerfuffle a few days before.

I began to burn up with shame and, quite frankly, wanted to die. "Everyone, I can't remember who knows my old college chum from Oxford, Tarquin Scott. Tarkie, I think you've met most of this lot before." Guy met my eye. "Oh, and here's the reason we're having this shindig. This is Arden Forrest, that chap who wrote those books that were in the window of Waterstones the other day."

I had a window display in a Waterstones? I should tell Verity. She'd be thrilled. Tarquin turned his devastatingly handsome face to look at me. He clicked instantly.

"Yes, we've already met." I squirmed in my chair.
Guy looked confused. "Oh?"
"He was the bloke in the Tesco car park who was the reason I turned up in a shitty mood the other day," Tarquin continued, only half-joking.
Sonia burst out laughing.
"Arden, what did you do?" Odette asked, staring at me with her bug-like eyes.
"In my defence," I started, as the entire room turned to stare at me, the evil incomer who had nearly driven beautiful Tarquin off the road, "I haven't driven a car in about ten years. Still think I'm on the Tube half the time." There was a smattering of laughter. I turned to Tarquin, my cheeks blazing with embarrassment. "Really sorry about that. Totally my fault. Lesson learned. Eyes on the road at all times."
"I think whatever Arden did, he more than atoned for it yesterday, racing to poor Ellie's aid like that. He had no qualms about being the Good Samaritan," Guy said. I was immensely thankful.
Ellie gripped my hand and smiled her thanks at me once again. "I agree," she said.
Lady F smiled benevolently at me. "That's settled. Tarquin, I hope you're happy with that? I remember someone many years ago once reversing into my flowerbeds when he came to stay over Christmas break?"
Tarquin chuckled. He was wearing a red V-neck jersey with no T-shirt on underneath, showing a good bit of his lightly haired chest. He was about six foot and slimmer and more angular than I usually like in a man (Ollie had been on his college's rowing team), but his natural swagger was hard to ignore.
That, and he looked like a young Clive Owen. He came forward and held out a hand to shake mine. "No hard feelings at all. The number of people I cut up on the King's Road, I'm being a bit of a hypocrite." He took my

hand in his, and I probably imagined it, but he briefly gave my hand a rub between my thumb and forefinger. My heart skipped a beat.

"Right, story time." Lady F clapped her hands together. "Everyone gather around. We'll change our usual routine of reading a passage first and then discussing the work as a whole. This time, we'll change it up to ask Mr Forrest any specifics of his working patterns."

I took my cue and read out the emotional passage about Freya's dead boyfriend. I omitted the swearing and a few pop culture allusions. It went down… well, not brilliantly. Margo looked completely unimpressed. Nigella pulled at some fluff on her top. John Parkinson busied himself with a cream cake. Tommy knocked back his drink and went for another one.

Sonia paid attention, Lady F stayed painfully politely attentive, Odette gave encouraging smiles, Rita was rapt, Eleanor appeared to enjoy it, and Guy and Tarquin shared a few looks but didn't mutter under their breath either, so I was taking it as a win.

Afterwards, the group asked me about my writing processes and the joy of struggling to get published.

"Were you always a writer?" Eleanor asked.

"No, I worked in a dull office job for several years before I started making enough to quit and do this full-time."

"What's your process?" Nigella asked.

"Mostly, I just imagine terrible things happening to my characters and then write it down on the notes app on my phone on the Tube," and then try and form it into something coherent back at home after I'd seen that Ollie was working late again and I had the place to myself.

"How… creative," Lady F offered.

"And what about the aliens in book three who murder the service station attendant? Where on earth did you think of that scene where they melt his body into a puddle of human goo and drink it in a paper coffee cup to absorb his likeness so they can shapeshift into him?"

Rita had asked this. Everyone turned to look at her. She was definitely one of my fans, with that deranged expression on her face. "Goodness," was the only reaction, from Margo.

The reading and meeting wrapped up after an hour or so. People started to gravitate more towards the drinks table. Odette Douglas stood up and yelled about photos. Everyone sighed and gathered around in a formation behind me while Odette snapped away on her phone.

"Now, how do I post these?" Odette asked. Nigella muttered something insulting under her breath. Guy made his way over to help Odette with her brand-new iPhone.

A few minutes later my phone buzzed with some new notifications – @LilburyVillageLife had another social media coup on its hands.

"Peace offering?" I looked around to see who had said that and saw a glass of Prosecco held out to me by Tarquin. I stood up to receive the drink and we made our way over to a window to escape the other conversations.

"That was a great reading… no, seriously. Whenever I come down here I have to sit through one of Lady F's interminable social gatherings, and this is the first one in several years in which I've not wanted to steal a bottle of port and go drink myself to death in the kitchen. I like the sound of your books. I might download some."

I was chuffed. "Thanks." I sought to keep the conversation going. I looked around: Simon was glaring at us from over at the drinks table where he was talking to Nigella. He said something to her, and she spun around and stared at us too. I looked away and noticed Eleanor was sitting on Guy's lap. Margo looked proud as punch.

"Do you come here often? To Honningtons," I clarified, realising how cheesy it was to fancy a straight guy.

"Yes, I spent basically every school holiday here. Guy and I did our PPE together. And Lady F was always welcoming. I felt like the third sibling with Guy and his sister, Rosie."

"Guy was raised here?" I asked, feeling guilty for being nosy, but hey, writers usually were. That or alcoholics.

"His parents were killed in a car accident when he was a child. Guy will inherit Honningtons when Lady F dies anyway, so it made sense for him to be raised here."

"That's horrible… about his parents, I mean. How sad to lose them both like that."

Lady F came over to us. "Thank you all for coming. I believe you're all decamping to the Fox and Lamprey?" This was the politest way I've ever had a party shut down. Lady F wanted her drawing room back. She took my hand. "Do come round for afternoon tea next week so we can chat one on one."

"I'd love to."

"Good, now, please do pass on my request to my goddaughter that she is expected for lunch tomorrow, and I want no excuses this time." I looked over to Eleanor, who seemed perfectly able to receive the instruction herself.

"She means Arabella," Tarquin muttered as Lady F moved off to kick everyone else out. "You've met her, I presume?"

"The other night. How many godchildren does she have?"

"I gave up counting years ago. The fate of a spinster, I suppose."

Ewa was bringing out coats as quickly as she could as we emerged into the foyer. She passed me a wonderfully expensive-looking jacket. "This isn't my coat," I said, noticing the Burberry label.

"Sorry, that one is mine," Tarquin said, taking it from me. I gave an awkward smile. Ewa passed me my own. I tried to hide the Asos label.

"Right, pub?" Nigella, back in her furs, yelled over the hubbub. "Come on, everyone. Even you, Odette."

"Are you coming?" Tarquin asked.

"Yeah, sure," I answered.

We set off walking together. Sonia hopped in her car ("I don't think Her Ladyship would appreciate me leaving it here overnight") and Eleanor and Guy jumped in the back, giggling like schoolchildren. The Parkinsons joined them (Rita in the front) and, once again, Eleanor ended up on Guy's lap. Only Margo stayed behind – to gossip with Lady F.

Nigella led the way on foot, with Simon at her side. The Douglases argued and sniped at each other with Tarquin and me making up the rear.

Sonia drove past, and Guy's face was a picture. His blue shirt with a gilet over it, squished under Eleanor gyrating to whatever dance track Sonia had pumping out of her car stereo. Even Rita was grooving along.

"Poor Frobez, Eleanor's been after him since she was in school."

"Isn't he about ten years older than her?"

"Twelve," he corrected.

We carried on walking. Eventually, we overtook the Douglases, who were walking in stony silence, and caught up to Nigella and Simon. "So, you need work doing on your place?" Simon asked, cutting off Tarquin, who had been about to say something. There's something forceful about being cut off in a Scottish accent that doesn't allow you to talk over it. I saw Tarquin grit his jaw a little against the redhead.

"Yes, the entire bathroom needs ripping out and doing again. I think it's from before the war. And my stairs are halfway to falling apart. My cooker needs replacing. My boiler is on its last legs."

"Tell you what, why don't I come over tomorrow and you can show me all the things that need fixing up and I'll see what I can do and what you'll need a plumber, electrician and the rest for?"

"That'd be great."

We reached the pub and saw Sonia already staggering in (she'd be taxiing home, I hoped) with the others behind her.

Inside, it was much busier than on Wednesday night, and Cytrine was glad to see us, especially when Guy ordered several bottles of Prosecco for the group.

Arabella was sent to fetch them. Her eyes were red and blotchy as she arrived at the trio of tables pushed together with ice buckets and glasses. I was the one nearest her as she leant over to put them on the table. "Are you okay?" I asked, being nosy again.

She smiled through her tears. "Just a long day."

Guy and Eleanor came over to her and she was whisked away from me. They took her to a corner where Guy propped himself up against the bar, shielding her from whatever her family were telling her.

I looked over; both Tarquin and Simon were staring at the goings-on. So was Tommy.

I scoured the pub for Arnie. Yup, he was looking at the event in the corner too. He was standing at the bar. Louchely, Pawel was leaning on the bar next to him. All the men were staring at the corner intently – surely Arabella wasn't giving the entire village her car park specials?

After a few minutes, Guy laughed and walked around to hug the girls. He stepped away and we could all see Eleanor and Arabella locking arms in a sisterly embrace. All seemed rosy again. Cytrine came over to talk with Nigella, her hand on the other woman's shoulder. Nigella was staring at the scene too, but still chatting away amiably. Was there no one in Lilbury who didn't have some sort of antipathy to the girl? It seemed you either loved or loathed her.

Arabella returned to her work and soon all returned to normal, but the longer we were there, the more things started to go haywire for the girl again. She was acting erratically, and by the time closing came (we were the only group left) I saw Guy making a special effort to shadow her. Even Tarquin at one stage pulled her away.

All of us bundled out into the light rain that had started to fall and made our goodbyes. I agreed to wait for the taxi Cytrine had rung for Sonia to take her back to Compney.

I stood with Guy and Sonia (Guy being a gentleman and waiting for her taxi too and receiving several compliments from her about what a charmer he was for letting her come) and we watched as Arabella took out some rubbish, just as she had the night earlier in the week when I'd watched her toss off Pawel.

The bins from behind the back door were then moved out to the big skips that sat at the end of the car park, next to the hedge on the roadside. Arabella carried the bags out from behind the pub across the car park. Pawel came running out from the pub behind her and didn't seem to see us.

He grabbed her arm and spun her around, yelling out something at her that I struggled to hear over the rain and Sonia's squawking.

"You cannot do this! You cannot!" I eventually heard him yell.

"Leave me alone!" Arabella screamed.

"You are being stupid!"

"Fuck off!"

"Stupid bitch!" he yelled.

"Hey!" Hearing the language, Guy yelled and began to make his way over, just as Sonia's taxi pulled in. Arabella stared at us like a deer in headlights, the actual headlights of the taxi highlighting her and her terrified face. The taxi blocked Guy from her and Pawel, but she stared at us all in horror, looking directly at Guy. I looked at him, noticing then that Tarquin had come out of the pub and was standing directly behind his best friend. Pawel swore loudly in Polish and waved his hand in defeat, then went back into the pub.

"Arabella!" Guy yelled, but the girl threw the bag in the skip and quickly followed Pawel back inside.

Guy made to follow her, but Tarquin gripped his gilet. "Leave it! You'll be here all night looking after her if you go comfort her. Let her fight her own bloody battles for once."

Sonia got in her taxi, muttering something about "Drama never ceases round 'ere!"

Guy looked troubled at this, but after a few seconds of inner turmoil, he nodded and agreed. They slammed the door to Sonia's taxi, and Tarquin slapped it on the back to set it on its way.

"Arden, lovely to meet you," Tarquin said. He gripped my hand and then brought me in for a hug. His hand resting on the small of my back. Oh.

Guy followed suit. He too placed his hand lower than I thought he would. Right. Okay.

I turned and made my way home after my night out in Lilbury feeling utterly confused.

Chapter 10

The next morning, I woke up with a blinding headache and the sound of rain drumming on my roof.

"Ugh," was about all I could manage. I hadn't been drinking much recently, despite the usual reputation of those going through break-ups. My ability to handle the copious amount of Prosecco I'd consumed last night was at an all-time low. I shuddered, shivered my way out of my bedroom, and somehow managed to crawl down the stairs to the kitchen, where I kept my paracetamol. I swallowed two and then drank a pint of water, hoping it wouldn't come straight back up again.

The edges of my eyes were dull and cloudy, and the room was spinning a bit. I attempted to make coffee, but it took several attempts. I eventually settled myself on the sofa to watch *Murder, She Wrote,* or whatever Saturday morning repeat was on TV. It was still children's cartoons. I checked my phone – it was barely 8am. Much earlier than I thought.

Simon had given me his number in the pub last night, and I thought about texting him to ask what time was convenient for him to come over.

My phone buzzed before I could, and I presumed it would be Simon asking the same thing.

I supposed that by the way he drank, he felt as fresh as a daisy this morning, and with a military background had already been up at 5am to go for a run and was currently regrouting his bathroom or something.

It was Sonia. I felt guilty for not texting her last night to make sure she got home safely. She was messaging that very same thing, adding a thank you for a nice night, and that she hoped to see me again soon. I smiled. Maybe Sonia and I could be proper friends?

I put my phone down, and after a moment of queasiness, I decided my best bet might be a shower and then food. I looked in the cupboards. I had no sort of hangover food readily available – I'd have to head down to the shops. I sloped off to the shower and made myself look presentable. In my bedroom, I threw on a woolly jumper and a big coat, with boots on my feet. I left the house and ignored my car. Instead of walking the path, I'd take advantage of the route John had told me about earlier in the week. It was easy to see – in a straight line across the fields you could see the cluster of trees and shapes that made up Lilbury.

It was still raining, ever so lightly, but it had got heavier during the evening, so the ground was muddy. However, I was determined to take advantage of the glories of nature on my doorstep.

I'd be lying if I said I didn't feel inordinately stupid climbing over the fence into John's sopping paddock and meandering through the grass and mud, but I was determined. For some reason, I had a strange feeling. Maybe it was waking up too early (I work from home – 8am is very early for me), but something felt… off. Something about last night had been in the back of my mind. Something had been amiss. The whole evening had been filled with sniping and looks. For a group of friends, they had all spent a long time at each other's throats.

I mulled over these thoughts as I wandered through the fields. I had to cross over into a new field a couple of times and made a specific effort to always close the gate, despite not seeing any of John's sheep anywhere.

After about fifteen minutes' walk across the fields, the wind and spitting rain had completely cleared my headache, but the bottom of my jeans and boots were caked in mud. I was wetter and colder than I'd bargained for and would definitely be taking the road home. Hopefully, this time I would be able to see any Land Rovers that sped down there, unlike last night, which had involved several near death experiences even on a short walk.

I came off the hill and walked across the last field. The pond John had mentioned was about a hundred metres in front of me. The garden at the back of the Fox and Lamprey was visible through the trees that it surrounded it. The houses and other buildings of Lilbury's high street were all practically invisible through the trees everyone had planted at the back of their sections. A demarcation line that the village ended precisely here.

There was one large oak tree standing over the pond, but aside from that, nothing else grew around it. I approached and looked into its muddy green waters. It was covered in weeds and algae. Surprised by its size, I wandered around its edge.

From the angle that I approached I went across to the left, to the side where the oak tree was, and from there it was a short walk down to the lane running alongside the pub.

I came closer to the oak tree, and that's when my heart began to beat faster. I rubbed my eyes, because surely what I was seeing was a mistake. But it didn't work, I could still see it. Amongst the tranquil natural surroundings was something that didn't belong. Something that destroyed the scene. Something that was very, very wrong. I approached cautiously, mentally begging any and all higher powers for it not to be what I knew it was.

"Please, please," I whispered under my breath.

I came closer to the tree, and there on the water's edge, half submerged, was a body.

It was face down, but I knew it.

It was Arabella.

Chapter 11

We've all imagined finding a body, haven't we? Stumbling across a corpse in the woods, a hidden grave, a body on the street late at night. The drama, the mystery, the intrigue.

I tell you now, at that moment, none of those thoughts crossed my mind. All I had was a deep, almost primal need for it not to be true, to not be seeing a fellow human being's corpse, bloodied and battered, lying in a pond.

My instinct was to run away. That this was dirty and foul, torrid, horrible and someone else could deal with it. Or that I was exaggerating it? Was it really a body? And so, what of it? Don't go to the police; murders don't need reporting; stop being a drama queen. It's a mannequin. Or died of natural causes. It's fine. Don't ring the police. They have other things to deal with.

I felt seedy – like I had walked in on people having sex. Like I had with Arabella a few days before. Was I looking for this? Would people think I was obsessed with Arabella?

Then I worried that whatever had happened to her might happen to me. I shuddered, and a cold sweat broke out. A bird squawking in the trees made me jump. She'd been murdered and the killer could be only metres away.

Maybe it was suicide? I looked again at the back of the head in the water. Nope. You definitely couldn't do that to yourself unless you had some very flexible joints.

I knew it was Arabella because the body was wearing the clothes she'd had on last night: high-waisted skinny jeans, black ankle boots and a long-sleeved black top. Her long blonde hair was even more of a mess, floating in the water covered in the blood from the huge hole in the back of her skull.

I thought I was going to be sick. Not because of revulsion, but of over-excitement. My blood was pumping, and my heart was going like it was battery-operated. Adrenalin seemed to be pumping through my body. Some sort of miscalculated fight or flight reaction, I presumed. My brain saw a corpse and thought the predator might still be around. Whatever it was, it was making me feel ill.

I bit my nails; I didn't know what to do. Should I go to the pub and find Cytrine and Arnie? Should I stay here? I debated internally for what seemed ages but was probably about thirty seconds.

I got out my phone, and as the screen was flecked with raindrops, my shaking hands dialled 999. The second time in three days.

I stopped for a second longer – what if they thought it was me? I lived alone. I had no alibi. What was this strange unmarried newcomer doing wandering through a field in the middle of a cold morning and stumbling over a pretty blonde? Why'd you do it, Forrest? Did she reject you? I'd be sent to prison. I wouldn't survive prison. I like long showers in private.

Did I need to ring the police; could I just run away? I didn't want this. I didn't want my life to become the story of the man who found the body. Being interviewed by the police, having to give evidence in court. I came here for a fresh start. This was not the fresh start I wanted.

I could go home and act like it never happened. Were my footprints here? Would it make me a suspect if I tried to cover them up? Someone else would find her soon. There'd be someone along this path sometime today.

My thoughts were interrupted as the woman on the end of the call greeted me in a curt efficient manner.

"Emergency services, what is your location?"

"Um, I'm in a field." I took a second to collect myself. "I'm behind the Fox and Lamprey pub in Lilbury. There's a body."

The call-handler took more details. "Are you sure the person is deceased?" she asked matter-of-factly.

"There's a bloody great hole in her fucking head."

"Right."

"She's lying face down in a pond and hasn't moved." I think she's well and truly brown bread. "I'm not gonna touch her, if that's what you're asking."

The operator ignored my bolshiness and told me to stay with her, that police and ambulance would be on the way. I laughed at the thought of an ambulance, but I suppose they needed to send one to make sure, and to cart her off afterwards.

About ten minutes later, they arrived. I had given them directions as best as I could. I heard the sirens, as did most of the village as they neared. I wandered down the lane to see the police and ambulance both there, looking stumped as to where to go.

I recognised a cop. "Arden?" Adebayo asked. He was in his uniform again, standing there by his car, with his partner, a skinny white woman. "You called this in?"

Instead of answering this, I pointed down to the pond. "She's over there." I leant against the wall as Ade, his partner, and the two paramedics all trundled past.

"Stay here," Ade said as they did so.

I heard a noise inside the pub and turned to see Cytrine and Arnie emerging from a door in their dressing gowns.

"Oh my God," Cytrine said, followed by something in a language that was not quite pure French, Creole maybe, which sounded distinctly like a much ruder version of what she'd said in English. "Arden" – she'd clocked me – "what's happened?"

I had no idea what to say. So, I started at the beginning. "I walked across the fields. I was going to buy some bacon and eggs for a fry-up from the Co-op and I saw her in the pond. She was floating."

Arnie looked at me. "There's a… there's someone in the pond? A body? A dead person?"

I nodded.

"Who is it?" Cytrine asked. My face seemed to answer that question for her. She began to walk down the lane to the pond, her arms out in front of her to grab the brick wall to prop her up. She was walking fast but not at all steadily.

"Cytrine, no!" Arnie called out, but she was halfway down there. I stayed leaning against the wall, my eyes not quite focusing on anything, just the flashing lights on top of the ambulance and Ade's patrol car.

I heard Cytrine scream a few seconds later. I sensed Arnie run down the lane after her, yelling her name. I heard Ade's voice yelling at her to go back. She was crying hysterically.

"Please take her inside," Ade was saying.

A woman's voice, the female police officer I presumed, cajoled her: "Come inside with me, my love. Let's get you a cup of tea."

I heard Ade's voice as he returned, speaking on his radio. He was saying something in police jargon. Lots of numbers and acronyms. He was calling for more units, for backup, for detectives, for forensics. "The homicide squad from Bournemouth too."

He called off. "Arden…" He came over to me. "Are you okay?" He was looking at me intently.

"Um, yeah, I'm fine. Yeah, yeah, I'm okay."

"Good, we're gonna need you to stick around, okay? Here, come with me. We'll go wait in the pub for the backup to arrive."

He guided me by gripping my elbow and walking me into the pub, where we joined his colleague and Arnie and Cytrine in the upstairs rooms that the Hugheses used as their living rooms.

The female officer, whom Adebayo addressed as Lauren, was busy making tea for everyone. Cytrine was staring out the window from her seat; her cheeks were covered in tears. Arnie was looking down at the table.

I felt uncomfortable as we all sat down. This was the Hugheses' house, not for customers to be sat in. It felt like we were invading their privacy when something horrible had happened.

To break the silence, I asked a stupid question. I was wondering if Ade and Lauren would start asking us about Arabella, but they seemed to be keeping schtum and making us comfortable in our horror while they waited for detectives. Above their pay grade.

My stupid question hung in the air: "Where's Pawel?"

"Pawel?" Lauren asked, or, as her badge said, Constable Trescothick.

"Pawel Gromorski," Arnie said, clearing his throat. "Our chef. He lives on-site with us, but he went out last night after closing."

Lauren wrote his name down. She spelled both names wrong.

There was a banging on the door. Ade left to go see who it was. I could see the paramedics and him talking through the window. I looked through another window at the front, holding my full cup of tea in my hands. This window looked out the front over the car park and small garden, with the service area and alleyway separated by the brick wall off to the side, just out of sight. If Arnie or

Cytrine had craned their necks, they'd have seen Arabella and Pawel the other night. Or, worse, me.

You could see the road clearly over the hedge and the first half of the lane from the high street before it went past the pub buildings. The ambulance and patrol car were still there, as well as a small crowd of people. About five or six so far. Amongst them, I saw Odette Douglas in her ugly green suede skirt again, and Nigella in her ridiculous fur coat. As I stood there, more and more people joined the group. Within two minutes, they numbered nearly a dozen. A bloke jogged along the outside of the pub, coming from the south where the turn-off for my road was, and after that the cul-de-sac of council houses. He was wearing jogging bottoms and a hoodie. He pulled his hood down and his bright red hair stood out in the crowd huddled in the drizzle. It was Simon. He leaned in to talk to Nigella and Odette.

As they stood there, they had to part ways as more police cars began to arrive. Another patrol car, and then two plain vehicles driven by the homicide squad from Bournemouth that Ade had called, who were having their Saturday lie-ins ruined. A fourth police vehicle arrived. A large van that had to be forensics. Ade went to talk to one of the detectives. Another uniformed officer began ushering people back and set up tape from the beginning of the alley all the way across the pub's front to the entrance of its driveway. The Fox and Lamprey was now a crime scene.

I watched as Ade led the detectives down the lane and through to the pond. They all disappeared for about ten minutes.

"What happens now?" Arnie asked, breaking my reverie.

Lauren answered: "The detectives will obviously need to speak to you all, and we'll begin a preliminary crime scene analysis for forensics to gather all the information from the location where the body was found."

"How long will that take?" Cytrine said, speaking for the first time since I'd arrived.

"I don't know, I'm afraid. But I wouldn't expect the pub will be able to open today."

Whether this was bad news or not for the Hugheses, I didn't know. I had no idea what kind of profit the pub made, if they desperately needed a Saturday night to keep things ticking along.

They seemed to be thinking as shell-shocked grieving friends and bosses rather than as small business owners having to maintain their finances above all else.

After a few more minutes, Lauren's radio buzzed, and she went into the hallway to answer it. A minute or so later the detectives came up. "Mr Forrest, we need to speak to you."

I followed the detectives downstairs.

Chapter 12

I've been interviewed by the police several times before. But this was the first time I was innocent of any wrongdoing.

The two detectives and I sat downstairs in the pub, Ade keeping a watch at the door. He seemed nervous and fidgety.

"Mr Forrest – Arden, is it? May I call you Arden?" I nodded. "I'm DI Gary Neuberger, and this is DS Cara Wales from Dorset Police." They both showed me their warrant cards in case I didn't believe them.

DS Neuberger was a white guy, about fiftyish with a square-shaped head and a short, spiky shock of grey hair. He was well spoken but unimaginatively accented. He was around my height, wore jeans with an adorned belt, and a tucked-in dark blue dress shirt. Over it he had a black all-weather jacket. He looked less like a cop and more like a café manager.

DS Wales was a beak-nosed white woman in her late thirties, with dark brown hair collected at the back of her head in a bun. She spoke with a northern accent. She was also, to my surprise, several months pregnant.

"Could you tell us your movements this morning, up until you found the body?"

I wanted them to call her Arabella, but I knew they couldn't until she'd been formally identified.

"Well, I was here last night." I pointed at the floor to show I meant the pub, unless they were dense. "This morning I was feeling a little worse for wear. So I decided to go to the Co-op to get food in for a fry-up."

Neuberger gave me a nod, telling me to continue. DS Wales was rubbing her belly.

"I… uh, I had asked my neighbour John Parkinson, he was here too, last night, about walking across his land as a shortcut earlier in the week, and he told me about the route to the high street, by the pond and down the laneway outside. So that was the route I took."

"You'd never gone that way before?" he asked.

"I only moved here on Monday," I said. They both appeared surprised.

"I'm sorry you've had such a shocking start to your new life, Mr Forrest," Neuberger said, reverting to my surname. "Where were you based before Lilbury?"

"London." I gave them my old address in Southwark. Actually, I gave them Ollie's address, just to complicate matters between him and me further.

I told them about my new cottage and my week moving in. "And the party last night?" DS Wales asked.

"It was a book club meeting," I said, and filled them in on the evening.

"And you saw the victim here last night, too?" Neuberger asked.

"Yes, she was working."

"Did you speak?"

"We shared a few words when she came over. She was talking to lots of people. Everyone knew her."

"Did anyone seem angry or upset with her, or vice versa?"

I knew I should tell them about Pawel, but I couldn't. This looked like a vicious crime, and to me, Pawel seemed like a nice guy. I was being naive. Naive and possibly hindering a murder investigation, but I couldn't drop the foreign guy in it.

"She seemed very upset about something. I don't know what, though. She talked to her cousin, Guy Frobisher, for a long time, and Eleanor… err, I don't know her last name. She's a goddaughter of Lady Frobisher like Arabella is, was, is. Um, they spoke to her for a long time. Like I said, though, she knew everyone, and everyone knew her."

"Everyone knew her?" DS Wales was looking up. "What do you mean by that?"

I gulped. "She was a pretty girl, Detective. You do the maths."

Neuberger looked at me. "Had you done the maths, so to speak, Mr Forrest?"

I sighed. Being gay means coming out again and again in life. "I'm not interested in women in that way, Detective. I noticed purely because it was so obvious, as a newcomer, that Arabella was popular with the men."

"Do you know any of these men in particular?" Wales asked.

I shook my head, once again dropping myself in it. I decide to go half-hearted. "She seemed close to the chef, Pawel." I gave a half-truth: "I saw them chatting outside on a fag break the first night I came to the pub."

"Just talking?" Wales asked, rubbing her bump again. Making me feel seedier.

"No, more than talking," I said, reddening.

"What, exactly?" Neuberger asked.

"She was, um, giving him a hand job," I said quietly. "Out by the bins, by the car park. I was walking past from my car. You couldn't miss them."

Wales and Neuberger gave each other a look. Whether or not he'd done it, I'd basically just given Pawel a murder sentence.

The detectives told me that'd be all for now and I was free to go. They took my number and address, said there'd be follow-up questions later in the week. and could I please keep any and all information to myself.

As I left, I passed Ade. He looked furious.

Chapter 13

I made my way outside in somewhat of a daze. I checked my watch. It was barely 11am but it had felt like much later.

As I approached the police tape by the drive entrance to the pub, I saw the police presence had multiplied. There were several cars and vans all in the car park with some out on the streets.

Officers milled about in the rain looking cold and drinking coffee.

I went under the tape and hadn't walked two metres before I was set upon by half the village.

Odette looped her arm in mine. "Arden, what's happened? The police aren't saying anything."

Nigella grabbed my other arm. "Has there been a murder? You don't get this sort of police show for a burglary. Even if they'd held up the pub by gunpoint, they'd have only sent a few cars. Not the whole dog and pony show."

Simon pushed them both off me. "Guys, let him be."

Nigella dropped my arm. "Of course, so sorry. Totally uncalled for. Are you okay?" She took on a mothering vibe. "Come back to my place and have a cup of tea, you look like you could use it. Come on, I'm only across the road here."

She took me, along with Odette and Simon, across to her house and let us all in. Nigella's place was like walking into a Dickensian novel. Everything was filled to the brim with something: books, ornaments, paintings, furniture, rugs, grandfather clocks; that shabby chic-boho realness that only truly posh people can get away with. Generations of accumulating *stuff*. Only in the newer part of the house could you tell that Nigella had lived in London for most of her life; there the country house feel dissipated slightly for a tastefully designed and clutter-free living space.

It was all distressed wood beams, the perfect furniture, the latest in design. The kitchen was a bright cosy room, both spacious and invitingly snug. The space between the sink and the kitchen island alone was the size of my cottage's ground floor.

Simon and Odette seemed less interested in the décor – obviously they'd been here before. As if to prove a point, I walked past a noticeboard with a photo pinned to it of the whole Lilbury Book Club. It was in the Fox and Lamprey, and everyone was wearing Christmas jumpers and paper hats. Nigella was in the middle, with her arm around a dark-haired man who must be her husband. Odette and Tommy were off to the side, Simon at the other end with the Parkinsons and, to my surprise, Arabella.

"We took that Christmas Eve last year," Nigella said as she began pouring our individual Nespressos. Just a couple of months ago.

Simon and Odette took a seat at the kitchen table, and I followed suit. "Strong and black?" Nigella asked, gesturing to her coffee maker. "White and milky," I answered. She shrugged and handed the espresso she'd already made to Simon.

He took a sip and looked at me with his blue eyes. "What happened? Has there been a murder?" He pronounced it in the Scottish way, a *maaarrrdur*. All the r's rolled.

For the first time this morning, my eyes filled with tears, and I could only nod. Eventually, I managed to squeeze out a name: "Arabella."

The effect was instantaneous. The coffee cup Nigella was holding smashed on the ground and she covered her mouth. "Oh my God," she said, the words muffled by her hand.

She clutched the kitchen counter to steady herself. Simon sat dumbfounded, his face not moving, but I could see that his mind raced. Odette turned pale and then went to Nigella. For two women who bickered like an old married couple, they clung to each other now, with Nigella resting her head against Odette's shoulder, the older woman's face covered in grief and shock.

They steadied one another for several minutes, and eventually Odette moved her to the stools on the side of the island in the middle of the kitchen. Simon abruptly stood up and walked to the French doors at the side of the room and stared out at the weak winter daylight, his hands in his pockets, his back to us all. In his jogging pants, it was hard not to look at his rather taut backside.

It must be hard for him. I presumed he'd slept with Arabella at some stage, if their moment in the car park was anything to go by. And why not? He was a good-looking, fairly young and attractive man, who, despite his current job as the lowly village handyman, seemed to be quite well off and had had an interesting life and career.

I felt bad. My comments about Arabella's habits with the men in the village would surely send Neuberger and Wales sniffing around every guy in Lilbury and check them one by one to see if they'd had a relationship with her. Simon would be on that list. I wondered if Odette and

Nigella knew their platonic friend had been one of many men having it off with the departed?

"I've known that girl her entire life," Nigella said, regaining her composure. "Ever since I used to come here to visit my aunt. Her parents lived down the road from here until they divorced. I was so happy when she moved back after uni."

"I know, I remember her as a teenager. She was so kind," Odette added. "Her parents' divorce did a number on her," she added. She didn't say it with malice, just as a fact.

"It was a bad divorce?" I asked.

"The worst. Her father was a bigwig in the City and then moved into construction. Pots of money. He left her mum for a model, and then got custody of Arabella, saying his ex was a coke addict and not fit to look after her. He won in the courts and then sent her to boarding school, while he buggered off to Dubai with his new wife," Nigella explained.

Nigella looked quite pale. She was taking this badly. "The last time I spoke to her" – she began to cry, her chest racked with sobs – "I was calling her a whore… and telling her to leave." She broke down on the island and sobbed, her head in her hands. "Oh, God."

Both Simon and Odette seemed unsure of what to do with this. Simon turned and looked at the women for a few seconds before returning to gazing out at Nigella's garden; Odette gingerly patted her friend on the arm. "Don't worry. I said basically the same thing to her yesterday."

"What?" I asked.

Odette looked at the floor. "She'd been up to her usual tricks. I was furious. I went around to the pub earlier in the day and ripped a strip off her in the car park. Not sure what came over me, never done anything like that before."

"When you say usual games—" I started to say, but Simon cut me off.

"Odette, why don't you take Nigella upstairs and get her to lie down? I'll run Arden back up to his cottage in my car."

Odette nodded and began to lead Nigella upstairs. Nigella gave me a weak smile and waved away Odette's steadying hand as she made her way from the kitchen.

"Come on," Simon said. He stopped briefly to pick up the shards of the smashed coffee cup off the tiles and left them in a small, neat pile on Nigella's countertop.

We went outside and I followed meekly as Simon led us back across the road to the pub, where I saw Sonia getting out of a car with *Bliss Real Estate* written on the side. As she emerged, a glam-looking Asian woman got out of the other side of the car and the two both stared at the scene in front of them at the pub.

Sonia noticed me as we walked past on our way to Simon's car. I was tempted to tell him no, I was fine to walk, but I realised I was still dazed. I would probably get lost on the way home. I then realised that the last thing I wanted was to be alone.

"Arden, what's happened?" Sonia asked. The woman next to her was pretty but looked mean. It is not often you see someone who you can just tell is a bad person, but she was one. "This is my sister-in-law, Dhapinder," Sonia told us. Dhapinder held out a hand.

I took it without registering her and dropped it a second later. "There's been a murder," Simon answered for me. Once again, his accent infusing it with a *Taggart* sense of drama.

The two women were horrified. "Great place to leave your car, Son," Dhapinder said, recovering fast.

Sonia was flabbergasted. "What? Who? Oh my God, how awful." She reiterated one of her previous comments: "Who was it?"

Simon took a deep breath.

"Arabella Sweet. The barmaid."

Sonia thought a second. "Blondie? The one we saw having a barney with the Polish bloke last night?" She was talking to me.

"What?" Simon asked me. Dhapinder had gone quiet. She was staring at the ground. Arabella's name meant something to her. I was looking at her, wondering what that could mean. Was Dhapinder from around here? Her accent was too posh to tell. She could be like Odette, born and raised in the five-mile radius, but could be from anywhere in the south.

Hadn't Simon said he'd played rugby with Sonia's brother, her husband? If he was a rugby player running a successful business with an attractive wife, surely he couldn't be too ugly and unattractive himself – had Arabella dug her claws in there too? I really hoped not. It was making me uncomfortable that every man who lived nearby seemed to be treating Arabella as his own personal cum sock.

Simon was looking at me. "Um, yeah," I answered hesitantly. "I don't know. I was pretty drunk. I can't remember much about it."

"Did you tell the police?" Sonia asked.

Why hadn't I told the police? It would seem open and shut. Slutty girl cheats on boyfriend one too many times. Angry boyfriend lashes out and then does a runner. You know what those foreign types are like.

No, it had to be more than that. If that was the case, then Pawel would've snapped ages ago by the sounds of things. And what about all these other men – Simon said their relationship was on a break – any other man could have stepped into the breach and taken on the boyfriend role while she and Pawel were on the outs. There seemed to be no shortage. Maybe I wanted the police to cast their nets a bit wider before they took the inevitable turn and arrested Pawel.

"They've already spoken to Arden," Simon told her. "Sonia, maybe you should tell the police that you saw her last night. You might have been one of the last ones – and maybe you were more sober than him."

"Him". My haziness seemed to have raised Simon's hackles. He didn't approve of my inability to remember. Or hold my drink.

"Yeah," said Dhapinder. "And maybe they'll be nice enough to give you your car back if you talk to them without them having to come to you."

Sonia was convinced. She nodded firmly. "I'll go grab one of them now." First, however, she came to me. "Are you all right? You're as pale as a sheet."

"It was me who found her," I whispered.

Sonia hugged me as tight as she could. When she released me, she stared me straight in the eye. "I'm going to talk to the cops, but I want you to know if you need anything, I'm here for you, okay? Don't be too shy to ring."

We moved off and Sonia and Dhapinder made tracks to find a police officer who'd take Sonia's statement about the argument. I looked back as Sonia was pointing at her car and jabbering in the ear of a uniformed constable.

Simon led the way, and we began walking in the opposite direction, crossing the road to the narrow footpath outside the few shops Lilbury had. The whole village was out in the high street watching. Several people called out to Simon asking what was happening, but he waved them away. We passed the village shop and then further on past the narrow turn-off for my road. There were several more houses before the tiny cul-de-sac of mid-century council houses started. Simon walked quickly down the street and stopped near the end, where there was a house with two front doors, a purpose-built maisonette. He loped up to the front step, while I stayed by the car in the driveway, which I presumed was his.

He let himself in the flat and jumped up the stairs two at a time. I watched his taut backside retreat into the gloom, then looked at his place. Not exactly salubrious, but the council houses (I presumed most were now privately owned like everywhere else in Britain, Inc.) were all well-kept with cars out the front and mowed lawns. I was being snobby. Of course Simon couldn't afford a mortgage on a bigger, posher place just on his own. In London, even doctors and lawyers couldn't afford mortgages on one-bed flats unless they were married to a partner earning the same as them all over again.

It's why Ollie had breathed a sigh of relief when my royalty cheques started coming with zeroes on the end, not the front.

Besides, Simon was a single guy. He didn't need a huge house to rattle around in. I didn't know anything about him; maybe he was divorced?

He came thundering downstairs again, and I noticed, sadly, he'd changed into a pair of cargo pants and a T-shirt with a fleece gilet on over it (they loved their gilets here). He had his tool belt around his waist.

He gestured for me to hop in the truck – yup, his car was actually a large pickup truck, and why yes, I was feeling more and more emasculated every second – as he unlocked it with the button on his keyring. I hopped in. It was nothing like the farm vehicles my dad had when I was a kid.

"I thought this might be a good way to take our minds off things. If you're not keen and wanna be alone, I can drop you off and leave you be?"

"No, please. Yes, let's get an inventory of everything that needs sorting. Good thinking."

I wasn't sure whether I wanted to sit around my cottage and stare into space or not, but I guess I'd find out.

He started the engine, which throbbed as if it was on steroids, and we reversed out. Simon was a sure and steady driver, who obviously had not spent fifteen years on the Northern Line and forgotten how to use a clutch. We got to the turn-off and then made our way up to the cottage in silence. Simon parked next to my car without even seeming to touch the wheel; he judged the angle perfectly and the truck pulled in.

He was showing off now.

He got out and stood in front of my wee cottage. "It's picturesque, I'll give it that," he said, smiling. "I nearly bought this place myself, you know."

"Really?" I asked, making my way to the front door.

"Yeah, but I tried to factor in how much it would cost on top of the restorations and work it needed. I couldn't see it happening without a lot of stress."

Ha. I was richer than he was, at least, I crowed internally. Then again, I hadn't exactly factored all the restorations into the cost in that much detail either. I was playing it by ear, to be honest. A strategy that was sure to go pear-shaped at some point.

I let us in, and Simon followed me through the house. We took a left to the small dining room, and then onto the rectangular kitchen. Simon inspected everything with an unreadable facial expression. We returned to the hall with the stairs, and a tiny downstairs loo behind them. Then to the other side with my cosy living room. Simon brought out a piece of paper and pen to begin making lists. In my mind, I realised I'd be living off Pot Noodle for a long time.

Upstairs we went, to the landing, then through to my boxes-of-books-filled spare room, and the bathroom beside it, then across to my room, where, embarrassingly, last night's underwear lay on the floor at the bedside, and the bed was unmade.

Simon pretended not to see my boxers before I picked them up and threw them into the washing basket. He inspected the corners, the windows, the doors, the floors, and then back to the bathroom for another look at the pipes and taps. I made my bed hurriedly as he did so.

"Tea?" I called out as he crawled around under my sink.

"Coffee. Black," he replied. He was lying on his back looking up at the pipes. His T-shirt was pulled up slightly revealing his lily-white stomach with a smattering of ginger hair.

"Coming up," I said, averting my eyes. I went downstairs and tapped the kettle on. I brought out the cups and stood at the window watching the clouds go by overhead. Grey. Wet. Dark. When I die, I'd like for the last thing I see to be blue skies and sunshine.

It was only 12.30pm. Arabella hadn't even been dead twelve hours, probably. Yet her body was probably already bagged up and on the way to the morgue to be prodded over and cut up.

Already there'd be press outside the pub, harassing people for vox pops. Detectives Neuberger and Wales would be on their way to amassing a mound of paperwork. She'd receive a case file and an operational name. She'd be on the evening news as "murder victim". She wouldn't be Arabella any longer. She was Arabella Sweet, twenty-two, bludgeoned to death in a field behind a pub.

And what of her family? Her supposed coke-addict mum? Her useless father? What of Lady Frobisher, Guy, Eleanor, and all those that knew and loved her? They'd be finding out around now if not long before. Poor Lady F standing there in her drawing room greeting Wales and Neuberger with polite indifference until they say the body was a relative.

I seemed to have worked myself up into a bit of a tizz. I was shaking as I leant at the countertop; I tried to calm myself but instead just let out something akin to a gasp but was more of a sob.

"Hey, hey, it's okay," said a deep voice behind me. Simon wrapped his arm around my shoulder and pulled me close. "You're in shock, it's okay. Nothing to worry about. There was nothing you could have done for her."

I'd love to say Simon smelled like fresh sheets and comfort, but he didn't. He hadn't showered after his run, and he'd been rummaging around on the floor in old work clothes. He didn't exactly stink, but he had a musky scent to him, for sure. On the other hand, his arms were warm and rock solid and I felt a little better. Inwardly, I shook my head at myself and sighed. I attempted to extricate myself from his embrace, lest he think I was overstepping boundaries and taking advantage of his charitable nature. Oddly, he wasn't pulling away. In fact, his other arm was now coming up to my side and stroking my chest. Oh.

"I'm just a bit, um, well, I don't want to be alone right now," Simon said as we turned to face each other. He put his mouth on mine. He tasted of toothpaste, but his lips were soft. His body was hard and warm, and he gripped me as we kissed. We scooted around and he lifted me up and deposited me on the kitchen benchtop.

We broke apart from kissing for a second, and he removed his T-shirt in one deft, breathless, move. I nodded appreciatively and gripped his chest, digging into his firm muscles. "This is very nice. Whatever you're doing to achieve this, keep doing it."

He chuckled and pulled up my shirt above my head. Over the next few minutes, every piece of clothing was removed until we were standing naked in my kitchen.

Simon's body was even nicer out of clothing; he had a pert penis with a rather comical thin crescent-shaped line of short ginger hair at the base. "You shave it like that?" I asked, incredulous.

"I like it trimmed but I don't like it bald," he said with a shrug. We retreated to the living room, where I ended up on the floor, with his head between my legs. I was torn between two things: one, did this mean he hadn't slept with Arabella? And two, it had been a good few months since anyone had been at that angle, and I was enjoying it immensely.

"Does all that noise mean I'm doing a good job?" he asked, coming up for air. I hadn't even realised I was making any.

"You're earning your money, that's for sure."

He laughed again. "Good, because I'm sorry to say, this place is in dire need of some maintenance."

"Not what I want to hear when there's a sexy naked man on top of me."

"Who said I was talking about the house?" He was still laughing. "I can do other things too if you'd like?"

"Oh, yeah?"

He got off me and ran to the kitchen, I saw him pull his wallet out of his trousers from through the doorway. He returned unwrapping a piece of silver foil he'd taken out of it. "I'll make it worth what I charge, I promise you."

Chapter 14

Afterwards, we lay on the living room floor panting like marathon runners and eventually managed to retain our dignity. "I need to go to a gym," I informed him.

"Trust me, your performance was great," he said, rolling over and grinning at me. "I have zero complaints."

I blushed, but it felt nice to be complimented. "Do you want that coffee now?"

"It's after midday, why don't you make us something stronger?" he asked. "We've earned it."

I went to the kitchen, fixed us two vodkas, and returned to the living room floor, where Simon had found my throw from the sofa and draped himself in it.

"Thanks," he said and took a sip. "You know, I meant what I said before – unfortunately – this place is lucky to still be standing. I'd be happy to do all the surface-level work and recommend you good professionals for the electrics and plumbing. But don't think you have to hire me because of what just happened."

"What, you think I'll throw you out because I wouldn't want to employ anyone who'd seen me naked?"

"I meant how I banged your brains out, but seeing you naked is a fine way of putting it too."

I lay on the floor and rested my vodka on my chest. "Well, as soon as you can start, I'm happy to have you. Money's no problem."

We clinked glasses. "Here's to not letting rogering you senseless get in the way of a perfectly good professional relationship," he said.

"You have such an ego."

"Someone's got to think I'm hot shit," he sighed. Maybe I'd been right about the divorce.

"Who knew there'd be more than one gay in Lilbury?" I said changing the subject.

This made Simon laugh, his giant muscles jiggling with the motion. "You have no idea, do you? You're in for a treat."

I was puzzled by that statement and was going to ask, but he got up and went upstairs to the loo before I could ask. When he came back, I changed tack. I stretched out from where I lay on the floor.

I wanted an answer about his relationship with Arabella. "Were you close?" I asked, tentatively.

"We were friends."

"You never…" I let the question hang.

He looked at me with a puzzled expression – "I'm gay," he said finally. "I would've thought that was obvious by now." He gestured at his naked torso. "I mean, I slept with women before I came out, but that was more than ten years ago."

"I just thought… I saw you two in the car park the other night after we had a drink in the pub."

He nodded. "She was crying. She was always crying recently. She told me she was having money problems and was a bit stressed out. I offered her a loan."

This was news. "Really? What did she say?"

Simon cleared his throat and reddened. The blush went down his entire body. "I was going to transfer her a thousand pounds on Monday when I had a cheque clear for some work that I did last month."

I had sat up but now lay back down on the floor and looked at my ceiling. Where did Simon get £1,000 to randomly give Arabella? He said a loan, but he couldn't have been that naive to think Arabella to be the sort of person who'd actually repay it.

I ruminated over this for a minute or two. "Did you know that she was… so popular?" I asked. I felt guilty.

Simon sighed. "Yeah, I told her she'd burn bridges. It became harder to be her friend the longer it went on. But she was fun to talk to, so I kept my thoughts to myself."

My guilt was back. "I'm not trying to slut shame her," I said. "She can have as much sex as she wants. With whomever she wants. None of my business and people can do what they like. Like I'm one to judge, anyway – be a bit hypocritical," I said and gestured at both of us naked. This was only the third time we'd ever met.

Simon sighed again. "I know. I'm a modern feminist too," he said, laughing. "I wasn't going to police who Arabella took her knickers off for or how often. It was her life. I just wish she hadn't always been after the married men."

This seemed to be upsetting him. He put his drink down and leant forward, his hands rubbing his temples. I hoped he wasn't crying. I jumped up and put my arm around him.

"I barely knew her compared to other people in the village," Simon said. "I've only lived here a couple of years; they've known her since she was a bairn. But I think I knew her better than them. I knew the real Arabella. The fucked-up lonely girl who wanted someone to tell her she was not a bad person. Instead of trying to make her wear frilly dresses at country dinner parties and set her up with some chubby aristo with no chin.

"She loved Guy and Lady F. But she told me she couldn't think of anything worse than living a life like them. All she ever used to talk about was running away somewhere warm and sunny where no one knew her and starting again."

That was a feeling I knew all too well.

Simon smiled at me. His eyes were wet. "Anyway, onto happier topics," he said, and threw off my throw rug. He pointed down at his dick, which was awake and ready for action. "I've got this to deal with. Round two?"

Chapter 15

After we finished, we dozed for a while, and I awoke at some point with my stomach growling. No wonder I'd had weird, dazed spells. I hadn't eaten anything all day. I went to the kitchen grabbed every item of food I could find and brought it out to the living room, where Simon was sprawled out on the floor on his side, the throw clutched around his chest, while his back and legs were left uncovered by the material. I slapped him on one of his very muscular and toned bum cheeks to wake him up. "Eat," I ordered.

We both dug into the toast, crisps, chocolate and other completely un-nutritious foods I'd ferreted out of my fridge. I noticed it was dark outside, and almost as a reflex grabbed the TV remote and switched it on.

I had managed to find the BBC News channel. I glanced at my phone. It was 8pm. At least the day was starting to go faster. The lead story was about Syria, and the horrors unfolding there, and then a quick piece on the latest Brexit shitstorm. Item three, however, was about Arabella.

"A dog walker discovered the body around eight this morning ("I don't even have a dog!", "Sssh!") at the back of this pub in the north Dorset village of Lilbury.

"The victim has been formally identified as Arabella Sweet, twenty-two, a local girl. Miss Sweet had worked as a barmaid at the Fox and Lamprey pub where she was found, for around eighteen months, after finishing her degree at Bristol University."

The footage showed the police in the car park, some aerial footage of the field too, with a white tent over the spot where she was killed. Simon grabbed my hand, and I rubbed his knuckles.

The report went on to interview some locals. Unsurprisingly, Odette Douglas popped up. "It's horrible. We knew Arabella well, so this is a devastating blow." She stopped to sniffle a little. "I can't imagine who would do this."

The reporter began to wrap up the item, Simon grabbed the remote and switched off the TV. We sat there in silence for a long time, holding hands. Simon took deep steadying breaths.

"Would you like to stay the night?" I asked, tentatively. I'd spooked myself a little in the kitchen earlier. It didn't have a blind or curtains yet and I'd spent a few minutes looking out into the darkness, imagining the person out there who had killed Arabella. They were still out there.

He took my hand in his. "Come on."

We lay in the darkness of my bedroom. There wasn't much touching. I wanted another person there in case I woke up in the middle of the night like I knew I would. I didn't want to imagine the murderers and bogeymen without another person there.

Simon fell asleep eventually and breathed quiet, steady breaths, while I fidgeted. I counted the hours until dawn.

Chapter 16

I must have fallen asleep eventually because I awoke to Simon leaving the bed. I followed him downstairs to see him putting on his underwear in my kitchen, where we'd left our clothes so many hours before.

"Morning," he whispered.

"It's early," I told him.

"I know, but I've got work to do," he said. "I've got wallpaper to hang for a widow in Sittingston." He put his shirt on – disappointing.

"It's not a reflection on you, I promise," he said, grinning. "Yesterday was the best possible antidote for all that crazy shit."

I smiled. I didn't believe him, but okay. He sensed it. "What day should I make a start on the work?"

"Um, I'm in London on Thursday night. Going up in the morning and coming back Friday. Aside from that, I'm here."

"Great. I'll be here Tuesday." He made his way to the door. He gave me a peck on the cheek as he left. "We're cool? About this?" He gestured up the stairs. I nodded.

"We've seen each other naked. It doesn't mean we can't be friends or work together."

He grinned again. “You’re a good guy, Forrest.” He opened the door and ran through the rain to his truck. It was just starting to break light over the horizon. I closed the door and heard his truck pull away.

I sat on the bottom step of my stairs for a long time after he left. I sighed. I had a list of things to do. I made a start on the novel again, but my mind kept drifting. Hours crept by and I eventually found myself on the *Guardian* homepage tapping on the link to the article on Arabella’s murder.

They had used a picture of Arabella relaxing on a beach in a bikini as the header photo. She was wearing sunglasses and a little pink bikini. Her skin was golden brown. *The victim on holiday in Malta in 2015* the caption said. Sourced from Facebook.

The victim.

I read the article. Twenty-two-year-old Arabella Sweet was the daughter of Miles and Jocasta Sweet (nee Frobisher. Oh). Her grandfather was the landowner and printing magnate the late Hector Sweet. At one stage, he’d owned almost every local newspaper in the south-west of England and numerous holdings overseas. Her second cousin was Guy Frobisher, the former stockbroker who’d made millions after he sold his holdings just as the price of oil crashed last year and had been basically able to retire at thirty-five. He was now on the board of Miles’s property company, Sweetly Made Homes, who were building several huge housing developments in Dorset and Somerset, including a huge block of flats in the nearby town of Blandford Forum that were nearly causing riots from the locals who thought they were going to ruin its quaint aesthetic.

The article didn’t imply Guy had done anything dodgy when he’d sold his stocks, but they didn’t imply that he hadn’t done something rather legally grey either.

Was Arabella killed because of her father and his dodgy dealing? The article went on to list the truly shocking number of lawsuits and court cases Miles Sweet had been involved in. Everything from illegal labour practices to insider trading and environmental lawsuits. He must have some very rich lawyers. I wondered if Ollie knew much about him.

I stopped that line of thinking. I clicked onto the *Daily Mail* website, which had a garish headline about her death; they showed photos of the properties her father owned, complete with price tags.

The *Daily Express* website had a picture of Arabella in a ball dress from some sort of debutante event, and a headline supposedly quoting her mother: *"Who's taken my ANGEL?"* with more mentions of how staggeringly wealthy her family was.

The *Telegraph* website had a photo of her in her university graduation gown, with her mother and Lady F beside her. *Murder in Tiny Village* read the headline. It went on to sensationalise the violence and quoted terrified locals. It criticised the lack of local police and the local county council for not closing the Fox and Lamprey down when they had a noise complaint made against them four years ago.

I got up and left my computer. It was late morning now. I showered, dressed, and attempted to make myself look vaguely presentable. I grabbed my car keys and drove as fast as I could in the opposite direction to Lilbury. After about an hour of getting thoroughly lost near Winterborne Minster, I eventually made it to where I wanted, and parked outside the retail complex in Poole with the John Lewis. Fucking on the floor was fine once, but only because Simon and I had deemed it necessary to stop due to the creaking of my ancient sofa every time we tried to do anything more athletic than sit completely still.

And now I had carpet burn on my back.

I spent a couple of hours in there spending every penny I had by making the bored shop assistant my bitch. She had to ditch the older middle-aged couples bickering over tablecloths when I announced I wanted to buy that, that, and that.

At the pub on Friday, Nigella and Odette had given me the names of several shops in the towns near me who were independently owned and had great, original pieces. But frankly I preferred new manufactured mid-range things from chain shops. I needed furniture that wasn't something I bought ten years ago from IKEA that had spent most of the last decade in Ollie's spare room.

I sat on the toilet in one of John Lewis's model bathrooms that I quite liked and gave yet another sigh. I had no desire to keep shopping (my credit card groaned with relief), but I couldn't face going back to Lilbury. My stomach rumbled. It was mid-afternoon, and once again I'd forgotten to eat anything all day. While finding murder victims wasn't great for your state of mind, it was doing wonders for my waistline.

"Are you all right there, sir?" said the shop assistant coming towards me.

"Yes. I'll take this." I waved my hand around the model bathroom. "All of it. Bring me the paperwork," I snapped. She scuttled off to do my bidding, and I settled on the toilet for a few more minutes.

Returning home, I remembered I'd gorged myself in a post-coital feast yesterday (as had Simon; he seemed to put away the calories, even if, unlike me, he was actually using his for energy) and had little easy food to make dinner with. As I approached Lilbury from the south, I passed the village shop and was about to pull in when I saw Tommy Douglas emerging from it, having what looked to be an argument with Tatiana about a chocolate bar. At least that's why I presumed he was holding a Twix in one hand while he wagged his finger at her and yelled.

I decided to give that a miss and drove the few hundred yards to the Co-op. I passed the pub on the way. Still closed. There was a huge array of flowers outside the front gate. Cards in the shapes of hearts and even a few teddy bears. I slowed to a crawl as I went past. Someone had printed off a photo of Arabella and pinned it to the gatepost with her name spelt out underneath it.

There was a small crowd around it. Mostly mothers with children. I sped up again when I started to receive a few looks. They must think I was some passer-by, rubbernecking.

I made it to the Co-op and saw, once again, that it looked deserted. I stopped to get a basket and noticed that the sign saying *Kittens free to a good home* was still there. Just one serrated strip was left. I grabbed it.

The bloke at the counter was picking his nose as I walked past so I hurried to the back where the frozen ready meals for one and pizzas were. I nearly walked straight into Cytrine. She was standing listlessly looking at a microwave lasagne. She looked very different. It took me a minute to work out what the difference was. *Oh*, I thought, when I clicked. *She doesn't have her weave on*. Her natural hair underneath was a short buzz of dark brown curls. She didn't have any makeup on either and was dressed in sweatpants and a grey jersey, with an expensive red coat she just seemed to have thrown on over it. She had crumbs on her lapel.

On her feet she was wearing a pair of trainers that were more holes than shoes.

"Cytrine?" I asked tentatively. She looked up, breaking her attention from the lasagne.

"Arden, hi." She cleared her throat and straightened her jacket a little.

"How are you?"

"Muddling along." She sighed. "Did you hear? The police are looking for Pawel," she continued to my surprise. "Guy Frobisher told them he'd seen the pair of them fighting outside after closing on Friday night." She sobbed and covered her mouth with her hand. "They think he did it."

I moved to comfort her, but she stopped me. "I'm fine. I'm fine, I promise." She looked heavenwards and shook her head. "I can't believe it. I've known Arabella since she was seven years old. She used to come into the pub with her parents when she was a kid and practise her French with me. She had the accent down pitch perfect but couldn't conjugate a verb to save her life."

We both flinched at the expression. "It was me that hired her. She used to come back for holidays and summer. She'd always come to the pub and chat with us over a gin and tonic. When she finished her degree, she was depressed. She said she'd turned down a job on a graduate scheme at some fashion company in London she'd been offered, and she didn't know what to do."

"Why?"

"She said she didn't like London. Didn't trust people who lived there." Cytrine shrugged. "I knew she'd worked in a cocktail bar in Bristol as a student, so I gave her a job. I said, it doesn't have to be forever, just until you figure yourself out. I remember being her age. I had no idea what I wanted to do with my life either. I ended up in Paris, marrying a soldier who couldn't speak French, and I could barely speak English."

I laughed. "Been there."

"She was good for a while. Seemed to enjoy the routine. But the past few months, since last summer, she'd been a different person. Emotional, flighty, arguing with customers. Disappearing during her shift. Did you know," Cytrine's voice broke, "I was planning on firing her yesterday? Friday night had been the limit. Her attitude. I couldn't take it anymore. I was going to sit her down yesterday and tell her to go." She was crying. Tears rolling down her cheeks. "I'd been lying in bed, wide awake, practising what I was going to say when I heard the sirens." Cytrine once again waved away my attempts to comfort her. "Excuse me, Arden. I think I must go home." She made for the door and dropped her basket off as she dashed out.

I stood there contemplating everything for a minute or two. So once bubbly and lovely Arabella had become antagonistic and depressed over the last few months. She was sleeping with every man in the village (minus those I now knew to be shirtlifters). Her father was a crooked businessman, and her boyfriend was about to arrested for her murder. I wondered what she'd meant by saying she didn't trust people in London. Maybe she meant her mother. Didn't Guy live in London most of the time? Surely she could have relied on her second cousin.

I eventually managed to pull myself together and buy my nutritious foodstuffs of pizza and wine and made my way home. I got in and set about stuffing my face with unhealthiness. Between bites, I dialled the number on the piece of paper for the kitten. "Hello?" said a vaguely familiar voice down the line.

"Hi, I'm ringing about the kittens."

"Right, yes. We've two left. A boy and a girl. Would you like to come see them? They're darling."

"Sure. Whereabouts are you?"

The lady gave me directions, and it was only when I realised how close the house was, and that I'd passed the sign for the farm she was telling me to come to on my way out earlier, that I clicked. "Rita?"

"Yes, who's this?"

"It's Arden. We met the other night."

"Of course it's you. I thought your voice sounded familiar." She told me to pop over whenever, and twenty minutes later, my battered car was driving over the potholes of Merry Wind Farm, the property that had been in John's family for a hundred years.

Rita waited for me at the doorway of the old stone farmhouse. She had slippers on and a floral dress, with the same rust-coloured cardie she'd worn on Friday night over the top of it.

She greeted me warmly and invited me out of the soft rain that was falling and into the Parkinson's warm and comforting kitchen.

It was like stepping into a chocolate box. A dog was warming itself by a fireplace, and John was sitting at the huge kitchen table with his feet up on a chair, his head lolled back, snoring softly. Rita had been making something delicious smelling on the Aga when I'd arrived and kept up a flow of conversation as she let me in and stopped to stir the pot of flavoursome meat.

"We inherited the cat, you see, from John's mum, who had to go into a care home last year. She got her as a stray and swore blind she'd had her spayed, so we never thought about it until she came and jumped up on me at Christmas time and I realised her belly wasn't that big just because of all the scraps people had been feeding her under the table. Should have known" – she made the universal sign for crazy – "John's mum has dementia. Of course she wouldn't remember whether she had her moggy done or not." She sighed wistfully. "Still, they're gorgeous wee things. I wish we could keep them all."

I followed her past the sleeping man and dog into the hallway, past a family photo. "Those are our boys. Daniel's in his last year at Cardiff doing business, and Blake and his fiancée have just bought a house near Reading." Rita turned to look at me. "She's Portuguese," she said of her soon-to-be daughter-in-law, as if this was the most exotic thing imaginable.

"Here we are." She opened the door and turned on the light to the spare bedroom and instantly meowing started from a cardboard box in the corner. Inside was a very bored-looking mamma cat, who was gorgeous – she was mostly white with big squidges of black over her. As if someone had squirted black paint on a canvas. She had a tiny bit of ginger around her mouth. Scampering around the box beside her were two kittens, one completely black, one black, white and ginger like its mum, who were scurrying up the side of the box as fast as their little legs could carry them trying to get to us. "They're big enough now they won't stay in the box for longer than five minutes. We lost one of them in the curtains last night. Took us half an hour to find it. We could hear it mewing but it had managed to get stuck in one of the folds and couldn't make its way back down."

I was in love. I stared at the kittens and thought my heart was about to break. "We've had ever such a problem getting rid of them," Rita continued. "I've had that sign up in the shop for weeks. I even put up a thing on Facebook. Well, Daniel did when he came home for the weekend. I'm no good with computers. Everyone turns their nose up at the black one, especially. They're too big for this box but I kept on thinking that someone'll take them soon."

"I'll take them," I said.

"Oh," Rita replied. "What, both?"

"Absolutely, I wouldn't want to separate them from each other. Siblings should be together."

"Are you sure?" she asked, but before I could answer, she decided for herself, and clasped her hands together. "Oh, that is good news. Do you hear that, Millicent?" I presumed this was the cat's name.

"Mr Forrest is going to take these last two. Isn't that good news, and that way, they won't be too far away from you, will they? You can wander over and see them, can't you?" She gave Millicent a celebratory stroke behind the ears.

We both sat down around the box and the kittens eventually made their way over the cardboard wall and came to me. The next few minutes proceeded in silence as they decided if they liked me enough to come closer.

"How are you feeling?" Rita asked me as I stroked the black kitten, a boy Rita said, and waved a toy in my other hand for his sister.

"About Arabella? Not great," I answered. "Not something I want to make a habit of."

"I went down to Honningtons this morning after church. Tarquin was there. He said that Guy and Lady F weren't up for visitors right now."

"Tarquin's still here? Surely he'd have to head back to London soon."

"Oh, he comes and goes as he pleases. I'm not sure what he does for money. I think he inherited something, a castle up north, or a town. I can't remember. He and Guy have flats near each other in Chelsea, I know that much. Although Guy's been living down here since he quit his job last year."

Rita was a font of information. "Ewa and I go to church together in Sittingston," she answered without me having to ask my question. Her Irish accent was a little more obvious now. I could imagine them sitting in the Catholic church gossiping away.

We began to organise how I'd get the kittens home. Rita lifted Millicent out of the box and handed it to me. She passed over some of the leftover toys and treats they had too.

I gave my thanks and promised to take her up on the offer to come over for dinner one night soon. She stopped me at the door and fixed my coat collar. "Don't think about it too much, doesn't help the soul to focus on why. That's for the police to figure out. And for God to judge them. You just keep writing those books, young man. I like them."

I waved to the sleeping John and made my way into the dark and rain with two small meowing kittens who were not happy to be kept apart from their mum. I got them home and put the box in the corner of the living room nearest to the fire. I got a selection of old towels and made a bed for them next to some meat and a bowl of water (all with lots of newspaper under them). I googled "how do you house train kittens?" and spent the next few hours watching them while intermittently checking them to make sure they hadn't weed on the carpet.

"Horrible carpet, anyway," I said to them as the black kitten took his first awkward steps across it. "We'll get Simon to replace it with something nicer." I went and made a sandwich and munched away as they explored the corners of the room. "What am I going to name you two little buggers? Starsky and Hutch? Dalziel and Pascoe? Mulder and Scully?" Was a duo too cutesy? Black kitten was climbing the sofa, while the ginger, black, and white one was sniffing the TV. Did it matter if one was a boy and a girl, and I gave them names of one gender – would the binary survive?

"Smith and Jones? Black and Decker? French and Saunders?" The kittens didn't seem to be interested in any of these names. "Mel and Sue?"

A knock at the door broke my concentration. I checked my watch. It was gone 8pm. A bit late for social calls in the countryside on a Sunday night.

A part of me hoped it was Simon round for another session, but I doubted it. Still, I ran to the door a little faster than I should, especially with a murderer out there.

I opened the door and stood stock-still. "Hi," Guy said, drenched from the rain and looking like a drowned rat. "Can I come in?"

Chapter 17

Guy was sodden. I made way for him to pass through into the house. "Did you walk up here?" I asked.

"I wanted to get out of the house. My aunt hasn't left her room all day and the four walls were driving me mad." I took his coat and waved him through to the lounge.

"Go sit by the fire." He went in as I hung up his coat on the back of the chair in the dining room.

"Hello, kitties!" he said loudly. "You've got animals!" he yelled out to me. "When did you get these?"

"About three hours ago," I answered as I came into the room. Guy, whose shirt was drenched down the middle where his coat had been open, but dry along the sleeves, was cradling both kittens, one in each hand. "They're so small!" He was adorably excited about them.

I realised this was going to be a recurring theme from now on; every conversation I had would be prefixed by ten minutes of cooing over these helpless balls of fluff.

Guy stood in the middle of the living room patting and stroking them. "What are their names?"

"Haven't got that far yet," I admitted. "I was thinking Merkel and Sarkozy."

Guy laughed. After a bit longer, he put them down in their pile of towels so they could curl up together now that their adventures had tuckered them out.

"Would you like a drink?" I asked.

"Yes, Scotch if you have it." I didn't.

I bought him a beer. "My liquor cabinet is a work in progress." I firmly believed that if you had alcohol in the house then you drank it.

Guy took the beer but didn't touch it the entire time. "I hope you're settling in well?" he asked. "I do apologise for not coming over properly to see you. My aunt did mention yesterday we should send you something as a welcome gift, but I think that's slipped her mind."

"Think nothing of it," I said, watching the kittens twitch in their sleep.

"I'm not quite sure why I'm here, to be honest," he said with a dry laugh. "I-I just wanted to talk to you, I suppose. The police told us yesterday that it was you who found her. Part of me was glad it wasn't a total stranger. I'm glad you at least got to meet each other. It's a pity you didn't get to know her. She was lovely, Bella."

As he said this, his face was blank until the end when he smiled briefly. A sad smile. The flames from the fire were illuminating his face. He'd aged about five years in a day. "Anyway, yes, that was my reason for this visit. Just to say thank you, I guess, for finding her. For ringing the police. I'm glad someone found her early."

"Early?" I asked. "Do you mean early in the day?"

"Yes, well," Guy swallowed like it was physically painful. "Early… the police performed a post-mortem on her. Obviously. They told us today that they put her time of death as… well, she'd only been dead an hour or two when you found her. They'd originally presumed she'd been killed late in the evening, after we all saw her, because of her clothes and the such. But no, now we know she was killed at dawn or thereabouts."

The feeling I'd had that the killer had still been around maybe hadn't been so far off the mark. I shuddered.

"Sorry you've been dragged into this," Guy said, noticing my reaction. "Most of the family will start arriving tomorrow for the funeral on Wednesday. My sister is flying in from Miami, and Arabella's dad from Dubai. No one's been able to find her mother yet. Luckily, some of my other aunts and uncles are at Honningtons now, so I can leave Aunt Georgina with them while I go down to London to find her tomorrow. I'm gonna rope Tarquin in and we should be able to track her down."

"Tarquin's up in London now?" I asked, mostly thinking of his cheekbones. And other body parts. "I heard he was at Honningtons."

"Yes, he left first thing on Saturday morning, before we'd even heard. He has a big meeting tomorrow morning for his company that he's trying to get off the ground, so wanted to spend the weekend going over figures. He rang me from Fulham when he heard and came straight back down yesterday afternoon. Such a good friend. He left just a few hours ago. He's devastated. Arabella and he had been close when she was a student. She used to stay at his place if she was over for the weekend and I wasn't around."

Ah. So, I could add Tarquin to the list of men Arabella had been sleeping with. Pawel. Possibly Tommy Douglas. Possibly Trevor Bliss. Possibly Arnie. And some others I was unsure whether to even speculate on.

"Did you hear that bloody Polish bloke has gone missing? Her supposed boyfriend." He spat out the word. I could tell the thought of his cousin sleeping with the help riled him. I felt my sympathy for him dissipating.

"You think he did it?"

"Who else would it have been?" Guy seemed confused that I wouldn't agree.

I kept my mouth shut. It was his relative. I had stuck my nose in where it didn't belong, and I didn't want to stir anything else.

"I was just having trouble processing it all," I answered meekly. The police knew about the fight now; hopefully, Neuberger and Wales wouldn't be knocking on the door to ask me about my reasons for omitting it. Hopefully, they'd believe me. Once again, I wondered why I'd just not told them. But I was convinced that Pawel hadn't hurt her. He seemed upset with her on Friday night about whatever their argument was, but I remember the expression on his face. It was genuine concern for her, I was sure of it.

I came out of my thoughts and looked up. Guy was crying, but trying awfully hard not to; he wiped his cheek with the back of his sleeve. "Oh, Jesus, look at me. Sorry, this is so inappropriate. You must think we're all mad. You barely know us."

I went over to him and sat next to him on my ancient, sagging sofa, which creaked like it was about to collapse under the weight of both of us. I put my hand on Guy's shoulder and had to resist the urge to caw over his ridiculous muscle tone. If the question was "Bro, do you even lift?" then Guy Frobisher's answer should just be to flex his upper arm, and it'd shut down any more questions.

Guy patted my hand. "Thanks, I-I'm so embarrassed. I did just come over to say thank you on behalf of the family. Um, well, I'll let you get on. You've got those wee things to look after." He cocked an eyebrow to the kittens. "I'll, um, see you around. I hope you'll come to the funeral. We'll host it at St Candida's down in the village when they let us have her body back. I want my aunt to see how many people really did care for Bella."

I couldn't think of anything I wanted to attend less than the funeral of a murdered posh girl. But I smiled politely and gripped his shoulder. "I'll be there."

Guy left to make his way home shortly afterwards – turning down my offer to drive him back to Honningtons. As he left, he grabbed me to him and put his arm around my neck like he was going to strangle me. He let out a muffled sob and pulled me even tighter. He let me go, but our faces were close. We stared at each other for a second. I felt a frisson of something, but then again, I sometimes felt a frisson from an electric space heater. He broke first. "Oh, and please, I know this is a lot to ask, but if the press come sniffing—"

"Don't worry, I won't be talking to the media."

Seemingly satisfied, he bid me adieu and walked back off into the rain. I closed the door and put the chain on. And then went back to my kittens.

Chapter 18

The next morning the kittens were mewing and causing a right old ruckus from the moment dawn broke. Luckily, I hadn't slept a wink and instead had been up all night at my computer stalking all those connected with Arabella on Facebook.

I'd learnt several things: Pawel Gromorski was covered in tattoos under his chef's jacket according to his holiday snaps in Ibiza last summer (I'm surprised many of the photos were still on Facebook, considering in every one of them there was one of a group of Slavic men flashing the camera) and had worked at the pub for two years. He also couldn't spell. His written Polish was worse than his written English, which was strange.

Tarquin Scott seemed to have a lot of very good-looking male friends who he went to nightclubs with, ran half marathons and colour runs with, went on lads weekends to Barcelona and Prague with, drank magnums of champagne with, in the gardens of their houses in Battersea and Fulham, and seemed to always be at the races and also seemed to have an amazing ability to have a different attractive blonde woman around him at all times, usually called Francesca or Tabitha.

Guy Frobisher was on the local council as a conservative councillor and was in fewer of Tarquin's photos than I would've assumed – he never seemed to be in crowd shots and the only women he was ever in photos with were Arabella and Eleanor and a few of his sister Rosie from when he seemed to have gone and visited her in Florida last year. I naturally scanned these photos closely for clues that may be hidden in those shirtless pictures when he was sunbathing on the beach.

Tommy Douglas was a GP in Sittingston, like he'd said, and his practice's website had a photo of the doctors and support staff all gathered around the reception desk, smiling and looking inviting. Tommy had his hand on the pretty blonde receptionist's shoulder. All his other photos were shots of him as the perfect father to Tatiana. Tatiana and Daddy go to the zoo, Tatiana and Daddy go swimming, Tatiana and Daddy in London for the day at the Natural History Museum. There was not one photo of Odette. Her profile photo was them on their wedding day.

Simon did not appear to have any social media.

At 9.01am, after I'd fed and watered and attempted another round of house-training with Eisenhower and Roosevelt (names were a work in process) I received an email from Verity.

> How are you?
> Heard what happened. Shocked.
> Let me know if anything I can do.
> Otherwise, see you Thursday.
> Vx.

I sighed. There was a kitten digging its claws into my bare leg as I sat in a towel after showering. "I regret adopting you," I told it, but it meowed plaintively and so I had to pick it up and reassure it. It thanked me by kneading its claws in the towel right over my willy and then reacting in a very put-out manner when I jumped up and screamed in pain.

I put Eisenhower in the bathroom with his sister, the toilet bowl lid down and newspapers all over the floor. "Don't drown," I warned them as I closed the door, with my phone buzzing in my other hand. I answered the message as I made quick progress to Compney Parva and found the pet section of Tesco, where I proceeded to spend my way to a feeling of calmness again. After I'd finished making sure my kittens would be catnipped up to their eyeballs, I went for a meander around the town. It was still drizzling, but barely noticeable. I wandered down the street until I reached Bliss Real Estate and the reason I'd come to town.

Sonia was on the phone in the window when I came through the door. She was just finishing up as I greeted her. "Okay, Mrs Lyons, have a wonderful day, and I'll see you at 4pm tomorrow. Bye. Hi!" she greeted me. "Thanks for calling. Are you ready? Can't believe I'm so hungry already, it's barely eleven."

I saw Dhapinder at the photocopier and gave her a brief wave. She went into full "satisfied customer" mode. "Mr Forrest… seem to be seeing a lot of you."

She walked around as if she owned the place. Whereas Sonia stuttered and crept around the office. I looked at the walls: Bliss Real Estate seemed to win a lot of awards and have customer satisfaction guaranteed. The office was two shops knocked into one. I presumed from the tiles and the look of it that one of those shops had previously been a butcher's. The second half of the shop was down a few wee steps in a gap in the wall, where more desks were set up. There was a man giving the sales pitch to a young couple with a pram at a desk just in my eyeline.

"I hope the cottage and Lilbury are treating you well?" she asked.

"Except for the murder, it's grand," I answered. Dhapinder flinched but Sonia nodded solemnly.

"It's a dampener, that's for sure."

The couple with the pram were departing, and a ridiculously – it was the only adjective for it – handsome man strode up the steps towards us and held out a hand. "Trevor Bliss – you must be Mr Forrest – my wife and sister have told me all about you. Nice to meet you."

I shook his hand and felt my underwear tighten as I did. Yeah, Sonia wasn't unattractive, but she was still average-looking, so surely all her family's good genes had gone on this specimen. He was about six foot five, with short buzzed blonde hair, and a square jawline. A lithe, muscular frame, and long legs in tight trousers that made me hope desperately he'd turn around. As he stood beside his wife, I had to hide a grin at their height differences; it always amuses me when a husband is a foot taller than wife – even when she's in heels.

He put his arm around Dhapinder and told me how glad he was I'd settled in.

I was wondering where he must've met Arabella. Maybe Simon had brought her along to his rugby game and introduced them, unaware of any intentions on their ends. Or maybe she'd been in a bar in Sittingston. Or they'd come to the Fox and Lamprey – he'd got her number while Dhapinder was in the loos or something?

"It must've been horrible, your first weekend here and… well," Trevor continued. Dhapinder stared at his arm around her with anger.

"Yes, it was rather a shock."

"Arabella was a client, you see. We'd been dealing with the Sweet house lettings for years. Ever since the family moved away after the divorce."

I filed that information for later. But I didn't want to talk about Arabella and the week in front of them. I was here to try to make a friend. I answered Trevor's questions politely and then told Sonia we must be off. We left amongst a flurry of good wishes and made our way to the café around the corner. Sonia ordered a sandwich and a coffee, and I got a latte and a muffin.

"Is Trevor still on the rugby team with Simon?" I asked casually. Sonia nodded and took a bite of her sarnie.

"Yeah, they both still play, I think. Neither of them puts much effort in, though. They're a bit older than the rest. It's mostly guys in their early twenties." Trevor was about thirty-ish.

That was a locker room I'd like to be in.

So, there were multiple ways Trevor and Arabella knew each other.

"Did you get your car back?" I said, changing tack. Sonia nodded and regaled me with a story of her afternoon-long effort to get access to the car park before Adebayo had seen her and just waved her through to collect it after they'd got her statement. "He's a peach, he is."

"Did you tell them about Arabella's fight with Pawel? You know he's gone missing now?" It was hard to miss. The *Bournemouth Echo*'s front page displayed a picture of him (one of the same pictures I'd seen on Facebook this morning – sadly, not one of those where he was in a state of nakedness and drunk on a beach) and he'd been mentioned on BBC *Breakfast* this morning in the item about the "Millionaire pub murder".

She nodded, hesitantly. "It's bad, I hope they find him." She stared out the window at a passing pedestrian.

"Sonia?" I asked. "Is everything okay?"

"The police are looking for him, aren't they? They think he did it, don't they? That he bashed her brains in?"

I nodded. "I think they're wrong, though."

Sonia cocked her head. "You think he's innocent?" She was ripping apart her sugar sachet packet and piling the tiny bits of paper. Her hands were shaking.

"Yes, I do. Sonia, why don't you tell me what's wrong?"

She gave a terrified look around the café. There were only a few other customers, all sitting several tables away. "What if I told you I know where he is?" she whispered.

"Who – Pawel?" She nodded. "Then you have to say something. He's wanted in connection with a murder." I mouthed the last word.

"But you don't think he did it?"

"No, but he needs to go to the police. How else will he ever get cleared?"

She bit her lip. "Sonia, where is he? We need to go find him and convince him to turn himself in to the police. It's the only way they'll ever find out who really hurt Arabella."

Clearly panicked, she held her hands up in agreement and defeat. "I know, I know. Okay, God, I am going to get in so much trouble for this." She picked up her phone and dialled a number. "Hi, Trevor, it's me. Yeah, I've just had a call about 14 Gore Road from a lady who says she can only do now, she's away on holiday next week. Yeah, I've got the key from when I showed it to Mr and Mrs Carter this morning. I'll just pop over to Sittingston now to show her around. I won't be more than an hour. Okay, bye."

Sonia seemed very good at that excuse. I wondered how many fictional viewings she had in a week.

As we drove to where Pawel was hiding, Sonia informed how she knew where he was. "I only found out yesterday, I swear. Darren has his weekend Sunday–Monday, so yesterday I went round planning on telling him everything about the murder, and then letting him have some fun… you know, we were planning—"

"I get what you were planning, Sonia," I snapped as we drove north to Sittingston.

"Well, he wouldn't let me in when I got there. I wasn't having that. I said, 'you got some tart in there?' and I barged my way in. Was a bit surprised when I saw Pawel on Darren's sofa in just his pants."

"How have the police not found him though?" I asked. "They'll have visited all his mates in the area to see if he's hiding out."

"Oh, no one knows Darren and he are mates," Sonia explained, as she took a pothole in the road far too fast, and we nearly lost a wheel. "You see, Pawel came to him a few months ago when they met at a pub in Sittingston – The Lucky Feather, the nearest thing we have to a club here – and asked him if he could get Pawel a cheap gym pass and a trainer as he was looking to get ripped. You know, like, proper ripped. Bodybuilder style. But he couldn't afford it all on the pittance he got at The Fox. Darren says yeah, come round after hours when you're done at the pub, and I'll let you in. They've been meeting for months in secret. None of Darren's mates at the gym know either, cos… well, Darren's boss's brother was the bloke who stood for UKIP in the election. He wouldn't be keen on doing favours for some Polish bloke. They're not even friends on Facebook," she added, showing how cunning they'd been, as if not putting every part of your life on social media was showing the utmost discretion.

Aside from that being an uncomfortable element of the story, I felt like Darren may have been a little easy with the truth to his girlfriend. It sounded distinctly like Pawel might have had a side business with Sonia's beau. Namely, one involving steroids.

I kept these suspicions to myself as we pulled up on Sittingston high street. Darren lived in a flat above the local branch of Boots in a small red-brick building. Sonia buzzed us up, and Darren sounded pleased, clearly thinking he was about to get his leg over.

We barged straight in. Darren was shirtless and in nothing but a pair of grey sweats and some socks. He really did have a lot of terrible tattoos. "Where is he, Darren?" Sonia asked.

"Who's he?" Darren ignored Sonia and instead seemed to be gearing up for a fight, glaring at me.

"Don't worry, I'm not here to steal your bird," I said, and barged past into the living room. I wasn't surprised to find Pawel sitting in his pants playing FIFA on Darren's Xbox, clearly not that concerned whether I was the long arm of the law. "Get up, it's time you stop this and go to the police," I said to him in Polish.

Sonia and Darren stood behind me, and I could sense their facial expression rather than see them. "You speak Polish?" Sonia asked. "I can't even get hello right in that language. *Dob-jah*," she said in a poor imitation accent. "It's too hard."

"It all sounds like a dial-up modem to me," Darren added.

"I'm not going back," Pawel said, surprising me by speaking in English.

"Why?" I said (in Polish again, hoping he might be more honest if he knew Sonia and Darren couldn't understand).

"They think I killed her!" he yelled, in a further surprise to me, in a language that was neither Polish nor English.

"Explain what's going on, Pawel. Now."

He hesitated, and I yelled it again, but this time I reverted to English. Sonia and Darren sat on the sofa, while I stood, my arms folded, over Pawel in the armchair. "I know you're lying. I saw you on Friday night at the pub car park. You say you'd broken up, but I saw you the other night in the alley behind the pub on Wednesday. You didn't exactly hide yourselves away."

Pawel stared at me, confused for a second before he clicked. He gave a choked laugh. "You saw us? Her giving me a…?" He made an unmistakable motion with his hand and then blew a raspberry to stand in for the money shot.

"Yup."

He sighed and squeezed the bridge of his nose. "Okay. Well, if you've seen that you may as well know everything. You believe me, right? That I didn't hurt her."

"Just explain what's going on," I answered.

I could hear Sonia muttering about the handjob behind me: "What does he mean by that? What were they doing?"

"My name's not Pawel Gromorski. It's Pavlo. It's the same as Pawel essentially, but a different country. My surname is Davidenko. I'm from Ukraine."

I nodded, the picture coming together. "You're here illegally, aren't you?"

Sonia gasped. Pawel nodded. "I grew up near the border. It's easy as fuck to get over into Poland. When I got there, I got a job at a restaurant serving tourists in Krakow. One of the guys and I became friends. I asked him to use his ID. And for every fucking cent I had to my name he let me take his passport and use it to come to the UK."

"Oh, Pawel," Sonia said. "I'm so sorry."

"That's why I ran. I knew once they found out I was illegal they'd pin it on me. But I didn't do it." He started to cry. "I'd never hurt her. I loved her. I thought she might love me too. But I found out what she was like. All those other guys."

"Is that why you broke up?" I asked. Even though the car park still seemed to say otherwise.

"Kinda, I didn't want to. I told her it was okay with me, that I wasn't bothered by them. I fell in love with her when she came to work at the pub. She didn't take herself at all seriously, and she was different from all the other English girls. We had a drink and a laugh every night after work. We'd go back to the posh house she lived in, and smoke and I'd make her food, and she'd tell me all these crazy stories about how fucked up all her rich relatives were. We were never properly like a couple. We never walked around holding hands. We screwed and we had fun, and it seemed to work. But she started to go funny before Christmas. I thought she was just getting bored – she promised me she wasn't – but she said we should try and spend some time apart and that it was better if we cooled it for a while. I begged her to come back. And she'd promised me we'd get back together, but first she had to get money from her dad and sort some other stuff out. She said we'd go to Spain and start a new life working in a bar or maybe go to Australia and live there. She had loads of friend from uni out there.

"She hated the pub. She wanted to go anywhere else. And when I told her I wasn't here legally she said she'd fix it but that it was gonna slow us down and complicate things. She said that once she had money she'd pay for a lawyer and help me get a visa. But she started to go cold on me not long after. I promise, I'd never hurt her," he repeated.

"Who do you think did then?" I asked.

"One of those rich bastards who was always fucking her," he said. His face was red with tears. He leant forward and covered his face so we couldn't see him crying.

"Pawel," I said in my best-accented formal Polish – so he could understand it clearly and give him a modicum of privacy from Sonia and Darren. "You need to go to the police. Tell them this. It's the only way you're not going to be sent to prison."

"You believe me? You don't think I killed her?" he asked me in his poor, broken, Polish.

"I think you're innocent. I have no idea who did it, though."

He watched me closely, tears streaming down his face, to judge if I was being honest. He nodded eventually. "Would you drive me back to Lilbury? So I can say goodbye to Cytrine and Arnie first? I'll ring the police from there."

Chapter 19

It was quite a complicated procedure to get back to Lilbury. First, there were many tears and goodbyes from Darren and Sonia, who promised to stand by him, no matter what. Darren offered him his bike "one last time" to get away, but I was firm.

Then we drove back to Compney in Sonia's car in complete silence. She dropped us off at my car and Pawel pulled a face at it but got in none the less. He and I drove in silence again to Lilbury, but a few hundred yards from the village, he asked if I'd pull over and let him out.

"I don't want the whole village seeing me go in and you don't want them seeing you drop me off, either. I'll go in around the back. Past the pond. I want to see the place where she died. I want to say goodbye."

A tiny part of me was concerned he'd leg it, but he was bigger and stronger than me and could've bashed my face in at any time, stolen my car, and driven off. I trusted him – though God knows why. I stopped at the northern end of Lilbury, and he got out and disappeared through the trees. I waited several minutes on the side of the road while I collected myself.

Eventually, I drove on. I stopped outside the village shop as I remembered I needed milk, attempting some sort of normalcy. I parked up and was greeted by Nigella, who was just coming out of the shop with her own bottle of semi-skimmed.

"I'm so sorry about what happened on Saturday. Please, come round and I'll make you that coffee." She seemed calmer and back to her old self, but quieter, with a tight, nervous smile.

I agreed and left my car and followed her inside to her beautiful house. She put the milk away and played with the buttons on her coffee machine. In no time at all we were sitting in her conservatory drinking our coffee and eating some of the red velvet cupcakes her housekeeper had made that morning. "We're having a little memorial thingy for her tomorrow night if you're up to it? It's nothing major. I've always thought funerals were very impersonal, especially in this modern age when no one even knows their vicar. Besides, they're mostly for family. And Lady F is deeply religious. It'll be a God-fearing ceremony, that's for sure. Hardly Bella's scene.

"I just thought we could have a few moments about Arabella's life here in Lilbury. She used to play here, in my garden, you know. I looked after her when she was little. We can play some of her favourite music, and light some candles. I know you only met her once or twice, but finding her like that, I just thought you might want some closure as well."

"I'll be there," I said. "This has all rather knocked me for six, so I'd like to try and make sense of it in any way possible."

I checked my watch. We'd been nearly half an hour. Surely Pawel had rung by now? I doubted it, to be honest.

"Sorry, are you supposed to be somewhere?" Nigella looked scared. I realised she probably didn't want to be alone in the house.

I smiled. "No, it's fine," I said, and instead launched into the story of my newly acquired cats. Nigella was enraptured and I showed her a video on my phone I'd taken last night of them in their box just before Guy had arrived. We passed another half hour or so of feline chat: Nigella surprised me by saying she was a cat lover and that she'd even been up to the Parkinson's farm to take one of them, but her boys wanted a dog and nothing else was good enough. "And a male dog. I'm all alone as a woman in this household."

I eventually decided the poor wee moggies had been shut in the bathroom long enough and had probably found a way to kill themselves by now. As I made my goodbyes on the doorstep, it happened. The same car from Saturday arrived outside the pub and out stepped Neuberger and Wales. Nigella gasped as they went inside and then brought out Pawel in handcuffs not long after. I saw Cytrine and Arnie follow him out, holding each other. Cytrine was in a dressing gown. She looked devastated. Her two surrogate children were now both gone.

"What's happening?" Nigella asked no one in particular. She made her way to the roadside, and I followed her. The officers lowered Pawel's head into the car, and he caught my eye for just a second.

Unsurprisingly, the same crowd who'd stood outside the pub on Saturday emerged from their houses to see him go. A dozen or so people stood, arms crossed, at the junction. "Murderer!" one woman screamed. A ripple of agreement went through the people. I looked over at who had yelled: it was Eleanor. She had her fists balled up. Her face twisted in anger. I was shocked that the sweet, bubbly young woman I'd met last week was so different.

Nigella burst into tears. "Oh, God, I can't do it." She made a break for her doorway, gasping and holding back sobs. I thought about following her, but she ran inside and slammed the door. I saw Odette Douglas standing in the street too, looking at us. I felt very conspicuous. I moved away after the car as it pulled off. I followed it out of the village towards the shop where I'd left my own car. As I approached, I saw Ewa, Lady F's housekeeper, standing outside, the crucifix she wore around her neck in her hand as she watched the car go past.

"He didn't do it," I said, giving my rusty Polish a workout for the second time in a day.

"That won't stop them from sending him away," she replied in the same language. If she was surprised that I could speak to her in her own language she didn't show it. "Arabella was a girl who worked in a pub for just a few months. She still lived in a big house in the village all on her own that her father bought. That's what people see. And then they see Pawel. Just a cook with an accent. All those tattoos and up to no good. They'll blame him. It's easier."

She turned from where she'd been watching the car disappear in the distance and smiled at me. "You should speak Polish more often. It suits you," she said, and walked off back towards Honningtons.

Chapter 20

I arrived home and let the cats out, who were, as you would expect, going stir crazy. I put them outside on the grass for a few minutes while I cleared my head. They both tentatively sniffed at things and tapped at blades of grass with their tiny paws. Eisenhower (that name seemed to be sticking) attempted to chew it and then pounced on a dandelion.

Roosevelt and his sister seemed much more relaxed and wandered about quite happily. She kept going too far and I would have to go and get her and bring her back to the space I'd deigned as their little patch.

When I'd made my peace with forcing Pawel to hand himself in, I bought them back in and plonked them on their little bed of towels by the fire. They curled up for a sleep. I then set about cleaning up their mess in the bathroom and consulted my house-training website again for more ideas.

While I did so, I rang Sonia. "You've found your Bliss. Make the most of it," her voicemail snapped at me. "Sonia, I've had a terrible idea, but I think it's gonna be great. Or terrible. Call me. And don't make plans for tonight."

A minute later, my phone buzzed as I was cooking. "Sonia, good, hey, so listen," I started.

"Check your phone's caller ID, ya daft pillock," came a growling Scottish accent down the line. He laughed though.

"Shit. Sorry, Simon. What's up?" I was blushing as I chopped a mushroom, and had a kitten trying to climb a leg each. Their naps were surprisingly short.

"Just wondering what time you want me tomorrow?" he asked.

I thought about my own motivation for early mornings. "First thing. Early as you can." Let's rip this plaster right off.

"Cool." I could sense he was waiting for me to say something else.

"Simon?" I asked as a kitten reached my knee and dug a claw in.

"Did you hear they arrested him?"

I exhaled. "Actually, I saw. I was at Nigella's when it happened."

"I went over to Honningtons this morning to pay my respects to Lady F," he said. "The police had just been round. They had shaken her up and sent Guy into a mardy as they were talking about how they hadn't found Arabella's phone. He was raging about how useless they were. They'd looked all over her house, and the pub and the place where the body was. They wanted to search Honningtons too. Frobisher was spitting tacks."

I took this information in with a grunt and kicked a kitten off at the same time. I got the distinct impression Simon was not Guy's biggest fan. "Anyway, just thought you might want an update to help reassure you, or not," he said, his views of the police not much above his views of Guy.

"Will you be at the funeral on Wednesday?" he asked. I replied in the affirmative. He told me to come sit with him at the back. "It'll be poshos and aristos at the front; you don't want to be near them." He hung up not long after, once we'd had some convivial renovations chat. As soon as did Sonia rang. "What's up?"

I was checking a kitten to make sure it was the sex I thought it was. "Oh, hey, yeah, okay. Cool – do you want to break into Arabella's house with me?"

Chapter 21

Sonia was less than happy at the prospect. "Listen," I said, my happy demeanour leaving me, "you're gonna click eventually, but not soon enough. Your boyfriend and Pawel are selling drugs together. Steroids. Now, it's illegal, but not *that* illegal. So they might get away with suspended sentences. But they will get prosecuted. They'll get a record. Darren will probably lose his job, maybe his licence to work as a personal trainer too. But this isn't important at the moment. What is important, however, is that it's a great way for the police to hold Pawel and dangle a murder charge in front of him and hope something sticks."

"But..." Sonia whispered down the line.

"Look" – I pulled a cat off my plate as I sat at my table and plonked the meowing hairball on the floor – "the reason Pawel went running to Darren and the reason Darren was so happy to hide a suspected murderer is because they were already in cahoots together. Pawel probably knows a guy back East who can get the drugs and then they get it over here from Poland, then sell it through the gym. I'm sorry, Sonia. They are not master criminals. They're going to get caught and a storm of shit is gonna land on your head."

Sonia sobbed.

Which led me to point number two. Arabella's family still owned the home she had lived in as a child. It'd been leased out while she was at school and university, but she'd moved back in upon returning to Lilbury. It had a large for sale sign outside it, but it seemed like no parties involved were in a rush.

I'd seen it months ago when on the website, and then had confirmed it this morning when Trevor explained that Bliss Real Estate was handling the lease on Arabella's house. It explained how Arabella and Sonia knew each other on Friday night when they chatted amiably, to my surprise.

"You have the keys?" I could hear her practically squirming down the phone. I shovelled more pasta into my mouth while I waited for her pragmatism to win out over her morality.

"Come on. You know I'm speaking the truth." I told her about Arabella's phone too.

"Maybe it's in the house? Have you ever met a twenty-two-year-old girl who went to work and didn't take her phone?" Sonia was wavering but she had a point. What kind of millennial left home on a Friday night without their phone, even if they were just going to work?

I heard someone call Sonia's name in the background. "Who was that?" I asked. I felt bad about slagging off Darren when Sonia was still in his place. But it was a woman's voice.

"My mum. Dinner's on the table."

I snorted. "You live at home?"

"I'm saving for a deposit," she said, exasperated.

"Look, the funeral is on Wednesday. The police are probably already dragging Pawel over a barrel right now. We need to get in there and find something that could lead them to think he isn't a murderer." I told Sonia in detail about my belief that Arabella was screwing half the town.

"That proves nothing," Sonia said, still wavering.

I sighed. Big guns. "I think she shagged Trevor."

Sonia went silent. "He wouldn't," she said.

"He's a bloke, isn't he?"

"He loves Dhapinder. They had a fairytale-themed wedding for Christ's sake."

Sonia was whispering. I heard a door slamming. I think she'd shut herself away in a room so her parents couldn't hear.

"You said yourself Trevor and Dhapinder ran into Guy when he was out with some blonde girl in a tiny dress. She knew Simon, Simon knew Trevor."

"Look, my brother used to be a bit of a manwhore, but he's under the thumb now. He doesn't do that anymore."

"Then let's prove it. All we need are some love letters, a note, a receipt from a bar even, to prove that Pawel wasn't her only gentlemen caller, and that Trevor wasn't involved. The police will have to keep interviewing people."

"Why are you so convinced it was someone around here? That it was one of the blokes she was getting off with," Sonia asked.

Because I didn't want this to turn into a game of line up to denounce the foreigner, I thought. But to Sonia, I said, "Because when do the police ever get anything right?"

Sonia had her boyfriend, and her brother involved. To help one out she had to implicate the other. Who did she think had the better chance of surviving the police breathing down their necks?

"I have to do this, Sonia. I keep seeing her lying in the water. I can't sleep. I'm too scared to look out the windows at night."

She sighed. I heard her mum yell her name in the background. "Your tea is getting cold," I said.

"All right, I'll help. What's the plan?"

After I'd hung up on Sonia, I went to get ready for our break-in – technically, "entry without permission", as the Americans call it or "trespassing" in plain old English parlance. Sonia was going to tell her mother she was spending the night at Darren's house and then come here. We'd walk to Arabella's house from my place and go through it, hopefully find something, or if not, at least we'd have tried to help Pawel. What I wanted was to find that phone.

Sonia was of course late, and it was nearly 10pm by the time she arrived, but just as she did, my phone buzzed again. It was a familiar name. I sighed. It was about time I acted like an adult and answered the call.

"Hi, Ollie," I said, as Sonia's bright pink VW pulled in, the white roof and the swirling *Bliss Real Estate* written on the side in black.

She locked it and waved at me through the window as she came in. She had, mercifully, dressed appropriately for a burglary.

"How are you?" Ollie asked. "I heard about the murder. One of the reports just casually threw out that a famous writer found the body. I knew it was you."

"I'm fine." I let Sonia in and pointed her towards the kittens.

"KITTIES!" she screamed, and ran to the cats. "Oh my God, they're just the best. Oh, I love you and I love you, too. Look at their little paws!"

With Sonia taken care of, I moved into the kitchen, "Thank you for calling. I appreciate it, but I assure you I'm fine."

"It's a shock, though," Ollie said. "I've met her father, that Miles Sweet."

"Really?"

Ollie rarely talked about his work, and obviously, he could never reveal a client's name. This was a much more useful conversation than another one of Ollie apologising to me.

"Chambers were very funny about when we took him on as a client. He has so many lawsuits and charges against him. He's some sort of gangster gentry. Corrupt as anything. I can't think of one of his deals that hasn't ended in legal trouble for someone."

Ollie was a barrister and one of our first dates had been us walking around the grounds in Temple not normally available to the public on a summer afternoon. "It's like a movie set," I'd said.

"Yeah, and that's where Maxine Peake has a fag break when she's here filming *Silk*," he had added, completing the glamorous look.

Back on the phone, I thought about Ollie's slightly dubious clients. "You've never represented him?"

"God, no!" he exclaimed. "Thankfully, someone else in Chambers picked him up as a client. The lawyers who do represent him usually come back with a new Rolex and a tan from a week in the Bahamas."

"Yes, I got the feeling she had a complicated family."

"Look, can I come and see you? Make sure you're okay? I want to see you. I need to make sure that—"

"What? That I've not gone all suicidal and weird?"

"No, well, yes. That I can miss you instead of missing you and worrying about you. Doing both is just too much."

I sighed and wandered around my kitchen. "I'll be up in London on Thursday afternoon. I have a meeting with Verity and was thinking about spending the night there. I suppose I could see you then instead, so you don't have to come down here."

"Okay. Is this so you don't have to let me see where you live now?"

"Mostly."

In the background, I saw Sonia through the doorway chasing a kitten round my living room. "I'm just going to eat you all up!"

He heard the noise. "Who's that?"

"My estate agent."

"Of course. I'll see you on Thursday evening then?"

"Yes. Hey, um, in the meantime, can you find out anything you can about the Sweet family, and any deals they might have on at the moment?"

Ollie sighed. "Christ. What are you up to?" I could hear him tapping at a keyboard and rifling through papers. He was working late in his office, I presumed. He didn't have me at home any longer to run to for burnt dinners.

"Nothing, nothing. I swear, but just find out what you can, and we'll talk about it later."

"Okay, I'm looking forward to seeing you, for what it's worth. Which isn't a lot to you, I'm sure," he added.

I stayed silent. I wasn't going to get drawn into this.

"I'll see you on Thursday evening, Ollie." I hung up before he had the chance to drag up any more emotional blackmail. Wherever my feelings for Ollie currently stood, I had neither the time nor the inclination to go on a massive introspection to figure them out. I had a petty crime to commit.

I went through to the living room, where Sonia was snuggled with the kittens. "What are their names?"

"Eisenhower and Roosevelt."

"Ya what?" she asked. Clearly not a fan of mid-century presidents.

"I'm gonna get a dog too and call it either Kennedy or Garfield."

"I think you're too clever for your own good. You'll end up giving yourself a brain injury," was her comment.

We sat across from each other on my tatty furniture for a moment of silence before she put Eisenhower down and looked at me. She gestured to her clothes: black jeans, black top, black trainers, black coat and a black rucksack. "I've never burgled anywhere before, so I wasn't sure of the correct outfit."

"I've robbed lots of places and you'll be fine."

Sonia gave me a wary look and then reached into her coat pocket and withdrew the key to Arabella's cottage.

"There's a small lane two houses over with a miniscule, little path running to the back of hers. I remember having to walk down it in winter one day in heels when the pipes backed up and there was a flood. Anyway, it means we can get in through the back door."

"Excellent," I said. Sonia was less than happy.

"This is super-duper extremely illegal. If I get discovered I will lose my job. I will lose any chance I have of having another job ever again."

I held up a hand in submission. "I understand. Trust me, I have no intention of us being there for long or getting caught."

She seemed unmoved.

"Do you even like being an estate agent?" I asked after a long silence.

She snorted but didn't answer. I looked at the clock; we still had hours to go before we could head over. I knew we should have probably gone at four or five in the morning to be safer, but frankly, I couldn't be bothered waiting up that long. "Go on then, tell me. What do you want to do?"

Sonia shrugged. "This is the family business. This is what I do. Not everyone's lucky enough to get a job for life guaranteed, you know. Up until Dad retired at Christmas it was nice. Him and Trevor and me, and we all just—"

"—and Dhapinder?"

"Her too, yeah, I suppose. But now all the staff there hate me."

"They've just started hating you?"

Sonia sighed again. "No, it turns out they always hated me, but they were just too afraid to show it in front of Dad. Now he's gone they have no problem doing so."

"Does Trevor not help? Not stick up for you?"

"Oh, he's oblivious. Too busy trying to figure out how to pay off all the debt from the wedding. They're drowning in it, you know. Dad and Mum said they could have either a fancy wedding or a deposit on a house. Trevor chose the deposit, but Dhapinder screamed blue murder and made him take out all sorts of loans and credit cards to pay for her to have a dream wedding too."

"Wow." Sonia's life seemed much more complicated than I imagined. I was interested about Trevor being in debt. "Does Trevor know Darren?" I asked.

Sonia's eyes flashed. "They… are aware of one another. Darren's not from Sittingston originally. He's from Brompton Hall," she said, as if Brompton Hall was hours away. It was two villages over, about six miles north of Sittingston.

"Well, I'm sure their paths have never crossed then," I said, a bit more sarcastically than I meant to.

Sonia didn't like the implication of her family being accused of dealing drugs as well as her boyfriend, but I wasn't going to let that stop me. "Are you going to keep seeing Darren?"

She stared pointedly in a corner of the room and not at me. "I don't know. I want some evidence about whether this is happening first. I'm not going to take your word for it." She glared at me. The London big shot arriving to ruin her life and treat her like a dunce.

"I'm not trying to be mean, or ruin your relationship," I said, feeling more than a tad guilty. "But I think you should be careful, is all."

She kept staring at the wall, and I gave up and decided to put the kittens to bed. They were zonked and happily allowed themselves to be placed in the bed by the fire.

Roosevelt wrapped his paws around his sister and the two were soon merrily purring away in a bundle of fluff.

"They're adorable," Sonia said. She pointed a finger at me. "You're a dick, but they're adorable." That was me told.

I went into the kitchen and tried to find something to do for a few minutes while Sonia sulked. My attempts at making friends in Lilbury weren't going particularly well. So far, I'd had sex with one, managed to lie to another and upset her over a girl she'd known since her birth, and now Sonia was annoyed at me for stating the obvious and forcing her into criminal deeds. I didn't even want to try and imagine how I could make any others. At this stage, I'd be lucky having Odette Douglas being the only person in the village who stopped to talk to me.

I looked at my ramshackle kitchen. Simon was due in eight hours and was going to rip everything out. I'd be living on microwave meals for the next however long. He'd said he'd bring in a couple of lads from Compney who he used as day labourers to help him clear everything. They would be around on Wednesday too while he and I both attended Arabella's funeral. My first thought, that by throwing money at the renovations I'd make them stress-free, was quickly coming unstuck. I wondered if I should book a hotel. There was one called Heston's Mill in Bottomingham, the village due south of Lilbury. But that was incredibly expensive. There was a slightly more realistically priced B&B in Compney. Maybe I'd have to go stay there for a couple of nights.

Sonia came into the room after a few minutes. She had her arms crossed over her chest and her nose stuck up in the air.

Between a rock and a hard place, she was biting her lip, a habit I had too. She looked at some of the books I had in a box on the dining table that I hadn't got around to buying a bookcase for yet and picked at some. She was upset, more so than she thought I realised, and was desperate not to show it.

It was obvious that Sonia was lonely and didn't have many friends. She'd clearly thought I was a lifeline and now I was making her break the law while telling her that all her nearest and dearest were crooks, users, and liars. No wonder she was unhappy.

"I didn't mean to upset you," I said, hoping we could avoid a scene. I focused on doing the dishes and trying not to look in her direction too hard. She gave a dismissive sniff.

"I'm not upset," she said, slightly forcibly. She was a little bit scary when she wanted to be. Sonia had clearly needed to bash a few heads together in her time. "Let's just do this and get it over with."

I dried up and sat down at the table, with her taking the seat opposite, and we formed a proper plan. In, out. No fuss. No mess. No time to spare. If we didn't have anything within twenty minutes, we got out as quickly and quietly as possible. We came up with some contingency plans, Sonia explained that the lawn was higher than the back entrance of the house. There was an upstairs window that could be used to enter/exit by clambering over the roof of the shed in the garden from it. As the lawn sloped upward from the back patio quite steeply, the shed's roof was a jumpable height from the far side of the garden shed.

"I know which one is the master bedroom. Anything she'll have hidden, it'll be hidden there," she continued to tell me as we made our way out of my house, leaving an upstairs light on so it looked like I was at home. Sonia Instagrammed a kitten. "It makes us look like we were in all night," she told me.

"It also confirms we're together," I argued.

"Okay, you do it then," she said.

And that's how Eisenhower and Roosevelt made their internet debut. As an alibi.

We tiptoed into the village, which took what felt like hours, but according to my watch was only a few minutes longer than usual. I clutched Sonia as we went through the pitch-black street. "Your phone is on silent, right?"

"Shit. Yes, yes, it is now." We both carried on walking, going past Nigella's house. As we did, an upstairs light went on and I nearly wet myself. We both flattened ourselves against a fence. I peeked out and saw someone upstairs through the window. The light went off again and I hurried Sonia onwards. We walked to the end of The Wedge and turned into the little lane that joined the circular street, Hedgewards, that ran around Lilbury like a pregnant belly. The street was called Kissing Lane and had the nicest houses on it. The Sweet house was four houses down on the left (there were only six on each side). A large stone-clad cottage with a low roof and which opened straight onto the narrow footpath. The street itself was only just wide enough for one-way traffic to go down. It was only two or three metres from the window by Arabella's front door to her neighbour's door across the street.

Sonia assured me that the houses went quite a way back and had multiple extensions to the rear. A hodgepodge of styles and ceiling heights that turned simple cottages into a labyrinth of rooms and hallways, with endless converted downstairs loos.

We slipped down the narrow passage that Sonia had mentioned previously and squelched our way down the path. "Ssh!" Sonia gave me an angry rebuke as my shoe made a sucking sound while I attempted to extract it from the thick mud.

"Shut up," was my whispered response. We opened the gate to Arabella's surprisingly large garden. It was a good fifty metres long and had numerous trees and shrubs growing around it.

"Told you the street front was deceptive. Now watch out, there's a fishpond somewhere down here at the end."

I gripped Sonia's arm and together we inched along closer to the house on the damp grass that sunk under our feet.

After what felt like an hour, we made it to the door on the patio and Sonia took a deep breath before she opened it. "Last chance to back out," she said to me, a note of pleading in her voice.

"Do it," I whispered. My resolve was unusually firm.

She slipped the key in, and the sound it made as it turned seemed to echo in the chilly silent night like a gun being shot.

The door opened with a muffled creak. We were in.

Chapter 22

Downstairs, as Sonia had explained, the house was a maze of small rooms joined together through a series of quite low doors that all seemed to be in competition for most likely to cause a head injury by being a foot too short.

"Anything we want will be upstairs in the master bedroom," Sonia whispered as we made our way through to the front of the cottage.

I broke my mind away from how lovely the kitchen was (that is, at least it was underneath the mess caused by Arabella, and, presumably, the police ransacking it for clues) and followed her upwards. "How many bedrooms?" I asked.

"Four. The front left one was the master. It has eaves running along the front with very practical storage space," she said in estate agents-ese. We made our way in. The police had definitely been in here. There was not a drawer in sight that hadn't been opened.

I put out my gloved hand (we both wore them) and picked up a framed photo on top of the drawers by the door. Arabella and several other girls all posing on a beach. Eleanor was one of the other girls.

"Is she, maybe, a lesbian?" Sonia asked. I chose not to respond.

We both went through the other drawers. Photos, receipts, incriminating notes with "It was Mr X what killed me" scrawled on them were all absent.

"The coppers must've taken everything," Sonia remarked.

"What about the eaves?" I said, seeing the moonlight reflect in the room and highlight the outline of a small door. Sonia pointed. I scurried down and opened one. Inside were bags and bags of old clothes and shoes. As I was out of sight from the windows down here, I dared use my phone to light the little cupboard up. I rooted around for an age, but all the bags seemed to be empty.

"Check side pockets," Sonia told me.

"I am," I said through gritted teeth. It was a particularly unpleasant way of sitting that I had to be in to angle myself the right way to get at the contents. It was cold and dusty, and I couldn't see properly, even with my phone, and was hoping I didn't interrupt a spider or a rat. My knees were taking a killing. I threw a bag out of the way, and it clunked against the internal wall of the cupboard. Sonia gave a surprised squeak. I popped my head out. The wall of the cupboard was nowhere near as far along as the wall in the bedroom itself.

"Sonia, does the room next to this one have cupboards in it as well?"

"Yeah, but they're sealed up. A tenant once asked if he could undo them and Arabella was quite insistent that he didn't," Sonia said.

We both looked at each other for a second and then scuttled into the next room over (I luckily just remembered to shut off my phone's light before it shone upwards into the room), where we emerged into a smaller box room.

“Over here, behind the bed frame.” I began to move it out of the way. The bed made a horrible scratching noise along the wooden floor.

Sonia gave a raggedy gasp. “Sorry,” I said. “Everywhere else has had carpet so far.”

Sonia glared at me despite this explanation. Together we moved the single bed slowly away from the wall, trying not to trip as we stumbled around the other furniture in the little bedroom.

The storage cupboard in the corner was there. And sealed up. “Shit.”

“Do we dare?” Sonia asked.

“We’ve come this far,” I said. “Go to the kitchen and see if you can find something that we can jimmy this with. I’ll try and do it without.”

Sonia hesitated. “What about our twenty minutes maximum?”

I’d completely lost track of time. I sighed as I ran my fingers along the edge of the door, looking for a piece that stuck out that I could grab or drive a wedge into.

“We can’t turn back now,” I answered. I didn’t turn back to look at Sonia’s face so I couldn’t tell in the slither of moonlight from the window whether she was mad or not.

She left the room, and I heard her make tiny footsteps down to the kitchen to look for something.

The door was nailed in around the frame. I could feel the tiny nails at the side. However, the door itself was just a flimsy piece of plywood with the catch painted over. I grabbed under it and made a tiny bit of space where I pulled. I was in no way strong enough to break it without a tool. Putting my boot through it wasn’t really an option either, without waking next door up.

Behind me was a desk that looked like at one stage it had been part of an office. Presumably, in the nineties, the desk had a PC on it and all the other forgotten mod cons.

There were drawers on one side. All were thankfully unlocked. I started at the top (even though I knew it'd be full of Post-it notes and staples) but found nothing helpful; the second drawer was all just paperwork. I read it quickly, nothing exciting – Arabella's gardener was ripping her off, though.

The third drawer I hit pay dirt with. A rudimentary toolkit. Screwdrivers… no hammers or crowbars though. But I could work with this.

At the same time, Sonia came back. "I bought a selection." She put them all on the floor next to me.

"Is that a knife sharpener?" I said, picking up a long steel pole.

"Yup. I thought you could…" Sonia descended into making a motion with her arms, "sort of lever it."

I shrugged. "Worth a shot." I went back to the door as Sonia held the tiny crack open and I managed to slide the sharpener in. "This is going to make a mess," I said.

"And noise," Sonia added miserably. The pole went in, and I pushed it to the side. There was a cracking noise almost instantly and the wood split along the top third of the door. Sonia grabbed it and began trying to snap it as I went for another round. After about five minutes of sweat and uncomfortable angles, we'd snapped the top of the door off leaving a mess of splintered wood around the nails. There was the small matter of it being locked too. "Fuck it," I said limbering up. My shoe connected with it as hard as I could.

Five years living with a fitness fanatic like Ollie had slight advantages; namely, he was horrified by my general physical abilities and had spent long hours trying to build my strength with ridiculous and monotonous exercises involving my legs and arms. He was annoying at the time, but I was quietly thankful right now. The door split with a loud crack down the middle. Sonia muffled a squeal. "Oh my God that was loud," she whispered.

"We'll leave straight after this," I promised as I pulled the two sides away and went into the cupboard, fumbling for my phone to light it up.

"What do you see?"

"It's a lot bigger than the other side," I told her as I looked around and saw several boxes. Proper archival boxes, like the sort that Ollie used to keep his legal documents in, not the shoeboxes most of us use for storing paperwork. "I wonder where these are from?"

"She must've been hiding them," Sonia commented. I saw her check the time again.

"Five minutes more, I promise, and then we're out."

I opened a box lid and looked inside. The papers in it were headed with several different companies, and were a mix of financial documents and official headed letters. There were documents from HMRC in there too. I grabbed a thick wodge of them and shoved them into the pocket of my jacket.

"Shouldn't we take all of them?" Sonia asked.

"No, the person who comes to this house next will see the door and realise it's been gone through. They might click and come and look here to see what was being kept in these."

"We want the police to know we've been here now?"

"The police didn't find this, did they?" I was losing faith in Neuberger and Wales. I looked into another box.

Bin-go.

Inside was what I would probably call Arabella's love letterbox. My more cynical side would call it her fuck list box.

"She kept it all, Son," I said in a tone of breathless glee. I was starting to understand why those tabloid reporters were always so proud of themselves.

Inside were love letters from dozens of men. A lot of them were printed-off emails. I handed a pile over to Sonia who put them in the bag she had strapped to her back. I got another pile. This seemed to include necklaces, bracelets and other trinkets. And photos. I passed them all to her. I took a third handful and put them in my empty jacket pocket.

I looked at the bottom. There were several more photos. Polaroids.

You can guess the subject matter.

"Interesting angle," was all I could think to say of them.

"What body part is that?" Sonia asked as I showed her them.

"Doesn't matter," I said as we quickly packed up. "Take the tools back downstairs. You have the other photos, right?"

"Yeah, there's loads of them here. I've seen Pawel's knob three times already."

"Good," I replied, referring to the fact that she had them, not her newfound knowledge of Pawel's wang.

I followed her downstairs and saw her make estimated guesses at which drawers she'd taken the kitchenware out of earlier. I followed the room through to what looked to be the main living area. In the middle was a large trunk with vases and ornaments on it. I placed a Polaroid on each one. Dicks looked up at me. Arabella's naked breasts being squeezed by a man as he fucked her, whose black skin showed he was clearly not Pawel, was propped up against a scented candle. "Try and ignore that," I whispered.

"Done," Sonia said as she made her way through the room back to the garden door we'd come in from. She glanced at what I'd been doing. She shook her head. "You're deranged."

I started to respond but stopped as we both heard a noise at the front of the house. "Is that a key turning?" I asked as quietly as I could.

"Someone heard you putting the boot in!" Sonia whispered back at me, and gave my arm a slap for good measure.

"Quick!" I said. The pair of us ran to the back of the house in a panic, desperately trying not to trip over. We reached the garden door and Sonia fumbled with the handle and lock, but I shushed her as she went to open the door. "Stop moving! Who has a key other than Arabella and Bliss Real Estate?"

"Ahh, um, her parents? I don't know, a mad ex-tenant. It was rented out for, like, eight years and they were always changing." Sonia was panicking, and clearly not in the mood to talk.

The front door swung open, and I heard a footstep come into the house. That was it – Sonia was gone. I saw her shadow sprinting across the garden.

But instead of the footsteps moving on, I heard whispers at the front door. And then louder whispers. There was an argument going on. I moved back towards the front of the house. Just far enough to hear whoever it was at the door.

I hid behind a partition wall between the living room and kitchen. I could see straight through to the front door. A tiny bit of light was coming through from the street. I could hear the voices.

There was a man. And he was drunk. There was a woman, and she was high-pitched and scared. It was Odette Douglas.

Odette was pleading with the man.

"Is it not bad enough that you rubbed my nose in this when she was alive? Now you need to come and do it when she's dead too? For God's sake, come home!"

The man, who I'd worked out must be Tommy, answered with a slurred voice. "Go home. Go home, Odette. You shouldn't be here. I need to fix this. I don't need you here."

What did he need to fix? I inched closer to the end of the wall to hear them better. However, in my haste, I didn't see the side table with a glass vase on it. It fell and went smashing onto the floor and made the loudest sound in the history of humanity. Tommy and Odette's squabbling ceased immediately. As did my heartbeat. I stood in total horror for several long seconds.

"Tommy, I think there's someone in there."

I heard Tommy's ragged breathing and then Odette's voice again. "No, don't!" Tommy barged through the house, looking for the person. For me.

Now, I was nearly ten years younger than Tommy, I had the element of surprise, I was sober, and I had several inches in height on him and possibly the advantage in strength. But this meant little to me right now. I did like Sonia did and scampered through the house.

"Hey, you, I see you! STOP!" Tommy yelled. The fuck I would. I legged it to the back door and threw a chair in my wake as Tommy tried to give chase. He got about five metres before he ended up on the floor and a loud banging and crashing followed him through the house. I reached the door and flung myself through it, not stopping until I reached the back lane. I walked as fast I could through the narrow passage in the mud and had to stifle a scream when I reached the street and ran straight into a person.

"Are you mad?" Sonia whispered at me. Though I could barely hear her over the sound of my racing heart.

"Let's fucking go!" and we did.

Chapter 23

We got home around 2am. The walk to my cottage was a distant memory even as it happened. At several stages we had to hide in hedges and bushes to avoid cars as they passed through the village, but eventually we made it back to my cottage.

Sonia and I descended into the living room, where we spent the rest of the night looking at the files. We made several piles: financial papers relating to Arabella's dad. Other papers relating to finances not involved with that, love letters and other messages, trinkets and whatnot, and, finally, the photos.

"Any faces?" Sonia asked as I looked through them.

"Pawel, obviously, and er…" I was hesitant to say.

"Trevor?" Sonia asked.

I nodded. She gave a long exhale. "What haircut does he have?"

"It's longish. Shaggy."

"That'd be pre-wedding then. He had it cut for the photos and has kept it short ever since. I suppose that's something." That her brother had only been cheating on Dhapinder when they were engaged rather than married was the best Sonia could currently hope for.

"Anyone else?"

I sighed. The seediness was overwhelming: a variety of penises. She had a thing for guys who were circumcised, apparently. Which must've been quite difficult in this part of the country.

I saw someone I knew. "Arnie." I held up a photo of him with one of Arabella's legs over his shoulder.

"From the pub?" Sonia said, pushing a kitten off the papers. "Poor Cytrine."

"Who do we think this Black guy is? He's in loads… so to speak… but never his face."

Sonia took the photo. "That's the living room in the house. I recognise that nice wallpaper. So, whoever he is, he must be fairly local."

"That narrows it down." The Black population wasn't huge. And this guy was young and had a great body. Shouldn't be too hard to find him.

"This guy is in lots too. No face either, but he's got a tattoo of a lion on his shoulder."

I'm not a big fan of tattoos but his was quite nice. It was a lion's head made to look like a sketch, which made its way over his shoulder and upper arm.

"That helps us," Sonia said. "That's very recognisable."

"Yeah, his were one of the photos I left on show."

"Do we have any of Tommy Douglas?" she asked.

I searched through again. "None with his face. Arabella has a type, and he seems out of sync with them. She likes them tall and manly. Frankly, I'm jealous."

Sonia thought on this for a second. "So, she was screwing every bloke in town. They'd come to the pub, or she'd meet them on Tinder and invite them over to her house for a wild night. And in the throes of it all, she'd bring out a Polaroid camera."

"Sounds about right," I said. "But was it for fun or insurance?"

"Insurance?"

"Well, blackmail, maybe."

Sonia gasped. "Arabella wasn't like that. She liked sex. She was a modern woman."

I didn't like casting Arabella as a slut either. What she did in her own home was her own business. It wasn't like I was innocent.

I tapped the papers. "Her dad is a notorious crook. He's been dodging the police for years. I'm not saying like father, like daughter, but she clearly knew how to get ahead in life."

Sonia looked at the papers. "Ugh. This makes me feel dirty."

"Is there anything in there we could use?"

"I have no idea. To be honest, I don't know what half of this means. All I can work out is that Arabella's dad gave her a lot of money and she had papers for a lot of his companies."

This didn't help exactly.

We went on for several more hours as we discussed theories and scrapped them straight afterwards. I eventually gathered up all the papers and took them to the sheds out the back of the house and hid them in a box behind the deep freezer.

"Why out there?" Sonia asked.

I rubbed my eyes. "Simon will be here in a few hours and this entire house becomes a building site. The last thing I need is for him to stumble over the photos."

We parted ways not long after. Sonia had to go home and try and look presentable for a day at the office. I wasn't jealous. God, I did not miss having a proper job.

As for me, it'd been so long since I'd had a full night's sleep that an all-nighter made little difference to me. My insomnia had been in overdrive ever since I'd first noticed Ollie was spending more time on his phone than usual about six months ago.

After Sonia left, I poured myself a bath and sat in its warm water. I put my phone beside me on the chair and listened to the news on the BBC radio app. The 7am bulletin came on.

> *"Dorset Police have made an arrest in relation to the murder of Arabella Sweet at the weekend. Pavlo Davidenko, twenty-eight, a Ukrainian national who had been living in the UK illegally under the assumed name of Pawel Gromorski, was arrested yesterday afternoon after being missing since the death of Miss Sweet was reported.*
>
> *"Davidenko was Miss Sweet's ex-boyfriend and was employed as a chef at the pub where Miss Sweet also worked. Witnesses say they saw them arguing heatedly in the hours before her body was discovered."*

I turned the news off and tried not to think about it. Pawel sitting in a cell. Arabella's body lying in a funeral parlour somewhere with Guy and Lady F fussing over which dress she should be buried in.

I thought about anything else. The water. The heat. My eyes began to fall shut and I let myself sleep for a moment. I jolted awake as a banging on the door reverberated around the cottage. I got out and went to the spare room. Through the window I saw Simon at the door with two lads huddled in the cold. Simon was still wearing a T-shirt and a gilet. He was just showing off now. I dried and dressed at superhuman speed.

"Morning," I said, as chirpy as I could. "Come on in! Tea?"

Simon grunted. "Arden, this is Leon and Levi from down the village. They'll be helping me out. Are your new kitchen units still coming in a few hours?"

After that, it was basically a case of me keeping out of the way as Simon instructed the two lads what to do, with me occasionally confirming my requirements. They all took a few minutes to coo over the kittens. Even Simon cracked a smile as Roosevelt miaowed helplessly in his hands.

Leon and Levi both looked barely old enough to shave let alone work full-time. Levi was blonde with curly hair and a quickly growing beer belly in a pair of grey sweats. Leon had slicked-back black hair in a fashionable cut and wore black jeans and expensive boots. His T-shirt was bursting around the seams at his biceps.

I retreated upstairs after they'd cleaned out my kitchen and shoved everything in the deep freezer. It was 9am by the time it was empty, and I heard the first of the banging begin. The sounds from downstairs as I attempted to email Verity were loud and insistent. From the window, I saw a pile of broken wood amassing in my front garden.

After about an hour of that, there was a brief respite when they had a coffee. Leon bounded upstairs and made for the loo. He winked at me as he walked past my bedroom before shutting the door.

I had the distinct feeling Simon had met Leon first, and an even more distinct feeling it might have involved a certain geo-location based gay dating app.

As long as he did the job.

About midday Simon called me downstairs. The delivery of my new kitchen was reversing into my driveway and there were a number of men standing around waving their arms, helping to make sure the driver didn't hit a fence post. Or because men just like to stand around and look at trucks. One of the two.

"Are you okay up there?" Simon asked as I came down to inspect the units.

I'd been attempting to write but so far all I'd managed was several brief naps.

"It's fine. But I'll be heading off to the pub this afternoon."

Simon nodded. "It's open again then?"

I nodded back. "You're welcome to join me when you're done," I added. Simon ignored the invitation. I reddened. Perhaps Leon had new underwear he wanted to show off.

The units were delivered off the truck with minimal damage. Up until a car turned up at the back of the lorry. "Go around, mate!" the delivery driver yelled. The driver of the car waved a warrant card at him.

"We need to speak to Mr Forrest," said Neuberger. He parked up on the verge and he and Wales emerged from the car. The delivery man appeared annoyed at what this meant for his ability to drive off.

Neuberger still had his trendy café owner look to him. Wales was attempting to navigate the narrow bit of grass from the passenger side to the garden with her natural sense of balance out of kilter due to the bump at her front.

"Detectives," I said coming out of the house and walking past a whispering Leon and Levi. "What can I do for you?"

I hoped any nerves would be put down to the fact they'd interrupted me during construction work and that my builders were on the clock, rather than anything more untoward.

"Is that Mr Anson over there?" Neuberger said, ignoring me. "If you wouldn't mind coming over too, we'd like a word with both of you."

Simon appeared pissed off with this development but complied. He glared at Neuberger.

"We received a phone call this morning informing us that Miss Sweet's family home had been broken into last night. Apparently, one of the residents heard noises and saw someone leaving the premises with several stolen items."

Bullshit. I arranged my face into one of shock. No doubt Odette Douglas had been on the blower straight away. I wondered if Tommy would've been quite so keen if he'd been on his own.

Simon, unlike me, was genuine in his shock. "Someone was robbing Bella's house?" He looked disgusted. Just as well we wouldn't be having lunch together then. I was tempted to ask the detectives if the break-in had led to any new discoveries but stopped myself just in time from asking anything that stupid.

"At this stage, we don't know. But have either of you seen or heard anything that you think might be related to this?"

Simon shook his head and so did I. "Afraid not, Detective," I said. "As you can see, we're a little preoccupied."

Neuberger viewed the cabinets. Wales, meanwhile, was strolling around my garden looking at things she really shouldn't. I made sure to not look at the shed where the documents were kept.

"Mr Forrest, one more thing." Here it was, Pawel had told them about my involvement in his return to the fold. Or Tommy Douglas had recognised me, and they'd been playing with me hoping I'd fess up.

"Miss Sweet's phone. Are you a hundred per cent sure you didn't touch it or see it when you were… near her on Saturday morning?"

They still hadn't found her phone? For a wild second I thought maybe it was in the cupboard at her house and nearly told them to look there.

"No, I'm afraid not. I saw nothing at the time." The truth for once.

"And Mr Anson, you don't know of anywhere she might have put it for safekeeping or someone she may have passed it on to?"

Wales arrived back to stand next to us. "What with you two being such good friends and all," she added ominously.

Simon was still glaring, his ginger-stubbled cheeks flaming underneath. It was kinda hot.

"No. I haven't got a clue." It was his final answer. "Lads, come on. We've got work to do."

He moved off, and Levi and Leon sauntered behind him back to the house.

Neuberger regarded me after sharing a look with Wales for a second. "We'll be in touch should we need anything."

"I hear you've charged Pawel?" I couldn't help myself.

Neuberger gave me a look. "Yes, but I'm afraid we cannot share details of an ongoing case."

"Shame it was the foreign guy who did it," I said. I was screaming internally at myself.

Wales glared at me. UKIP-voting troll. "Yes, we can see why you would sympathise with his situation," she added.

Neuberger pulled her to the car. "Thanks for your time, Mr Forrest. We'll be in touch."

He drove off (awkwardly past the truck – it took several minutes) and I exhaled audibly as I saw his car go down the road and out of sight.

Almost instantaneously my phone started to ring in my pocket. "Can I not have five minutes to myself?" I groaned, and answered.

It was an unknown number, so I steadied myself to hear an offer on solar panels or an automated voice asking if I'd been in a car accident that was not my fault.

Instead, I heard a wavering voice down the line say hello. "Is that you, Mr Forrest?" the voice asked in Polish. "It's Ewa Zurko. I'm ringing on behalf of Lady Frobisher. She was wondering if you were available for afternoon tea?"

I was taken aback and had to stop to gather my thoughts. "*Tak*, *tak*," I answered after a second. "I'm available."

"Would this afternoon be okay? Around three?"

"Ah, yeah. Yeah, I'll be there." I said goodbye – in English for some reason – and stared at my phone after the call ended. "Okay," I said to myself.

I looked over and saw Simon standing in the doorway looking at me. "Problem?" he asked as I came back inside.

"No… hey, listen, I'm just getting in the way here so I'm gonna have lunch out and then I'll be gone most of the afternoon. I'll be back four-ish."

Simon seemed mildly interested in this but not overly. "Okay, we'll finish up for the day not long after, so I'll probably see you at Nigella's for the memorial."

I slung my jacket on and collected a few things to make myself look productive. "Of course. Good luck. Look out for the kittens."

I made my way down the lane back towards the village and turned over everything in my mind. The police still thought Pawel did it even after presumably seeing the photos this morning. I wonder what they made of the break-in and the Polaroids. Maybe they thought it was a rival of her father's coming to do a bit of corporate espionage domestic style? They must have found the upstairs bedroom. Must have seen the boxes of files that Sonia and I hadn't had a chance to go through. I don't know what they must have made of it.

But I know what I made of it. That one of the men that Arabella had been sleeping with had been as likely to kill her as Pawel had been. Tommy Douglas. Trevor Bliss. Arnie Hughes. There were a dozen other possibilities. Pawel had seemed genuine when he'd cried about his love for her, but I was as susceptible to liars as the next person. He didn't come across as the jealous type. He and Arabella had what seemed to be an open relationship. Arabella could sleep with who she wanted, so presumably Pawel could shove his dick wherever he pleased as well?

I just hoped that the police treated it with some degree of impartiality instead of an open and shut case.

Chapter 24

I went down to the pub and noticed that the memorial to Arabella was still there, but just moved ever so slightly off to the side. The gates to the car park were open again, though there were no cars to be seen inside it.

I walked in and found myself in an empty bar. Oh dear.

I was hoping this was fear of the idea of being somewhere a murder had taken place in and not because anyone thought that Cytrine and Arnie had done something wrong. It was making me especially uneasy after the sight of Pawel being led out in cuffs yesterday was seen by half the village.

I stood in the empty pub feeling like a ninny for several moments before Arnie emerged from the back of the bar and looked surprised to see me. "Thank God, we haven't had a customer all day."

I was shocked at that news. Not even any journalists looking to rubberneck? "How's Cytrine?" I asked as I took a seat at the bar.

I'd seen pictures of Arnie having sex with his barmaid earlier in the day and I wanted to jump the bar and grab him by the collar and shout, "You deserve to be in a cell just as much as Pawel does!"

But I didn't.

Arnie sighed before answering. "She's all right. Bit stronger today. The police coming for Pawel yesterday was a bit much for her, but she seems to be getting to grips with it. She's shoved herself out in the kitchen to keep away from everyone for a while. Well, and because we haven't got a chef for the moment. We'll have to get an agency bloke in for a few days or one of the lads from the kitchen over at the Farmer's Arms in Compney if things pick up again."

I was angry with Arnie, but I still felt sorry for his current predicament. His wife was hysterical, and his business was in free fall due to something that was probably ninety-nine per cent nothing to do with him.

"Did you know Arabella well too?" I asked after ordering a plate of the corned beef and potatoes and a pint of the local lager.

"Not like Cytrine did," he said. I bet that was true. "They were more like mother and daughter at times. They'd spend hours gossiping. I suppose that's why it hurt Cytrine so much when Arabella started acting all funny a few months ago. Normally Bella would tell Cy what was wrong. Cytrine's a romantic, you see. I think she hoped Pawel and Arabella were going to get married and take the pub over from us."

"What did you do before the pub?" I asked, sipping my lager. I had an hour and a half to kill before my presence was desired at Honningtons.

"Royal Air Force," he answered. "I was 42nd Squadron RAF Regiment at RAF Leeming when I met Cytrine while I was on leave in Normandy. She was this skinny girl with bad English from Martinique, and I was a little scroat from Sunderland hell-bent on ruining my military career in any way possible."

"It must have taken a while for you two to get together?"

"No, it was love at first sight. She took my order in this little café. I waited all evening for her to get off work and then walked her home. I made all sorts of promises. I'd take her to England. I'd marry her. I'd teach her English. I'd get her a visa. I'd leave the RAF, and I'd buy us a nice cottage somewhere."

"And what happened?"

"I sobered up," Arnie said with a laugh. "It takes a long time to quit the air force. But I eventually managed to get all the things I promised her. Just took a long time. Much longer than I ever thought."

There was a story there, but I didn't want to pry. So, I changed the subject. "The police came to my place this morning. Apparently someone broke into Arabella's house last night."

"Aye, I heard in the shop this morning," he answered. The shop? Was I missing out on vital village gossip by not paying a twenty per cent markup on milk and bread?

"Shocking. Then they asked me if I knew where Arabella's phone was too. Apparently, it wasn't on her person, or in her house."

A shadow passed over Arnie's face. Jackpot.

Although was it? If Arnie had killed her then he'd be aware of where her phone was. No, that was the shadow of a man who'd been playing away and knew there was evidence. Or so I assumed. I wasn't an expert.

"I wonder if it's in Pawel's room," I said, half wondering if I needed to break into the pub as well.

"The police have been over Pawel's room pretty thoroughly," Arnie answered, sounding more than a little pissed off.

The door to the kitchen opened and Cytrine, this time thankfully better dressed and with her hair back on, emerged into the bar. "Ah, hello, Arden," she said in a voice that told me she did not particularly appreciate my custom. My lunch was placed in front of me, fresh from the microwave.

"Yum," I offered, with nothing else to say. The Hugheses both stood behind the bar and kept stoic, blank faces.

I began to feel it was time for me to leave. They were open in name only, really. I ate a potato that was more molten lava than food and swallowed it painfully, trying to stop the burns on my tongue.

"Are you coming to Nigella's memorial tonight?" I asked. Cat + pigeons = answers.

"I think it best we don't," Arnie answered. Cytrine fiddled with something behind the bar to distract herself. "Several people in the village have made it abundantly clear we're not flavour of the month."

I had been right in my previous assertion. When push comes to shove, foreigners, incomers, people with accents are always the ones likeliest to be blamed. I wondered who'd said it.

"Nigella was very polite about everything. She came over last night and wanted to know about Pawel – I mean Pavlo, that's his real name." I cocked my head pretending that I was unaware of this fact.

"She seemed kind enough. It was this morning we had the problems," Cytrine added.

"You had no idea Pawel – Pavlo – was here illegally?"

"None. He had a Polish passport; we showed the police a photocopy of it. That horrible DS Wales said she'd have no choice but to report us to the Home Office anyway."

Either Pavlo had spent a lot of money on a fake passport or his friend from the restaurant could've passed for his brother and he'd just gone for the old "Yeah, I've changed my hair since I had the photos done" routine.

Cytrine let out a sob. "That bitch," she said – I presumed she meant DS Wales – "then had the audacity to ask about my right to be here too. I said I'm allowed to be here. My husband is British, I'm a French Citizen, I've lived in this country for twenty years. Poisonous cow."

Arnie put his arm around his wife. "Hey, come on now, pet. Don't let her get to you. She was just needling you cause it's her job. She has to do that to everyone."

Cytrine was in no mood to be mollycoddled. She shrugged off her husband. "Enjoy your meal, Arden." She stormed back into the kitchen.

Feeling that the atmosphere was souring somewhat, I finished my food in record time and left quickly after that. I had been planning to sit in the pub and do some work until 3pm but found myself now without anywhere to sit to while away the time with over an hour until I had to go see Lady Frobisher.

I could go to the little tea shop on the high street, further towards the cul-de-sac where Simon lived, but as I was going to have a surfeit of tea and cucumber sandwiches later with Lady F, I thought it might be overkill. I decided in lieu of anything else to wander the streets of Lilbury for a while and see what occurred to me.

I made my way up the short street that curved around Nigella's house, past where it turned off to Kissing Lane, to the church.

The church, St Candida's, was a handsome but not particularly inspiring piece of architecture from the late Norman era. It had the requisite big square tower made of the greyest of stone. Lifeless. It was stately but not pretty. Especially not on a cold and blustery February afternoon with complete cloud cover and a general sense of being an almost non-day. I walked up the small, steep rise to the church itself from the street and looked out over the graveyard. There didn't seem to have been anyone buried here for some time. Possibly a century. I looked at the nearest gravestones to the entrance of the church. The surname of the person buried there was "Frobisher".

"Quelle surprise," I muttered to myself. There were several more all along the line of graves. The Frobishers seemed to have been coming to this church to cark it for years.

I made my way down the line noting off all the "Johns" and "Marys" of the Frobisher line and nearly walked straight into the only other person in the graveyard.

"Oh, I do apologise," I said, backing up. I was on the slope standing above them so I had to grab out so the person wouldn't stumble backwards.

Odette Douglas made a drama of the situation and acted like she was about to fall down a crevice. She clutched my coat and dug in.

"I nearly broke my neck!" she said, her face turned away from me at an *Exorcist*-style angle, gurning at the spot of grass a few feet below where she would have gently rolled onto her bottom.

I resisted the urge to shake her off and send her flying. "Yes, wasn't looking where I was going," I mumbled, hoping to extricate myself from her clutches.

She pulled me up the hill, away from the danger zone. "Naughty Mr Forrest!" she said wagging a finger in my face. "Could've killed ickle me."

The urge to walk us back over there and demand a "best of three then?" flashed through my mind, but instead I plastered an absurd and hopefully apologetic grin on my face.

"How are you?" she said, turning the conversation around before I'd had a chance to register her intent. She stared at me with her insect eyes. Today she was wearing a frilly red coat over a woollen jumper, and what can only be described as jodhpurs on her lower half. "Terribly distressing, I'm sure. But thankfully we can all breathe easier now that horrible Polish man is locked away."

I regarded her as one would regard shit on their shoe. "Yes, quite."

"I've just been putting some flowers on my grandmother's grave. She was one of the last people to be buried here, you know. It's her birthday today. She would have been one hundred and eight. Except she died when she was fifty-two. Fell off a cliff on the Isle of Wight. Never met her myself, obviously, but Daddy cries over her every year."

I gave my best half-smile at this information. "Fascinating," I told her. "How thoughtful of you."

"Isn't it just?" she said, smiling. "What brings you to the graveyard, Arden? Researching for your latest novel, a thriller? Are we all going to feature in it?" She gave a high-pitched guffawing noise that at a push could be generously described as a laugh.

"I was just mooching around, really."

"Mooching? What a turn of phrase you have. Wonderful. Well, come on, we can't have you *mooching* around the village like a beggar, making the place look untidy. Maybe in London that was okay, but here people will think you're a prowler. Come home and have some coffee at mine. Come on, now. Quickly!"

Like a fool, I had entered her territory and now she was going to make me her plaything. I meekly followed her back to her house. The Douglases lived on the corner of The Wedge and Kissing Lane in a large Tudor house. They were four houses down from Arabella's, and about six or seven houses up from Nigella's on the previous corner, with the road forking in front of the house. One way went to the road out east where I had found Eleanor and the other riders, the other fork going south-east along to the village's tiny primary school. The road, imaginatively named "The Pottages" was a tiny narrow lane I had never been down. "What's a pottage?" I asked as I went past.

"Some food thing from ye olden days. Apparently, it was all the rage during the plague."

The house, situated as it was on the corner, and unusually for the village set fairly far back from the roadside, afforded the Douglases an optimum view of all those who passed it on their way hither and thither. It was a large house, with the black beams and a series of odd angles and sizes of windows and gables that showed its true age and that it wasn't some hideous eighties attempt at the style.

The house was also covered in a riot of colour, even at this time of year. Odette, to her credit, was clearly a mad keen gardener and green-fingered. It was a bit like stepping back in time, with the little wooden gate and the charming front garden full of flowers and shrubs.

Odette had to push against the door to get it to open. "Always something, isn't there? Sticks like mad. I've asked Tommy to fix it once a week since we moved in."

"How long have you lived here?"

"Six years," she answered. Clearly, Tommy was not mad on DIY then. The house's internal design was as to be expected: low, snug rooms full of comfortable, slightly dilapidated (I believe we called it shabby chic these days) furniture around picturesque fireplaces with heavy beams of blackened wood acting as mantelpieces.

Odette's kitchen, however, was all soft blues and filtered light. I felt like I was walking into the post-coital breakfast scene of a French arthouse movie. The weak sunshine coming from the window highlighted the dust particles in a ray over the plain wooden tables, festooned with flowers and chintzy crockery.

Odette had been spending the morning making jams or some other sort of domestic habit as the kitchen was covered in jars and the air had a sickly-sweet smell of burnt sugar.

"Excuse the mess. I've been having a bout of productivity and that ends in the place looking like a bomb's hit it." Odette would hate my house.

She cleared a space, and we sat for coffee. Odette got the cafetière out and I kept up social norms by pretending I could stand plunger coffee. What is it with people and their posh coffee? I just want some instant powder with hot water on it and some milk. But no one was willing to do that these days.

"Will you be coming to Nigella's tonight?" she asked.

"Yes, I have afternoon tea with Lady F, and then I have to make sure my house is still standing, but I'll be there."

Odette scrunched her face up just a tad. "Afternoon tea at Honningtons? How nice."

Sensing I was walking on thin ice, I put my foot straight through. "Do you go round to see her often?"

Odette gave a happy – nearly mentally ill – smile. "I've only ever been invited for tea once. When Tommy and I got engaged and we bought this place. Despite the fact that I grew up in the village."

I back-pedalled. "You didn't go over even as a child? I just assumed with you organising the book club meetings and the like?"

"My mother was unmarried," Odette said, fixing her glasses. "She married my stepfather when I was four, and he was the best father I could have ever asked for, but Lady F likes propriety. My mother and I were never asked for tea. Lady F seems to be modernising rapidly, though," she added as an afterthought. Clearly, it wasn't so long ago the great lady had a less positive view of sodomites. I was also shocked to discover Odette Douglas had any scandal in her life. My view of her as a demented Stepford wife now had a large crack through it.

"I'm sorry to hear that," I offered up, taking a sip of my drink and getting a nice mouthful of coffee grounds. "Did you hear there'd been a break-in at Arabella's house?" I continued, hoping for a reaction.

Odette didn't disappoint. "Terrible, isn't it?" she said, as I nestled in to hear her story, or whatever version she'd tell me. "It was me who rang the police. Tommy had been working late" (a lie) "and said he saw people in the house" (a lie – kinda) "and he said he was going to investigate" (the truth – kinda) "and I begged him not to. That it wasn't safe. I was convinced it was the murderer back to pick up some evidence he'd left behind. Tommy said it was just some opportunists burgling the place now that they know it's vacant."

"The murderer? But Pawel had already been arrested. We saw him."

Odette shrugged. "I don't know." She was wavering – did Odette not believe Pawel did it?

"Do you think it was him?"

Odette shrugged. "It has to be. It's always the boyfriend. And he was a liar – living here illegally. She probably threatened to report him to the immigration services or something."

I decided to publicly concede this point, though I knew it was incorrect. I wanted to know about Tommy and Arabella. "And Tommy going to fight them or something, I hear? Were he and Arabella close?"

Odette gave me an inscrutable look. "Not particularly."

"But you'd said you'd gone to tear a strip off her the previous day. What was that about? Was she overstepping the boundary?" That ice felt very thin right now.

Odette didn't answer. Instead, she busied herself. "More coffee?"

God, no. "I'd love some, thanks." My bladder might not recover from having to drink all these beverages to snoop. I still had innumerable tiny cups of tea at Lady F's to go yet, on top of the pint at the pub. It might not sound much, but my tiny bladder has been a burden all my life. Ollie used to make fun of me for it mercilessly as I would run home from the pub to the flat, after going for a pee five minutes earlier before we'd left.

"Is everything all right between you two?" I asked as Odette got up to make the coffee. Odette and I weren't friends. Her opinion of me didn't bother me, but if her husband had gone crawling to Arabella because he wasn't getting any love at home, then that really did put the spotlight on him. Sick of watching her paw over every man in the village? Maybe he'd seen her with Pawel and had no problem in stirring the pot? Maybe he antagonised them on Friday night? Provoked an argument between them at the pub and then watched on as they screamed at each other in the car park?

It wouldn't take much; a whispered comment in the ear or two between most couples could set off an almighty row. Ollie and I could scream blue murder at each other over a misplaced comma in a text.

Odette's response was not what I expected: she started crying. Not full-on bawling, but she gave a few weepy sniffles, and all of a sudden her head was in her hands, and her shoulders were heaving.

"Hey, hey, come on now, it's all right," I said. I went over and gently guided her back to her seat. "It's okay. Tell me what's wrong. Whatever it is, I'm sure it's not that bad."

Unless your husband killed a girl.

"It's Tommy. He's so unhappy. Oh, God. He's been so angry and miserable. For months he just shouts, and he's always in a bad temper. I didn't know what it was until…" Until what? I daren't ask in case she ran away like a frightened forest animal.

"Until I found these…" She got up and walked over to a desk in the next room. I heard her open a drawer. She brought a pile of papers back over to the table. I saw the names of the companies on them. Oh.

Credit card statements, final demand notices for bills, letters from the bank. "We're up to our eyeballs in debt," she said, stating the obvious.

"We already had a huge mortgage on this place, and Tommy hasn't finished paying for medical school. Not to mention everything else."

By everything else, I presumed the brand-new car in the driveway and Tatiana's school fees. "We're not spendthrifts. Half the furniture for this house is from my mum's. We live within our means. I have no idea where all this came from." She angrily slammed her fist down on the table. Everything jolted.

"I'm sure it'll be okay. Have you talked to Tommy about this?"

Odette stopped blubbering for a second and shook her head. "Arden, I'm so sorry to burden you with this. You barely know us. And here you are, my confidant. But I can't tell anyone else. They wouldn't understand. Or they'd just judge me. Especially Nigella. She's loaded. No problems in her bank account." She groaned. "Everyone here is so perfect. This village is full of snakes."

That took me by surprise. "What do you mean?"

"Oh, you know. The usual. People can't wait to tear you down behind your back, but to your face, they couldn't be a better friend. They're all liars. I hate it here sometimes. But it's my home. Where else would I go? Unlike all of them, I've lived here all my life. I won't be driven from my home just because they want me gone."

"Who is *they*?"

She snorted. "You know, the poshos. The ones with all the money. The people who eat up villages like this and chew them out." I didn't know who she was talking about and said as much. "You'll recognise them when you see them."

This was news to me. Were there property developers sniffing around? I clearly knew nothing. And the things I thought I knew were a complete misunderstanding. I had thought of Odette as "jolly hockey sticks and lashings of ginger beer", but the way she was going on she sounded more like she'd just stepped off a sink estate somewhere. She sounded like me, basically.

Odette blinked away some tears. "Never mind, just the rantings and ravings of a crazed old woman." She was embarrassed and began fussing around with all the bills, clearing away the debris of her little emotional spat.

I checked the clock; I had ages to get to Honningtons. "Look at the time," I said, sounding about as convincing as the worst actor in the worst movie ever made. "I really don't want to be late for Lady F. Can I just use your loo?"

Chapter 25

Ewa was giving me a very odd look as she poured the tea. Lady F was also giving me a look, but that was because she was getting as close to baring her soul as posh people ever did.

I'd been here under ten minutes and had already had a hushed conversation in Polish with Ewa. I had begun to speak with her much more loudly, but she'd put her finger to her lips. "I speak quietly if I talk Polish," she said, and beckoned over her shoulder. She'd asked me if I'd seen or heard anything of Pawel, and when I said no, she told me he was having some sort of bail hearing the next day at Court. "Could you drive me?" she asked.

"The funeral's tomorrow," I said. "We'll be a bit occupied."

"Yes, the hearing is early though, and I've been to these type of things before. They only take two minutes. He just says his name and they read off the charges." I knew the procedure too. I'd been to several. "I asked Cytrine, but she said she wasn't going to go. She can't face it. He needs to see someone in there, he needs to know not everyone thinks he's guilty."

I said I'd take her just as Lady F greeted me. Ewa scuttled away with my coat and said something about tea.

Her Ladyship and I returned to the same drawing room I'd been in on Friday night. That seemed a very long time ago.

Lady F seemed older; her movements were slower. Arabella's death had added a decade onto her. There was no glimmer in her eye. She was an old lady, posh or not, and death was now shadowing her.

"I understand my nephew has been to see you? To ask about your discovery of… Arabella." She'd clearly been about to say "body".

"Yes, Guy came over on Sunday night. I told him the circumstances. Explained how I'd found her." Ewa came in as I said this. She gave a tiny shake of her head after she'd given me the look.

"Please tell me about it." Lady F asked, holding her cup and staring intently at me. "She was my niece, my flesh and blood, and I have to know how she died."

I stuttered. I couldn't think of anything to say that wouldn't be needlessly upsetting or morbid, or gruesome. Ewa stood by the door, obviously wanting to know too. Maybe for very different reasons.

Eventually, as the seconds dragged on, my mouth came up with its own version of events separate to the blockage in my mind. "It was very calm. The pond, the field. It was a beautiful spot, actually. It was quiet, there were birds, a few leaves rustling. It didn't feel lonely. It felt peaceful. It felt calm. Something horrible had happened but it almost felt like it was okay." I had no idea if she'd baulk at this. I would have. "It felt like Arabella wasn't angry about it. I've seen other crimes, horrible crimes, and I've felt uneasy every time I've gone past the places where they've happened. Stains on the roadside, a wreath on a lamppost, that sort of thing. This didn't feel like that."

Lady F had tears rolling down her cheeks. "The police said she was hit with something heavy and metal. They have a feeling it was something from a car. A crowbar or tyre iron or something like that."

"She was lying face down in the water," I said, not really listening to Lady F. "Her body was floating, gently moving with the water's own movement. There was the injury at the back of her head, all the blood, it wasn't nice. Her head…" I gestured and pulled a face; how do you tell an eighty-year-old woman her niece's head had been bashed in so violently that it looked like papier mâché?

Lady F nodded. She understood.

She stood up and walked over to the windows. "Arabella wasn't a bad person. I've long watched the news with tales of murders and their victims, and the victim is often in the murderer's orbit. The idea of" – she struggled to articulate her ideas – "guilt by association, that they'd strayed down a path they didn't understand, that things got out of hand, but that they knew, *they knew*, what the person they were with was capable of when they first began their association with them, and it had always been obvious. Arabella never did that."

I puffed my cheeks out at that and gave a slow, silent exhale. A liberal newspaper columnist would have a field day picking apart that victim blaming argument, but me? I could see it. People didn't often come into contact with major crimes unless they had led a certain style of life. One time, in a posh gastropub in Clapham, the police had burst in and pushed past on their way to sort out some scuffle in the back function room, where there'd been a private party. Ollie and I had only been dating a month or so and were both still desperate to appear perfect in each other's eyes. When a bearded hipster constable brushed past and jolted me, I muttered a string of expletives, perhaps a little too loudly. I'd finished off with "Fucking pigs" (quite innocuously, I thought). Ollie was shocked – as far as he was concerned, the police were a noble, if deeply flawed, profession containing people doing their best and they deserved respect. He was uneasy around them as they so rarely came into contact with his cloistered little world. Poor, sweet, middle-class, son of an architect, Ollie. It had changed him in my eyes, and me in his. What you thought of the police was such a quick way of understanding someone's background. Friend or foe? Were they someone you ran to or from in an emergency?

Lady F was still speaking. "Arabella wasn't like that. She didn't do drugs; she didn't go to raves or try and smuggle illicit goods in from Thailand. She wanted to live here in the village. She wanted to be close to where she was from. To be where she'd been happy as a child. She was rooted, but she was lost. She needed me. She needed Guy.

"I should have done more. I should have been more patient. But I'm too old for that. I've already raised children who weren't mine. I didn't have the energy to do it again. So instead of listening, I lectured. Instead of caring, I condescended."

She looked out the window, over the grass on the drab February day. One of those painfully English days of weather not too cold, but nowhere near mild, not raining, and yet with a dampness that worked its way into your bones.

"The police told me things I didn't want to know about Arabella," she said. "Things about her private life." She shook her head, trying to remove the information she didn't want from her mind.

"Are you going to Nigella's memorial service tonight?" she asked suddenly, turning back to me and giving me a big smile.

I gulped. "Yes, Nigella has invited me." I thought to describe it as a memorial service was a bit much. We were going to drink cider and listen to whatever terrible pop music Arabella liked when she was seventeen.

"Nigella was always very fond of her. She used to look after Arabella when her parents were away. Jocasta, Bella's mother, and she were – are – dear friends. She went to live with her for a few weeks during the worst of their divorce." Lady F said "divorce" a lot more quietly than the rest of the statement – it was a dirty word to her.

"Anyway, I shan't keep you. I just wanted to thank you for your discretion and kindness in finding Arabella the way you did and looking after her while you waited for the police. They said she was killed not long before you found her. It gives me comfort to know she wasn't alone for long."

I stood to meet her, deciding it would be uncouth to drain my cup before doing so. There was only a little left. I hadn't even had a dainty. Lady F took my hand and walked me from the room.

"You seem like a good man, Arden. No wife, though? We must work on that. We have lots of garden parties over the summer. A handsome writer would be a welcome partner for many of my goddaughters." She gave me a mischievous look. Lady F liked to matchmake.

I suppressed a shudder at having to make small talk over sandwiches with "horsey" Sophia and "art gallery assistant" Antonia. I'm sure they're lovely, but I don't want to hear about their "gap yahs", and new flats in Parsons Green.

"That sounds lovely."

Ewa brought me my coat. Lady F said goodbye and Ewa showed me to the door. Then she leaned closed to me and said, "Bournemouth County Court at eight thirty. Pick me up outside the village shop at half seven." She then moved away and said much more loudly, "Thank you, Mr Forrest. Until tomorrow."

Chapter 26

Simon seemed less impressed with me than I'd expected. Levi and Leon were packing up when I came home. I received a lascivious wink from Leon and instantly felt dirty.

Simon was glaring at me as I walked in the door. "Your cats are a menace. And your house is a bombsite." He scratched his bicep, and I had to resist the urge to ask if I could feel it. Oh, dear. I had the horrible feeling I was developing quite a crush on Simon. The worst situation when I'd already had a taste and decided I quite liked it.

"The kittens are adorable, and you know it, and my house won't be a bombsite for long, right?" I questioned him.

He shrugged. "Strange about the coppers this morning," he said, changing the subject.

I walked through my kitchen. Bombsite. It had no units in it any more. It was bare. The walls were covered in the marks of cabinets that had stood there for fifty years and were now in a skip on my driveway. I sighed. At least I had my decade-old microwave. Well, I'd bought it a decade ago. God only knows how old it'd been when I answered the ad off Craigslist from a flat full of Hungarian guys in Tooting.

"Yes," I didn't know what to add. "I can't get the feeling out of my head that they don't really care about the killer, they just want someone behind bars."

Simon shrugged again. "Can't say I blame 'em. Have you seen the papers today? Full of Arabella. There's gonna be a scrum at the funeral tomorrow."

I watched his ruddy face as he spoke and tried to focus on what he was saying, not on the line of his jaw. Luckily, my inability to control my animal instincts was not a problem as Levi or Leon tooted the horn and Simon made his departure.

"I'll see you in an hour or two at Nigella's?" he asked.

I replied in the affirmative and hurried him to the door, hoping he'd not realise my impatience was caused by a confluence of horniness and antisocial behaviour, but more that he was the help, and I wanted him gone.

I admit it wasn't a great solution.

After he'd departed, I turned the shower on and slowly washed away my long day. I began to try and put together the timeline of Arabella's last night.

Around midnight the pub had begun to close, and Arabella had been to-ing and fro-ing as she set about her jobs at closing time – collecting glasses, cleaning, setting the furniture, cashing up, and the million jobs waitresses do at the end of a night.

Yours truly and a gang of hardened drinkers were the last to leave. Who else was there? Nigella and Simon had not long made their departure, leaving Guy, Sonia, Tarquin, and me as the last customers. Arnie, Cytrine and Pawel had all been around too, especially Pawel, who'd made himself known.

Arabella had recently fallen out with her surrogate mother Cytrine over her behaviour and had been (I sighed) screwing Arnie at least at some point in the past, if not currently, which I was ninety-nine per cent sure Cytrine did not know about, and if she suspected, she wasn't dwelling on it.

They were suspects one and two.

Pawel and she had fought. She'd promised him fidelity in the future if they were able to go on a break now so she could work through some things. They were still sleeping together at least semi-regularly but Arabella's need for freedom and her desire to get away from Lilbury had driven her further from Pawel. He was heartbroken and angry by this development. Pawel knew her habits with other men but didn't appear to know – or wasn't bothered – by their identities.

Suspect three.

The previous day, Odette Douglas had yelled at Arabella. She was sure her husband was playing away. Perhaps the credit card debt was Tommy trying to buy Arabella's affections? Maybe I need to ask around oh so subtly if Arabella had bought any new clothes or jewellery over the past few months. If Odette had found those receipts so easily then they can't have been very old, otherwise Tommy would have got better at hiding his newfound financial recklessness.

So, hubby cheating on you and spending all your money with a tart?

Suspect four.

Your wife figured out you're playing away and the younger woman you were trying to capture the affections of still doesn't appear all that interested in you, despite pouring money over her for months?

Suspect five was Tommy.

And Nigella. Clearly devoted to her. She'd left the party not long before. She could have gone back to her house, but later slipped out. Told Arabella to meet her, as they needed to discuss some things. Nigella and Arabella were old pals. Nigella had babysat her, for God's sake. She would've trusted her implicitly. Nigella's anger at her frivolity and reckless behaviour manifests itself as a violent outburst. She only went to give her a stern warning, but instead she lost her temper and began to beat her.

I sighed. Suspect six: Nigella.

And there were more: what of Trevor Bliss and the lovely Dhapinder? Sonia said Trevor went for early morning runs to Lilbury, specifically the pub, three times a week. The distance wasn't that far for someone of his fitness level so he could maybe get here faster than his wife realised leaving him more time when he was here. He would meet Arabella round the back of the pub, she'd slip out from her room and silently run across the field to have a shag in the woods. Trevor got his leg over and then ran back to Compney, as fresh as a daisy.

Would anyone do this? Hell, I remembered how good-looking Trevor Bliss was. I'd lie down in a sewer full of heroin needles for a chance of five minutes with him naked. Arabella probably thought the same.

Maybe Dhapinder clicked on this, one night when they came to the Fox and Lamprey for a nice meal in the cosy pub; she'd seen her husband ogling the barmaid and suspiciousness had raised its ugly head.

The next time he went for a run she followed him in the car. Saw him disappear into the bushes with a leggy blonde. Dhapinder waited till he'd pulled his sweatpants back up and then followed in there with whatever she'd found in the boot of her car and BLAM! Arabella's brains all over the field.

Or maybe Trevor himself did it. Angry at her cuckolding him while he cheated on his wife. A torrid love dodecahedron gone wrong.

Suspects seven and eight: Trevor and Dhapinder Bliss.

I sighed again. And then there were all the other men in those photos. Oh, God. There'd be hundreds of motives for this. Every man in a ten-mile radius seemed to have had a go on the Sweet fun train. Every one of them, and their wives, had a reason to kill her if you looked close enough.

And God help us if it turned out Arabella was secretly bisexual or something. They'd need to DNA test the whole of bloody England.

Then there were the events of the night. The pub would've closed around midnight, and the final cleaning would've taken them up until 1am-ish. Arabella would've headed home not long after.

Cytrine and Arnie went up to bed, while Pawel apparently went off into Sittingston to go and get drunk with Darren all night.

If I turned up around 8am then Arabella must've been killed around 6.30-7ish. Had anyone seen her to make sure she went home? I was sure the police must've asked her neighbours. Maybe they had heard her opening her front door? Was she alone? The absence of her phone must've confused matters there.

The police must've taken her laptop, found iMessage on it, and seen who she was texting that night. But if she didn't belong to the Apple hegemony then they were fresh out of luck. Whatever admirer of Arabella's turned on her was probably not on there.

What would've happened? Arabella got a text at dawn, maybe.

We need to talk

Can we meet somewhere?

Why would they have chosen the pond? Presumably, Arabella hadn't wanted them coming to her house, and it was a secluded spot, with easy access. With the pub and several houses not far away, Arabella could've screamed if she'd needed to. But, unfortunately, she had needed to and hadn't been able.

So, Arabella throws her clothes back on from the night before, leaves her house and wanders through the village to meet the person. A fight must've broken out, an argument. Arabella and he (or she) get angrier. Maybe Arabella has enough, turns to leave, and then he/she whacks her over the head. She either falls into the water, or they drag her there. Maybe she wasn't dead yet?

Then, as it's a cold, damp, February morning in the middle of nowhere, the killer manages to get away unseen because I'm the only person stupid enough to be wandering around at that time.

And they get away.

I pondered these possible scenarios as I got ready for the memorial. I wasn't sure how formal Nigella wanted us but decided to play it safe. Some charcoal-grey suit trousers, black Chelsea boots and a black long-sleeved shirt. I'd need my suit for tomorrow.

As I dressed, I realised that I was trying to make myself look good. Like this would be an opportunity to show off a little. For whom? For Simon, obviously. God, I needed to nip this in the bud. He'd made it obvious he only wanted some company that day. Maybe there'd be another guy to come along. Some tall, dark, and handsome stranger. Someone like Tarquin. His face popped into my head. If only. I would give a kidney for a roll in the hay with that.

That would never happen though, I told myself, as I had already told myself several times since Friday night. Guys like that were a) straight, and b) out of my league. Put that to one side and focus on not saying or doing the wrong thing tonight.

I gave the kittens some food and a scratch behind the ear. They were too tired to misbehave so Simon can't have hated them that much. Clearly they'd been played with all day. The selection of knick-knacks that surrounded their bed informed me there'd been several handymen on their hands and knees all afternoon rolling things backwards and forwards in front of them so they could pounce on a rolled-up ball of scrap paper and a ballpoint pen attached to a bit of string. I should tell Simon their toys were behind the sofa, as he was clearly either playing with them, or letting Levi and Leon play with them when they should be decimating my kitchen.

"Behave, you little buggers," I ordered them as I left.

Fifteen minutes before it started, I made my way down the hill to Nigella's house, hoping I'd be several minutes late and not the first to arrive, and luckily, for once I timed it right. When a dark-haired man I didn't know opened the door, I could see several others already there.

"Hello?" he asked.

"Hi, I'm Arden. Nigella invited me tonight."

"The writer! Of course. I'm Matteo, Nigella's husband." He spoke in a heavy Italian accent, but his English was fluent. He was a handsome man, in his mid-fifties wearing a roll-neck jumper and chinos. Matteo had his sleeves rolled up to reveal hairy forearms. He was tall, well over six foot. He beckoned me in. "'Gella has told me all about you. Please come in, the others are through in the living room."

"It's terrible," he said, as he took my coat, and I hoped he meant Arabella and not my clothing. "I'm in Milan two weeks a month, then two weeks back here, but Gella was so upset I came back as soon as I could. I can't believe this is happening; Arabella was like a member of the family." He gave a sad smile and sighed as my coat made its way onto a hook. "Come through, we've got refreshments." It was a reflex to offer me food and drink, rather than from any joy at having taken in a guest.

Nigella stood up and kissed me on both cheeks when I entered and gripped me by the arms. "Thanks for coming. I hope you don't think we're morbid."

"Not at all." I was glad to be involved, to be honest. From somewhere I suddenly found myself holding a glass of red wine. I had no memory of who gave it to me. The Pettonis had lovely glassware.

"Let me introduce everyone. Obviously you know Odette and Tommy," (the Douglases gave a wave), "and John and Rita," (the Parkinsons did too), "and Simon," (loin quiver), "and you remember Eleanor Hetherington." (She gave a sad smile.) She turned to people I didn't know. "This is Roz Staines. She runs the village shop."

Roz was a woman in her late fifties, who was as short as she was fat. She had swept-back brown hair that has been dyed and cut to make her look a little younger but hadn't worked. She was around five foot tall, with a full bosom which made me worry she'd topple over. Around her neck was a series of beads, and her earrings must've needed building permits.

"'Ello, my love," she said, holding out a tiny, podgy hand.

"And these are her boys," Nigella said, gesturing to the trio of young men behind Roz as I shook the matriarch's hand. "Padraig," (who was tall and painfully thin, with a bird's nest of curly black hair) "Philippe," (who had long hair swept up in a man bun, and was even taller than his brother, and at last a foot and a half taller than his mum) "and Phineas." (Phineas had his mother's height and was dressed like a homeless guy with a bushy beard and a beanie on inside.)

The three sons all had a series of women hanging around them and I couldn't work out who was a girlfriend, a cousin, a Lilbury local, or a groupie. Clearly, Nigella didn't know either as she dithered to introduce them. "They all knew Arabella," she eventually declared, diplomatically. "Friends when they were teens. Used to wreak havoc with a bottle of Strongbow at the bus shelter."

We moved swiftly on to the next person I had never met. I was surprised to clap eyes on someone I presumed was our local vicar. "Arden, this is Jedrev."

"What?" I asked dumbly as she sidled me up to a vaguely handsome blonde man in his early forties.

They both laughed. "Jed… well, Jethro… actually Jethro Fulford," he said, holding out a hand. "I'm the vicar at St Candida's, but everyone around here calls me Jedrev. I don't know why."

"Because Jedvic sounds like a type of wet behind the ears Viking," Nigella said. "Jed's been the vicar for about five years after our previous vicar died on the job."

Jed was laughing. "Such a caring manner, Nigella. Poor Reverend Douglas had a long and happy career here in the village, but sadly, yes, he did succumb to a heart attack right in the middle of the Lord's Prayer on a Sunday morning."

"Douglas?" I asked.

"Tommy's dad," Nigella confirmed. "And, anyway, I don't have to be caring. Us Catholics aren't known for mincing our words."

Jed gave a laugh. "You're only a convert, Nigella. Don't let it go to your head. The Anglican church will take you back when you see the light."

Nigella saw my expression. "Matteo's parents insisted. No way they were letting him marry a Protestant."

"Can I expect you in the church on Sunday, Arden?" Jed asked, knowing the answer already.

I at least gave a pretend grimace. "Afraid I must join Nigella. Catholic as well." I had gone to church with my grandmother, but when we'd moved away my mother had never taken us again. I didn't even know if my grandmother was still alive. She wouldn't be much past seventy, so there was still a good chance.

"Lapsed, I presume?" Nigella asked.

"Collapsed, more like," I said, and we all tittered at the joke.

There was the sound of tapping on glass behind us, and everyone turned to look. Matteo was standing in the centre of the Pettonis' mouth-wateringly well-designed living room. "Everyone, thanks for coming." Nigella excused herself from our chat and made her way over to her husband. "We both just wanted to say that there's no pressure tonight. We gathered you all here to say goodbye to Arabella in our own way." Matteo gestured to Jed. "I'm sure the vicar will do a lovely service tomorrow and we'll all have a good cry, but tonight is about celebrating her, not saying goodbye."

He put his arm around Nigella as she began to speak. "Arabella was a handful, always was, hands down, a little madam from the moment she learned the word 'no'. I presume most of you know that Matteo and I had trouble having a child. For years we tried… how many rounds of IVF we had before the twins came along, I shudder to remember. I nearly lost hope so many times, but all through it, I always had Arabella to remind me why I wanted children. When she wasn't throwing a tantrum because Jocasta wouldn't let her wear her ballet tutu to bed, she was my favourite person. It was Arabella who taught me how to be a mum. I learned any patience, any compassion I have, from her. She was my little friend, and it was a privilege" – Nigella's voice cracked as she continued – "an absolute privilege, to watch her grow up into the wonderful young woman she became.

"I'll not lie. I'm devastated. I'm heartbroken that someone has come into our world and done this horrible thing and taken her from us." There was a momentary pause as the door was opened and a latecomer popped their head in and gave a grimace of apology at interrupting – it was Tarquin. "Thanks for coming, Tarq," Nigella said without breaking her flow. "I was just saying how shocked we've all been at this happening here in Lilbury. It just shows us that the life we have, the community, the friends and family we all have here, everything is so precious, and we must always remember that. We must always remember how easily it could be snatched from us and how we must be so vigilant to make sure it isn't."

There was a smattering of applause, and Nigella, who was nearly in tears, waved it all away. "So, in that respect, please eat, drink, and be merry, and please try and remember Arabella the way she was – full of life, full of laughter, a handful, a great friend. Padraig and Philippe have got a Spotify playlist of all the songs she likes. This one is her favourite." She held up her glass. "We've got all her favourite foods. This is the jumper she bought me for Christmas a few years ago. Tomorrow we'll all be in tears, but tonight let's laugh and love her for who she was."

There was another smattering of applause. "To Arabella!" Matteo said, and held up his glass.

"Arabella," the room chorused.

I looked around. Roz was batting away damp eyes, Eleanor was gone, floods of tears rolling down her face. She went with a few of the others to the kitchen for some privacy and stopped to get a hug from Tarquin on her way. Odette was standing at the fireplace, dabbing her eyes with a tissue, while Thomas rubbed her shoulders and gently rocked her back and forwards a little.

I felt like an intruder; my own grief was almost non-existent. I hadn't wanted her to die, but I hadn't loved her either. I trained my eyes on Simon. He was sitting on the sofa, looking blankly ahead, lost in thought. I decided to go offer a word, but I was caught up by Tarquin. "Bit heavy, isn't it?" he said by way of greeting, taking a slurp of his wine.

"Not really good at this stuff," he continued. "I'd much prefer to remember her in my own way, in private, but I thought I should make the effort."

I gave my agreement, but we were interrupted from continuing by Nigella appearing at our elbows. She hugged Tarquin, and he apologised for coming in late.

"Oh, don't worry. I'm glad you could make it. Were you able to find her?"

"Find who?" I asked.

"Jocasta," Tarquin answered with a grimace. "Guy and I have spent the past two days ripping London apart trying to find her. We eventually managed to track her down through the grapevine to an old flame of hers in his druggie flat down in Wandsworth. Some ageing rock star whose name I won't mention in public. The pair of them jacked up off their tits. We've just got back. She's drying out in a guest room at Honningtons, with Lady F looking over her."

"Jesus…" Nigella let out a few more choice words. The news hit her like a tonne of bricks. "Sorry, Jed," she said as her voice travelled and the vicar had frowned at the litany of swear words. Her one-time best friend was a junkie and a drunk and nothing seemed to be able to change that. Not even the death of her daughter.

"I think she'll be okay for the funeral. Fragile, but she'll make it," he finished.

Nigella wasn't paying much attention. "I'll go check on Eleanor," she announced brusquely. She wanted a battle she could win; putting Eleanor back together was easier than dealing with Jocasta.

Tarquin and I stood for a few seconds in silence. "I need some air," I announced. Simon was staring at us, and it was making me feel uncomfortable.

"Good idea, I'll join you," Tarquin said, and guided me with a firm hand out to the garden. There was a formal dining room beyond the living room that ran beside the kitchen, which also had French doors in it that led to the garden, so we didn't have to go through the kitchen and interrupt Nigella and Eleanor and the other women. We opened the doors and stood out in the cold February night. Tarquin took a big lungful of air and exhaled, looking up at the stars.

"Tomorrow is going to be hell," he announced, and then finished his wine. He rubbed his hands over his face. He had dark circles under his eyes; the past couple of days had been hard work. I felt sorry for him. It wasn't even his family, and yet his loyalty to Guy, to the Frobishers, to Arabella, meant that he, like Nigella, was determined to help them and make sure everyone was present and accounted for.

"You must think we're all crazy," he said to me.

"Not at all. I think what you're all doing is admirable. Coming together like this, it's good."

"Guy heard about tonight and was not impressed. He thinks it's morbid. He thinks Nigella's being disrespectful. He can be a right snob when he needs to be," he said with a hollow laugh. "He's still got a touch of the landed gentry about him. Doesn't like the commoners interfering in business that doesn't concern them."

My views on Guy took a nosedive with this news. "And you?" I asked.

Tarquin reached up under his black roll-neck jumper and scratched his midriff. It was firm with a little bit of hair. My loins gave a quiver. Clearly being single was messing with my head. Half the reason I'd been shocked Ollie had gone looking for more was that our sex life had been fine. We'd still been having it just as much and the nature of our intimacy hadn't taken a nosedive or anything. The night before I'd found him with his dick in another man in our bed, we'd been up half the night doing the same thing.

But now, apparently, after my hormones had died a death on our 'marital' bed, they were roaring back into life. Like a spring bloom, they wanted to pollinate and open up for all the world to share. What a pain. It was like going to be a fourteen-year-old boy all over again. If I didn't watch out, I was going to get an erection in maths.

"Arden?" Tarquin said. I realised I'd been too busy thinking about my how horny I was to take in that he'd been speaking to me for several seconds.

"Sorry, on a different planet. What were you saying?"

"I was asking if you were okay. You know, after finding her. I once found a dead fox on my front doorstep, and it gave the shudders for weeks."

I frowned at the comparison but put it to one side. "Yeah, I'm fine. Mostly. I try not to think about it. As soon as the funeral's over I'll be better."

"Well, now they've arrested Pawel, it's all over and we can go back to normal."

"You think he did it?"

"Who else would it've been?"

I chose not to answer the question. Tarquin seemed to notice that, and he instead turned back to the sky and took in the night.

"The last time I was in Nigella's garden was Bonfire Night last year. With Arabella, oddly enough. She had a spliff. We got high and sat at the end of the garden, giggling. Guy wasn't happy."

I came to stand by him. Not for any reason other than human company and to look at the stars. You didn't get stars like this in London. Tarquin must've been thinking the same thing, for he commented on the night's brightness and stillness.

"Yes, it's lovely."

We stood together in companionable silence. I thought he must've been dreaming of Arabella and the fun times they'd had when he and Guy had played surrogate older brother to her for all those years. We were shoulder to shoulder, our arms just about touching. If I wasn't imagining it, there was a definite urge for our arms to brush… I'd had these moments before with other men. There was a frisson.

I thought about coughing to clear my throat and remind him of what he was doing in case he'd zoned out. Before I could do anything else, several of the other people in the room came out to join us. I looked at Tarquin, and he gave me a smile before he merged into the group.

Breathing a little heavily, I made my way over to them too. The group were speaking softly and sharing stories of Arabella. After a while I reached my limit of both how much sadness I could take, and how appropriate it felt to be there for someone I'd only ever met a few times. I slipped away and walked home.

When I made my way through the door, I checked on the kittens and made sure they were all tucked up and then turned in. As usual, sleep was a far-removed goal unattainable in the current mindset, so after an hour of tossing and turning I got my laptop out and started writing. I managed a few pages of half-arsed work, but my heart wasn't in it.

I got up and wandered around my house, going from room to room, occasionally passing through the kitchen to pick at things to eat. I was stuffing brioche into my mouth when I caught myself looking out the kitchen window. The night was black and cold outside. In my mind, I always feared windows in the dark. The idea of a face appearing through the pane at night was one of my paranoid fears.

I purposely stared at the glass, daring a murderer to arrive and stare at me. Whoever had killed Arabella was still out there. Unless I was wrong about Pawel.

No face arrived. No gurning murderer out to skin me and hang me up by my nipples from the rafters.

I was shaking as I looked out the window. How close were the Parkinsons, my nearest neighbours? Would they hear me scream? I tore off another chunk of brioche. Roosevelt miaowed and galloped clumsily towards me.

"You come to protect me?" I asked, picking the wee thing up and nestling it to me.

"Miaow," was the tiny contribution.

"I'll take that as a yes."

I tore off more bread and stared out the window. Daring the face to appear.

Chapter 27

The next morning was bitterly cold. The skies were clear, and the ground was covered in a hard frost.

Ewa, like a Polish trooper, was waiting patiently outside the shop at the designated time. She was in all black.

"This country is so damp, it always feels colder here," she said sniffily as she got in beside me.

I couldn't remember the winters of my youth so I could never judge. We were too poor for thick coats, so whether I was cold for whatever reason they were specifying I couldn't say.

I kept silent as we drove. The countryside whipped past us in the half-light. "Radio?" I asked, and Ewa shook her head.

"I want to be alone with my thoughts," she said in Polish. Conversation, understandably, was rare after that.

The city's limited rush hour was in full swing as we arrived, but through some miracle I managed to avoid most of it. I parked on a side street, and we made our way to the ugly mid-century building. Painfully perfunctory. I was nervously checking the time every chance I got. Ewa clamped her hand down on my wrist the next time I checked my watch. "We will make the funeral."

Being a high-profile and serious charge, Pawel – sorry, Pavlo – had the earliest slot of the day.

We sat in the Court. The guards and lawyers milled, and the tiny public gallery was empty bar us.

Not even a reporter. Probably all at the funeral.

Eventually they brought Pawel in. He was unshaven and wearing a grey tracksuit. His hair was greasy. He looked tired and cold, and his eyes were red. He kept his head down and his face obscured.

The judge entered and sat with great aplomb. If you could instantly take against someone, I took against her. A sharp-faced woman in her forties with leopard-print kitten heels on.

There were some preliminary questions, but we held our breath when she asked the big one: "Pavlo Davidenko, you are charged with murder. How do you plead?"

He was in a glass booth with a microphone in front of him. He looked to his lawyer. Ewa's fingernails found the most tender flesh of my arm and dug themselves in.

Pawel looked at his feet, but he spoke clearly: "Not guilty."

The judge nodded. "Take the prisoner down. The trial will be set for the date of June twenty-third."

When she said this Ewa let out a loud gasp. Her fingernails dug down to the bone. Everyone in the courtroom looked at us. Judge, lawyers, police, ushers, and Pawel. The judge narrowed her eyes.

I jutted out my chin. She might see just two Eastern European immigrants, but we were not for turning. I stared at that judge with all the strength of character I had. *When you look at me*, I spoke to her in my mind, *you will see every prejudice you have. I am not some minimum wage worker with bad English. Anything you throw at me I will throw back with a rock buried inside it.*

Pawel was taken away, and as the Courtroom cleared, Ewa dabbed her eyes. "We must go home. I need to prepare for the day."

It was nearly 10am when we got back to Lilbury. Ewa strutted in her heels through the village when she got out of my car. Her head held high. Victimised but never a victim. If communism and the Polish winters couldn't break Ewa then no reprimand from an Englishwoman for being late would.

I returned home. I had just enough time to piss and change my shirt for something less court-y and more funeral-y before I had to leave again. I walked back down and found myself in the midst of a village possessed.

Hidden from the high street was the circus outside St Candida's. The media was in force and Arabella's popularity meant her funeral was well attended.

"Sky News, BBC, Channel 4 and ITV are behind those trees," Simon pointed out as I walked up to join him where he stood near the church. There was a group of around fifty mourners all gathering outside. A police line separated us from the reporters. I'd had to make my way through to be allowed in – "I live here. I knew her" – was luckily enough to get me through.

The Parkinsons and Douglases were both nearby. Rita remembered her manners; "Arden, these are our sons, Daniel and Blake," she said, gesturing to the two tall, handsome men beside her and John. I greeted them and gave my condolences, remembering they had known Arabella well.

"No Nigella?" I asked Simon.

"She's with the Frobishers," he answered. One of the family.

While we were speaking, Matteo hurried through the police line with two dark-haired boys beside him. Archie and Luca were dead ringers for their father, but minus forty years. Matteo was scolding them for being late in an Italian-English hybrid I presumed was the lingua franca of the Pettoni household.

"We had issues with finding shoes. And ties. And combing hair," he explained, giving his sons a look that spoke volumes.

Archie and Luca seemed cowed by their punishment for any transgressions but clung to their father in the company of all the adults. They both gathered around Matteo's coat-tails and looked out at us all sheepishly.

Rita gave them a hair ruffle each. "You both look very smart," she told them. Archie was making no secret of the stares he was sharing with Tatiana Douglas. The pair were apparently acquainted. Ah, young love.

"Shall we go in?" Simon said, shortly.

We made a large troupe as we joined the long line of other people filing their way into St Candida's gloomy interior. The church was packed to the rafters with black hats and flowers. Women of varying ages and face-lift quality scuttled to their seats in head-to-toe black dresses and thick tights against the cold.

The temperature was lower in here than outside.

I took a seat in the middle of a pew near the back. At the front, the Frobisher/Sweet extended family was apparently such a voluminous clan they required multiple rows.

On the other side was a large group of blondes in their early twenties. Arabella's high school and uni friends, I assumed. The men all had smug looks on their faces; the girls all had messy locks they allowed to splay over their faces then pushed back – just like Arabella had. Why wouldn't posh girls buy a hair tie?

The rest of the pews were filled with villagers. Everyone I had met in Lilbury was here. Roz Staines was with her sons; to my surprise Cytrine and Arnie were nestled into a far corner. As even more of a surprise I saw the Bliss family walk through and take some of the last seats at the back. Sonia was with Trevor and Dhapinder, and an older man and woman who I presumed were her parents (no Darren, though, I noted). The family took their seats, and we all waited. Sonia gave me a wave.

The immediate family began to waft in. First up was Lady F with Guy on one side of her, and Eleanor on her other. A man and woman who must have been Eleanor's parents followed them with several more family members I had no idea of. A beautiful blonde woman was next, her arm linked with that of an equally handsome Hispanic man. Before I could ask, Rita Parkinson leant over:

"Rosie, Guy's sister. And her fiancé, Juan. Or Jose. Something Spanish-y. He's Cuban."

Rosie's life in Miami was going well then.

Rosie turned back and gave an eye to the person behind her. It was Nigella – in her vast furs, her raven hair was a contrast to the flaxen family (aside from Juan/Jose they were a light-haired procession). She was cradling a shrunken woman with a messy blonde beehive on her head. The woman was pale and seemed to be clinging onto Nigella for dear life. She had sunglasses on indoors and was whispering continuously to Nigella. I couldn't hear what, but it looked almost like whimpers. Rosie's look was noted, and Nigella nodded. Rosie removed her arm from her man's, and she took the woman's other arm. "It's okay, Aunt Jocasta. Come find your seat. Come on, just a few more steps."

So that was Jocasta. It's not often you met someone whose only effect on you was one of pity and, well… disgust, a wee bit.

She was a husk of a woman, barely able to stand, propped up by a friend and niece who had long given up on her.

There was a lull after the women went to the front before the last of the procession arrived: Miles Sweet.

Arabella's dad had a bald head and grey ringlets swept back and curling on the nape of his neck. He was not a tall man, and neither was he slim. He wore an expensive suit, dripping with accoutrements over his person. The main one of which was his young bride who glided along the floor beside him. She was a little older than me: tall, willowy, with chestnut hair and a tight black dress.

"She's Lebanese, I think," Simon said. "Poor English. And she hated Bella."

I sighed. I stared at Miles and his silent wife as they proceeded with a smug wiggle to their walk down the aisle. They could barely keep the smirk off their faces.

Instead of watching them, I looked to the rest of the family. Nigella was just settling Jocasta into her seat next to Lady F. As they fussed, Tarquin stood to help. He was in a black suit with a red tie. He turned and caught my eye for just a second and gave a smile.

I hoped Simon hadn't noticed.

As we sat, Jedrev made his way to the pulpit and the service began. Lady F had made the choices for songs, psalms, and the others had been correct: it was a religious occasion. Lady F had arranged a proper High Anglican ceremony for proceedings. We stood and sat, and I tried my best to hum along to songs I had never heard, or at least not in English.

Jedrev spoke once again. He was a good public speaker; his voice was deep and clear with no stuttering or notes of uncertainty.

As I sat there, I noticed that more and more of the grouped people were weeping. Sometimes privately, sometimes openly and quite dramatically.

At the first eulogy, "Binky", Arabella's best friend from school, began to speak, and a horde of blonde hair in the front descended into snotty sobs and tears. A plethora of them all hugged and held one another through the moment. Binky told inappropriate anecdotes of drunkenness, of missing lectures, of spending their money on drink, of batting their eyelashes at men until problems went away.

Eventually Jedrev puffed out his cheeks and it was over. Binky gave a strangled sob and left to sit back down. The next speaker was Rosie.

Rosie was a tall woman with immaculate skin and short thin blonde hair she clearly didn't like on her face or getting in the way. It was severely cut, and she had pinned it to keep it away from her face.

She spoke in a resolute transatlantic accent that couldn't cover its public school tracks.

"Arabella was my shadow when we were young. It used to annoy me so much. Wherever I went, she would be five steps behind. Hiding if I was mad at her or walking openly if she was feeling cheeky. She always had that blankie, that filthy blankie, do you remember, Guy? The one she used to carry around sucking on the corner. That's still how I picture her. My baby cousin. I still think she's a baby. She'd never be a grown-up in my eyes." Rosie's voice broke on the last words. She wobbled and pulled a tissue out to dab.

She took several deep breaths and tried to continue, but every time she started her voice wobbled again. "Sorry," she said. She took another second to console herself. Both Guy and her fiancé stood to go to her. They both gestured to one another to continue. In this instance, brother was needed more than lover, and Guy clapped him on the shoulder before he vaulted the steps up to her.

Rosie clung to his arm as he helped her finish her words.

"I wish I could go back to those days. I'd be kinder to her. I wouldn't get mad. I wouldn't yell at her. Arabella was more of a sister than a cousin. The three of us were off on our own, orphans." There was a murmur, and a lot of eyes swivelled towards Jocasta and Miles who had essentially just been called out by Guy for their parenting skills by the sound of it. Neither showed any reaction.

He and Rosie left the stage, holding one another. Guy kissed his sister on her forehead as he took her to her seat. A gesture of pure affection. I was a little jealous of people being so close to one's own siblings. God knows I wasn't.

The next speaker was another friend from her school days, who gave an unexpectedly funny eulogy that was mostly a recount of their antics as teens together, which seemed to involve a lot of Arabella getting stuck in the tiny fan windows of nightclub toilets as she tried to sneak in while underage. It succeeded in breaking the strained air and it was nice to see those in the church smiling. Even Lady F laughed during it, when she'd sat in stony silence during Binky's.

Next, surprising everyone, Jedrev asked Jocasta to speak. There was another murmur, but after several seconds it was Nigella who stood.

"Now, what's going on here," Simon muttered just loud enough for me to hear.

Nigella took to the microphone, her ridiculous furs draped over her shoulders.

"Hello, everyone." Nigella's voice was strong and clear. This was Nigella the PR professional and political spin doctor. This was not Nigella the heartbroken surrogate mother.

"Jocasta has asked me to speak on her behalf, and I am glad she did. I have many things I too need to say. Arabella was like a daughter to me. I cherished her. I helped raise her and I was so proud of who she became."

Nigella scanned the room for anyone daring to disagree.

"And now she's been taken from us. She hasn't died from an illness, nor has she been killed in an accident, a car wreck, or some-such. No, someone has made the decision, the conscious choice, to take her life, and take her from us.

"We don't know for sure who did this, but I want everyone to know this: we are angry. We are upset. They say women are emotional. Well, you're damn well right we're upset. I am upset.

"I fed Arabella, I bathed her, I drove her, I read her stories, I cared for her when she was sick. I helped her write university applications. I held her hair back when she came home drunk. I held her when she cried, heartbroken over some boy. But most importantly, I want everyone here to know that Arabella's death is not a tragic waste. It's not a statistic, and you better damn believe it's not fodder for a tabloid. It was murder. It was a crime. I want everyone here to remember that. No euphemisms. No polite phrases. None of that. She was taken from us in a violent and cowardly act by some man – it'll be a man – who thought she wasn't important enough to let her live and be the person she could become."

Nigella was breathing hard when she finished. Her nostrils flared. She was steely eyed and staring down anyone in the room who was willing to face her wrath.

Jedrev, who had been a benign presence through the other eulogies, appeared at Nigella's arm as she gathered herself to leave the pulpit.

They shared a look. Whatever look it was, no one saw other than a stricken look on the vicar's face.

As Nigella sat, Guy, Jose and two other men from the family side rose. On the friend side, a walking brick of rugby-playing Tory youth stood and hovered over the coffin.

"Her first boyfriend." Rita answered the question we hadn't asked but wanted to know. "Giles, or something. Lady F approved. Old money. And a lot of it. I think his dad owns Wales."

The sixth pallbearer was Nigella, who pointed the men where to go and silently organised them. Even the male relatives of Arabella's (including Eleanor's dad, who was at least sixty) did not dare to question or backchat her.

The procession made their solemn way out of the church and into the daylight. Slowly we all followed out and made our way to the hearse outside. "They wanted to bury her here, you know," Rita whispered to me.

The coffin disappeared into the back of the hearse. Rosie stood beside it, with Lady F and Eleanor. All three were holding their heads resolute. Jocasta was unsupported for a second as Nigella was busy. She made her way forward to the coffin and clawed at it. Before I knew what was happening, she was scratching and screaming, desperately trying to get into the back of the car to be with her daughter. Nigella was at her side immediately.

"Shh, it's okay, it's okay," she whispered to her old friend. Jocasta started to recover but was now giving out the most mournful of sobs. Nigella began to take her away, but Jocasta was clinging to the car. Her friend patiently extracted her fingers one by one, as we all stood watching the drama, too English to do much about it except watch and pretend it wasn't happening, in a horrible paralysis.

Lady F appeared at Jocasta's side and was far less diplomatic than Nigella had been. "For God's sake, Jocasta, get it together." She gripped the younger woman's arm with a ferocity I hadn't been expecting. Nigella was trying to help Jocasta up, but Lady F was in control. "We'll have no more of this, thank you. Stand and move on."

"But—" Jocasta started.

"Move. On," Lady F hissed. She stood tall and proud and waited impatiently as Nigella scurried around her getting Jocasta bang to rights.

Nigella watched Jocasta with something akin to hate. Everyone else kept their distance. The principal mourners trooped to their respective cars, while us plebs all made our way to our own. "Want to ride with us, Arden?" Matteo asked. "We're bringing Simon as well."

"Sure."

I hopped in the back of Matteo's Mercedes (that didn't seem to suit having two young children) and found myself hemmed in by small boys on each side, while Simon sat up front with Matteo and chatted away quite amiably.

"Do you like Spider-Man?" one of the boys asked me. I don't know which one.

"Um, he's okay, I s'pose," I answered. "I prefer the X-Men, though."

This didn't please whichever boy had asked me this and he made a face and turned away. His brother was more interested. "I like Wolverine!" he told me. "Who's your favourite?"

I thought for a moment. "I always quite liked Storm."

I distinctly heard Simon scoff.

"Cyclops was okay, too."

The boy who liked Spider-Man was looking at me with disgust. "But Storm's a *girl*." Clearly Nigella was not raising feminists.

"And Cyclops is gay," he continued.

"Luca!" his father snapped. "What have I told you about that language?"

"I thought Cyclops was gay when I was young too," I said. *That's why I liked him.*

"He's married to Jean Grey," Archie told us. "They have a house and a frying pan."

Simon snorted. "What?" I saw him mouth to Matteo.

He shook his head. "Nigella wanted a new pan, so I took the boys up to London to shop for one and they were very confused about why Mummy wanted it, and I told them that lots of people take cooking very seriously and you needed good kitchenware if you wanted a happy life and marriage. In their heads it now means they hand you a frying pan at the church or something when you get married."

I imagined a bridal Nigella accepting a frying pan from a priest in a church somewhere in Italy and smiling graciously, if a little forced.

"I'd be happy with someone who could fix my TV aerial," I said without thinking.

"I think I'd need a new power saw for a happy home," Simon added.

How masc, I thought to myself. The boys were largely quiet after that, and we made our way to the burial site in a grateful silence.

Arabella's plot was a long way into the cemetery. There was a slow procession of mourners making their way across the path to her graveside.

Amongst the faces I saw the Bliss family just ahead. Sonia was drifting behind her relatives looking morose. "'Scuse me," I mumbled to Simon and Matteo, and jogged the several metres to catch up with her.

My feet crunching on the gravel alerted her to me as I neared. She turned and gave me an inscrutable look. "You okay?" I asked, giving a small wave to Trevor who had turned around to look and saw us falling back a few more steps.

He looked better out of his clothes.

"All right? Of course I'm not all-bloody-right. How are you not freaking out?" Sonia asked, her nails digging into my arm. "The police are all over the house, they'll find our DNA."

I extracted my arm and instead put it around her shoulder. "It's okay. We won't get caught. If they find your DNA, you're her letting agent, you have a perfectly valid reason to have been inside the house recently."

Her attention had moved on though. She was eyeing her brother. He had his arm around Dhapinder and was stroking her lower back in a comforting gesture. Sonia looked horrified.

"You have to act normally," I said, my mouth practically in her hair, our heads were so close together.

"How? My lying slag of a brother is one of the men who was shagging the dead girl. He could have easily been the one who kill—"

"Normal, Sonia," I said. "You will make everything ten times worse if you don't stay calm. The important thing is to act normally. Remember, you saw nothing, you know nothing. Just smile and nod, okay? Everything is going to be all right. I promise." It was a lie.

"Do you think Trevor was involved?" she asked in a tiny whisper.

"Of course not."

I stood awkwardly on the side of the Blisses as we watched Arabella's family throw clumps of dirt into the hole. It was still freezing cold, with a grey mist blanketing the landscape. Being outside, and standing still, was letting the cold seep into my bones and I was beginning to feel angry with Arabella and her murderer for not choosing to do this in the summer. Matteo and Simon were somewhere behind me, and I could hear Italian being muttered threateningly as he scolded his sons on several occasions. I distinctly heard a young voice utter "I'm bored" just after Rosie had thrown her lump of soil in the ground and sobbed loudly. The contrast forced me to bite my lip from letting out a snort of laughter.

Sonia stood in perfect stillness and watched the mechanical procession of people throwing soil into the hole. Her eyes never moved, but occasionally I saw the muscles in her neck contract as she swallowed painfully. I gripped her hand below our coats. If she freaked out and confessed to breaking in then we were both fucked.

We made our way back to our rides as the ceremony ended. The wake was taking place at Honningtons, so poor

Ewa would be spending the day serving tea and sandwiches to the extended Frobisher/Sweet clan, plus any gawpers from Lilbury who felt like turning up.

As we made our way, Sonia pulled me in. “I’m fine, I’m fine, don’t worry.”

I patted her other arm gratefully. “I know it’s hard, but we did nothing wrong. We were looking for the truth. We didn’t hurt anyone. We were just making sure the police did their jobs.”

She looked at me. “Do you really think Pawel is innocent?”

I shook my head. “I don’t know, but he looked like a broken man this morning at Court.” I had seen guilty men look just as ashamed and broken too. My father was a perfect example.

“Those statements we took… how much trouble could we be in for those?” she asked. Reasonably.

“A lot. But they point to there being more to Arabella’s dad than meets the eye,” I said as the man himself passed us with his hoity-toity wife. They were given a wide berth by the rest of the mourners.

“I’m going home. I can’t face the wake,” she said.

“Okay. Oh, wait. I had a favour to ask you.” She gave me a look. “How would you like to look after my kittens for a day or two? I’m going up to London tomorrow morning and I’ll be staying the night. You’re welcome to stay up at my place if you want to be free of the family.”

Sonia thought about it for a moment and then grinned. “Yes, that would be good. Wait – you’ve got Netflix, right?”

I sighed. “Yes, of course.” I was about to give more details, but I felt a hand clap around my shoulder, and I jumped in fright.

Tarquin was beside me looking amused at my startled reaction. “Sorry, mate, should have made a racket coming up to you. Didn’t mean to scare you.”

I blushed a deep, boiled, crimson, while Sonia tried to hide her amusement.

"You two coming up to Honningtons? Please say yes. I'm not sure how much more of today I can take."

"I am, Son's off home." I turned away from Tarquin and his square jaw to look at her. "I'll text you later about the arrangements for tomorrow." We said our goodbyes, and we both awkwardly kissed her on the cheek before she left to go join the rest of the Bliss family, who had paid their respects but weren't family, Bristol friends, or Lilburians, so felt they'd be intruding if they came to the wake (despite Tarquin scoffing at this: "Lady F has enough food back at the house to feed the whole of the south-west. I hardly think she'd mind.").

"What are you two arranging?" he asked as we headed in the direction of the cars.

"I'm off to London tomorrow," I said. Categorising seeing Ollie as a meeting felt a bit cruel. "I just have to figure out exactly where the train station in Sittingston is."

"The train? Don't be silly. I'm driving back up to London tomorrow as well. Leaving about ten-ish. I can give you a lift if that time works for you? The train takes bloody hours from here. You'll be on it all day."

"Really? You wouldn't mind?"

"No, of course not. It'll make the journey fun, actually having someone to talk to for once, instead of just hating all the DJs on Radio One."

"Thanks, that'd be fantastic."

As we approached the gates to the cemetery, I saw Simon waiting by the car. He had his arms folded and was making no secret of glaring at us. I swapped numbers with Tarquin, who agreed to swing by and pick me up at 10am the next day. I parted to join with Simon at the car as Matteo and Nigella were talking on the other side of it. Simon was staring intently at the other side, possibly because, as I approached, I noticed the Pettonis were not talking so much as having an argument in hushed tones.

"Matteo has never liked Jocasta," Simon said as I came to stand by – not near, by – him. I kept my distance at almost a metre. A movement that Simon noticed.

"Would you just do it this once? For fuck's sake," I heard Nigella hiss at her husband, and to cover the awkwardness, of which I was glad, Simon spoke again. "You and Tarquin best of mates now?"

I cleared my throat. "He's very kindly offered to drive me up to London tomorrow, so I don't have to faff with the train." I made circles in the gravel with my shoe.

I heard a distinct "Hmph" noise emanate from the Scotsman, but I ignored him. "Yes, he's very generous. Sometimes."

"What's that supposed to mean?"

"He's very forthcoming when he gets to benefit from it."

"And what is his benefit with this?" I hardly think having to add several miles to his journey and listen to my inane prattle for two hours was his idea of a benefit.

Simon looked at me like I was a moron. "Seriously? And you're the one from London?" I was about to ask what he meant when Matteo and Nigella broke apart and she made her way to us.

"Thank you both so much for today. So nice to have you here." She stood between us and gripped our arms. "See you up at the house for a drink."

We all piled in the car when Matteo promptly explained he was taking the boys home and would just be dropping us off at the house before going back to his own. His mouth was clenched. "We can walk if that's easier?" I offered.

"No, it's best Lady F at least sees me enter," Matteo said, sounding put upon. The five of us made our way back to Lilbury in a strained silence and arrived at Honningtons, where the boys let me out and then I waited for Simon to exit too, but he instead stopped and chatted with Matteo at the car door for several minutes. It eventually became so awkward for me to stand there that I waved to the twins and walked off. *Fine*, I thought, *play your little games. I'm really not interested. No*, I corrected myself internally, and mentally slapped my wrist for my petulance, he wasn't playing games. *He's just a lot closer to Nigella and Matteo than you are and probably wanted to discuss something privately and not in front of the Londoner they've only known a week.*

Even though I'd slept with Simon.

Hell, as if that meant anything. Probably less than nought. Just cos I'd seen his dick didn't mean I knew anything about him. And he was being quite sulky and two-faced, if truth be told. *And* it also seemed he didn't like Tarquin, who, let's face it, was probably a posh knob, but Simon was hardly working class either? Aberdeen was the Surrey of Scotland.

It was one of those things – you never really counted as a local in these places until you'd lived there twenty years. And frankly I couldn't be arsed playing the game. I wanted to be back in London, with my familiar surroundings, where everyone was a stranger, and we could all just get on with our fucking lives. I wanted to be with Verity in a wine bar in Soho getting sloshed on a Wednesday night. I wanted a takeaway and a night in with Ollie, who, despite all his faults, I knew inside and out, and who was physically incapable of surprising me. Even his affair had been predictable.

Feeling absolutely, ruinously, sorry for myself, I made my way indoors and attempted to be seamlessly part of the wake before Simon came in and saw me. Unfortunately, what this meant was having to let Odette guide me in. "How have you found today? I suppose murders in London are so common you've done this all before. Well, it's quite shocking for us. I must've wept a bucket during the funeral. I saw you whispering with Simon, not to judge, but I wouldn't have done that in a church, it's very rude, but you've probably not been to many village churches. Oh, look, is that punch?"

Ewa was one of several staff working the wake, and she had been entrusted at the punchbowl, where she had a helper, a waitress in all black, who she was talking to in Polish. We made our way up and Odette had begun to say something. "I wish she'd talk in English. It's not really appropriate—"

"Hi, Ewa," I said in Polish. *Cześć, Ewa*. "Can I have two glasses of punch? One for me and one for this annoying witch beside me. She's just been saying she doesn't like people not speaking in English around her so I thought saying all this in Polish would piss her off." I turned to the waitress and continued my non-English. "Hello, I'm Arden."

"I'm Polina," she said in Polish, and meekly poured us two cups.

"Thank you, Polina." I took them and passed one to Odette. I hadn't looked at her when I'd been speaking to the others. "It's lovely punch, isn't it?" I said to her, as she gaped open-mouthed. I wandered off to the sandwiches.

The wake was taking place across what seemed like the whole ground floor of Honningtons. The drawing room that I had been in on both my previous visits was open as the main sitting area, but the food and drink was being served in the dining room across the foyer. And another room on from that, which was some sort of informal living area, was also being used too, by a group of women sitting on pouffes drinking tea while their children ran around and made a racket. I saw Tommy Douglas being flirted with by a blonde at the fireplace while two other little girls were bullying Tatiana.

I took my sandwiches and eventually found a glass of wine and made my way through to a sort of study, which was at the back of the house, and a huge, light airy room with windows on three sides, all of which seemed to be floor to ceiling. What wasn't window was green-and-white-striped wallpaper in a frilly pattern and great ruches of fabric around the windows. In the middle there was a large desk that Lady F must use for her correspondence.

It was occupied, surprisingly, by Rosie's boyfriend and John and Rita Parkinson's sons. They were gathered around the desk all eating sandwiches from tiny plates and watching a video on someone's phone.

I made my excuse to leave again upon seeing them there. "No, no, feel free to stay. We were just watching some clips on Jose's phone," said one of the Parkinsons.

Jose stuck out a hand. "Jose Martinez, I'm Rosie's boyfriend. From Miami," he added, as if I might think she'd met him in Swindon.

I introduced myself and hung back awkwardly as I couldn't remember which of the two Parkinsons was which. "I'm Daniel," said the one who'd spoken before. Daniel was the younger one I remembered at least. Still at uni. He had light brown hair and was taller and thinner than his brother, Blake, who was much stockier and a hair shorter (but still six foot-ish; thankfully, Jose was no giant, so I didn't feel completely emasculated) and had his lighter blonde hair swept back off his face in a style that you usually only see on WWII soldiers. He had a slightly puggish face when he wasn't speaking or laughing (as he was now, but when it was animated in conversation it was more attractive, as I would see later).

"I was just showing Jose the video of Arabella when she was hammered at our New Year's Eve party last year."

He pressed the buttons to play it again, and I scooted up to see it. In the video Arabella was drunkenly singing karaoke in a living room that had the same homely décor and low beams as the Parkinsons' kitchen, which must mean it was at their house. She was in a leopard-print top, with messy hair, screeching out the chorus to "Spice Up Your Life", with the microphone up the wrong way. A few seconds in she took a tumble and narrowly missed the TV and Christmas tree as she landed on the ground at an odd angle, before, Terminator-style, bouncing back up to finish the song like nothing had happened, while screaming laughter filled the room around her.

I couldn't help but guffaw with them too. "Yeah, Bella was an absolute champ," Blake said a bit more wistfully than I think he'd intended. He got a clap on the back from his younger brother.

"She was a laugh. I'm gutted. I'm gonna miss her."

"You knew her well?" I asked.

"Since we were kids," Blake answered. "I was the year above her at school and Danny was the year below her. When Rosie and Guy were too old to hang out with her, she started hanging out with all the other kids in the village when she came home from school during the holidays."

They settled in on the desk and went back to eating their sandwiches, and gave me a full rundown of their antics as teenagers, which were much more entertaining than those I'd heard at the funeral: Arabella as the loose cannon teenager, with a fistful of £50 notes and who would supply booze and weed to all those around her, who was often left alone at her house through a complicated system of telling Lady F she was being looked after later by Nigella, telling Nigella that Guy was there, telling Guy that Mr and Mrs Parkinson were chaperoning her. She had the entire village wrapped around her finger by the sounds of it. It must've been a shock to her in the past few months when her bullshitting and antics were beginning to wear a bit thin, after so long as the golden child no one could stay mad at.

Jose's phone began to ring, and he groaned. "It's the office. Nine AM in the States by now. Sorry guys." He loped off into a different room.

Blake looked sheepish. "I should ring the missus too, let her know I'm gonna be home late." He had been drinking a couple of beers when he'd been talking. "Best leave it a while before I get on the motorway."

He left in the same direction as Jose. It was just Danny and I now. He was quite a bit more drunk than the rest of us, as he seemed to be drinking his beers at twice the speed of Blake and Jose. He was staring into space, thinking about Arabella, and occasionally giggling to himself. "Man, this one time," he started after an awkward minute or so of silence. "This one time, right, it was my eighteenth birthday, but I was fucking grounded after Mum and Dad found weed in my bedroom. So, I was sitting at home on my own feeling really sorry for myself. And Bella rings me up and screams 'Happy fucking birthday, you fucking loser! What are you up to? You gonna get wankered?'" He had his hands up by his face with his thumb and pinkie out in the classic "phone" gesture. "And I tell her what's happened, and how lame it is, cos Blake's off with his mates in Magaluf and he's sending me all these texts about how fucking awesome it is, how all the girls are just up for it, yeah, and how he's just getting shitfaced all day. And Bella goes, 'Well we should just go meet up with him.' Her exams at uni had just finished and she had, like, two or three days before all her mates had finished, and afterwards they were going off to Australia for like a month, so I'm, like, 'We can't!' And she goes, 'I just booked us on EasyJet from Bristol Airport this evening. Sneak out and meet me there.' I was, like, 'Shit, mate, how am I gonna get there?' I had to pay my friend Rob, like, thirty pounds to sack off his job for the day and drive me up there, and the whole time I was cacking myself cos Mum and Dad were gonna go apeshit.

But I get to the airport and there's Bella and she's like, 'Isn't this fucking hilarious?' And she has this mate whose brother or something owns a villa in Magaluf, so she's like, 'Text Blake and tell him to go there, but don't tell him we're coming too.' So, we get there, and he's with all his mates, and it's hilarious. Blake is pissing himself. All his mates think it's great. It's mad banter. Arabella, man, everyone always loved her. And she was just throwing money out, right, paying for all the drinks. She's like, don't worry, it's my dad's, he's trying to buy my love again. She used to joke about, but I knew she hated him, but you know, it sure did come in handy sometimes. So that night we go into town, after Mum and Dad ring and are fucking a-po-plect-ic. They are raging at me. But fuck it, we go onto the strip and get fucking wasted. At about four in the morning we're in this tattoo parlour – Blake and I have always had this idea of getting matching tattoos, and we say it, and Arabella's like, 'Do it, he's turning eighteen, it's the perfect time.' So, we did it. Man, it was hilarious."

I laughed along, an odd feeling coming over me. "What was the tattoo of?" I ask.

He got up. "I'll show ya," and started to remove his shirt. "Blake and I always wanted these tattoos, right, as, like, brothers. We'd done the designs, and Blake's a real good artist, so we had the sketch of it on his phone, and he shows this guy in Magaluf, and he's, like, sure, so we got the outline done there and then came back to the UK to get the rest done properly. Cost us a shitload. But we had to do it there that night cos Arabella said we'd chicken out otherwise and never get them."

He unbuttoned his shirt and pulled it down to reveal his shoulder (and a completely hairless chest and bright pink nipple) on which there sat a lion's head. All the way from his shoulder down his arm and across his shoulder blade.

Made to look like a sketch. It was a tattoo that was very recognisable. I gulped.

"And you and Blake have… matching tattoos? Of these? E-exactly the same?" I stuttered.

"Yup," Danny said, doing his shirt back up.

He flopped back onto the ground, just as the door opened and Blake walked back in. "Missus is placated. She's got yoga tonight, anyway, so won't be home till late either."

"Daniel's just been telling me about your trip to Magaluf."

Blake grinned. "That was a fucking riot. Two days, and I think we drank the place dry." Daniel started telling another story, but my mind was somewhere else. I was busy thinking about what this meant. Had Daniel slept with Arabella? Had Blake? Had they both? Were they in love with her? Could either of them be capable of it? Blake was definitely a big enough guy to drag her around and knock her head in. And he had more to lose if their affair was made public – a doting fiancée back in Reading. Daniel was young, free and single. Or young, dumb, and full of cum if the truth be told. No one would be hurt there.

He was still talking, even as I only pretended to listen: "Arabella had snuck off from her school and had come back to the village. She texted me in the afternoon telling me to get some booze and come over to her place. It was late and we were shitfaced. Blake was already away at uni at this point. She'd have been… yeah, she'd have been in her last year of sixth form, and I was doing my A Levels.

"So we get trollied and then, lo and behold, who turns up, but her dad. He's in a foul mood. We could hear him yelling on his mobile as he comes in, so we run and hide, but we were trashed and so it's obvious someone's been there, but he's in the kitchen for ages on the phone, and we'd been in the living room, which you have to go like two more rooms to get to. Arabella's house is crazy old, and really big," he explained. I nodded along, because of course, I had never been there.

"So we hide in this wardrobe between the living room and the door outside, and we can hear her dad in the kitchen screaming his nuts off at someone on the phone, about how this guy's a useless prick, and he'll bankrupt him, and really going at him." He put on an imitation of her dad down the phone: "'You work for me, you hear me? If I say to do, you do something.' Man, he went off on this poor guy, calling him all sorts of names. Telling him everything he owned, he had given it him."

"Danny," Blake warned him.

"So, we're hiding there, and Arabella's freaking out. She's like, 'He's actually going to kill us for this', and—"

"Danny!" Blake snapped. He looked furious. He shook his head. "Not appropriate."

Danny sighed. He looked at me and then shrugged. "I thought it was a funny story."

The two brothers muttered between themselves for a few moments, before Blake took charge and decided his little brother needed parental supervision. "Nice to meet you, Arden," he said as he dragged his sibling away towards the rest of the wake.

Well. Okay.

I got up from where I'd been sitting cross-legged on the floor and tried to breathe through the pain. Oh, being in your thirties sucked. I decided it was probably time to take my leave, but needed to use the loo before I went. I vaguely knew in which direction it was and headed off into the recesses of the house to find it. Along a dark corridor, which was lined with various sketches of bucolic scenes.

At the end of the corridor just before the door to the loo was a sharp corner, where I neatly walked straight into someone. I gave a small intake of breath as I saw it was Arabella's father, Miles Sweet.

"Excuse me, sorry," I mumbled, as he knotted his eyebrows together and gave me a look of absolute venom.

"I should think so," he said to me.

You were the one skulking in the fucking shadows, was my first instinct, but I bit my tongue and instead disappeared into the loo, and hoped he'd be gone by the time I came out. I relieved myself and then spent several minutes staring at myself in the mirror.

In little over a week in Lilbury, I'd found a corpse, had sex with the local lothario on my living room floor, broken and entered, harboured a fugitive, and stolen evidence. Frankly, London beckoned.

Instead of feeling sorry for myself any longer I put my ear to the door and tried to listen to Miles Sweet's conversation, but he seemed to have left his position, and I couldn't hear anything. I opened the door and headed for home instead. On my way through the rooms, every resident of Lilbury seemed to be glaring at me. The Parkinson brothers were in the corner, Rosie and Jose in another, Guy and Tarquin, the Pettonis, the Douglases, Jed, Ewa. Thank God the Hugheses weren't here.

I made my departure quickly and headed home. It was only mid-afternoon, but I felt like the last week was catching up on me. As I climbed the hill my eyes were getting heavy. I'd barely put my foot through the door when I started yawning. I managed to feed the kittens before throwing my suit on the ground and slipping between the sheets. I slept, but it was a fitful, restless sleep of nightmares.

Chapter 28

I woke up in the dark. According to my nearly dead phone it was a little before six. I'd been asleep for nearly fourteen hours. I felt groggy. My head was pounding, and my throat was dry.

I was a little worried I'd been drugged, but I decided my body had just simply had enough of me and was telling me to sit down and shut up for a while. I lay in the shower and let scalding water do its job.

Eventually I started to feel more human and capable of making life choices. I went back into my room and packed a bag for a couple of nights in London, while still wrapped in a towel. My phone was charging, so while I was there I wrote a long rambling message to Sonia explaining the kittens' routine and what she needed to do for them, where their food was, and how they were slowly, unevenly, being house-trained.

I had my breakfast, thinking over what Daniel Parkinson had told me yesterday. Both he and his brother were also some of Arabella's past gentleman callers. Was it possible for either of them to have done it? I'm not sure why I was so fixated on it being one of her exes. Her death hadn't been at all sexual. There had been no rape. She'd been whacked over the head. A stranger could have done it.

One time, at the pub that the last of my stepdads had run, a man was beaten half to death in the car park by his own brother-in-law. When they dragged him off him, they all asked why he'd done it, but he gave no explanation. The next day everyone on the estate had come in to ask why, but we had no clue. His other relatives shrugged too. There were no affairs, no debts, no vendettas, no slights. In Court, it turned out they'd never liked each other; he'd just snapped and after twenty years decided to do him in. My stepdad had shrugged too. "Sometimes people just do crazy shit," was his explanation.

Maybe someone had just killed Arabella because they were passing by, and they saw a defenceless blonde sitting by the water on a quiet, early morning. It definitely made more sense than either Daniel or Blake driving from Cardiff or Reading respectively and bashing her head in and then being able to drive back without anyone noticing.

I put the key outside by the door, like I said I would to Sonia in the message and played with the kittens while I waited for Tarquin, trying to think of possible conversation topics with a posh straight guy. What did they do? We could talk about polo and rugby, I suppose. Not that I knew anything about those subjects, but he might have some homoerotic locker room tales to tell.

Twenty minutes after he said he'd be there his Porsche swung into my driveway, thankfully, at least, before Simon turned up. He jumped out of the car. "It's such a nice house," he said as I came out to join him. Instead of setting off straight away, he came in for a tour and was distracted for a moment or two by how cute the kittens were.

I felt bad to be abandoning them again, but after today I'd be home lots to look after them, and Sonia had replied by this point saying she was only doing a half-day at the office this morning and she'd be round at lunch.

We set off in Tarquin's ridiculous Porsche. It was so low to the ground I felt distinctly unsafe as we went over some potholes.

"It's a beauty, isn't it?" he said as we zoomed through Lilbury.

"Do you often have people wondering if you have a small penis?" I asked before I could stop myself.

Luckily, Tarquin put his head back and roared with laughter. "I hear the comments. All lies. I have several exes who can verify it's a great size."

We passed through several more villages as we made our way north to the A303. I stared at the countryside whizzing past me. It was a comfortable way to travel, and I was thoroughly enjoying it compared to the train. Tarquin was a steady driver, despite his choice of vehicle, and he knew what he was doing. Unlike my driving style, he never second guessed, or hesitated at roundabouts. He diligently checked at all intersections, but never seemed to cut his speed.

He noticed me looking and laughed. "Yes, I am a safe driver. The car is mostly just for show."

"It must've cost a pretty penny," I said. He shrugged. "What exactly do you do?"

"I invest in several businesses," he answered. "I did PPE at Oxford with Guy; he went into banking, and I decided to be my own man. I managed to make a little, then invested that, made a little more, and then so on and so forth. I'm never going to be as rich as Guy, but I do okay. I'm launching my new project in a few weeks."

I was intrigued by his comparisons to Guy but chose not to ask him about it. "Where's home for you then?" I asked, tipping my head towards the direction of far-off London.

"Fulham. I bought a little place a few years ago." He rolled up the sleeves of the cashmere jumper he was wearing and took a moment to collect his thoughts before continuing. "Arabella used to stay with me a lot when she was a student. You see, she hated her dad. But she was like family, so always welcome at mine, and I'm often not there. I don't – didn't – nag her like Guy and Rosie do. I'm an only child, so I can't really tell if it's a familial thing. I'm the only child of two only children – well, Dad had a brother, but he died before I was born and never had kids, a bit of a weirdo, so I never knew what the relationships between cousins and siblings were like."

"That must've been a bit lonely growing up."

"Not at all. I've been in rugby teams since I was old enough to walk. That's an unbreakable bond. And Guy has been a brother to me since we were at school."

I dreaded to ask about his parents, in case there was more death, but he answered before I said it. "Mum and Dad retired after the financial crash. They lost quite a lot. They moved to Portugal, where it's cheaper for them."

"Do you see them often?"

If I'd been able to see his face better, I'd have sworn a shadow passed over his face, but instead he cracked a smile. "A few times a year," he answered gaily. "Christmas in the sun, what's not to love?"

We were passing through the Wiltshire countryside, near the turn-off to Salisbury. I was staring out the window, hoping I'd feel something for the rolling hills of the English countryside, but instead it was just a dreary February day. Salisbury made me think of the bed I had ordered a few days ago from the craftsman.

"How's the house going?"

I explained about the kitchen and how most of the furniture was Mr Jeffries poor quality knick-knacks and basically firewood.

"Do you want modern?"

"I don't know. I'm not interior decorator minded. I thought about looking at antiques, but I wouldn't know where to start."

"I do," he said. "That was Dad's business before the crash. He ran an antiques business, import-export stuff, but he had a shop in London too. I could show you a few of the good ones around Lilbury if you want. Stop you from getting ripped off and buying yet more firewood."

"That'd be excellent!" I said, with complete sincerity.

We passed several miles in silence until Tarquin pointed with his finger at the distance: "Stonehenge." The car came to a stop as we were held up in the procession of tourists and rubberneckers looking at the ancient circle.

I had questions I wanted to ask, and I was burning to. As Tarquin muttered to himself about the traffic jam, I built up the courage. "So… Arabella used to stay at your place. Didn't Guy live in London, though, up until last year?"

Tarquin cleared his throat and flexed his fingers on the steering wheel. "He did. Yeah, he had a flat in Chelsea. Now he lives in the old groundskeeper's cottage at Honningtons. A plusher cottage you'd struggle to find. The amount he spent getting it done up. A family of four would rattle around in that place."

I felt a "but" coming on.

Tarquin pursed his lips. "Guy's… look, I love the bloke. He's my best mate and I'd jump in front of a bus for him, but the chap's a prude. He hated that Arabella was, well, let's be honest, the local bike. He hated her for it, was always lecturing her about it."

"Whereas it didn't bother you?"

Tarquin shrugged. "Not really. A few times when she stayed over at my place there was some guy in my kitchen in his pants making a coffee the next morning. Hardly the crime of the century."

"Was Guy ever violent? How far did he go?"

"It was nothing like that. He's just got a strong moral centre." Tarquin laughed. "A shire Tory, you know? He had to grow up fast after his parents died, be there for Rosie. I don't think he understands what fun is. Guy's sexual history mostly consists of the missionary position and looking at a dot on the wall."

"How did his parents die?" I felt guilty for asking. It was something that'd be widely available on the internet. And despite Tarquin's crudity, he was making me laugh.

"Long story, well, not really. You see, Guy's dad, Harry, was a bit of a chancer, a bit older than his mum. He spent a lot of his life out in Kenya where his parents had been based. On a flight, he meets Charlotte, Guy and Rosie's mum. He went out on holiday to Australia and came back with her. She was a trolley dolly for Qantas. Proper Aussie blonde type, the full Bondi package. She was still quite young. His parents, and especially old Auntie Georgina, were not impressed. Along came Guy, then Rosie. One family holiday out to Kenya and boom. Head-on collision. Both killed instantly. Guy was eleven."

"That's…" I couldn't even imagine.

"Awful? Yeah. So, Lady F became the new mum. She was over fifty already. No kids of her own. She loved them, but, ah, you know. Her husband left her because she couldn't conceive. He remarried and has about eight sons now. She's bitter. She resented them all, I think."

"I meant that I couldn't imagine Guy's mum being Australian."

This made Tarquin start laughing again. He slapped his knee, he was tickled pink, and then gripped my knee for a second. "You're a funny bastard, you are."

We'd made it as far as the junction to join the M3. Traffic was light, and we made our way through the damp and misty countryside from one big road to an even bigger road.

"What brings you up to London, anyway?" Tarquin asked after a few minutes of companionable silence. "Surely you're glad to be rid?"

"I have a meeting with my agent," I answered, while also giving serious thought to his comment about whether I was better to be shot of the place. Not like Lilbury was going swimmingly so far, though, either.

"Writers have agents?" Tarquin looked confused.

It was my turn to laugh. "Yup, that's who we send our manuscripts to. And if they like 'em, then, and only then, do they get sent to a publishing company."

"And what's your agent like? I'm imagining he was like one of my tutors at Oxford. All leather patches in a tweed jacket and quoting the ancient Greeks while staring at my arse."

"Actually she's a four foot eleven Welsh harridan with dyed hair and a tramp stamp."

Tarquin paused. "Not what I was expecting. Do they put you up in a hotel?"

"No, I'm sleeping in her spare room tonight. Apparently, there's no bed. They've taken it out to the ramshackle farmhouse they've bought in Surrey they're pouring money into. They're going to be on *Grand Designs*."

"Really?" Tarquin seemed to respect this, so I gave him the full story of how Verity had married a South African investment banker and now had more money than God. Her penthouse apartment in Canary Wharf was little more than a starter home compared to the country pile they'd splurged on. It made my cottage in Lilbury look like a feudal hovel.

"If there's no bed, why don't you stay at my place instead tonight?"

I looked at him in what must've been a shocked manner. He laughed again – his laugh was incredibly sexy. "I have three bedrooms. Two of them have beds in them.

I'm having some friends over for dinner tonight, anyway. It'd probably be more fun than sleeping on the floor after having to trek all the way over to Canary Wharf."

I looked at him again and gave it a moment's thought. I barely knew him. And it was never a good idea to get a crush on a straight guy no matter how gorgeous and flirty they were (in fact that was the worst kind). But he and the rest of the Frobishers (of which he seemed to be an honorary member) had been incredibly kind to me since arriving and had treated me with a level of inclusivity I hadn't expected. Especially from posh people. Was I overstepping the mark? And more importantly, would this make me look poor and scrounging in their eyes? Posh people had a different set of standards when it came to give and take than the rest of us.

It wasn't like sleeping at Verity's house, where I had a thousand times after she and I had drunk all the wine and she'd lectured me about my career, and we'd fixed the latest problem in her marriage because her husband was an idiot.

"Sure," I said – my mouth running off without me again. "It'd make more sense for the train, I suppose."

Tarquin seemed pleased and drove on as we passed through the boring commuter towns of the south of England. Each dull housing estate morphing into another one. The countryside in between was a mix of mossy green fields and grey skies, with empty black trees lining the motorway.

I never got why people who live in the south-east of England were so proud of their countryside. It really was the most boring-looking scenery. Squat houses filling dull, rain-clogged fields and not a hill or a forest in sight. At least the north managed scenery that is more dramatic.

As we entered London's orbit, we snarled our way through Slough, then the outer suburbs of west London where the houses suddenly got a lot closer together, and the sea of loft conversions started. Raised train lines started appearing everywhere and by the time we hit Brentford the tower blocks surrounding the motorway were dominating the skyline. We managed to get to Chiswick before stopping again. Everything in the city seemed dirtier. I had expected the buildings to seem bigger than I remembered, but instead everything seemed smaller. A hodgepodge of styles and size, all crowded around roundabouts and narrow pavements where they jostled for space with the endless supply of pedestrians.

A Thursday afternoon at lunchtime seemed to be no deterrent for anyone. There were gangs of schoolkids running beside the motorway, with dodgy men in tracksuits, and old ladies bundling along with their shopping carts. We stopped at traffic lights as we came into Fulham. Everyone who crossed the road in front of us was non-white and on their phone. Lilbury it was definitely not.

Tarquin took us around Hammersmith station, down past the hospital and into the heart of yummy-mummy Fulham. We turned off to a side road at Parsons Green station and then down another smaller road, then stopped at the narrowest mews entrance I had ever seen.

"Eel Brook Mews," I said, reading the sign.

"Home sweet home," he said. "I've lived here for about three years. Thankfully got in before the prices were absolutely crazy, back when they were just terrifyingly horrible."

We drove up alongside the tiny mews, which had just enough room for Tarquin to park his Porsche. It was a simple row of sandstone brick cottages, all of which I assumed would be deceptively large inside. Tarquin's was three floors, with a small garage door on the ground floor beside the front door. I followed him inside and up the stairs, into what I'd been expecting, plus more.

The interior was white and grey with big windows and high ceilings. A large open-plan kitchen with sitting areas at the back. "My office and the lav are down the back through that door. I say office, I haven't stepped foot in there in months, other than to get my workout equipment.

"Upstairs are the two bedrooms with actual beds in them. I've got an en suite up there, but I'm afraid you'll have to jog up and down the stairs for any night-time functions."

I waved my hand away. "You're already being too generous. I'm not gonna complain about needing to go downstairs for a wee."

He showed me upstairs to the small guest room, which was comfortable but hardly stylish. On the wall were a few framed band posters ("relics of my youth I refuse to throw out no matter how sad it makes me look in my thirties") and an England rugby jersey.

"I'll be in all evening with the others; they won't be here late. We're just having a catch-up, so don't worry, you'll get some sleep. When you rock up after your meeting you can join in."

"Oh, I have dinner plans this evening. Sorry, should have mentioned. I won't be back in until late."

For a second, I could have sworn Tarquin looked disappointed, but once again, I was presuming too much.

"Is Verity taking you out somewhere?"

"No, um, I'm… seeing my ex. For dinner. We're trying to be friends. At least I am. Maybe. I don't know."

Tarquin gave me a look at this information that I couldn't have understood with a PhD in psychology and a million years.

"Right, well I'll see you later… much later then. I'll be in, just knock on the door."

I dropped off my bag and left him to get ready for this evening. As I slunk out, he was on the phone, talking rather firmly to someone about something that sounded work-related. As I closed the door behind me, I heard him raise his voice to the person down the line. Probably best out of that. I walked the few minutes back to the Tube and enjoyed being back in London.

I'd lived here from the age of seventeen to my early thirties. I was moved up in school and finished my A levels a year early. Not to brag, but that was rather good, considering that I couldn't speak English when I arrived, which was something I used to love telling my teachers when they brought up my brother.

When our family had moved to England, he'd been twelve and already falling in with the wrong sort. Turning up to a British comprehensive and speaking only the basics of the language wasn't going to help his academic performance. He barely stayed long enough to scrape a couple of GCSEs, to my mother's disappointment. My sister, who was ten when we arrived, fared slightly better and managed to get on her college course. Neither of my siblings had doused the family name in greatness though, so when I arrived two years later, having moved to the UK at age eight and picked up English quite quickly, they were shocked. Then when I ended up skipping year nine and going straight into a class with a group of angry fourteen-year-olds, they were even more shocked.

I was good at history, geography, and a voracious reader. It was easy; the words for things in these subjects were mostly the same so I could move my encyclopaedic knowledge over from Polish to English. Polish history classes were dates and battles, English history was themes and opinions. It was a doddle.

Besides, the only place I could escape the pub was the library, so I never had a shortage of books to help with my homework.

I left home at seventeen, deferred my place to study English lit for a year and came to London to earn some money. I slept in a dodgy flat, which I shared with a variety of students, losers, and dropouts from all over the globe. I worked first as a waiter, then at a music shop, then as both, then at a nightclub (which I stayed at through uni). By the time I graduated I'd been living in East London for four years, which after the farm I'd lived on until coming to England, and then our council estate, I thought I'd seen it all.

I hadn't. A teenager in a dodgy flat in Whitechapel who earned his money in high school giving handjobs to truck drivers quickly learns he knows nothing. It was a tough time, where I cried myself to sleep more than once, with an empty stomach growling and my bruises throbbing, but I learnt. I got stronger. But anything was better than my brother coming into the room we shared above the pub steaming drunk and looking for something to punch. I'd never remembered my mother being a mother so I didn't miss her, as much as I missed the knowledge that she was there, and I couldn't rely on her. It was nicely reliable in its own way.

I changed at Earl's Court and took my seat on an Upminster train. I sat in the empty carriage and brushed my hand across my face. I wasn't crying but my eyes were itchy. I tried not to think about family because it wasn't as if it ever lifted my mood.

The train trundled along to Embankment, where I got off amongst the well-heeled office workers and made my way to the backstreet in Covent Garden where Verity's tiny office was.

Across from the Waterstone's on New Row, on the first floor I could see the sign as I walked along. I hit the buzzer for the agency and was let up by Verity's latest intern.

He bundled up to me as I entered. "Hi, Arden! Wow, lovely coat! You look great! Can I get you a coffee, oh wow!" Hitesh, the intern, was possibly the gayest and most hyperactive twink I had ever met. And I'd met a lot of twinks. He was wearing a white shirt with braces over it, and a bowtie. He had diamante studs in each ear, thick-rimmed black glasses and the current fashionable haircut of a short back and sides with a swishy fringe added to the front for extra aplomb.

On his bottom half he wore tight, tapered shiny suit trousers that were cut off a few inches above the ankle.

Everything he wore looked like the sort of thing I'd decry as being too much bloody effort.

"Hi, Hitesh. I see you're still here." It was a surprise. Verity got through twinky interns at a quick rate.

"Oh, you know, that singing job on the cruise ship fell through. So I've been here all winter. C'est la vie, innit, babes?"

"Yes. Very c'est la vie."

"I'll let Vez know you're here." He wandered off and left me at the entrance, his little bum swishing as he walked off. Was I ever that young? I can't remember what it was like to wear primary colours and not wake up tired.

And did Verity know he called her "Vez"?

The office looked the same. The usual tiny white foyer with blonde laminate floorboards and a tired-looking pot plant. Hitesh's wee desk in the corner, and a watercooler that hadn't worked in years. One small sofa, with a plethora of books scattered around to show its credentials. I sat on the uncomfortable couch for a few minutes and contemplated how dirty my boots were. I hadn't cleaned them since I'd trampled through the field the day that I'd found Arabella.

Hitesh's head popped round the door. "She's free-*yaaahhhhh*," he sang out, and his head disappeared again.

"Shouldn't you man the front desk?" I called as I followed him through. He didn't answer. A narrow corridor led down to a small central office where the other staff worked. On the doors either side of the corridor were supply rooms and a miniscule conference room.

In the large room was Appolina, the grande dame of the agency who oversaw all finances. She was ancient, French, and reeked of Gauloises. Her tiny dog came to work with her. Her domain took up half the office, filled with her personal effects. Verity had long ago given up trying to control her.

"Bonjour, Appolina." She greeted me with an eyebrow raise. It was a gesture of love. I got a hug from Gracie, Verity's junior, who was the "operations manager" for the company, which meant she did every bit of admin for the company that Hitesh was too stupid to do, or that Appolina decided wasn't to do with money so refused to touch. From HR and events to IT and marketing. She was a charming bespectacled Chinese girl who'd always been kind to me. I kissed her on the cheek and made small talk for a few minutes.

We were discussing her impending nuptials to a charming accountant called Gary from Finchley when a sour-faced white woman came through the door, threw a sheaf of papers at Gracie's desk and walked out again.

"Who?" I asked.

"Ffion," Gracie answered. "The new agent who joined us from Rebus, McDermid & Welsh. She's an expert on poetry, apparently." Gracie fixed her glasses. This was as close as Gracie got to throwing shade.

"What happened to what's-his-chops? The Don?"

"The Don" was Donal Callous. The formerly only other agent of the company. He and Verity divvied up the stock. His group of pretentious toffs that his posh circles sent him as clients were all white, privileged, and wrote gut-wrenchingly hackneyed tomes about upper-class adolescents in the 1950s who inherited a family secret. There was always someone drowning in a lake and families where no one spoke in anything but ominous foreshadowing.

Pre-Hitesh there'd always been a literary intern who eagerly read through the pile of shit that was sent to the agency every day, but they'd dried up when Hitesh was hired, and now Ffion was number three. A paid employee, so Verity must be doing well. I wondered why she hadn't mentioned her.

Gracie led me through to Verity's office (the smaller of the two, while Donal got the bigger one when he joined. I had no idea where Ffion worked). I walked in without bothering to knock and was greeted by Verity on the phone, sitting behind her desk staring at an A4 piece of paper looking pensive. She was sucking on the end of her glasses and appeared both bored and angry at the phone call's topic. As I went to close the door behind me, I heard a roar of laughter from Donal's office. His door was ajar, and I peeked my head back out and saw him reclining in his chair, also on the phone. "Squiggers, old sport, how the hell are you? Listen, just got your manuscript! Marv-el-lous."

I shuddered and closed the door to Verity's office. I took one of the two seats she had facing her desk. She gave me a massive grin as I did but reverted quickly.

"And how much is that going to cost?" she asked down the phone. I heard the person at the end give a distinctive "*Weeeeeelll*, it's hard to say." They talked for a few more minutes, while Verity became more and more visibly annoyed. Eventually she hung up.

"Oh my God," was her conclusion.

"Problem?" I asked, hoping there wasn't.

"My house has subsidence. But not normal subsidence. Oh, no, some special sort of subsidence that evades detection until the eleventh hour. Somehow, a surveyor, an inspector from the council, some bloke from English Heritage and two bloody architects all missed it, but Kyle, the builder, noticed it straight away. Half the east wing is about to fall down or something. And naturally, this is the week Gravz is in Benoni for his great aunt's Petula's funeral."

Verity's husband's – real name, Travis – surname is Graves. Naturally, he hadn't been called that since childhood. He introduced himself to her as Gravz. She herself had officially become "Mrs Graves" on her wedding day (though still Jones for work). To those who knew her through her husband, she was just Mrs Gravz.

"Gravz has a great aunt called Petula?"

"I don't know. She's called something. She died when he was near there, so he flew out to help his sister organise the funeral."

"He was in Africa for work?"

"He was in Dubai."

"Those places aren't close, Verity."

"They are when your company foots the bill for first class."

"God, I wish I'd done finance at uni."

"Same. We'd have to learn to count past ten, though, Ard. Right, famished. Lunch?"

We made our way out. On the way, Ffion gave us a dirty look. "Okay, explain her."

"She's awful. Donal found her. She was his protégé at the other agency. She's a stuck-up cow and I want to push her in front of an Uber. Closest she'll have ever come to a Black person. You know she called Gracie 'Oriental'? Not even in private – to her face!"

Verity's parents were from Barbados originally and she'd spent most of her career in publishing trying to not to grind her teeth down to nubs over the attitudes of the establishment in the profession, which had stopped developing at, oh, about 1952. A Black girl from Swansea who'd grown up in a single-parent family and had put herself through university was shocking enough to almost induce heart failure for some of them.

"She only started on Monday, and already she's ruining my life."

"You never said you were hiring someone new." I was a little miffed at being kept out of the loop.

"Well, you've been a little busy," she said as we walked through the door of the Carluccio's near the office.

"You take me to all the classy places," I said as we sat.

"Gotta treat me bird right, ain't I? Anyway, where's your bag. You're travelling light. I thought you were staying at mine tonight."

"Funny story. I'm staying with a friend."

"What friend? You don't have any other friends."

"Yes, I do. James and Harry, and Gus, and Lisa and Clive—"

"Those are all Ollie's friends. You don't even like them."

"Just because I didn't like them doesn't mean they're not my friends."

"Well, that's an enlightening insight into your psychology." She shook her head and picked up her menu to cover us from the rest of the small, and mostly empty, restaurant.

"Anyway, tell me everything. I need to know – how are you, really?" She slipped her hand over mine on the table.

Had it been anyone else doing that I would have rolled my eyes and jerked my hand away. But this was Verity, my oldest and dearest friend. I knew she cared for me.

So, I told her everything, from the moment I met Sonia to this morning's ride with Tarquin. The book club, Eleanor and the horse, meeting the villagers, Nigella, Odette, Lady F, Guy – even the night I saw Pawel and Arabella out the back of the pub.

When I came to explaining about Arabella, Verity looked suitably aghast, but with the hungry look behind the eyes that everyone had when they heard about murder.

Verity played with the food on her plate as we talked, seemingly put off while hearing about death.

I told her about finding Pawel at Darren's. I told her about Simon staying the night (her eyes widened: "I completely approve") and the funeral yesterday.

"That all sounds like a week and half."

"It doesn't feel real." I pinched the bridge of my nose to try to ease the feeling of exhaustion that came when I thought about Arabella too much, and then pushed my pasta around the plate. I'd taken a few bites.

"And you don't think Pawel did it?"

"Not at all. He's a goofy idiot. I can't imagine him being violent."

"Does he have a record?"

"Probably. Petty stuff, likely: theft, teenage shit."

"And what about the steroids?"

"I have no proof of that. It's just a hunch."

"If he's doing that, then maybe he could be—"

"Verity, since when does dealing some pills make you a murderer? I've sold drugs in the past."

"Yeah, but he might be getting into all sorts of scraps, money problems… it could be easy to go from one to the other."

I stared at Verity with horror. Was she convinced of Pawel's guilt too? Was I the only one who didn't think it was right? What the police said went though. The British trusted their police. In Poland, no one trusted the police. They were thieving thugs you kept out of the way of. I'd never been able to shake the idea that they were just as bad everywhere in the world. I'm not saying that Neuberger and Wales were corrupt, but that the police had reasons to make quick arrests. Pawel wasn't squeaky clean. He'd fit. He'd do. Anything to keep the politics to a minimum, and the tabloids out of it.

“Besides,” Verity said, spearing a chunk of chicken with her fork, “it’s always the boyfriend.” This, actually, was largely true.

I felt like I was fighting a losing battle. Why did I even care? Had what I’d told Verity about Arabella’s corrupt dad meant nothing? Had it not at least opened the possibility that maybe there was something we didn’t yet know?

Verity had moved onto business. “Guess what, you’re going to Comic Con!”

“Which one?”

Verity’s face fell. “There’s more than one?”

Chapter 29

After that, the lunch turned into a business meeting that I thought would never end. Cover designs for the new book ideas must be discussed, promotional and marketing strategies, where was I in the writing process? A little behind? Well do more writing, it's not hard.

The only exciting moment was the eventual spectre of the TV adaptation. A production company had raised an interest last year about adapting it for the BBC, but the ideas had ground to a halt, and the budget just wouldn't make it worthwhile. And the producers had been morons who'd gone for the most clichéd ideas I'd ever heard. Verity had been so excited, but I had acted like a petulant teenager during the meeting after they raised the idea of "a few tweaks" – which included making a gay character straight, a Black character white, and completely changing another character's personality to make her a bit more "likeable to a wider audience".

"You mean cut out all her feminist politics and her mental health issues?"

The meeting finished soon after, but Verity had kept pushing and they'd been interested in us for months longer, despite my reticence. "Arden, just think about the money, you selfish prick. Sell out, for God's sake. Everyone else does."

But now, there was an American company that were interested, after the last book had made half-decent sales in the North American market. This was the holy grail. "They'll want to relocate it from Scotland to California or something, obviously. They can't have TV shows set outside the US, God forbid," Verity had said.

"I'm honestly okay with that. Hell, I'll write in a Latino character if it helps." I was thinking about my bathroom. I wanted one of those massive tubs with claw feet. They weren't cheap.

And a walk-in shower. And underfloor heating.

"I mean, it wouldn't be my ideal, but I think I can live with them sounding like Valley Girls instead of Rabbie Burns."

"Fantastic. I'll set up some meetings. We're gonna be rich, Ard, RICH!"

Afterwards we parted, and Verity seemed a little offended about by me not wanting to go get drunk with her like we always did; I cried off with a headache. "I can't really face it." We hugged. As we went our separate ways, I felt guilty about bringing up the drawbridge after she'd sided with everyone else about Pawel's guilt. Truth is, I was feeling a little lost. No one agreed with me. No one thought I was right. I was just going around antagonising people like Sonia and making myself a nuisance for no good goddamn reason.

I huffed and puffed to myself as I walked through Covent Garden in the watery afternoon sunlight and made my way to Foyles bookshop. I spent a happy hour in there, trying to distract myself from all my problems by reading the blurbs of every novel I'd been meaning to buy for years, and then not buying them still.

Later, I walked my way over to Oxford Circus, through the crush of people, and briefly looked in a few clothes shops. I didn't have the money to buy anything too expensive, so I stayed away from Selfridges. I eventually managed to find myself in front of a section selling overpriced men's underwear: £30 for a pair of boxers was outlandish. The model on the box made me feel fat and unattractive.

I made my way to a pub behind Tottenham Court Road station and sat there with a pint and felt even more desolate. I had never spent much time in a pub on my own in the past. But I had decided, fuck it, it was the new me. The same thought that, which always did at times like this, made its usual appearance in my head: "I can't believe this is my life."

My phone buzzed as I got to the end of my drink. I looked at the time and it was already five thirty.

The message was from Ollie. I can meet you at the usual place in half an hour?

I replied in the affirmative, drained my drink, and made my way out to the dark and cold, my hands stuffed in my coat pockets and my general mood as low as it had been in months. I made my way through London's streets feeling like an alien. Like I stuck out as some abnormal weirdo they could sense was not one of them. I hated people, I hated noise, and I was sick of being in my own head.

When I got to the restaurant, I was surprised by the maître d' when she said, "Booking under 'Ross'? Yes, your companion is already here. He's downstairs, please follow me." Ollie was never on time. He always rushed in twenty minutes late, looking aggrieved, but also insistent it wasn't his fault and that if you kicked up a fuss it was you who was being unreasonable.

He'd chosen Le Garrick, one of London's many attempts at a stereotypical French brasserie, which never quite seemed to make it past provincial caff. It was awkward and angular upstairs, and dark and dingy downstairs – they attempted romantic, but it came across as more of a converted Gothic cathedral with proper old-style wine bottle candelabras and an air of the forgotten.

The tables, rare for Central London, were miles apart, and you could have proper private conversations without some app developer getting the sleeve of his AllSaints leather jacket in your Korean fried chicken fusion burger.

I followed the maître d' downstairs, and she pointed at the table in the corner. Ollie had been on his phone, reclining, looking as he always did when *he* was kept waiting for more than three seconds: like he was the most put-upon man on the planet.

He saw me and bounced up onto his feet. I took a second to look at him properly. He was looking absolutely gorgeous. Dressed in a navy-blue suit with a crisp white shirt, undone at the throat (his tie was in his pocket where I'd fished them out of to put them in the washing a million times). His light brown hair was cut shorter than usual, and his wry little smile was hidden for once, underneath a rare crack in his veneer of sneery indifference. He was nervous.

He was also a ball of energy. "Hi!" he said as I neared.

"Hi," I gave in return.

He hesitated for a second then gave me a massive hug. "God, it's good to see you."

I felt like a Wookie next to him. He was clean-shaven. I was stubbly. His hair was perfectly coiffed; mine was a bird's nest. He was suited and booted. I was wearing a jumper with a massive black coat over it, a scarf (one I'd bought purely because it was about two metres long) and a pair of skinny jeans and my mud-flecked boots.

"You've lost weight." *Excuse me?*

I made a scoffing noise and ignored the comment. We sat, him still in a high-strung ball of energy mode. He gave me a look. "You look… it's great to see you."

"What's that supposed to mean?" Instead of keeping my emotions in check, I was jumping straight to defensiveness. No, Arden, stay calm. Keep it pleasant. Don't do it.

"I mean, are you all right? You're skin and bone."

"I'm fine. And thanks for mentioning my weight. I know I've gained a bit, but I've been living on microwave pizzas. I'll start eating again properly once I'm more settled."

"Gained? Babe, you look unwell. You're gaunt. Your cheeks are hollow."

"It's just muscle tone. I haven't been to the gym. Apparently, all those days you dragged me to CrossFit actually did make the world of difference."

"Babe." I wish he'd stop calling me that. It always used to make me smile when we were together, and I knew he was saying it out of habit, but it was already pissing me off. "Are you sure you're okay, though?"

I was flushed and embarrassed as I sat there removing winter layers. "Can we stop discussing my weight, please?" I hadn't seen him in months, and this was how he chose to open the conversation?

"God, yes, so sorry. None of my business. I was just worried you weren't eating. Sorry." He didn't know where to put his hands. He fumbled with his water glass. "Just a bit nervous."

"I don't think I've ever seen you act like this. Am I really that intimidating?"

Ollie gave a smirk – like he always did. "You always made me nervous."

That stopped me in my tracks. I looked up from the wine list – Ollie was paying – and focused on him. "I do… did? That's news to me."

He let out a sigh that sounded more as if it was steadying his breathing than anything. "You have no idea. You have no idea what you're like, do you?"

I slammed the wine list shut. "No, I don't. Why don't you enlighten me?" *Stop it, Arden. For God's sake, stop it.*

He stammered and took a huge gulp of air, hunched over at his stomach, like he had cramps. "You… terrify me. Not in a bad way," he added quickly, "But because you are just so… you.

"You're never scared of anything or anyone. You have this whole secret side of you. Your brain goes at a million miles an hour. We could go to a party, and within five minutes you've summed everyone up and picked exactly who's worth talking to, who's annoying, and the exact vibe of the place. It would be off-putting, but you're always right."

"You make me sound like a serial killer."

He grinned. "You'd make a brilliant serial killer. They'd never catch you."

Maybe he thought that was a compliment, but it made my innards go cold. I knew I was a bit odd, but I had no idea my own (ex-)boyfriend had long thought I was one step away from serial killer. I knew I could be cold; I knew that once I made up my mind on something, it was done for good. I was judgemental and, to use an old phrase, I didn't suffer fools gladly.

I was looking at the table. I hadn't said anything for a minute or so. I saw Ollie's hand snake across the table and make a beckoning gesture. I put my own hand in his and he gave my thumb a stroke.

"I never meant to hurt you. I was a fool. I'm so sorry."

I was about to say something. Maybe I was about to say I forgave him, and he should come to Lilbury, but we'll never know.

"Hi, you guys ready to order?"

Ollie looked strained, but I replied with a bright smile and rattled off my order. The good thing about not really caring about food is that you always just order the chicken.

Ollie gave a flustered look at the menu. I stared at him. He was never self-conscious. He was much too confident for that. He flustered because he wanted to make sure he got the best choice for himself, not because he was holding anyone up. He was the same as he'd always been. Losing me hadn't dented that confidence, despite whatever he might claim.

He gave the waitress a smile as she left after he'd eventually given his order.

"So, have you found out anything about Miles Sweet?"

This didn't seem to be the question Ollie wanted me to ask, but it was the only reason I'd agreed to come. He ducked under the table, to where a gym bag was nestled under his feet, and pulled out a thick wad of paper. "One of the chaps in the chambers used to do a lot of work for him. Never quite liked the guy, apparently, but he was impossible to say no to. Everyone in his office reaped the benefits. All of this is public record, but if anyone asks you didn't get this from me."

"So everyone knows he's corrupt?"

"Yes, absolutely. Hence why there was so much concern when we did take him on."

"Is there anything in his history out of the normal? Not just backhanders and the sort, but…"

"What sort of out of the ordinary?"

"Violence."

"Not as I know of. He has security guards who are quite intimidating. Tim, that's the chap at work who knows his goings-on, said they used to come to the office with him and stand around in the doorway smoking, making the place look untidy like a bunch of gorillas in suits."

Tim was new. Tim must've joined since we'd broken up. I hoped Tim was in his fifties and fat.

"Anything else?"

"There's a rumour going round he was investigated by the Serious Fraud Office last year. But that was all hush hush. No evidence."

"What about Sweetly Made Homes?"

"The property development work that he's doing down in the south-west?"

"Yeah, anything untoward?"

"Surprisingly little, actually. It barely makes a mention."

"Oh. How big of a deal is it to be investigated by the SFO?"

"Fairly. They investigate a lot of people, but they don't do so without a serious hunch. It's a pretty big black mark against someone's name. They have a lot of power."

"How would you get around it?"

Ollie shrugged and laid into his beef, which the waitress had put down in front of him. My chicken was dry.

"There's a lot of ways if your pockets are deep enough: keep everything offshore, put it all in someone else's name."

"Like a relative's?"

"No, too close. I'd choose someone out of the family. I checked on Companies House and couldn't find anything for his wife or Arabella. I can check more relatives if you like?"

But Arabella's name had been on some documents: were those properties listed in the UK? I thought over this while I ate a bit. But the chicken tasted of nothing in my mouth, and I soon gave up, while Ollie dug into his own.

"How much criminal law did you study at university?"

"Enough to know that a life on legal aid was not what I wanted. Why?"

"How often is it actually the boyfriend who does it?"

Ollie chewed a bit and looked thoughtful. He swallowed and then gulped down some wine. He was stalling.

"Tell me."

"Almost always. And if not him almost always at least someone the victim knew well enough. If you were to look through the last hundred women under thirty murdered in Britain, you'd get the boyfriend or husband doing it ninety-five per cent of the time."

"And the other five?"

"Muggings and rapes gone wrong, honour killings, that sort of thing."

"So it's possible?"

"Of course, it's just very uncommon. You're much more likely to die of a million different diseases than get murdered. And if you are, chances are it's someone you've been with in a relationship or a family member who did it."

"Looking at the facts, would you say Pawel did it?"

"I've barely read anything about it. I've been busy."

I looked at him. He hadn't read up about a murder in the village where I lived? That I was involved in the periphery of?

"I mean I've glanced at the coverage." Better.

"And?"

"Boyfriend with a record of petty crime, in the country illegally, which only she knew about. They'd just split up. You all saw them fighting the night before. Looks pretty open and shut, really."

"No mention of the fact she hated her dad who's immensely powerful and shady to boot? Or that she was sleeping around?"

Ollie's eyebrows went up at the second point.

"They've not mentioned that in the press. Who with?"

"Everyone in the village. Arabella was into free love."

"Any of them have the means?"

"I don't know, but some of them have motive—"

"Means and opportunity is much more important than motive. Motive is for scriptwriters."

"Oh."

"Who would have the means?"

A face flashed in my head. "Loads of them. Thomas Douglas, the local GP. His wife's annoying as hell. They live a few doors down from Arabella. I think he was screwing her."

"A wife kinda ruins his means. Proximity could be key though, but she wasn't murdered in her house."

"That means it'd be someone who had no one monitoring their moves but who had to go to a new location to get the privacy to kill her?"

"One way of looking at it. This is all very sensationalised, though. It really is just likely to be her boyfriend or a male relative."

"Her only male relatives are her dad, or Guy Frobisher."

"Guy Frobisher? Hmm."

"You know him?"

"Our paths have crossed."

"The world is very small if you're posh, isn't it?"

He ignored the jibe. "Arden, I wish you'd stay out of it."

"It's all right. I'm a big boy."

"You're tough, but you're not as tough as you think you are."

"No, it turns out I'm even tougher."

"Ard—"

"How is he?" I asked, cutting him off. "How is the wonderful, buns of steel, young enough to be your son, Jamie?"

Ollie was staring at me with a mixture of hate and hurt in his eyes. Good.

"I haven't seen him in months. He finished his pupillage and moved onto work at another chambers. I think he's based in Surrey or somewhere now, nearer to his parents."

"You must've been heartbroken."

"It was just a stupid fling. It meant nothing. I just had my head turned. I regret every second of it."

"It went on for six months."

"I—"

"You fucked him in our bed."

"I—"

"In the sheets we picked out together, while all the time criticising me for going away on a book tour."

"I acted like a colossal shit. I will say sorry every day until I die. It was the stupidest thing I have ever done. I'm sorry, I'm sorry." He grabbed my hand and clung to it. "Please, just give me a second chance. We were together for five years; we can't just throw it away."

I pulled my hand away. "You already did."

"I would move heaven and earth to get you back."

I shook my head. "Then fucking act like it."

Ollie went quiet. This seemed to have shocked him more than anything else had. That his demeanour and his actions had consequences.

The waitress approached. "Thank God," I muttered.

"Would you guys like dessert?" she announced in her bubbliest Australian accent.

"Yes, can I have the chocolate fondant? Apparently, I'm too thin."

Ollie was staring at the picture on the wall, studiously looking anywhere else but at me. This went on for quite some time. "Are you okay?" I asked eventually, trying to sound less bratty than I wanted to.

He nodded and darted a look at me. His eyes were glistening. "I'm just going to the bathroom," he whispered and made his excuses.

"Fuck's sake," I said quietly as he walked off to the loos. *He cheats and, somehow, I'm the villain because I won't take him back?*

Maybe I'm too nice?

My phone buzzed again while I waited for Ollie. I opened the message and received a photo of Sonia with the kittens bundled up on the sofa. I couldn't help but smile.

Hope they're behaving, I texted back.

I looked up as Ollie came back, his face dry but red, presumably after some scrubbing with a paper towel.

My chocolate fondant followed him. "Lovely," I said, and dug in while he stared at me, red-eyed.

"Do I have any chance?" he asked eventually.

"Of us getting back together?"

He gave flicker of a nod.

"Not a chance, mate."

I didn't look at him for a while, instead focusing on my dessert.

I finished and wiped my mouth with a napkin. He was staring at me. "I will win you back," he said.

"Ollie…" I wanted to be so far away.

"You might not believe you'll ever forgive me, but I promise I'll prove it to you that we should give it another go."

I gestured at the waitress to give us the bill.

"Oliver, listen to me." I took his hand in mine. "I forgive you. I really do. I made mistakes in that relationship too. I didn't treat you as well as I should. But please, let's just call it a day? Let's just focus on trying to be friends."

He shook his head and gulped. "I can't be your friend," he said quietly.

It was the first time anything he'd said this evening had got to me. I gripped his hand a lot tighter. "Having you in my life but knowing that you're going home with someone else every night would kill me."

"You melodramatic poofter," I said, cracking a smile, but Ollie's face was still set in stone.

I tried a different tack. "Give it time. You'll be okay. There have been a lot of times in my life when I thought

I'd never survive, but I did every single time. And things got better. Just focus on you for a while, and what you need. Forget about me." The waitress brought over the bill, clearly wondering what the hell was going on between us.

I put my card down. "Quick as you can, love." I'd pay if it got me out of here faster.

Ollie was probably about to start crying again. I'd only seen him cry a couple of times before this evening and those times involved dead relatives. Where was the man who acted like he'd done nothing wrong when the affair became public? Where was the guy who pretty much shrugged in the face of my heartbreak? My ego was, in a way, loving that my disappearance from someone's life could turn them into a snivelling mess.

"Go on holiday, start an evening class. Join a sports team. I don't know. Take your mind off it somehow. But I'm not the one, Ollie. We both know it deep down."

My card came back. "Will you cover the tip?" I said, letting go of his hand and standing up. I put my coat on. "Thanks for the info." I grabbed the papers he'd bought me and shoved them in my coat pocket. "I appreciate it."

He looked so forlorn. Almost broken.

"For God's sake, Ollie. You're thirty-four. You've years in you yet. Stop acting like I'm the only fish in the sea."

He snorted. "You're the only man I've ever loved, though."

"Well, I'm sorry about that." I wrapped my scarf around me. "Look after yourself."

I walked off and left him sitting there. I didn't look back.

Chapter 30

I'm a fast walker and I can usually get fair distances in times most people would struggle. A lifetime of strong calf muscles and an inability to afford a bus fare. But even for me the hour and a half it took to reach Tarquin's house in the rain from Covent Garden was a bit much. It was frightfully cold by the time I stepped outside the restaurant; some late winter cold snap was apparently going to hit us with a week or so of low temperatures and frosty nights. But being England, of course, no snow.

I managed to get lost as well, when I eventually left the King's Road and couldn't find Novello Street, which Tarquin's charming little mews led from.

I wandered around Fulham looking vaguely menacing (I mean, by Fulham standards at least). Truth is, I was desperately killing time. I'd left Ollie in the restaurant much earlier than planned. I was quite happy not to go in and disrupt Tarquin's dinner party with my morose and unkempt presence.

As I made my way there, I passed the nice pub on the corner and thought about keeping myself company in there until closing so I wouldn't have to face a crowd. My plan was scuppered when I walked past and saw it was doing a roaring Thursday night trade and was full to the gunnels. I didn't know Fulham well enough to try and find a quieter pub to hang out in instead. I was beginning to hate the fact I'd taken up Tarquin on his offer. Could I book myself into a Premier Inn then just go and get my bag in the morning? I could say I'd ended up staying at Verity's after all, and thanks anyway.

It was ten o'clock. I stopped being a miserable git, plucked up my courage and gave myself a talking to.

I arrived at Tarquin's place and gingerly knocked on the door. It opened a few seconds later. An attractive blonde woman stood in front of me. "You must be Arden! Tarquin's been telling us about his new lodger! Come in, come in!"

"Tarquin!" she yelled as we made our way back upstairs. "You can put your telescope away, he's here! You never mentioned he was hot!"

I blushed. Luckily, Tarquin was as well as I made my way into the living room. He was wearing an annoyingly tight denim shirt and glasses (I didn't know he wore them. He looked most becoming in them). I made a beeline for his pectoral muscles that were forcing the buttons at chest level to gape a little. I was glad it was freezing outside otherwise I'd have been a little hot under the collar.

"Arden!" he roared, and passed me a glass of wine before I could even respond. "Everyone, this is Arden. Arden, this is Millie," (the blonde who'd let me in) "she was at Oxford with Guy and me. This is Victoria," (a stunning brunette) "and Chiara," (another blonde who I'd turn straight for). "And my boys Freddie," (fuck me gently with a chainsaw – Freddie looked a bit like if Jonny Wilkinson had a younger brother who worked in the City) "Toby," (thankfully Toby was the token fat one in the group; I presumed he was the comic relief) "who's Vic's husband." I mentally did a double take. He must be loaded or have a dick that could perform miracles.

I gave my polite greetings. "Go put your coat upstairs and come back down. We're about to break out the Cards Against Humanity," Millie slurred at my general direction. (I groaned internally – was I the only person who hated that game?)

But of course, what I said was: "Great. I'll be back in a sec."

I made my way upstairs and dropped my coat off, hiding the paperwork in the bottom of my bag as I did so. My bladder was about to burst so I hurried into the loo and came out to find Tarquin hovering at the door, clutching the wine glass I had left in the bedroom, which he sheepishly passed to me.

"Sorry, I would've totally rescheduled this but Vic and Toby are off to India for a month on Saturday so this was the last night everyone could do."

"No, no, it's fine. It's your house."

"Well, I didn't mean for there to be a party. I thought it'd be just us two."

Either that was a sign, or I was terrible at reading signs. I was terrible at reading signs, though. I chose to ignore it.

I made an awkward gesture that was meant to show I'd follow him back into the living room. He gave me an inscrutable look then made his way.

I followed him back into the room, where a drunken debate was in full force.

Millie was holding court and grabbed my arm as I came back down. "Have you met Guy?" she said, boozily breathing at me.

"Of course," I said, unsure of where this was going.

"We're trying to set him up with Chiara. Don't you think they'd make the most beautiful babies?" Millie was framing Chiara's face with her hands. "The bone structure alone should get a *Vogue* cover, not to mention all that blonde hair." Millie forgot she was blonde too. And I assumed the money they both had would prove far more convenient than the cheekbones.

"Are you interested in Guy?" I asked Chiara as innocently as I could.

"I mean, who isn't?" Victoria guffawed, playing with the cards for the game.

"Oi!" her husband chided. "Actually, I'd probably do him as well."

"We'd all do him," said Freddie.

"Yeah, didn't you used to be on the rowing team with him at uni, Fred?" Millie asked. "Surely you've seen him in the buff in the changing rooms? What's he packing?"

"Briefly," Freddie said. "Rowing was not my forte. Rugby. Guy gave it up when we left school, and I packed in rowing." I could see why. Freddie was not someone who looked like he'd be happy in a canoe, or whatever it was they rowed in.

"Is everyone going to pretend he didn't ignore the other part of my question?" Millie asked. A girl who couldn't be distracted from discussing dick sizes was a girl after my own heart.

Tarquin appeared very awkward about this conversation. "Can we just play the game?"

"But we're matchmaking, Tarqz. You know how I love to." Millie was much drunker than everyone else.

She glided me along to the seat where she'd been perched and made me take the cushion, while she settled herself on its armrest, her tiny bum fitting easily on it.

"Tarquin's right. I think you'll find Guy is not in the mood for love right now," Freddie said, with a brief glance towards Tarquin.

"But that's exactly when he needs a shag. He spent so much time playing Daddy to that girl—"

"Her name's Arabella," Tarquin snapped. "Not *that girl*. For God's sake, Millie, you met her a hundred times. She was called Arabella."

There was an extremely awkward silence. Tarquin's jaw was set. Chiara, Vic, and Toby all sat on the sofa looking at their shoes, while Freddie made brief eye contact with me and puffed out his cheeks.

"Tarq, mate, come help me clear all the plates and stuff, yeah," Vic eventually said. "Come on, you've got your kitchen laid out like a crazy person. I can't work out where anything is."

She stood up and cleared the clutter away while she bullied him into going with her.

"Well, that was awkward," Toby muttered. "Well done, Millie."

"Yeah, try to keep your gob under control, will you, Millz?" Freddie added.

Chiara kept silent and drank more of her wine.

"How was I supposed to know?"

"They only buried her yesterday!" Freddie whispered angrily.

"Yeah, and I don't think Tarq's happy none of you went. We're supposed to be friends with Guy too, you know," Toby said. "Even though he's a boring sod."

"None of you came?" I asked. Surely, in the front in that huge group of poshos there'd been at least one of them…

"Vic and I did," Toby answered. "She's Vic Hetherington. You probably met her sister, Eleanor?"

Wow, it's a small world. The family resemblance was clear now. No wonder she was unhappy with Millie and Chiara joking about Guy – her sister had eyes on him.

"Couldn't get time off work," Freddie said.

"Lady F hates me," Millie said. "And so does Rosie."

"Chiara?" I asked. If she was trying to get set up with Guy then surely she went to the funeral? "Well, I meant to. But, unlike these guys, I'd never actually met Arabella."

I thought that odd in the limited posh circles that this lot moved in. There was only so many of them to go around, and if Ollie – who was only on the periphery of these types – knew Guy, then I couldn't see how Chiara didn't know Arabella. Chiara looked to be a wee bit younger than the others (still in her twenties), so their paths must've crossed at some stage.

Many books have been written about the dynamics of posh people and their strange ulterior world where up is down and down is non-U and whatever else. Frankly, it didn't interest me, and I had no intention of interrogating these people for answers. Despite the files on Miles Sweet burning a hole in my jacket upstairs and how I was overthinking about Arabella. I had enough of my own problems to deal with.

Pawel killed her. He must have.

"Right, we're off," said Vic as she came back to us.

"Really? What about the game?" Millie said, gesturing at the cards.

"We're off," said Vic again, more forcibly this time. She tilted her head towards the kitchen.

Tarquin followed her out and there was a prolonged charade of everyone saying they'd love to stay but "work in the morning", and Tarquin saying, "never mind, have one more", "oh no, we can't, have to get an Uber back to Notting Hill". The process went on for nearly twenty minutes as they fannied about getting coats and *mwah-ing mwah-ing* each other on the cheeks as they left. Millie started crying as she was convinced Tarquin was angry with her and needed briefly consoling. Chiara lost a shoe, and then, when she found it, wandered off without telling anyone, leaving Vic to sprint after her. Freddie's taxi to Clapham arrived and Millie hopped in with him. "She lives nearby?" I asked Tarquin.

"No, she lives in Primrose Hill. But her boyfriend is skiing in Courchevel."

"Oh."

"Yeah, she's lovely. But fidelity's never been a strong suit of hers."

Once the second taxi pulled away northwards to Notting Hill with Vic, Chiara, and Toby in it, he slammed the door with a contented sigh.

"Do you ever dread seeing your friends? Like, I've been putting off hosting that get-together for months. I can't take them all at once."

"Why didn't you cancel?"

"I'm in a masochistic mood. I can't feel any worse after the funeral, so I thought I'd just get it over and done with. Rip off the plaster."

He poured us another glass of wine and flopped on the sofa with his legs spread wide, put his head back and groaned loudly. "Oh, how were all your meetings?" he asked as I took a seat next to him.

"Great. Yeah, I might be getting a TV show made from my books."

"That's fantastic!" He held his glass up and we clinked. "And, I presume, somewhat lucrative?"

"I have no idea yet. But I hope so."

"It's good to hear someone's career is doing well." He was staring at a spot on the wall as he talked.

"Problem?" I asked. *Not your place, Arden. Back off.*

"No, it'll be fine. Just… headaches, that's all."

"Sorry to hear that."

"Yeah, well…" He shrugged. "I knew it'd be this way. Just thought I'd be less stressed about it all. Anyway, you still up for some antiques at the weekend?"

"Definitely. I'm now very sure I want my own house and want it nicely done."

He raised an eyebrow quizzically. "Should I ask about how the dinner went?"

"It went as well as it could under the circumstances. He wants to get back together." There were two sizeable bits of information I'd just given him there. Some hints.

"And you don't want to?" he asked after a pause of several seconds.

"Not in a million years. I think one day I can be his friend, but not until I see some character growth from him." I put my head in my hands. My resolve was cracking a little. I was desperate for Tarquin not to see this. "Five years. Five fucking years."

Tarquin's hand was rubbing my back. I wasn't sure if my emotions were in check, but I leant up from where I'd been crouched over to hide my face.

"I'm sure he's a prick. He doesn't deserve you." His face was only a few inches from mine.

I was lost in his eyes – yes, literally, cliché-ridden as it was – lost. I forgot myself for a second. God, he was beautiful.

You're single and free to do what you want. I could feel his breath, see the stubble on his jaw. His hand was still on my back.

I cleared my throat and broke the moment. "I'm going to head up to bed." I drained my glass. "Thanks so much for the room. I do appreciate it. I know you're not from Lilbury, but you've all made me feel so welcome."

Tarquin looked briefly miffed but recovered with a killer smile. "Think nothing of it. It's my pleasure."

"Well, I appreciate it, nonetheless. I'm going to be up early and get a train back to Dorset, so I probably won't see you, but we're still on for Saturday?"

"Absolutely. I shall text you tomorrow and we'll make a plan."

I smiled and left him there to make my way to his spare room. The room was cool, but not cold, and the bed felt like it had fresh sheets on (a blessing). There was the awkward moment as both Tarquin and I attempted to use the bathroom as silently as possible – Tarquin was one of those men who directed his stream dead centre of the toilet bowl and therefore made a cacophony when he pissed, audible through about three walls.

I heard him cough, clear his throat, and the springs as he got into bed. I was very much trying to convince myself I had made the right choice not to be in that bed with him. Oh, I was sure he had a body like a Greek god and would fuck me stupid, but was it worth it?

He was nice. I needed to make new friends. And I'd already made a mistake with that once since going to Lilbury and ruined a chance to make a friend with whom I presumed was the only gay man living in the village.

Besides, I was only surmising Tarquin was gay from a few awkward moments. He could be as straight as they come for all I knew. He could have had his turn with Millie and have passed her onto Freddie.

I briefly wondered what Ollie was doing now. I hoped he was sitting in his (formerly ours) living room crying over photos of me on his phone. But what he was probably doing was being very productive and healthy like he always was. He'd probably gone home and done a few hours of work, or a brief workout session, or something else that made my moping look bad, just like he always did.

Thinking about one Scotsman inevitably led to another and my mind turned to Simon. What an arrogant horrible person he was. Convinced of his abilities in bed, convinced he was so smart with his judgemental comments about everyone. His sneery face.

I tossed and turned and then as usual eventually gave up on sleep and settled with lying in the dark.

Chapter 31

I was up at 6am and was out the door of Tarquin's house by ten past. A note left on his fridge door saying thanks.

I walked to the Tube station and made my way inside with a few dreary commuters. I boarded a half-empty train and trundled along in near darkness to Westminster, where I exited to an empty, wet, and windswept street and made my way across the bridge. Waterloo station was already full of people, most of whom were miserable and trudging along looking like they were heading for the gallows.

Heading out of London, it was easy to find an empty seat, and I sat with my bag, a dishevelled mess. I went to the loos and nearly baulked in fright seeing myself under the train lights. I looked like a ghoul. Huge grey patches were prominent under my eyes and my skin was deathly pale. The only thing that made me look alive was the stubble on my face that was getting into beard territory. When had I last shaved?

I had been planning to get drunk with Verity, put the world to rights, and wake up with a leisurely brunch at an overpriced café near her flat. Here I was instead, speeding through the dormitory suburbs of south-west London at 7.30 on a freezing Friday morning looking like a zombie.

I made my way back to my seat and was pleased to at least see no one had tried to nick my bag in the minutes I'd been away.

I got out the papers Ollie had given me yesterday. There wasn't a lot. Basic information about Arabella's father and her stepmother, a woman called Noor Khoudy, the daughter of a telecoms billionaire. She had French-Lebanese dual citizenship.

When I pulled out my phone to google her, the first hit was a profile with *Vanity Fair*, who'd interviewed her several years previously when she was described in gushing terms.

> *With her exotic beauty and natural grace, acquired from several years training as a ballerina when in her teens, Noor slinks in and out of rooms, nearly invisible. Her footsteps don't seem to make a sound, even though she wears the latest Louboutin on her feet, which aren't yet available in the stores.*

I presumed the writer hadn't intended to make me want to hate her with the paragraph but … hey, surprise! Noor Khoury was thirty-four at the time of the profile meaning she was thirty-seven or so now. Fifteen years older than her stepdaughter. More than twenty years her husband's junior.

Despite my insistence to myself last night that I didn't care for anything more about Arabella's death, here I was rooting through her family's background once again. Could Noor have killed her stepdaughter? Did she hate her? Was she in the way for her inheriting if old Miles kicked it prematurely? No, her own family had billions. She was surely set for life either way.

She'd been in Dubai when the murder had happened anyway. But with those sorts of resources maybe she'd hired some goon to do her bidding for her. I was getting into dangerous territory – fantasist territory – but her family were billionaires in a corrupt country, and she was married to a man with a list of police investigations for sleaze a mile long. Was it believable that all that money was acquired through clean and open business practices? No, I think Noor probably knew her way around a dodgy deal.

As I continued to read the details of Companies House records, we passed through Woking and then Basingstoke. The view from the train of commuter towns started to thin out and the beginnings of rolling green hills took over. We passed through Andover and eventually I managed to nap, just before my phone buzzed.

Sonia was texting me letting me know she'd left for work and the kittens were fed, watered, and happily left to their own devices in the bathroom and that Simon and his lads had been busy doing whatever it was builders actually did.

I sighed and stayed awake for the train to reach Sittingston.

The taxi options at Sittingston left a lot to be desired, so I was given short shrift when I stepped into the tiny office at the station. "Forty-five minutes at least," the woman at the desk said to me before I'd even opened my mouth, and then she turned back to her solitaire game. *Fuck.*

"Right, well, I'll be over at the café. I'll be back in forty minutes. Unless there's a chance the driver might be any earlier?"

She shrugged. "Unlikely."

I felt like I was about to lose my temper with her so instead chose a sensible option and made my way out into the rain and trudged across the car park and into the narrow section of the high street. The village had expanded out to ridiculous proportions so it could connect to the railway line as it went past on the way to Exeter.

Presumably, in Victorian times there had been some serious town planning issues to sort out from a disgruntled populace. Now it just had the effect of Sittingston being over a mile long but never more than one or two streets wide.

It was raining a lot heavier here than it had been in London – and unlike London, there was mud in Sittingston. A lot of it.

I groaned internally and made my way down the steep hill to the main road and prepared myself for a long, annoying sit in a café after a walk in the rain but had to jump as a Land Rover nearly took me out and ended my waste of a life there and then.

There was a hoot. The driver waved at me. I gave an apologetic wave back and carried on. The driver wasn't happy with this and wanted their pound of flesh. He leant over and wound down the window.

"Oi! Forrest! Are you getting in or not?"

"Guy?" I said in a gormless manner. I peered at him, before darting across the road and jumping in the cab.

"How… how did you—"

"Tarquin texted me this morning. He's had the train schedule to Lilbury memorised for years. Told me you'd be on the seven thirty, so I knew what time you'd get in. Sorry I'm a bit late, but the rain made me drive a bit slower."

"That's… that's so nice of you. I have no words."

Guy blushed and revved up the hill, where he did a quick loop of the car park and turned around. "The steering on this thing is shocking. I need Belgium to turn around in."

I was grinning at him. I didn't care. This was one of the nicest things someone had ever done for me.

I wasn't sure if it was technically Tarquin or he who had done the nice thing, but I was giving the praise to Guy.

And before I knew it, I was making a right fool of myself.

"Um, oh, are-are you crying, Arden?"

"No," I said through tears. "I've just had a long couple of days. I'm a bit emotional."

Guy quickly switched his gaze back and forth between the road and me. He pulled over as we got to the high street proper, outside the local branch of Barclays where a parking space had just appeared.

"Don't cry, mate. You'll set me off."

I looked at Guy. My tears had gone as quickly as they'd come, and now I was just snivelling and looking even more bedraggled. Guy gave me a watery smile. "This week's been hell." He'd turned to look at me. He was unshaven, his hair was tousled, and he had an old rain jacket thrown over a white checked shirt and an olive-green pullover on top. He was equally dishevelled. But still better-looking.

"Look at the fucking state of us," I said. To my relief, Guy laughed.

"God, I know. I've got a dinner with the local Chamber of Commerce tonight," he said, and looked at himself in the rear-view mirror and pulled on his cheeks. "I look like shit. I suppose the moment Tarquin was back in London he popped on a pair of blue suede loafers and some chinos and was off out to the King's Road with a bunch of his acolytes. Compared to him I must be wretched."

"It was a dinner party at his place, actually. I met Eleanor's sister."

Guy laughed and then an odd look came across his face. "Victoria? I know her well. My first ever girlfriend."

"Oh?" I said as we sat in the rain, and both stared ahead.

"She has the dubious honour of being the girl I lost my virginity to." It was odd to imagine Guy losing his virginity. *To anyone*. He was somewhat old-fashioned; I thought he'd be more the type that lost it on his wedding night, like some *On Chesil Beach* scenario. "Oh, Beryl. I say, that was some jolly good lovemaking. I ejaculated most rewardingly at the end."

"And now her sister is after you?" I said without thinking.

"Yes." Guy was laughing again. It was a nice sound. "I'm a firm favourite with the women in the Hetherington household. Her mother's been trying to get one of her daughters to marry me since I started shaving. They're nice people, though. It's a pity all this has happened on top of what they've got going on at the moment."

I was too shy all of a sudden to ask, but Guy clearly wanted to talk. "Ellie and Vic's dad, George, well… I think he's made a few dodgy investments. And they've gone south. That's why she was riding one of my horses the other day; they had to sell Ellie's."

I nearly started laughing. In Guy's world, poverty was selling a horse. I should take him to the pub where I grew up.

"It's been a horrible time. Apparently, it's been going on for a couple of years. Gradually they've been selling more and more things, really stripping back. Now it's dire. They've put the house on the market. Ellie's going to start a new job in the spring up in Bristol working at a PR agency."

This was news. I stopped feeling sorry for myself for two seconds and focused on what he was saying. Eleanor and her family were skint and trying to pretend otherwise. Arabella's family had more money than God. Was Eleanor jealous? The two were like sisters. Had she asked for a loan? A rescue for her parents?

I buzzed at the idea. But shook my head again. Back to the fantasist tag.

Guy started up again. "Come on, let's get you home."

Chapter 32

The weekend was greeted with a downpour. It did nothing on Friday but rain and rain until surely the skies had nothing left. It didn't help my mood. Guy had driven off after he dropped me at my cottage. I'd invited him in for a coffee; he'd stared at it with an odd look on his face, which a more optimistic person would call lascivious, and then shook his head. "I have to get back to check on my aunt and make sure she's okay. Now that the funeral's over, it's just her and me again."

Instead of having him join me for tea and cake, I was alone in my house. The rain made it impractical for Simon and his lads to come, so when he texted me asking if they should be there today, I said no.

Instead, I sat on the living room floor in a pair of old sweatpants and thick socks and tapped away at my laptop until my fingers ached. The kittens played beside me. They chewed my toes and scampered about in their sickeningly adorable way.

At some stage Tarquin texted me and said he'd be there the next day to take me shopping. "I know a bunch of places we can go."

Friday afternoon gave way to night-time. It was late in the evening before I even stopped for food, and well into the night before I went to bed. I lay there listening to the rain and wind, and worried about my gutters.

Maybe the roof will leak too, and I can get Simon round for that. Maybe he'll hate me less if I keep paying for his services?

Saturday dawned to more rain. The garden was a sea of mud. The road past it was more of a canal. I put on the same clothes I'd worn the previous day and returned to the same spot.

Tarquin said he'd be there for 10am so naturally I'd woken up at 6am in the barest of light. My mind turned to the papers I had beside me in a pile from Ollie. *No. No*, I thought. *No fucking more.* I had spent enough time making a fool of myself and chasing shadows around trying to find my version of the truth.

Well, Pawel probably did it and I should learn to live with it. I threw all of Ollie's documents in a drawer out of sight.

After I rescued a kitten from the top of the curtains where they'd got stuck during a climbing expedition, I sloped off to the bathroom and took a scalding shower to wake myself up.

Okay, a lie. I was totally going to make myself look pretty for Tarquin. After my shower – my hair clean and smelling of peach conditioner – I took stock in the bathroom mirror (speckled and aged though the mirror was with a peeling back, the first thing that needed replacing). I was, as Ollie had pointed out, gaunt and pale. I had lost weight, yes, but all it had done was make my belly shrink into a ball of fat that hung off my sunken stomach. Any sort of tone that had once been there had now dissipated into nothingness. I was a corpse who'd had a big meal, with sunken eyes and chapped lips.

Jesus, I thought. I looked awful. How had I lost so much weight? I then remembered I'd only eaten once yesterday. No wonder I felt so tired all the time.

Half an hour after he'd said he would, Tarquin arrived in his penis-replacement-mobile. He tooted the horn as he approached, jumped out, and came to the front door before I could get to it. He near bashed the door down and I opened it to see him smiling in the rain in a very fetching leather jacket. His perfect smile was beaming at me with his big teeth all perfectly in line and whiter than a Scotsman's arse.

"Morning," he said, and brushed past. He stood in the hall and gave my house a once over, giving the downstairs rooms a thorough look. He, like everyone else, retreated to being a child around the kittens and instantly got down on the floor to play with them. He whipped off his jacket to show the navy-blue long-sleeve T-shirt he wore underneath. A T-shirt that rode up over his stomach. I tried not to look.

"This one's much braver than that one," he said, pointing at Eisenhower. Or Roosevelt. I'd forgotten which was which.

"He keeps coming over to me, but the other one just wants to watch."

I shrugged. "Some people are happier watching."

He gave me a look. "He's a cat."

I shrugged again.

"We'd better make tracks, or it'll be a wasted journey."

I threw on my old coat over a green jumper, put my muddy boots on, and shooed him from the living room, giving the kittens instructions on good behaviour as I did.

We got into Tarquin's Porsche. "So, I've got a few places I've found. These are all shops I know Dad used to have dealings with, the best types; no ruffian Lovejoys here, all gentlemen who'll give you a fair price on… what was it you wanted, again?"

"Dining table and chairs, a couple of chairs for the living room, a cabinet, maybe a bookcase, and a sofa if they've got anything in that I like."

"I can't imagine any of that being a problem." He grinned at me as we sped off eastwards. The first village we headed to was a place called Tisbury. It was possibly the most picturesque village in England, to be fair to the place. As usual, Tarquin saw speed limits and then ignored them, and drove through the rain-sodden fields as if he owned them.

"Doesn't put a crimp in your style having to to-and-fro so much between here and London?"

"Not at all," he answered. "I used to help Dad out with work, so I spent most of my weekends when I was at home actually down here. And my grandparents live not far from Lilbury, near Poole. If I didn't get out of London as often as I did, I'd go insane and turn into one of those miserable people on the Tube who look as though they've just escaped a warzone."

"And you and Guy are basically two halves of the same person."

He laughed at this.

We pulled up outside a large warehouse on the edge of the village, which was more of a ramshackle barn than a shop. A long half-timbered building with a sign outside saying, *Hillary's Emporium*.

"Hillary is an old friend of my dad's. He has everything."

We were not the only people out shopping for antiques on this cold and wet Saturday at the start of March. Around us were a mix of the old shires middle class and a few young white couples down from London who were all blonde hair and Barbour jackets. Behind us, one of the blondes was hectoring her boyfriend who had dropped something expensive. "For God's sake, James. If you're not going to act like an adult, why don't you go wait in the car."

James's response was less polite, and Tarquin and I shared a look. Not a relationship that was strong enough to survive a shopping expedition.

"I wonder what they're like in IKEA."

Tarquin grinned. I could make him laugh so easily; either he thought I was very witty, or his sense of humour was completely basic. I hoped for the former.

We plodded on through the shop until we reached its innards, as the man I presume we'd come to see came out of the shadows. "Tarquin! Goodness, you get more and more like your father every time I see you!" Tarquin grinned again, an even bigger one this time, and loped off towards a tall, erudite-looking white man in rolled-up shirtsleeves and pair of very worn-looking corduroy trousers. They shook hands vigorously.

"Arden, this is Hillary Carter. An old friend of my dad's and, obviously, the owner of this here shop."

"Pleasure," I said, shaking his hand. Hillary was friendlier looking than I expected and had a natural jovial attitude that rubbed well with Tarquin's own happy demeanour. The two spent a good ten minutes filling each other in on their respective families while I stood beside them like an idiot. Tarquin didn't ignore me, though, and put his arm on my side to include me. "Arden has just moved to not far from here, a great old place that's desperately in need of a bit of TLC."

Hillary surmised me with glasses that were like bottle tops. "Well, let's see what we've got. A dining set, you say? We have some lovely ones in. Any specific style you're after?"

"Anything that isn't mid-century modern. I loathe it. But aside from that, I'm fairly open."

He turned on his heel and beckoned us to follow. Tarquin's hand was still gently guiding me as we walked, occasionally brushing my side.

We made our way through the huge warehouse of lovely things to a far corner, where the dining tables and chairs were all laid out in sets. "My wife's handiwork; she thinks the shop's a mess and spends most of her life sorting the furniture. She'd love nothing more than for it to look like one of those big box retailers with everything in a specific place. I try and tell her that's not how antiques work, but she refuses to listen." Hillary pointed to a large oak table that was a bit too long. "Now this has several chairs I think would go with it."

Tarquin and I both inspected the table. "Like it?" he whispered as we bent down to look at its legs.

"It's too big," I whispered.

Tarquin shot up. "Too big, Hillary. He needs a bit smaller."

"Righty-o. Ah! What about this lovely one? From an old dear in Salisbury who dropped it off a few weeks ago. It's surprisingly light but might need some work."

It was a brighter wood than the first, but in much worse shape. There were scratches and scuffs on it. It was rectangular and large, about two metres long, without feeling like it was enormous. Tarquin picked up a corner. "It's not that heavy," he informed me.

We both bent down to look at its legs and the woodwork. "It's seen better days," Tarquin said after a minute.

It was my turn to bolt upright. "I love it. I'll take it."

Tarquin startled himself and rose to match me. "Really?"

Hillary was pleased. "Good, good. I like a man who knows what he wants. It'll be a bit of work to get it back to its former glory, but worth it in the end."

"I have plenty of spare time for a bit of sandpapering," I told him.

Tarquin leant over to me and whispered out of the corner of his mouth: "You don't want to look at some more?"

"No, this is the style I want, and it needs work, so it'll be cheaper."

Hillary was examining the table. "I've got some chairs in the back that would work with this—" There was a loud crash.

"Oh, JAMES!" said a harassed voice.

"That was your fault!" a man bellowed back. "Your handbag swung and hit it!"

Hillary rolled his eyes. "Let me just go sort this and then I'll go root around for those chairs. I think I've got a few that could work with it."

Once he was out of earshot, Tarquin turned to me with a big grin. "You don't muck around, do you?"

I shrugged. "I'm too impatient to spend all day on one thing. You'd tell me if he was ripping me off and selling me something that was only a bit better than firewood, though, wouldn't you?"

Tarquin gave me a rare serious look. "Of course." He put his arm on my side again. "And besides, Hillary's an old family friend and he's as straight as an arrow. He's an honest businessman."

He kept his hand on my side, just above my waist. Though I was wearing a jacket, I could still feel its reassuring pressure, and I was liking the sensation. I could hear other customers as they wandered around – there was a middle-aged woman perusing some desks a few metres away, but she had her back to us and was busy inspecting the inside of a drawer. I had a furtive look around.

Tarquin's hand was still there. He was staring at me with a coy smile on his lips. If I didn't do it now, I was never going to do it. I took a step towards him. Tarquin was only too happy to have me there and put his other hand on my waist too.

I was so close I could feel his breath on my face and the warmth coming off his body. I lifted my hand, took hold of the material at his throat, gripped it in my fist, and pulled him towards me.

It had been a long time since I'd had a proper first kiss with someone. My first kiss with Ollie had been in a drunken fumble in a nightclub, Simon and I had been as part of some frantic foreplay. But this was a proper one, with the harnessed passion of being fully clothed, sober, and in public. There was a proper frisson. When his lips reached mine, a jolt went through me, from my toes, up through my crotch and all the way to my head. His hands were around me and embracing me properly. My hand went round to cup one very firm and round arse cheek.

We went on for almost a minute; he pushed me up against one of the nearby tables, and held me, almost pinning me down, while his tongue went in my mouth. He was so beautiful, his body incredibly firm and muscular. It was firm everywhere.

We heard a noise, and I jolted upright. The woman behind us had closed the desk drawer with a slam and was now making her way across to the tables. We broke apart and smiled benignly at her as she wandered past.

"Hello," we offered blithely, sharing the English head bob and polite mutterings.

She made her way past us, and we gave each other a look. I was panting slightly and leaning on the table. We both had wet, shiny lips.

Tarquin looked down. "Do you think she noticed I have a boner?"

Before I could answer, Hillary arrived. "Ah, good, you haven't moved. Come look at these chairs."

It was another half an hour before I could finish up with Hillary and the chairs. Tarquin and I followed him around the chair area listening intently as he described woods and carpentry skills, making me sit on every single one and telling me I should check for important factors like lower back support, height relative to the table, and of course, dead-bum-creation.

All the while, I couldn't keep my eyes off Tarquin. I wanted to drag him into the toilets and have a repeat of earlier. And then more. He clearly had the same thought, as several times as I brushed past him while Hillary beckoned me here and there, his hands found their way over my body in the brief second we were close, leaving me feeling violated in the best possible way.

When we came to the counter to settle up the amount of money I'd spent (I don't want to think about it), Tarquin's hands somehow found their way up the back of my shirt for a few seconds, and only came back out in the split second before Hillary noticed. "So, this will all be delivered to the house. And I must say it's been lovely to meet you, Mr Forrest. It's so rare I get to see Tarquin these days, and always lovely to meet one of his friends."

Tarquin went a little red at this.

"Tell me, Tarquin, how is your lady friend?" Hillary asked as he argued with the card machine.

Tarquin stopped blushing. "What lady friend?"

"Why, the one you used to always be with whenever I saw you with your father in London. That young blonde lady, you know. Your father assured me the last time we saw you two together that wedding bells couldn't be far away."

I was confused. "Does he mean Arabella?"

Tarquin laughed. "I don't know what you mean, Hillary. There's no woman in my life. It's my dad listening to Mum again about her wanting grandkids."

Hillary shrugged. "Oh, I must be mistaken. I could've sworn… anyway, that's for you, Mr Forrest," he said, handing me back my card and a sheaf of paperwork. "Thank you very much for your custom, and please do come again. Even if it's without this one." He gave Tarquin a friendly shove.

As we left, the two shared a handshake and a few private words, while I waited near the door, surveying the nearby river that the road from the shop lead down to.

Tarquin met me at the door. "What was all that about?" I asked as we both put our hoods up to dash to the car.

"Nothing. He's old. Bit confused."

"Was it Arabella he was talking about?"

We made it to the car, and Tarquin let us in before he answered. "Might've been, not sure. Could have been Millie. I used to run into them in town occasionally when he and Dad were having one of their boozy lunches."

"And him thinking you two were going out?"

Tarquin was about to turn the key but roared with laughter at that. He turned to look at me and then kissed me again. After we broke apart, he gave me a wry look. "Like I said, I think he's confused. Does it look like I'm interested in women?"

I bit my lip in what I hoped was a coquettish way. "No, you seem fairly determined with this line of questioning, officer."

"Well then, there's your answer. So why don't we go celebrate your purchases with a nice lunch somewhere? There's a great pub on the other side of the village that does Thai food."

I shrugged.

"Or we could go back to your place, and I could rock your world? Up to you, I'm not fussed."

I laughed. Images of what he must look like under his clothes flashed through my mind. I was going to be good, though. "Let's go for lunch."

Tarquin looked like he regretted bringing up the idea of lunch now. "He wants lunch. Lunch. Course he does," he muttered to himself.

We drove to the other end of the village and went to the pub, which was doing a fairly busy Saturday trade, so we had to wait for ten minutes at the bar before we could get a table. I got us a drink, while Tarquin waited for me. I stared at him, and this time not with lust. So, he was gay, and he fancied me, and he was absolutely phenomenally gorgeous. What was wrong? Was I just nervous because the last time I'd slept with a guy, Simon turned out to be a bit of a dick and was now a permanent feature in my life? Yes. Now I was forever committed to having to make awkward small talk with the Scotsman who was fitting my kitchen instead of being able to just keep it to myself.

I took our beers over to the barrel where Tarquin was waiting; he was looking out the window, rotating his phone in his hand. "Penny for them?" I asked as I slopped half my pint over on the uneven surface.

"Nothing, just hungry." We'd entered a weird patch of not being comfortable with each other.

I took a deep sip then grabbed the bull by the horns. "What happened in the shop – that was nice. It was fun."

Tarquin examined me. "There's a 'but' coming, isn't there?"

I sighed. "I only just got out of a long relationship. And you live in London, and you're friends with my neighbours, and I need to focus on making some new friends and not snogging them in antique shops."

He cocked his head to the side. "I mean, that's very conservative of you," he said with a laugh. "Look, I'm not saying we have to get married—"

"I'm gonna stop you there," I interrupted. "I'm not interested in a shag for a shag's sake. I mean, I'm not against the concept, just not with someone I know who I am probably going to have to keep seeing from now until eternity."

"But you don't want a relationship either?" he asked.

"I see you've found the flaw in my plan."

Tarquin sighed. "So you want nothing, then? You just kissed me back, and ground up against my crotch while doing so because…"

I blushed (yet again). "You're nice. And so very good-looking. I am attracted to you, and if down the road things have changed, I'd be happy to grind against you some more. But not now."

"Okay. Understood." He sighed again.

"Don't be like that. It's not a completely wasted journey for you. I mean, you're not gonna get laid, but—"

"Bloody hell, give me some credit. I didn't come down here just cos I thought I might get my dick wet. I do enjoy your company, and all that. We can be friends, surely?"

I went the deepest shade of red I'd ever been. "Oh my God, I-I didn't mean to be such an arsehole," I stuttered. "Yes, of course. Of course I'd like to be friends. Very much so."

At that moment, the barman came and told us our table was free. "You still want to?" he asked.

"Of course. Friends can have lunch too."

Chapter 33

Tarquin drove back through the rain at a slower speed than earlier. We'd had a pleasant couple of hours in the pub after the initial awkwardness. Our legs had brushed under the table a few times, and our hands had met once or twice reaching for the mustard. It was awkward because of the fact it wasn't awkward. He was a lovely guy, and I had an extreme attraction to him. Part of me was still yelling at myself even as we drove through Lilbury to renege on my stupid idea of staying neutral – just bang his brains out and go for it from there.

But I couldn't. A bit of fun, a fling, nothing special – those were all the words that Ollie had used to describe the posh, handsome, tall, flexible, twenty-two-year-old from his office whose dick pics had been cluttering up his phone.

I had come to Dorset to be my own man. I'd never lived on my own before, and so much of my life had been about pleasing whatever man was in my orbit at the time, by making myself thinner, or more muscular, or quieter, for him to be more pleased with me.

I couldn't face the idea of being with anyone. I wanted time on my own. I wanted to build myself from the ground up and hope, by some miracle, one day I could be happy with being Arden Forrest. So I could respect him and not cringe at the thought of everything I had ever done.

We eventually made it back to my house just as it was getting dark. The rain was bucketing down and drumming on the roof of the car. Tarquin pulled up as close to the edge of the path as he could, so I'd have a few steps less to run in the rain. "Are you driving home in this weather?" I asked, hoping it wouldn't open a can of worms.

"No, I'll stop at Guy's."

"Okay, well, thanks for everything today. I appreciate you coming with me, even if it didn't have the ending you wanted."

Tarquin gave a crooked smile out the side of his mouth. He leant over and gave me a long kiss. "I still totally would, if you ever change your mind."

"Goodnight."

I got out of the car and rushed in from the rain. His car was gone by the time I got inside and twitched the curtain to see. The house was freezing. I quickly made peace with the heating gods, while the kittens mewed themselves silly over my arrival home. I heated up a microwave meal and grabbed a bottle of red wine.

The three of us left my dust-covered kitchen and retired to the sofa in a part of the house that wasn't a bombsite, where we sat in perfect harmony. By harmony, I mean they tried to eat my food and Eisenhower tried to get in my wine glass several times. There was a crappy romcom on that I managed to get involved with. Pretty people in perfect New York apartments who had what must be exceptionally well-paid jobs that seemed to require little to no attendance.

I couldn't eat the microwave meal, and after a few bites of the lasagne I pushed it aside and focused on the wine instead.

The kittens curled up in a ball on my lap and were soon just a warm mass of indistinguishable fluff. The rain drummed over the closing credits of the movie. "So, guys, what are we gonna do, eh?" I got Roosevelt to open one eye before I was dismissed, and the ball of fluff was reunited.

"Even you're tired of me."

I looked at the clock. It was nearly eleven. I slumped off to bed, where I tossed and turned for what must've been an hour. I went to the bathroom to splash water on my face. The rain was still lashing the house, and the wind had now picked up.

I headed downstairs to forage for something to eat, because my body had finally digested the pub lunch. As I came down the staircase, headlights came into the foyer and the sound of a car pulling up was just audible over the rain and wind.

Oh, God. Was I about to be murdered? Was it Neuberger and Wales come to arrest me for tampering with a crime scene, breaking and entering, or whatever else I'd probably done?

I stood at the foot of the stairs, rocking back and forward, wondering what was coming. Maybe it was just a lost nocturnal traveller who was using my drive to do a three-point turn?

I heard footsteps up the path, and then banging on the door.

I hesitated for a second before I made my way over. I was wearing nothing but a pair of boxers, so whomever it was, I hoped they would be okay with the sight of rather a lot of my exposed flesh.

I opened the door a crack. Tarquin's face stared back at me. He was drenched from the rain, but his eyes were on fire.

I pulled the door fully open, and he came in, his clothes leaving a puddle on my floor. "Tar—" I started.

“Shut up. Just shut up, okay? We don’t need to get married, and we don’t need to just have a shag. You don’t need to make any commitments to me or vice versa. I’m attracted to you, and I know you feel the same. There’s nothing we need to decide on now, but if we don’t do this, we’ll be idiots.”

How many times in life have you felt an instant attraction to someone?

Tarquin breathed heavily and looked me in the eye. “I want you. And I know you want me too.

Chapter 34

Reader, he looked even better out of his clothes. I kissed him on the doorstep, his soaking wet clothes chilling me, and before I knew it, our tender kisses had turned into panting, furious ones. I led him upstairs, where he threw me on the bed and then stripped off.

His body was muscular and wiry. Ollie had a body that was more like blocks of muscle; his chest carved and his stomach flat and taut. Simon had been a burly man of bulk; his chest and arms were large, and his stomach was never going to be completely flat. But Tarquin was different to both; he was triangular, with a narrow waist and broad shoulders, ripped abs covered in dark hair. As he stripped off in the light flooding through my windows, I had to stop myself from gasping at his frame.

He undressed down to his underwear and then climbed onto the bed.

"You are so beautiful," I moaned as he kissed my neck.

"I want to make love to you so badly, you have no idea," he whispered as he moved down my body.

The old bed creaked as we rearranged ourselves and cavorted. We could've made all the noise in the world; nothing would've distracted me.

When his underwear came off, I was pleasantly surprised. Not ginormous, but big enough to do the job. He was tender, kissed my neck, and pulled my hair, whispered things to me as he went harder. It seemed to last forever, and the moment it ended, he seemed to be hard again and wanted another round.

Panting, sweaty, and buzzing, we eventually finished and wrapped each other in our arms. He lay in the crook of my elbow with his head on my chest. "Arden," he whispered to me, as the rain pelted the window and we both listened to our heartbeats.

"I am so glad you came back."

"I'm so glad I snuck out of Guy's house," he said, laughing.

We slept fitfully, and then I woke at daybreak, to see, to my shock, Tarquin getting into his jeans.

"I will come back. I just have to do the rigmarole of leaving Guy's. It's easy, you can slip in and out of that place without anyone noticing you. But I have to pretend I spent the night there before heading off, otherwise I'll have to tell him everything."

Tell him everything – was I a secret? Or would it just be sensible not to say anything? No, it wasn't my business what Tarquin chose to tell his friends. It was common courtesy for him to be at breakfast.

"I'll be back in a couple of hours. Sleep," he commanded, and leant over and kissed me.

I heard his car leave, the rain had finally stopped, and I got up to get myself a glass of water. I inspected myself in the mirror. Tarquin was a vampire judging by the love bites on my neck. I had a quick shower to wash the sweat off my body from the unplanned night of exercise. When I got back to my bedroom, I saw the state of my sheets and wondered if it was worth changing them. They'd definitely need to be cleaned, but I might wait until after we'd completely finished.

I looked at the time; it was just before seven on Sunday morning. Was I to wake up every Sunday with a man spending the night?

I must've drifted for an hour or two, because I heard my phone buzzing and jerked up. I saw Tarquin's name on the screen. "Oi, let me in, I've been knocking on the door for ten minutes. Unless you've changed your mind?"

"Sorry, I fell asleep." I raced downstairs, to where Tarquin was standing with food for breakfast in one hand and trying to put his phone back into his jeans pocket with the other. I put the breakfast foods in the living room and then pounced on him.

"Again?"

"I had a power nap," I said, ripping off his shirt and licking his chest.

"The kittens are looking."

"Is that gonna stop you from getting hard?"

He grinned, and then groaned as my hands made their way into his jeans. "Wild horses wouldn't stop that right now." He squirmed as my hands explored more, before letting out a long moan of pleasure.

Afterwards, after I'd eaten my cold bacon roll and attended to the traumatised kittens, I went upstairs to get dressed. Tarquin shut himself in the bathroom for a shower.

I was coming back downstairs again when there was a knock on the door. Fuck. I could hear Tarquin fiddling with the shower pressure upstairs and occasionally swearing as he searched for the hot and cold balance (it didn't exist on that shower). I hoped it wouldn't be anyone who could make things awkward.

I peered at the window before opening. Nigella was standing in her furs and waved a gloved hand at me.

"Nigella, what a lovely surprise," I said as I opened the door. "Come in."

"Sorry to call so early." It was gone ten, but I suppose on a Sunday everyone has a different scale. "I'm just coming back from Birmingham where I dropped Matteo off at the airport. Annoyingly, the only flight which goes today to Milan leaves at stupid o'clock, and there aren't even any weekend flights there from Bristol. Usually he goes in the evening, or the first flight on a Monday but he has a packed schedule to make up for coming home a week early."

It was a lot of info on a Sunday morning. "Oh," was my response. I looked behind her. Inside the car parked at the side of the road, Archie and Luca were in the back seat, too tired to even misbehave.

"And with the boys too – such fun!" I gushed.

She rolled her eyes. "Never have children. I don't know why I was so desperate to. Anyway," she clapped her hands together, "I'm glad I caught you. I have an invite for you." She pulled a card from her coat pocket.

"For me?"

"For you. We're having a dinner party next Saturday. We have all been so horrible to you, making you come to memorials and funerals, and oh, that day at my house when we found out. Too, too horrid, all of it. This is the 'leave the past in the past' party. Honestly, this is what it's normally like here, not all murder and police."

"That sounds nice. I'd love to come. Who else are you inviting?"

She grinned. "The usual: there'll be you, me and Matteo, obviously, the Douglases, the Parkinsons if I can drag them away, Jedrev, Roz… oh, and Guy too, of course. And probably Tarquin as well, depending on if he's down—"

At that moment, the bathroom door swung open. "Arden, there's a problem with this shower. Apparently you have to work at fucking NASA to understand it."

I turned around, and Nigella's eyes also went upwards, to where Tarquin was standing on the landing with nothing but a small hand towel covering his privates, his gleaming wet body on display.

"Morning, Tarquin. Just inviting Arden to that dinner party – I texted Guy about it yesterday. I presume he told you?"

Tarquin was a man without repose, and didn't appear at all fazed by the situation, whereas I wanted to die from embarrassment. He didn't even bother to grab a bigger towel to cover any more of himself, but just continued to stand there for all to see, the towel doing nothing except drawing your eye to the dark wet hair on his inner thighs. "Yes, I'll definitely be there. Especially if Matteo is cooking."

"He will be," Nigella said, with a glint in her eye. "I should be off. The boys' school uniforms won't wash themselves. See you on Saturday."

She gave me the most lascivious wink I had ever seen, turned on her heel, and left. "Ta-ra," she shouted over her shoulder as she made her way back to her car. I waved as she sped off, then slammed the door and raced upstairs.

Tarquin was still fiddling with the shower. He'd dropped the hand towel and was starkers, his dick bobbing up and down as he strained with movement to get the shower working to his satisfaction. His face screwed up in what was probably incandescent rage at its refusal to cooperate.

"There is definitely a problem with the shower," he said before I got a chance to start my freak-out about Nigella seeing us.

"Oh?" I said – my voice an octave higher than usual.

"Yeah," he answered. "Problem is, I'm ready and all soaped up, and, well, you're not in there with me."

We used up all the hot water that morning.

Chapter 35

Tarquin left late that Sunday, just in time for me to go to Compney and stock up on proper food for once. I ate a healthy meal that night and sat in with the kittens in a much better mood than the previous night.

The week started off as I presumed it would: Simon and his crew arrived at sparrow fart on Monday morning and waylaid into the house with their usual subtlety. The milder weather was beginning, so Simon, naturally, turned up in a T-shirt. We managed to be civil with each other, but I knew I'd have to find someone else to do the work on the bathroom.

We spent the morning discussing colours, finishings, and other assorted decisions that hadn't been made the week before. After several hours, I had made all the decisions I could, and Simon seemed happy with what I'd set out. The plumbing and wiring would be done this week, and he'd have to hire other contractors for it. I sighed and let him make the arrangements, horrified at the costs.

After that, my week took on a pattern: I divested the house as soon as they arrived in the morning to go to work in a coffee shop in Sittingston every day. Being the most awful plonker in a café this side of Dalston, writing copious pages of the novel and keeping abreast of the deluge of information Verity was sending me. TV rights sniffing around had sent her into overdrive. I had several calls betwixt her and the publishing company where we hashed out more details, and then, as soon as that was done, Verity would email me with a list of details of literary festivals and comic cons she wanted me to appear at.

"There's a sci-fi convention in Dublin, a book tour in Germany in October. There's a podcast with two million listeners that wants to interview you."

I could never complain. I never thought I'd be lucky enough to do this for a living, let alone be making a better than average income from it.

I heard from Tarquin daily, just the odd text. A couple of pictures… of an adult nature. He seemed interested when I told him of my work, and occasionally dropped a detail of his own, which didn't appear to be going all that well, but he seemed to be keeping positive.

I got to Friday before I even realised that we'd passed the halfway point of the week. I arrived home earlier than planned to discover Simon still at my house, but Levi and Leon gone.

"I let them off early to enjoy their Friday night."

The cabinets were mostly installed. The floors were done; it was just the wiring and plumbing to be done next week, and then the paint job and new appliances to be installed. As of now, though, I had a kitchen again. I stood in wonder at the door. "Looks great."

Simon grunted, his head in a cupboard, his T-shirt riding up again to show that pale, muscular flesh. "Will I see you at Nigella's tomorrow?" I asked.

He grunted again. I gave up on conversation and instead gave myself a tour of my new kitchen, withholding squeals of glee at everything.

I stood in the middle and surveyed. I couldn't help but give a contented sigh. Simon eventually came out of the cupboard and looked at me. "Happy with it?"

"I love it."

He cracked a smile – I didn't know he was physically capable of them. "Good, I'm pleased. It should all be done by next Friday."

"Great. I appreciate all your hard work."

He shrugged. "You're paying me." He sounded surly but grinned at me after he said it.

I snorted at him. "Thanks anyway." He put his tools away and made tracks to leave.

"See you tomorrow night," he said cheerfully.

"See you then!" I heard the door swing but not close.

"Oh, Arden?" he called.

I was opening and shutting a drawer repeatedly, marvelling at it. "Hmm?"

A pause. "N-nothing. Never mind, see you tomorrow."

The door slammed. I put my shopping away for the dinner I'd concoct from a microwave and looked around again at my kitchen. It was lovely. A pleasant, sunnyish day too, with spring on the way. Tarquin had already called. He would be here in a few hours. I hadn't thought of Arabella all week.

He got in about 8pm and about an hour later we got dressed again and he marvelled at the kitchen too. "It looks lovely. Who knew that angry Scotsman actually had some skills?"

I managed to not ruin the evening by saying he had a lot of skills, actually, in the bedroom.

We cooked, chatted, and drank the wine he'd brought. It was nice to share an evening with someone again. Tarquin told me about his frenetic week in London and how several meetings had gone awry.

"Is everything okay?" I asked as he paused through another story about a business setback.

"It's just teething problems. When I have to sell my house, car, stock options, and go live in a bedsit under the Westway, then there'll be a problem."

I smiled. "As long as you're sure."

"You know what I'm sure of? That this was a great idea. How about I take you out to lunch somewhere on Sunday? Or maybe down to the coast for a bracing walk and then a pub lunch? I need to prove I'm not hiding you away."

"Don't worry, I'm okay with us keeping it private."

"Are you?" he said, slinking an arm around me. "I feel like it's not your favourite…"

"I don't want everyone up in our business. I'm happy to toddle along like this for a while, see where it goes."

"Good. And you don't mind me going off tomorrow?"

"Of course not. Where is it you and Guy are going again?"

"Well, I'll pretend that I've turned up from London about eleven, and then we're going to watch Bath get pummelled in the rugby."

"Sounds hetero."

"Oh, it will be. It matches up all but one of my favourite things: rugby, getting drunk in the day, and burly men in mud hitting each other."

"What's the other favourite thing?"

"Rampant sodomy. But that's why I've got you."

I was just about to ask for a demonstration when the microwave dinged. "Ah, good. The haute cuisine is ready."

Later, in the middle of the night, wrapped in each other's arms, I couldn't sleep. All week I'd pushed it to one side, but now I couldn't any longer.

"Tarquin," I whispered. From somewhere to the back of me (he was big spoon) there was a grunt. "Are you awake?"

"No."

"Do you still think about Arabella?"

His hand, which had been gently rubbing my arm, stopped. "Why do you ask?"

"I just… I can't stop thinking about her. About finding her."

"That's normal. You found a dead person. That's some heavy shit."

He went back to rubbing my arm.

"So, do you think about her?"

"I try and remember her as she was, and not how she died."

"Do you think Pawel did it?"

"The police arrested him, that's all that matters."

I turned to face him, fighting with the wound-up sheet to do so. "Is that what you really think?"

His eyes were open in the dark and shining brightly; it took me by surprise. His grip on my arm hardened.

"There's a lot we don't know about people's lives. Sometimes it's for the best."

"I can't help but think the killer is still out there."

He wrapped his arm around me. "Go back to sleep, there's nothing we can do now. But you're safe. No one's going to hurt you when I'm around."

The next morning, Tarquin left bright and early to pretend he'd just driven down from London to go with Guy to the rugby game, while I took advantage of a day at home and did some cleaning and washing, played with the kittens, and then wrote for a while.

I got a text mid-afternoon from Tarquin: he and Guy in the stands, scarves on, Barbour jackets buttoned up, pints in hands, big grins. It's bloody freezing! was Tarquin's message.

I don't know where Tarquin and I were going, or if this would last, but it felt good, and I quite liked the idea of letting Guy know. He had such a good friendship with

Tarquin that the three of us were going to be bound up with each other for as long as Tarquin and I were dating or seeing one another or whatever we called it… well, screwing.

I tried not to think about it as I got ready for the dinner party. I'd bought a new shirt in the week. A red-and-black check number, which I was wearing with black skinny jeans. It was slim fit, and I actually didn't feel self-conscious about my stomach in it for once, so clearly Ollie had been right about my heartbreak diet. Ollie. His face flashed in my head. I should message him. Maybe I could build a bridge to try to fix the damage done the other night.

Or maybe he could run after me some more. If he wanted me in his life, he'd have to settle for friends, and in that case, I'd leave the ball in his court.

Nigella had said it began at eight, so I set off at five minutes to, hoping I would be a little late and therefore not the first to arrive. I didn't consider country punctuality, so when I arrived at ten past, I was the last to arrive. But luckily it was just drinks for a while yet.

"*Mwah, mwah.*" Nigella greeted me as Matteo took my coat. Archie and Luca were atop the stairs in their PJs, giggling and waving. "Hi boys," I said and waved back. They giggled more.

I was ushered into the living room, where I was festooned with a glass of wine the size of my head.

"Arden!" Odette cooed, and made a beeline for me, but was beaten to the quick by Guy, who clasped my shoulder.

"How are you?" he asked, clinking my glass. I looked around; Odette looked most miffed at not getting my attention, while Tommy spoke to Simon and – my loins quivered – Tarquin gave me a sly glance as he spoke with Nigella and Matteo, who were diving in and out of the kitchen to check on the food.

"Glad I caught you, listen—"

"Arden" – Simon was at my side – "how are you?"

"I'm well, thanks."

"I was just about to get some fresh air; you lads care to join me?"

Guy looked pained but came with us. We stood outside in the air and chatted amiably for a few minutes.

Simon was staring between Guy and me with a look on his face that would chill anyone.

"Where are Jedrev and Roz?" I asked Guy, noticing our numbers were down.

"Roz had a family emergency, nothing terrible, just an aunt who'd had a fall, and Jed had to cry off with a dodgy tummy. The Parkinsons have gone up to Reading last minute to see Daniel. Apparently, there are wedding dramas they need to sort out. They sent their apologies."

Nigella popped her head in. "Um, Guy, I need your expertise in the kitchen," she said hesitantly.

Guy gave me a look and then seemed like he was about to refuse before his manners caught up and he smiled. "Of course. 'Scuse me, chaps."

Simon and I both drained our glasses in sync after being left with each other.

"So—"

"Listen, I don't care," he said. "But be subtle about it, don't just go around getting into mischief for the sake of it," Simon said.

"What?" I was confused.

"Don't play dumb. I saw what was in your bin."

I was even more confused by that, but before I could say so, Simon stormed off back into the house as Guy was coming back out. He blushed as Simon stopped for a second and gave me an open look of disgust.

"Wow, what's crawled up his arse?" Guy asked.

"No idea."

"Listen," Guy said, producing a bottle of red and topping up our glasses. "Um, oh God, this is a bit awkward. I'm rubbish at this. So… you're a lovely guy, and, oh, um, Jesus, I hope I'm not making a fool of myself, but I was wondering if maybe next week you would like to go for a drink?"

I choked on my wine and started coughing and spluttering. Guy Frobisher just asked me out.

"I'm sorry?"

"Yeah…" He was beet red. "I feel like a teenager. But if you're free, maybe one night next week, or during the weekend, we could go into Sittingston for a drink at that wine bar… you know, the one at the end of the high street; it's nice in there."

I was making fish faces, my mouth opening and shutting; no air was coming in. I was so surprised. Inwardly, my bowels were cringing.

"Guy, that is such a nice offer. Such a nice offer." His handsome face was already falling.

"You don't have to spare my feelings. It's fine if you're not interested."

"It's not that. I didn't even know you were gay for a start, but no, it's, um… I'm seeing someone at the moment."

"Oh."

"It's very recent, but it's going well."

"Oh."

"I'm really sorry. Honestly, if it wasn't the case, I'd have loved to go for—"

"Please, please, don't say what you're about to say," Guy interrupted me. He gave a wan smile. "I'm going to go inside." He pointed in the direction he was going with an awkward hand. "Um, sorry about this."

"No, Guy, it's not a problem. I'm flattered, honestly…" But he was already off inside.

Shit.

Odette's head peered around the corner. "Dinner is served," she said in a faux-Victorian butler voice.

Fuck off, Odette.

"Great, be right in."

Inside the Pettonis' lovely dining room the table was set for eight, with Nigella at the far end and Matteo at the garden end with his back to the French windows that looked out on the patio where I'd just been ambushed.

Along the far wall sat Odette, then Tommy, then Simon. Simon was glaring at me, while Tommy was sharing a hilarious joke with Matteo.

On our side, I was somehow in the middle between Guy and Tarquin. Guy wouldn't look at me at all and Tarquin wouldn't meet my eye.

Nigella and Matteo had laid out a fabulous feast for us, of an Italo-Sino fusion mix that all seemed to revolve around duck.

"Is everything on this table duck?" I asked.

"Everything," Odette said with a maniacal glint in her eye, eating a duck pancake in one bite.

"How… lovely," I answered.

"Tuck in!" Matteo ordered, passing me plates and setting off a chain reaction of endless dishes being passed around the table.

Eventually, after seventy-six rounds of pass-the-duck-parcel, I managed to get a plate full of dead *canard* in a variety of sauces and styles.

"So, Arden, how's the renovation work going?" Odette asked after stuffing her gullet in a most unladylike way, which I didn't expect from her.

"Mostly fine, I think we're nearly there."

"And Simon has behaved himself?" Tommy asked, with a tone I couldn't quite place.

"He's been great." Well, the work he'd done had been.

"And how are you settling into Lilbury?" Matteo asked, which I just caught as I'd been looking in Nigella's direction, who shot her husband a look of death.

I started to answer, but Nigella spoke over me. "Tarquin, how's your work going?"

Tarquin shrugged, and then started to answer, but soon narrowed his eyes at the group.

"It's fine," he said, after a pause. "Ups and downs, but we're getting there."

Nigella was frantically smiling at everyone, while Matteo was mouthing something at her.

"What's going on?" I whispered to Tarquin.

"So, Arden, seeing anyone?" asked Tommy as he chewed on a massive piece of duck, with the fat around his mouth.

I took a large gulp of wine that Matteo had just poured in my glass to a most generous level. I laughed, hoping I could ignore the question and that someone else would say something to interrupt. Unfortunately, after a few seconds, I realised that the entire table (even Tarquin) were staring at me.

"Not really."

"But I thought you just said—" Odette started to say to Guy.

"Can we talk about something else?" Nigella asked.

"But I thought that was the whole point of tonight?" Tommy responded.

"Wait, what?" Tarquin and I said in unison.

"Is that true?" Tarquin asked Nigella, with a snap in his voice.

"What's going on?" I asked after Nigella didn't answer.

Simon sighed, took a long sip of his wine, and stared at me. "Guy fancies you. Nigella thought she'd help. She didn't know you were seeing someone else until after she'd organised it, because unlike me, she hasn't been to your house. Hence tonight."

"Well, who is he seeing?" Tommy asked.

"It doesn't matter—" a clearly embarrassed Guy said firmly.

Tarquin gave me a look, sighed, and then threw his serviette onto the table, cutting off Guy. "It's me! Okay, he's seeing me. We are seeing one another."

There was a long moment of silence. Tarquin turned to Guy. "I'm sorry, mate. I didn't know you… I had no idea any of this was happening. If I had, I wouldn't have made a move."

Guy at least tried to look at peace with this, but his smile was more of a grimace. "It's okay."

"Shall we move on to dessert?" Nigella said airily.

"So, you two are at it?" Tommy asked. God, he was obnoxious.

Tarquin gave him a look that could break glass. "Yes, Tommy. We're sleeping together. Any other questions? No? Okay, great. Can we move on then, please?"

"Couldn't agree more," Matteo said, getting up and grabbing dishes. "Let's clear up, shall we?"

"I'll help," Guy said, jumping up to grab more plates and dishes.

Odette was staring at Tarquin and me with a befuddled look on her face.

"Living room, everyone! Simon, put on some music. Oh, I know, shall we play a game? Let's have a proper party." Nigella was in hostess overdrive mode but wouldn't meet my eye.

Tarquin went past me. "I suppose there's no point in hiding it now, is there?" he said, and brushed his hand up the back of my shirt. "Let's be subtle, shall we, though? Good." He had the conversation completely one-sidedly and went back into the kitchen where I could see him and Guy standing beside each other sorting food out. Tarquin made several comments, all of which were met with stony silence from Guy.

Feeling just about as awkward as I'd ever been, I made my way into the living room, where Simon had put on some music. Nigella had found a bottle of tequila. Beats

International's "Dub Be Good to Me" was playing on the Pettonis' hi-tech sound system. Nigella was controlling it.

"Alexa's racist," Simon said. "She refuses to understand Scottish accents. Alexa, play soft jazz."

Alexa's electronic voice came back: "Sofas are a form of seat that are usually large enough to sit two or more people."

"Alexa, play 'Ace of Bass'," Nigella called out in a plummy voice.

The song started. Simon marched over and grabbed the bottle of tequila.

Matteo appeared at the door with a solemn Guy and Tarquin. He was carrying a tray of cocktails. "Drink's up." He saw the bottle of tequila Nigella and Simon were knocking back. "Really, guys? Are we at university?"

"I've had a hard day," Nigella responded.

Tarquin took two glasses, then came over and passed one to me. "Stay calm, and don't act like anything is weird," he said.

"How exactly I am supposed to do that?" I hissed, a little too harshly.

"Shall we play a game?" said Odette, who could read a room.

There was a general murmur of agreement, and we all took our places. "Shall we play Charades? Teams of two: Tommy and me, Nigella and Matteo, Guy and…" She looked awkwardly around.

"Tarquin," Simon said. "Arden and I will be a team too."

Yay. I gave Tarquin a look and made my way over to Simon, where he sat on the edge of the sofa.

"Really?" I mouthed at him as I took my place beside him. He shrugged, tight-lipped.

Tarquin and Guy were avoiding eye contact as they sat on the edge of the sofa opposite us.

“We’ll go first,” Odette said, jumping up and beginning to act out.

“A film,” Tommy said, as his wife did the symbol for cinema. “Six words,” he continued.

Odette began, and as anyone would imagine, Tommy was a mix of terrible at the game and fiercely competitive, and it wasn’t long before he was frustrated with his wife and her abilities while the rest of us tried to act chipper in the face of social doom.

“*One Flew Over the Cuckoo’s Nest*,” Simon whispered to me as Odette reached the second word after Tommy eventually realised the first word.

“Odie, I don’t understand!” Tommy yelled as Odette careened around the room with her arms out.

“Dance? Are you dancing? *Dances with Wolves!* Um, um, ballroom dancing? *Moulin Rouge?* Are you a plane? *The Aviator! Snakes on a Plane!*”

Matteo shook his head. “None of those are even six words or start with ‘one’. And English isn’t even my first language,” he muttered.

Odette burst into tears. “Stop yelling at me! You’re always yelling at me,” she screamed at her husband, and then fled from the room.

“What the—” Tommy spun around the room in a bewildered state, looking at us all for an explanation.

“Oh, for God’s sake,” snapped Nigella, who got up and followed Odette from the room. “I’ll go sort her out.”

“What did I do? What was that about?” Tommy asked in a peevish voice.

“Well, she’s sensitive,” Tarquin said, knocking back his drink.

“I know that,” he snapped, turning to look at him. “We shouldn’t have come tonight. Last thing I needed is a bunch of gay guys having a drama to tell me how my wife is.” Tommy gave Tarquin a filthy look. He had got up off the sofa and was glaring at him.

There was a silence. Both Tarquin and Simon perked up giving Tommy a look of pure violence.

"Oi, none of that," Matteo said, gripping Tommy by the shoulder and easing him back onto the sofa.

I could feel Simon tensed next to me. "Why don't we go and get the women?" Matteo added, noticing the room. He led Tommy from the lounge.

The silence between the four of us left in the living room was lingering. I was alone in a space with two men I'd slept with and a third who'd asked me out. Not at all awkward.

What if Simon decided to tell Tarquin about us? God, my penis was really getting me into a lot of problems recently.

The minutes dragged on with the four of us sitting in silence. "Who won the rugby?" I asked after what felt like an hour.

"Bath got trashed," Tarquin said after sharing a look with Guy, who had been unaware that I'd known where they were going. Guy downed his drink and shook his head. "I need a piss," he said and left the room.

Simon whistled. "Well done, you two."

"How were we supposed to know?" Tarquin hissed back at him.

Simon had finished stirring, lifted his hands in surrender, and left the room too.

"Maybe we should go?" I mouthed at Tarquin. He shrugged.

From the kitchen, there was laughter. I got up and walked out into the hallway to see what was happening. In the kitchen, Guy and Simon were having a laugh. I thought they didn't like each other.

"Tommy!" I heard a voice call, and then a sound of thunder on the stairs. Tommy came down at pace, nearly bowling into me. "I have had e-fucking-nough of being blamed!" He grabbed his coat and stormed out the door.

Odette followed him down, and then a bewildered-looking Nigella. The front door was wide open, and Odette followed him out. At the end of the path they were screaming at each other. "Tommy please!" Odette yelled, crying.

"The last thing I need right now is to get involved with that lot about who is bumming who!"

Nigella pulled the door to the side so we couldn't see.

"I'm so sorry. Guy came up to me on Saturday and mentioned how much he liked you," she whispered in a hurried voice. "I thought I'd be helping. When I saw you and Tarquin, I knew I'd made a mistake, but I had no idea how to stop it. It was so stupid. I'm sorry."

"It's no problem," I said, and put my hand on her arm to try to comfort her. "No harm done – from me, at least."

Tarquin emerged from the lounge at the same time Odette came back inside, crying and shaking.

"Odette, oh, come here." Nigella escorted her into the living room and shut the door.

Matteo came back in and gave a long exhale. "Well, this went badly. As I said it would," he said and finished his glass.

Guy came out and collected his coat. "I'm going to call it a night. I'll just say goodbye to Nigella." He knocked lightly, put his head round and had a brief chat.

"I think I should go with Guy," Tarquin whispered to me. "I'll come over tomorrow and see you, but I think I need to go and try to patch this up."

I smiled at him; glad he wanted to right things with his friend. "Okay."

Guy put his hand out to me, and we shook, but he wouldn't meet my eyes properly.

"Well, at least we can all agree that Tommy's a tosser," Tarquin said as he and Guy left. Tarquin slapped his old friend on the back as they made their way up the path. "C'mon, mate, let's have a beer and you can yell at me."

I said my goodbyes to Matteo, and he was positively relieved to usher Simon and me out before he had to go and face his living room full of weeping Odette.

We made our way to the top of the path and walked across the road together.

"Thanks for not saying anything," I said.

"About Guy?" he asked, looking confused.

"No, about us."

He rolled his eyes. "My private life is private."

"Well, I appreciate it."

"Yeah, well, what you do is your business. Just be subtle about it, please." His voice had darkened, and I could feel yet more of his attitude seeping out. "I'm not an idiot. I rocked up on Monday morning, went upstairs to take a leak, and there were condom wrappers in the bin."

I blushed. "I'm sorry, I didn't think… but it's none of your business who I'm sleeping with. You've made it perfectly clear you're not interested in anything to do with me."

"Just as well, as it doesn't seem like you can keep it in your pants."

"Fuck you!" I yelled, losing my temper. "I don't know what I did to make you go from sleeping with me to thinking that I'm something on your shoe, but enough is enough. We don't have to like each other, and we don't have to have anything to do with each other."

"Sounds good to me."

"Fine. Then you're fired. I'll find someone else to do the rest of the work on the kitchen. You can come and collect your things and do whatever you have to do, but after that, I'd rather have nothing to do with you."

Simon was silent for a second, and then cracked his neck, angrily, his face contorted in rage. "Fine," he answered. "Whatever sire wants. I'd say it was a pleasure, but it wasn't. If you could remind Tarquin to put some clothes on when I come over."

“Grow up,” I snapped, and stormed off into the dark, taking the lane back by the pub and up through the field to my house. I replayed the conversation over in my head the entire way and called Simon Anson every insult I knew.

Chapter 36

"We talked for all of five minutes and then he went up to bed. I knocked on his bedroom door this morning, but he didn't answer. Eventually, he came down though, and we had a brief chat. He said everything's fine, and he'll text me in a day or two."

It was lunchtime the next day. I was lying on my front in bed, while Tarquin was on his back, his hands clasped behind his head. He was staring at the ceiling, recounting his night.

"Sorry we won't get to do our pub lunch today, but it doesn't feel like a good time," he added.

"No, it's fine. I'm not in the mood either."

"I think maybe I should cool it with my trips to Lilbury. I've been hitting it pretty hard lately; maybe I should give Guy some space."

I must've looked aghast because Tarquin chuckled and patted me on the bum through the sheet. "Don't worry, I'm not ditching you. I mean that maybe we should start getting out of here. What about spending a few weekends in London, or we could go somewhere. Maybe Oxford, or Brighton, stay in a nice hotel?"

I relaxed. "Lovely."

"Guy mentioned yesterday at the rugby that he's considering getting out for a while too, anyway. He has his grandma still alive and a million cousins in Sydney, not to mention a bunch of uncles and aunts he's barely seen in ten years. His grandma hasn't got much time left, so he wants to go see her, get out of the UK."

"That sounds like a good plan. It'll be weird for him not to be here, though. What about Lady F?"

"She's got other relatives who'd jump at the chance to come stay at Honningtons to keep her company." He nodded at my room. "We can come back here when you've got a working kitchen and a bathroom that's post the industrial revolution."

I put my head in the pillow at that. "That'll be a while. I may have fired Simon last night."

Tarquin cocked an eyebrow. "Why?"

I shrugged. "He's an arrogant arse who's super rude all the time."

"Uh-huh. And now you're builder-less?"

"There's not *that* much to do," I countered.

"There's a fair amount to do."

"I feel better for doing it." I was resolute in my opinion.

"You'll get a reputation," he teased. "Bringing all those builders around and then chucking them out the next morning, like some sort of renovation floozy."

He was closer to the truth than he thought, and I buried my head farther into the pillow. "Change of topic, please."

"Okay, how about I book us a hotel and we meet there on Friday night and have a nice weekend with no complications?"

"Sounds divine."

The week started off just like the previous one had. I busied myself with writing and a constant stream of correspondence with Verity, but unlike last week, I was doing it in my own home. Sitting in my new, half-finished kitchen, twiddling my thumbs over the gaps where the appliances were. Every so often, I came across a new builder online in the local area and made a call to see if they could finish the work.

There was a general consensus of "several weeks" before any of them were free. My half-bottle of wine and a cocktail or two-induced firing of Simon seemed rather stupid now.

Luckily, he wasn't as bad as I thought, because on Tuesday the plumber turned up and started the work. When Simon turned up to collect his tools, our conversation consisted of about ten words, even when I tried to thank him for not cancelling the tradesmen. "The electrician's coming next week," was his simple answer before leaving.

On the Wednesday, I took matters into my own hands, collecting paint, and supplies from the DIY shop in Sittingston to make a start at it myself. On Thursday, I went to the local shop to stock up on supplies. I only went in because I saw Tommy going into the Co-op with a tantrum-throwing Tatiana.

"Hello, love!" said Roz the moment I arrived. She was behind the counter, speaking to her son – the one with the man bun, whichever one that was. She was talking through a mouthful of the banana she was eating.

I picked up some drinks and microwaveable foods.

"How are you?" she said, coming towards me, her son banished to the back. She leaned forward in a conspiratorial manner. "I heard about what happened at the weekend."

My blood ran cold.

"It's so sad Odette and Tommy are having problems."

Oh, that.

"Yes, I must admit it was quite horrible to watch. I felt sorry for Odette," I added. Roz had the look in her eye of a keen gossiper; the banana was held up to my face as a reference point.

She checked over her shoulder to make sure her son was busy in the back. "You know, they've been having issues for a while. And I'm not surprised Tommy stormed out, he's always had a bit of a temper."

"A temper? What do you mean?"

"He and his father used to have rows that could shake the foundations of the house. Tommy would eff and blind and it would break his dad's heart. The two of them never saw eye to eye, even when his mum died, and he went off to university in Southampton. He never came back to visit. When he moved back after he graduated, everyone was so worried he was still… well, the brat he used to be."

This was a new side to Tommy I hadn't expected. "Hello, love," Roz interrupted herself, waving the banana, as one of Lilbury's older dears came in the shop. "Doris, this is Arden who's moved into Old Mr Jeffries house up on the hill."

"He looks foreign," Doris said of me before walking off to go get some milk.

"So, Tommy and Odette often have problems?" I asked, somewhat nonchalantly.

Roz was in her element. "All the time. If they aren't arguing about money, it's about Tatiana, or about his wandering eye."

I cocked my head. "No one in the village likes to talk about it – out of respect for Odette. Everyone here's known her all her life – but we all know what he's like. Honestly, it's so disrespectful. Men!" she finished, with a shake of the head. "This is why I've been married so many times. Every time you think you've found a good one…" She absent-mindedly squashed the banana in her hand. "Oh, bugger."

As I turned to leave, a familiar flash of red jogged past outside. Roz waved as Simon went by.

"Such a lovely man, that Simon. You know he lives next door to Doris, nothing he won't do for her. Mows her lawn, cleans her gutters. Honestly, couldn't ask for a nicer young man."

I kept my disagreement to myself and instead bought my food with a smile plastered over my face.

On Friday afternoon, I eventually pulled off the M3 just after Basingstoke and drove to the station in the village of Hook. The train was just in the distance. To my amazement, I had timed it perfectly. A few minutes later, my gorgeous man emerged from the Great Western train and sauntered out of the station with sunglasses on and a bag thrown over his shoulder. God, he was beautiful. He saw my little green car and made his way over.

"You actually drive this?" he said after he kissed me hello and got in on the passenger side.

"It's not that bad."

"It hardly goes."

"Rude."

He gave a deep laugh and ruffled my hair. "Thanks for picking me up."

I'd driven up to meet him, as it made more sense for only one car, and it was much easier for him to get from London to here than it was for me to brave provincial train connections. However, this meant that the Porsche was back in London and Tarquin was slumming it in my car.

We made our way through the village and were soon winding down the garden road towards the hotel, its gorgeous grounds making the sweet springtime sunshine seem even better.

Beside me, Tarquin sat in the passenger seat and chattered away, filling me in on his week, and asking after mine. I couldn't have been happier if I'd just been told I'd won the lottery and found a key to everlasting life.

We pulled up in front of the country manor hotel and got out. Tarquin took my arm as we walked in and smiled politely at the elderly couple who were going out. Ever the gent, he held the door open for them and smiled at their unease at our physical closeness. He grinned widely, causing his sunglasses to fall back from on top of his head and over his eyes.

"Cheesy," I said as I walked past him to the reception desk. "You are the definition of cheesy."

The girl at the reception desk was painfully polite, and a lot more efficient than the staff at the hotels I was usually booked in for my book tours. The lodges and travel inns, where a room with a window is £46 extra per night and running water is on request.

A charming young Portuguese man took our bags up to the main part of the manor, along the sprawling wooden staircase, and past suits of armour and tapestries to our room. The door opened to a huge space with a four-poster bed and a roaring fire.

"The last time I stayed here they put us in the extension with floral bedspreads and magnolia wallpaper," I said.

"When did you last stay here?" Tarquin asked as he gave the porter a £5 note from his wallet.

"Apparently, whenever it was, I didn't say the secret code word to get the good room," I said, purposely avoiding the tale of when I'd been here several years before…with Ollie.

"Come see this bathtub!" I yelled as I explored the bathroom, which was the size of the downstairs of my house.

"Can we have sex in it?" Tarquin asked, warming his hands by the fire.

"I think so!" I said, hopping into the whirlpool tub fully clothed. It was deep enough for my head to be almost under its rim when I slid all the way inside it.

"Cool," Tarquin said, arriving in the room and already stripping his clothes off.

That evening we dined in the restaurant in the hotel and later found ourselves walking through the grounds to work off some of the four-course meal we'd just consumed.

We stopped by the lake, enjoying the mild night. Tarquin stared out over the water, and I stared at him.

"Happy?" he said, noticing me, and turning to look at me.

"Very."

The next morning, of course, he ruined that when he announced that there was a running club for guests. "It's run by the hotel gym's head trainer, who organises a daily five-K jog for any guest who wants to join."

"I don't have any sportswear," I said from under the covers in the bed, hoping this would be enough.

"They can provide some, and I bought a spare pair of shorts and a T-shirt, just in case. So, you'll just need the trainers."

"Which, of course, they can provide."

"Exactly," he said, pulling back the duvet and dragging me up. "Come on, you'll feel great afterwards,"

I had never felt great after exercise in my life, ever. Not when Ollie used to make me do CrossFit. Not when my PE teacher used to make me play football in school. Not when my brother used to make me box with him in the back garden at the pub when we were boys. Not whenever I forced myself to sign up for a gym in order so that, one day, I'd have a body I was proud of.

To make matters worse, when we got downstairs the trainers that they provided turned out to have last been worn by a particularly BO-afflicted baboon who had used them to run through a slurry pond. They stank to high heaven. While Tarquin made charming small talk with the half a dozen or so other guests who'd decided to join for a run, I was joined by the coach.

The hotel gym's head coach was a Black American man called Caleb. He looked like he could be hit by a tank and not be fazed, let alone stopped. Caleb made a beeline for me as I attempted to stretch with some coordination. Luckily, the one talent I have in the gym is really, really good balance. I can stay on one foot, stretching my leg, for a long time. Admittedly this was never going to help in the main event when my chest was about to explode after running only a few hundred metres, but at least he thought me just about capable.

"Your boyfriend told me earlier when he came to sign you both up that you're not the most athletic person in the world?" Caleb said with what he thought might be a jovial tone.

"Boyfriend?"

Caleb looked stricken in that way liberal straight people do when they worry they've put their foot in it with queer sensibilities. "Tarquin, sorry, I just assumed – he isn't your boyfriend?"

I was taken aback. "Did he say he was?"

"Yeah. Is he not?"

I was stunned for a second but regained. "Yes, sorry, he is my boyfriend. Yes, he is." I cracked a grin. Caleb, wary of me already, moved on, so I was spared any more awkwardness when he tried to assuage my feelings of inadequacy while I struggled to maintain pace with everyone else.

Tarquin came over after Caleb had shot off. "Everything okay?"

"Yup, just getting my stretch on."

"Why did the trainer leave?"

"He was scared of my athletic prowess. H-hey, did you…" I stuttered. "Anything you want to tell me?" I asked, feeling awkward.

Tarquin looked confused and shook his head. "No. Why? Have I done something wrong?"

I shook my head too. “Nope, you’re perfect.”

My skills as a runner, however, were not. I came in dead last, miles behind everyone else. Even the fat lady beat me; it turned out she frequently did half marathons. As I sat at the end, my face bright red while the waiter from the restaurant bought everyone a protein smoothie, Tarquin came over from doing his stretches. I was pouring with sweat, and my chest was hurting.

“You know, I had terrible asthma as a child,” I just about managed to gasp out, desperately reaching for the smoothie and gulping it down, before actually tasting it and nearly throwing it back up again.

“I thought it might be something like that,” Tarquin said, laughing, and leant over and kissed the top of my sweaty head. “Luckily, my ego benefits from having an unfit boyfriend. It makes me look better.”

I glared at him. “I’m not unfit, I just hate running.”

He was grinning. “I’m only teasing.”

I shook off his hand, which was gently massaging my shoulders. “I like you calling me your boyfriend though.”

“I like calling you it,” he said, and leaned over to kiss me again. “I plan to keep doing it for a long time.”

Chapter 37

"Come to London next week, and then stay for a few days. I have a cocktail party my main investor is throwing, and I want you to come to that," Tarquin said, as he leant in my car window early on the Sunday afternoon.

After a wonderful night at a restaurant in the town, and another moonlit walk, we'd spent the morning swimming in the hotel pool. It was time to head home. I had a kitchen to finish, and Tarquin had work to do.

"Okay, I'll take the train." I grinned at him. It was an extremely mild day; the weather forecast said it might hit sixteen degrees that afternoon. Tarquin was wearing a denim shirt, unbuttoned low enough to get a glimpse of his delicious chest, his coat slung over his arm and his sunglasses back on his head. Lost in the mess of his glossy black hair.

"I already can't wait, boyfriend," he said, and kissed me goodbye. "Drive safe." He looked at the car. "Or not. Total this car and buy a new one. I'll nurse you back to health if you injure yourself in the process."

"Charming!" I yelled to his departing figure.

"Everyone says I am!" he called back, and blew me a kiss.

He'd told me not to wait for his train, so I sped off homeward, with the windows down and the radio blaring out the worst in top forty pop. Teenage love songs filled the car as I cat-shrieked in addition to the better voices the singers on the radio had.

I'd never been happier, and I refused to let anything dampen my spirit, even though the weather never got as warm as the forecast said, and by the time I pulled into my driveway it was spitting with a cold wind blowing from the north.

I had to have the laziest kittens that had ever lived. If their litter box didn't need emptying (I had meant to ask Simon to install a cat flap, but obviously that wouldn't happen now), I wouldn't have thought they'd even moved from their spot. Sonia had stayed again on Saturday night and had left me a note, saying thanks, and that her parents were still driving her mad.

When I checked my phone on my return home, I saw, aside from Tarquin telling me his train had got in on time and that he was now home in London – and in the pub with Freddie watching the rugby – I had a message from her too.

Can we meet for coffee this week? she asked.

I sent back a message confirming and told her to name a time and place.

Tomorrow lunchtime – 1pm, same place we met the last time? she replied, only moments after I clicked send on my own message.

I emptied a tin of cat food for the kittens and their mewing told me it was appreciated. I replied again to Sonia, saying yes, and wondered what she was clearly so desperate to talk to me about.

The next morning, I headed over to Compney Parva and picked up a few bits and pieces. The electrician had arrived early that morning and had set about doing work that I hoped wouldn't burn the place down before I returned. He was a gruff West Country type and seemed to only have three words in his vocabulary, none of which I understood. I was glad to leave.

When I made my way to the little café after doing my trips to the Compney shops, I was still early so I sat down for a coffee on my own and checked my emails. More drivel from Verity, and endless notes and requests for things I couldn't think about right now. I set my phone down and drank my mocha in silence until Sonia burst in about a quarter of an hour past our set meeting time.
"Sorry, sorry, I had a house viewing that overran. The buyer wanted to look in the loft and wouldn't leave until we'd called the seller back from work to help show where things were. I'd have said no but this guy's keen and he's the first person who's after the place and it's been on the market since November."

"No problem. What did you want to talk about?"

Sonia burst into tears.

Everyone in the café turned to stare at us; Sonia was not a subtle crier. After several minutes of gentle cajoling, I managed to get her to calm down and bought her a chocolate muffin to get her settled.

"I'm sorry… it's just – well, it's all a mess. The police came to visit me after Bella's house was broken into, not because they knew we'd—"

"Yayayaya!" I interrupted. She was speaking loudly, and we were in public.

"Right, yes, well, they came to ask us about who had keys and to check out a few things. It was Ade who came. And then, that night, I was having a drink to steady my nerves down at the Cock and Feather—"

"The what?"

"It's a pub in Sittingston. An old man pub, so I wouldn't know anyone there. I thought I'd be safe. Anyway, who walks in, but Ade!"

My blood was going colder with every word she said. "Really?"

"Yeah, turns out he loves a pint of real ale. So, I'd already had three glasses of wine, and then he sits me down and buys me another glass of wine."

"Because, of course, four glasses of Chardonnay on a weeknight is really steadying ya nerves," I commented.

"So, anyway," Sonia continued, ignoring me. "We sit, and he asks me all about the murder, and I start jabbering, and he asks about you. Apparently, the police are seriously suspicious of you."

"Me?"

"But I told him that's rubbish. Of course you weren't involved. How could you have been? Why would you? You'd never met her before, and I said 'why would he hurt her? In love with her, was he? He's as queer as a nine-bob note'. My dad says that – it's not offensive, is it?"

I shook my head. "Don't worry, the gay council said you're allowed to use it."

She didn't hear me. "So then he starts talking about Pawel, and he mentions how the investigation is progressing with all the loose ends being tied up."

"Such as?"

Sonia started crying again.

"Sonia, Sonia, for God's sake, control yourself, woman."

"I'm sorry." She took a tissue from her (knock-off Louis Vuitton) handbag and dabbed at her nose. "He was asking about Darren. I think the police know about the steroids."

"And then what happened?"

"We had another drink."

"Naturally."

"And then I went back to his place."

"Of course, you did— wait, what?" I leaned forward and whispered conspiratorially, "You shagged Ade?" I was impressed.

She nodded, still crying.

"Does Darren know?"

"Kind of…"

"What does 'kind of' mean?"

"I told him it was over. But he started crying, and I said, okay, we'll have another go, but then Ade called and said he wanted to be with me and had ever since we met. And, oh, Arden, he's so lovely and warm and kind, and his house has really nice natural light, and a big outdoor space, and those things are great for both resale value—"

"Sonia!"

"Sorry, yeah, Ade's great. And, I don't know, he's just so much more mature and worldly than Darren. He's been places, you know? He's been to Florida on holiday, *twice*." At that moment, Sonia's phone started ringing in her coat pocket; she pulled it out and looked at the screen. "Ade."

"Answer it," I said.

"No, I can't. Last night, Darren called and said he loved me. And I said it was too late and that I was going to go and get all my stuff from his place and take it back to mine."

"So, you're choosing Ade?" I was so confused.

"I'm not choosing Ade." She had stopped crying. "I'm choosing me."

I was impressed by her quasi-feminism. "Okay, but what does that mean practically?"

"I'm taking a break from Darren – while I sort me head out, but I'm not jumping into bed with Ade – again – I'm going to figure it out first."

"This is sensible."

"So, will you come with me to Darren's to get my stuff?"

"What? No! What, no, what?"

"Oh, please." She grabbed my hand. "There's no one else I can ask." She started sobbing again. The lady at the counter gave me a venomous look like it was my fault. "You know, I don't have many friends, and I thought that you've been so kind…"

"All right, all right, I'll do it. Come on, let's get this over with."

We bundled out to Sonia's car to drive over to Darren's flat. Darren was at work, apparently, and Sonia had a key that she was going to give back. "It's only for emergencies, he said. That's why I didn't use it for Pawel." Apparently, murder didn't dictate an emergency.

"Sonia, focus, what did Ade say about the murder investigation?" I said, wanting to get back to serious matters.

"Well," she said as we sped through the countryside from Compney to Sittingston, "that Wales and Neuberger think you're well dodgy and that you're up to all sorts of no good. And that there's been so much press coverage that the higher-ups are riding their asses to make sure there's a watertight case against Pawel… Pavlo, whatever his name is."

"There are people not convinced he's the killer. Did Ade mention the photos we left in the house?"

"No, no specifics. He said he wasn't supposed to know any of this, but that one of the junior detectives on the case down at Bournemouth is a mate of his, and that he hates Wales and Neuberger – apparently everyone hates them – and they've completely taken over Sittingston nick, and they can't wait to be shot of them."

"This is interesting," I commented as we approached the outskirts of Sittingston. "This means the police might still be open to other lines of enquiries. Did you know, for instance, that Tommy Douglas has a violent temper, apparently? He used to have massive… I don't know, temper tantrums, I suppose, even well into his twenties? He and his dad never got along."

"I never liked him. He was well rude to my mum once about her bunions."

"Sonia, don't you see? This means there are other people in the police force who aren't as case shut about the whole thing as Wales and Neuberger. This means there's still a chance someone could investigate about all of Arabella's other paramours, or even better, about her dodgy dad!"

"Yeah, but from what Ade thinks, it means they'll turn on you."

Oh, yeah. Bugger.

We got to the part of town where Darren's flat was located. Sonia parked down a small side street about fifty yards from the front door and we walked there, checking over our shoulders to make sure no one was looking. "You've got a key. No one's going to notice, and having a key means it's not illegal… I think."

Sonia's hand was shaking as she put the key in the lock. We hurried in.

"Right, what's yours?" I said. Darren's flat was a tip, and I couldn't make out where furniture finished, and dirty underwear and socks and left-out dishes began. The sink was overflowing with unwashed plates and cups, and the bathroom was something out of a warzone.

"Clothes… all my clothes should be in the bedroom. I've got some CDs in the lounge. Get them, will ya?"

"Which ones are they?"

"Literally any by a female artist."

I rummaged, Adele, Katy Perry, Kelly Clarkson, more Adele, another Adele. "How many albums has she bloody well released?" I found a couple of female singers I'd never heard of who I just assumed were off *X-Factor* or one of those shows. I picked them up as Sonia came back from the bedroom with an IKEA blue bag full of clothes.

"Right, this is most of it. You take all this out to the car, and I'll do a quick sweep for the rest."

I took the bag – which weighed a tonne – and made my way out to the narrow stairs leading down from the first floor flat to the entrance, and just as I got to the steps, Darren appeared at the door.

"What're you doing 'ere?" he asked.

"Darren, stay calm, we're just here picking up Sonia's stuff. There's nothing to get worked up about."

He lunged at me, ripping the bag from my hands, and tried to get upstairs. "Darren, don't do anything stupid!" I yelled, and caught his arm trying to get the bag back. We fumbled, and he let out a blood-curdling scream of "Soooooonia!" as I held onto him, grappling for the bag.

"Gimme that!" I yelled. We wrestled some more, and he pushed me back into the door. I caught it in the middle of my back, right on the frame's corner, and howled in pain as the heavy metal deadbolt jabbed me in a particularly non-fleshy part. I stumbled, winded, and Darren made a grab for the bag that I'd managed to get one handle of.

As he did, I made a break for the outside, and stumbled out onto the street still clasping the bag, with contents spilling everywhere. He made a grab for it again, still screaming Sonia's name. He pushed me away, this time sending me into the street. I let go of the bag, and all its contents spilled across the narrow pavement. I fell backwards onto the ground.

The street that ran alongside the shop where Darren's flat was located was essentially little more than a service alley. There was no space to park on it, so cars would come down it and only slow down at the intersection with the high street, a dozen or so yards from Darren's front door.

I lay prostrate in the street, mentally cursing my inability to handle myself in a scuffle. Sonia arrived at the scene and started screaming Darren's name as he screamed hers. She noticed me, and interspersed her choruses of "Darren!" with a one-off "Arden!" before they went back to calling out.

As I lay there in the street, with the sky spinning, wondering if I'd hit my head, and observing Darren and Sonia tussle with the bag, a car came careering down the narrow street.

"Ardeeeeen!" Sonia screamed again, as she noticed it first.

More preoccupied with my double vision, I didn't even notice until I heard the squeal of brakes and saw a bright red Peugeot hurtling towards me with an L plate on top advertising "Frannie's Driving School". The teenage girl in the driver's seat had her mouth open in what I presume was the longest scream of her life, while her instructor looked up from her phone and applied pressure to her own set of brakes.

The car skidded to a halt just inches from me.

Within a second of that, Darren grabbed Sonia and tried to drag her back inside the flat, yelling that they should work it out, and how much he loved her. "Sonia, get away from him!" someone yelled. I think it was me.

"Oi!" Frannie was out of the car, and she was a big girl. She bundled over to Darren in her sweatpants and hoodie, with a beanie on, and rugby tackled him, sending him flying along the pavement. Sonia started screaming hysterically at this point. She wasn't saying names any longer, but instead just letting out a high-pitched shriek that could raise the dead.

Frannie and Darren proceeded to engage in a scuffle – well more of a full punch-up – on the street as she unleashed a volley of punches on every aspect of Darren's upper body, while her legs kicked out viciously at him, aiming for his crotch and shins, her feet, with sandals and socks on, up in the air.

Sonia, in her high-heeled boots and leopard-print jacket, with her (fake) Louis Vuitton on the crook of her elbow, circled them, screaming and crying at them to stop.

The driving student, meanwhile, had her phone out and was sobbing down the phone to her mum, or the police, to come and rescue her.

My head was pounding from my fall, and when I reached up to touch where it hurt, my hand came away bloody. "Well, that's not good," I said to myself. The road was covered in debris from the IKEA bag and an Adele CD lay next to me, broken. "That's a pity. They're so rare."

Another car had pulled up behind Frannie's and the driver had got out and run over to help… pulled Darren off of Frannie, or Frannie off Darren… I wasn't sure which, and judging by the way they ended up hanging back, I don't think they were either. The man noticed me in the street with my bloodied hand and came over to me. "You all right, mate?"

"Yeah." I dragged myself to my feet. Then promptly slumped on the bonnet of the learner's car.

"You look very pale."

"That's just my natural complexion. I have a winter palette." My head started to throb even worse; I leaned over the other side of the car, out of view. "Excuse me," I said, and vomited up my lunch.

While I was busy, the ruckus continued, and the nice stranger tried to help me stand again. It took a moment, and it was only then I realised part of the ringing in my head was actually sirens.

A police car had turned up and parked at the entrance to the street, the officers emerging, and one looked familiar.

"Sonia?"

"Ade?"

"You!" Darren yelled. He flung off the driving instructor and lunged at Ade.

We all stood and watched as Darren and Ade went for each other. Ade was a restrained police officer, who shouted warnings and tried to stop Darren. Darren made a run for him, and Ade's fellow police officer (the same woman who'd been with him at the pub that day) was able to pull him off and the pair quickly had him under control.

Darren was held on the bonnet of the car next to me, while the officers handcuffed him. All the while, Sonia was still screaming.

"You are under arrest," the female officer shouted at Darren over the din, and read his Miranda rights.

"Fuck you!" he yelled back at her, or at me. Or at everything. It was all a bit hard to tell.

Darren was bundled into the back of the police car. "Right, I'm going to need statements from…" she said, and sighed. "Oh, all of you."

"You okay?" Ade came up to me and patted me on the back. "Noticed you chucked up your breakfast there."

"Yeah, I hit my head when I fell over. I feel a little dizzy, to be honest."

Ade looked at me properly. "We'll take you to go see a doctor after we've taken a statement." He looked across at where Darren was seething in the back seat of the police car. "So, did you actually fall or were you pushed?"

I screwed up my face. I didn't want to drop Darren in it. He was clearly heartbroken, and being arrested by the man your girlfriend had, for all intents and purposes, left you for was never gonna be a great way to spend your day.

"I don't want to get him in any more trouble."

"He's just assaulted a police officer so it's a bit late for that."

Chapter 38

Sittingston police station was a spectacularly ugly building in the middle of the village. It was 1960s through and through, with lino floors and cold white walls.

After we made our way over there in a variety of cars (both civilian and police), Sonia and I sat in the waiting room while Ade and his partner organised the process of statements. The station was small, and from what I knew, there was a tiny force based here: no more than seven or eight officers.

As we sat there, Sonia attempting to regain her composure, I looked around. Through the doors, I could see Ade talking with an older white guy in uniform, who I assumed was the sergeant in charge of the station. Ade must've explained what was happening, and the older man laughed heartily.

I was glad Sonia was on her phone at that moment and not seeing her private life shared as a joke between police officers. "Do you have a loo?" I asked the officer at the desk. He pointed to a door off the side. "I'll be back," I whispered to Sonia.

Through the door was a corridor with a series of offices and storerooms off it. To the right were doors with male, female, and disabled toilet signs. To the other side was an office with an open door. In the room was Neuberger.

He saw me before I saw him. I presume he'd known I was here since I'd arrived. "Mr Forrest, how lovely to see you again."

I gulped. "Hello."

He came up to me in the corridor, carrying his coffee cup, his puffa gilet on. He had a smarmy smile on his lips and was eyeing me as if I was dinner.

"I hear you've been in a fracas."

"Something like that."

"Seem to make a habit of being around when trouble kicks off, don't you?"

"I would hardly put this in the same category," I answered, in as polite a tone as I could manage.

"No, I'm sure you wouldn't." He smiled. "How are things going with your new boyfriend?"

"E-excuse me?" I stuttered.

"I heard you and Mr Scott were together. Am I mistaken?" As he said this, Wales walked past him and went out the door back to the main room. She gave me a horrible thin-lipped smile.

"How did you know that?"

He smiled and then took a sip of his coffee. "We had to speak to Miles Sweet again last week, after the break-in at the house. Mr Scott was at his home in London, I forget how we got onto to the topic, but he mentioned you were seeing one another."

What was Tarquin doing at Miles Sweet's house?

"Well, it's true, but that hasn't got anything to do with this."

"No, of course not. Just interested me, that's all. I'd been looking into your younger years, so hearing about how well you're doing now, it just struck me."

"I had a difficult upbringing, but I'm past that now."

"Quite."

The door opened. "Arden?" Ade asked. "Sonia said you were in the loo – we're ready for you now." He leaned through the doorway, his head sticking out into the corridor, and noticed Neuberger. "Is everything okay here?"

Neuberger smiled, and then turned away. As he sauntered back to the office, he called out, "See you soon, Mr Forrest."

Instead of waiting for Ade to ask me to come with him, I decided to ignore my full bladder, and quickly made my escape from the hallway and saw the waiting room was empty. "My colleague is interviewing Sonia. Sorry about that, by the way. Neuberger and his team have requisitioned the meeting room while they conduct their investigation."

"How much longer are they going to be here?"

Ade shrugged. "Not long, I hope." He returned to business. "Come through, and we'll get a statement. I rang the doc too; he's on his way over after he finishes his surgery hours to look at that head of yours."

"My head's fine," I lied. I had a headache and had been holding a cloth to the back of my skull on the way to the station. The bleeding seemed to have stopped now though. "But thank you, anyway."

I followed Ade through the doors and sat by his desk in the backroom. "You know my colleague, Constable Trescothick. She'll take your statement." It was the same woman Ade had been with the morning of the murder.

Constable Trescothick held out her hand for me to shake. "Call me Lauren."

Lauren was a small, skinny woman in her late thirties with mousy brown hair held back in a vicious-looking bun that seemed to require every bobby pin in the world. But she had a friendly face and a charming Dorset accent that put me at ease. "Now, let's get all this written down so we can work out what's happened here. Why don't you start off with how you know Ms Bliss and Mr Pascoe?"

"Who?"

"Darren. Darren Pascoe."

"Oh." I didn't even realise Darren had a surname.

I explained how Sonia and I had met, while skirting over the day I found Pawel there.

"You'd never met Darren before today?"

"Er, no, I ran into him once when Sonia took me to his flat."

"Right. Are you sure you're telling us everything?" She leaned in closer. "If there's anything that can help us get a closer understanding of what happened?"

Subtle, Lauren. Wow, what an excellent detective you'd make. I felt guilty for thinking this. The constable was doing her job. And yes, I was lying. I should admit what I'd done, but obviously that was not going to happen.

She gave me a disappointed look but returned to the task at hand. We wrapped up not long after that.

"What'll happen to Darren?"

"We'll keep him in overnight. Technically, this could be counted as either a domestic or assault. It's up to you to charge him."

"I want no charges brought. He's an idiot but he didn't mean to hurt me." *Besides, Sonia would never forgive me.* And I was already worried that Sonia was busy spilling the beans about everything that has just happened in the next room, telling Ade's boss about breaking and entering and all the photos.

"All right," said Constable Trescothick. She sighed and shuffled her papers. "Sign here. The doc'll be here any second to get a look at yer head."

I leant back in my chair and watched her go. I checked my watch. Somehow, it was already approaching six o'clock. Between all the excitement I had barely noticed how long it takes to actually have a fight and get people arrested.

I barely had time to breathe heavily and worry about the consequences of the day before Ade put his head around the door. “Arden, doc’s here.” I got up and followed him to one of the smaller offices in the back of the station that seemed to double as a sickbay. There was a stool and a desk in the middle of it, and, to my surprise, Tommy Douglas.

“Well, well, well,” he said as I walked in. “What have you been up to?”

I froze for just a second, before continuing. He was bound by an oath of secrecy, so there was only a ninety-eight per cent chance Odette would find out all about this.

“Wrong place, wrong time,” I answered with a forced smile.

He patted the stool. “Seems to be your MO. Come. Sit.”

I did so and he began to prod around the back of my head. “This is surprisingly nasty,” he said. “Ade said you bashed your head on the road after taking a smack, that right?”

I could sense the male bravado in me wanting to say no, but obviously it was true. “Pretty much,” I answered.

“I’m just going to check for concussion. You vomited, didn’t you?” He shone a torch in my eyes and did several other tests for my responses, his face becoming increasingly screwed up as he did so. “I’m afraid it’s affirmative, for the concussion. This is your first, I hope?”

I shook my head.

“Arden,” he took on the tone of a concerned mother. “That’s not good. Concussions are serious, despite the way they show ’em on TV. You’ll need to be careful for the next few days. Do you still feel sick?”

I nodded. I wasn’t sure if it was nerves, adrenaline, or the actual injury, but several occasions in the last half hour

I'd had to keep my jaw firmly clamped shut to avoid spraying the police station floor with what was left of my lunch.

Tommy was touching my jaw on each side with his hands and gently flexing my head. "Deary, dear," he said. He was very close to me, staring at my face. *I suppose he's handsome*, I thought to myself, trying to see what Arabella saw in him. She had money of her own; why would he think bankrupting himself to buy her gifts would make her want him?

"Did you hear about the break-in at Arabella's old house? The sarge was just telling me all the details," he said.

Was he allowed to do that?

"Photos of men lined up on a table," he added. "All the blokes Arabella was shagging."

He pushed my head to the side with force. I winced. "Sorry, just checking your neck."

"Let's get this cut sorted out." He stepped around behind me and there were several uncomfortable sensations, which I preferred not to think about. "This'll need stitches. I can do them here. I assume you'd prefer not to go to A&E?"

"Yes." My throat was dry. "Do you often come to the station to patch people up?"

"It's a small town," he said after a long pause. "The sarge is my godfather. It's easier this way." I winced as something sharp dug into my scalp. "Sorry, just putting some numbing liquid in."

"So, you're in on the goss here?" I said jokingly, as I dug my fingernails into my palms. He was doing a fucking shoddy job of that numbing.

"I know everything," he said. I started. "Just joking," he said, clapping me on the shoulder. I couldn't see anything except the door in front, and occasional flashes out the corner of my eye as he worked behind me. I hope he couldn't hear my heart beating like a drum.

"It's been useful these last few weeks, getting an update on what's happening with Arabella," he added. Another sharp sensation. "Odie doesn't like me talking about it at home."

I could feel something tugging in my hair. He was putting a stitch in. "You'll need to get these removed in a couple of weeks. Just hop down to the hospital and it won't take them ten minutes. Ask for Cynthia, she's got the gentle touch." He laughed again. "Not that you're interested in a woman's touch."

I pulled a face he couldn't see but had also started to sweat.

"Relax, Arden, it's almost over."

Tommy the Surgeon was creeping me out. The whole room was closing in on me. The headache and nausea were making everything a bit of a challenge.

"So, you and Tarquin?" he chuckled. "That was a shock. Frobisher was fuming. Always a fun sight."

"Do you not like Guy?" I was happier to discuss Guy than Tarquin. Tommy was in a revelatory mood, so I would take advantage.

He scoffed. "Let's just say I'm always happy when a Frobisher has a bad day."

"Does that include Arabella?" I said after a pause.

There was no answer.

"You're finished."

"What?"

"Your stitches. They're done," he said. I turned to look at him. He was staring me dead in the eye.

"Arabella wasn't like them," he said. Then he smiled. "But she's free now."

He turned around and began to pack away his things, throwing a few bloody paper towels in the bin. "Quite the little investigator, aren't you?" he added. "Always with the questions. You'll get yourself in trouble that way."

"What makes you think that?" I asked.

"I've seen you. In the corner… with Ewa. Going into Nigella's house, having little meetings with Lady F, Odie tells me."

"I'm a bit nosy, is all."

"You're putting your nose where it doesn't belong," he said. His eyes flashed. I backed up a couple of steps and walked into the door.

"Knock, knock," Ade said. "Everyone decent?"

"It's a cut on his head, Ade. I'm not checking his prostate," Tommy snapped.

"I meant more about any blood. I'm not good with blood. You all right to get home, Ard? Do you want someone to drop you off? Sonia said your car is back in Compney. Probably best if you leave it there for the night and go get it in the morning."

"It's also best you're not alone tonight," Tommy said. Ade raised an eyebrow.

"'Scuse me?" I asked.

"Your concussion. Have someone with you. It'd be best if you wake up every hour just to make sure you're not in any danger."

My churlish nature kicked in. "I'll set an alarm on my phone."

"I'm sure Sonia wouldn't min—"

"I'll be fine," I snapped. "Am I free to go, Ade?"

Ade nodded and moved out of the doorway as I pushed past. Sonia was hovering at the front desk. Ade and Tommy followed me out. "Come on, Son," I said, going towards the door.

"Erm… I'm going to wait here for a bit," Sonia said. She was blushing.

I scanned the room. Ade was staring at his shoes, and Tommy was smirking. I sighed. "When's your shift finish, Ade?"

"About twenty minutes," he mumbled.

I turned to Sonia. "Have a pleasant evening," I snapped.

"Tommy'll give you a lift," Ade said quickly. "Won't you, Tommy?"

"Course," said our charming local doctor. "Come on, Ard. Boys' road trip back to Lilbury."

I was fuming. And, quite frankly, terrified. "Have you checked in on Darren?" I snapped again at Sonia as we departed.

Tommy whistled as we made our way to his car. Not the SUV Odette drove, but a sleek Audi. "This looks pricey," I said without thinking.

It was wet outside; it had evidently rained while I was inside the station. It was a chilly night. I was still feeling quite ill, so the idea of driving back to Lilbury was making my stomach do flips.

My phone buzzed as we got in the car, Tommy still whistling tunelessly. "Buckle up," he said.

I checked my phone – Tarquin, asking why I was being so quiet today. I pocketed it.

We pulled out of the car park and sped through the village. Like Tarquin, Tommy enjoyed the sensation of driving too fast, and saw corners as challenges. I gripped the dashboard.

"Don't be a pussy, Forrest. Live a little," he said as we went around a roundabout that marked the southern edge of Sittingston and headed out onto the pitch-black road at high speed.

"You know, driving a car is almost as good as sex to me," he said.

You need to get better at sex, I thought to myself.

"Freedom, a bit dangerous, and if you do it right, a bit dirty."

I don't think Odette would want any of those words used with her sexual performance, so I assumed he wasn't discussing his conjugal duties.

"You asked before about Arabella," he said as we went around a corner twenty miles an hour too fast.

"I did."

"Of course, you know what you know."

"What do I know?" I asked as my head throbbed, and my stomach lurched. I was sweating profusely, but the last thing I wanted to do was to ask him to stop so I could puke on the side of the road.

"She meant nothing to me," he said as we came to a stop at a T-junction. I nearly bashed my head on the windscreen, so sudden was the stop, despite wearing my seatbelt. "I'm a very happily married family man."

"Are you?" The seatbelt had gouged into my neck. I looked around. The middle of nowhere. My skin covered in goosebumps. A happily married man, my arse. I started reciting a little prayer to myself in case I never saw my cats again.

"Let me give you a warning, Arden. Stay out of things. You don't understand what was going on."

"But you did?"

"She told me."

"Oh, pillow talk was it?"

For a second, I thought Tommy was going to punch me. Instead, he flexed his fingers on the steering wheel. "You don't know *anything*. So, let me give you a warning. Stop digging in things you don't understand. Pawel killed Arabella. We're all very sad."

"Did he?"

Tommy accelerated suddenly, turning the wheel violently; we sped off down the narrow road, going through a huge puddle, which sprayed my side of the car in a torrent of water. "Of course he did. There was no one else who could have."

"Why do you want Pawel to be blamed?" I was trying to lean away from him, up into the corner of the car. I could see the speedometer. We were hitting 80 mph on the tiny road.

I was terrified that Tommy was going to kill me or kill us both, intentionally or unintentionally. "Because it's easier for all of us if he is, isn't it? Definitely easier for you."

I had no idea where we were, but Tommy came to an abrupt halt on a piece of the road. I was breathing as if I had just been running. "Easier for me? How?"

He leant over and I flinched. He smirked. "Just think about it." He undid my car door. "And keep your mouth shut."

He gestured with his head. "You're home."

Chapter 39

I won't lie to you. I ran into my house, straight to the kitchen, and vomited copiously in the sink. I sat on the floor, back against a cupboard door for several minutes trying to get my breath back after losing everything I'd eaten that day.

Eventually, I slid down to lie on the floor and lay there panting for several moments. My head was absolutely pounding.

Had Tommy killed Arabella? Had someone discovered their affair? Had Odette found out? Everything he'd said was flying around in my head and I couldn't grasp the thoughts long enough to make sense of them.

I stood up on shaky legs and gulped down a glass of water. I went to the bathroom and gripped onto the wall for a long hot shower.

That night was not great. Like Tommy said, I woke myself up every hour to check I wasn't dead. Not that I needed it. I lay in my bed, with the kittens at my feet, and turned off my alarm every hour it went off. Sleep proved an elusive beast.

I got up early and padded around my house trying to feel better by tidying and making the place look as good as I could.

I texted Tarquin, but got no response, despite him being an early riser.

About mid-morning I received a call from Nigella.

"I heard you had a scrape yesterday?"

"Does everyone know?" I asked.

"No, Odette has been positively discreet… when she rushed over to tell me first thing this morning. But are you okay? And she mentioned something about your car."

Touched by her concern, I explained the situation about both my head and my car. "I'll be over in five minutes," she said.

True to form, fifteen minutes later (hey, who was counting?) Nigella pulled up outside my door in her ridiculously large SUV.

We drove the quick trip to Compney Parva as I properly filled her in on yesterday's shenanigans. When I got to the part at the police station, however, I faltered.

"And then what happened?" she pressed.

"Then… then…" I looked out on the road as we made our way into Compney's environs. "How well do you know Tommy?"

Nigella pursed her lips. "As well as we can ever know our neighbours, I suppose. He's not my favourite person." She gave me a look before turning back to focus on the road, her hands gripping the steering wheel a little harder than previously.

"Do you…" She faltered.

At that moment we passed my car sitting happily along the side of the street and my answer died on my lips. I hopped out.

Nigella sped off and I followed her (the Green Machine starting on the first try, so thank God for small miracles). We drove convoy-style back to Lilbury, where we parked up in front of the tiny tearooms on the high street. I'd promised Nigella scones with cream and jam to say thank you. It was the most English thing I think I had ever done.

We sat down and a scowling old woman took our order. "Don't mind her, that's Betty. She was that age when I used to come in here as a teenager."

I nodded to Roz as I saw her across the room, chatting intently with another woman. Nigella leaned in and spoke quietly. "What do you mean about Tommy?"

I considered the question. To say the wrong thing could lose me any sort of hope of an "in" with the Lilbury set. I could easily cast myself as a social pariah. But to say nothing would be to leave my thoughts in my head.

I chose the road less travelled.

"You know that Tommy and Arabella were—"

Nigella nodded. "Even a blind nun could work it out."

"You don't think…" I said, stumbling over my words. "You don't think he got jealous."

Nigella didn't answer as Betty brought our orders over and set a huge selection of teacups and cake stands around us until I could barely see Nigella over the sea of tannin and pastry.

"Jealous of…?" Nigella asked after Betty had shuffled off muttering something about "two soups".

"All the others," I tried to say as nonchalantly as possible, and buttered a scone. It was rock hard, but as the shop was doing a roaring trade on a weekday morning in March, it must have been just me who had a complaint.

Before she could answer, we were interrupted again, this time by a smiling Eleanor. "Hello, darling," Nigella said, and stood up to hug her. "How are you?"

Eleanor gave me a polite greeting before answering Nigella. She looked tired, and her normally shiny, bouncy hair was somewhat greasy and wrapped up in a messy bun at the base of her skull.

"I'm fine," she said in an unconvincing voice. Nigella made eyes with me before turning back to her. "Why don't you and your parents come round for dinner this week? It would be lovely to see you all."

"I'm not sure that's going to be possible..." She saw Nigella's determined look. "But I'll ask. I have to go. Just came in to collect my wages and thought it'd be rude not to say hello."

Nigella gave her a hard look, the kind I assumed she'd been giving Eleanor all her life, but said nothing. Eleanor said goodbye to us and went off on her day.

"What was all that about?" I asked with a mouth full of scone.

"People in this village keep acting very strangely lately. I don't know." She gave me the same look she'd just given Eleanor. "You think Tommy hurt Arabella?"

I buttered my remaining bit of scone for as long as I could without being rude. "I'll put it this way, I don't think Pawel did it. The only other man I can think of in the vicinity is Trevor Bliss."

"The estate agent?" Nigella was horrified her goddaughter would stoop to screwing someone of that profession.

"He looks like a Hemsworth," I said in his defence.

Nigella was unimpressed with that information. "I don't know what to believe," she said.

She looked out the window. "Did Pawel kill her? I have no idea. He was a nice man, but that doesn't mean he didn't do it. He could've been jealous—"

"But if that was his motive, then it was the same as Tommy's. His and Odette's marriage is on life support, and everyone knew he and Arabella were having an affair. What's to say he didn't get jealous?"

Nigella was staring out the window. "I would be careful with the opinions, Arden. It's not that I can't see your point, but people won't like you going around saying these things. People do stupid things when they feel threatened."

After I left Nigella at the café, I went home and wrote my book until I went cross-eyed, and my fingers ached. I played with the kittens, ate some unhealthy food, and went to bed.

Unable to sleep, my mind raced on thoughts about who was responsible.

I must have fallen asleep at some stage because I awoke with a start to the sound of my phone buzzing. It was just a message not a call. It was from Tarquin. Wish you were here, it said, with a video attached. I won't explain what the video was of, but it perked my mood right up.

I was due up in London that week to see him. He had a cocktail party on Thursday night, which I was cordially invited to, but I headed up on Wednesday afternoon as he'd said it'd be great to spend more time together. I dropped the kittens off at Sonia's on the way ("The hell am I staying in your creepy cottage in the middle of nowhere again. I didn't sleep a wink last time."), as we had reached an entente cordiale after the police station, and then made my way up to London. On the drive I tried not to think about anything dark or depressing, just taking in the lovely spring weather. It was sunny and mild, though the forecast had said that morning that the weather would turn in the next day back to grey rain.

London was as large and foreboding as always; it started off small with service areas on the motorways and new-build housing estates jostling for space in commuter towns, and before you knew it, you were on a dual carriageway, crawling alongside dilapidated office blocks advertising huge spaces available for rent. Everything in London wanted to be as central as possible. Everything it didn't want was pushed to the periphery, creating a thirty-mile-wide ring around it of "offcuts", which kept the City itself running, but the guidebooks for tourists never showed that.

I eventually made it to Fulham, and Tarquin came out to see me as I attempted to park on the pathetically narrow bit of drive outside his mews house. He stood in jeans and a white T-shirt with socks on, but no shoes, drinking a cup of coffee, his biceps bulging every time he raised the cup to sip. His presence was distracting to my attempts at parallel parking. He eventually knocked on the window. "Do you want me to do it?"

"I can do it, thank you!"

"Babe, I say this with the best intentions… no, you really can't."

We compromised. By which, I mean he parked, and I went upstairs and took off all my clothes and waited for him in bed.

That evening, Tarquin's friends had asked to meet me properly, so we headed to a local bar for a few drinks. Millie and Freddie, who I had met at the party at Tarquin's, were to join us. We walked to the end of the mews, and I was surprised to see an Uber waiting for us. "Can we not walk?"

Tarquin scoffed. "In these shoes?"

I had been looking forward to a nice walk after spending half the day cooped up in a car, but acquiesced. I hoped this wasn't a sign of differences starting to show up in our relationship.

We went to a trendy bar on the Fulham High Road. Freddie and Millie were already there. And several drinks in if the glaze in their eyes was to be believed. Freddie had his hand on Millie's thigh, and not just above the knee, if you know what I mean, but rather going as far up as he could in public.

They stood as we approached, and Freddie and Tarquin gave each other a straight guy-style bear hug while Millie gave me a sloppy kiss on each cheek. Her breath was about fifty proof.

"I'm so excited to see you two together," she said sitting back down and beckoning at the handsome, but short, waiter. She ordered a bottle of Prosecco and tapped the table impatiently when the waiter had gone off to fetch it. "Tell me everything."

"What do you mean?" I asked.

Tarquin rolled his eyes. "She'll want the full story. The antiques shop, the dinner party, me turning up in the rain."

"You turned up in the rain?" she squealed. Freddie was already bored by this conversation and had his phone out. When the bottle arrived, Freddie and Tarq took a few polite sips, then downed their glasses and retired to the bar for beer instead, leaving me with Millie. She eyed me like a tigress. "I've been investigating you." She twirled a finger in my face. "Finding out all about your past."

I had half a mind to tell her where to go but instead played nice. "Anything interesting?"

She gave a tight smile and tilted her head – her immaculate posh girl shag of choppy blonde hair (just like Arabella's) fell to the side – "It turns out your ex is a friend of a friend," she added. "He's very good-looking."

I took a drink. Sipped it slowly. "We broke up six months ago."

"My friend told me you cheated."

I rolled my eyes. "No, *he* cheated."

"And he'd do anything to get you back." Millie didn't even bother to counter my correction. She'd made the mistake on purpose to test me. She wasn't as drunk as she was acting.

"Tarquin needs people in his life he can depend on," she said. "He doesn't need complications. In his line of business, they can be the difference between millionaire and pauper."

I leaned in real close. "I'm no one's complication. If Tarquin is easily distracted from his goals then that's his business."

"Be warned. The people he works with aren't playing."

Rich City boys murdering an escort while high on cocaine is not really the same as the IRA or Chechen rebels, but sure.

I smirked. "I can handle myself."

I was clapped on the back, and before Millie could reply, Tarquin placed his pint down on the table and put his arm around my shoulder. "What are you two gossiping about?"

I didn't like Millie much after that. But I did replay what she'd said in my mind as we got progressively drunker. I ran over in my head that Tarquin had been with Miles Sweet days earlier when the police had come calling. Okay, so maybe *mi amore* was in business with the old bastard. Not a great look for someone who didn't want to be associated with sleaze, but he must have connections and favours he could pull, so maybe Tarquin needed to call in some friends to help.

The next morning, I wasn't too hungover and decided to broach it over breakfast. Tarquin had already finished eating his and was looking for his keys, wandering from room to room while I sat on his expensive kitchen breakfast stools eating organic muesli and drinking plunger coffee. I'm still not a fan, give me instant any day.

"Why were you with Miles Sweet?"

His eyes flickered for just a second in the mirror as he did his tie. "How did you know that?" he asked after a slightly too long pause.

Not the answer I was hoping for. "The police told me the day I got into the fight in Sittingston. Neuberger decided to pin the murder on me and thought I'd be rattled."

"He what?" Tarquin quit working on his tie and came over to me. "How does he spin that one out?"

I shrugged. "I found the body. I have a past."

Tarquin put his arm around me and kissed my cheek. "There's no need to worry about any of that. Neuberger is a fool, and no one will listen to his crackpot theories. All you need to do" – he released me and smiled – "is get your glad rags on and be Mr Hospitable at the cocktail party tonight. There are a few rich widows I need you to flirt with."

He gave me another kiss on the forehead and left for his meeting.

Was I worried that Neuberger was concluding that I hurt Arabella? Yes, of course. Was I going to let that ruin my day? Only on the inside.

I had arranged to meet Verity for lunch. After a pleasant morning perusing the bookstores in Piccadilly, I made my way to a small café near her office and waited for her. She arrived late, as was her tradition, and launched into a story about the latest construction disaster at her house before she'd even sat down.

"Do you want a coffee?" I asked after she'd described how her builder was a con artist, a fool, a ne'er do well, and a scoundrel.

"Yes, I've no energy today," she added, taking a bite out of the brownie I'd ordered. "I see you've got your appetite back."

"It's just a brownie," I responded, feeling a bit miffed I couldn't have even one treat.

"It's good to see. You're all skin and bone." I ordered her a coffee and sat down as we waited for it to come. She drummed the table impatiently just like Millie had. "Am I going to have to beat it out of you?" she said.

"Beat what?"

"The story behind you and the luscious Mr Scott. I've stalked him online. He is everything a man should be. I don't understand your weakness for posh guys, but that's your cross to bear."

"There's not much to tell. There was a spark. We went for it – after some hesitation on my part – and it's been a great couple of weeks."

Verity's face fell. "Gee, it's lucky you don't rely on describing things in interesting language to put food on the table, isn't it? With explanations like that, you'd have people only reading you as a sleep aid."

"I'm doing this new thing where I keep my private life private and don't jinx things by getting my hopes up about them before anything has happened."

"You don't think it will last then, do you?"

"It's in the lap of the gods."

Verity kissed her teeth and then took a very passive-aggressive sip of her coffee. "And what about the investigation?"

"It's on hold. Well, my attempts are anyway."

"Is this because you got your ass whooped in a fight?"

"It wasn't a fight. I wasn't whooped and, in general, no."

Verity gave me a look. A look that was all "what then?" but with more scorn.

"If you must know, I'm keeping a low profile."

"Running off to London for a midweek sexfest with your boyfriend is keeping a low profile in your world?"

"I'm staying out of the way of the local constabulary down my way, who, and you'll struggle to believe this, don't much like me."

"Whose sheep did you steal?"

"They think I might be the killer."

Verity paused. Then she laughed. Then she went silent again. Then she began laughing again. "I'm sorry, it's just… it's you. The guy who gets scared of old ladies on the bus. The guy who made us run away after a cyclist got knocked off his bike by a delivery van in case we had to help—"

"I'm aware I'm somewhat of a scaredy-cat."

"Did they think you trampled Arabella to death in a panic to get away after a gate shut loudly? Was there a gust of wind?"

"Your sarcasm has been noted." She'd stopped laughing, though.

"But for real though? They think you had something to do with it—"

"Yes!" I said a bit too loudly. "And my theory on who did it is never going to gain traction if they think it was me."

"Why would you do it? You're a massive homo, and they don't usually kill pretty little white girls. You guys butcher each other on Grindr."

"I'm foreign and always in the wrong place at the wrong time."

"Bit of a stretch." She finished her coffee and took the rest of my brownie. "Who's your suspect?"

"Tommy Douglas, the adulterous local GP."

"Evidence? Motive?"

"He was shagging Arabella. Everyone knew except his wife. He was loading himself up with debt trying to impress her but to no avail. Renowned for having violent outbursts and is a right little creep. Emphasis on little. Proper Napoleon syndrome."

Verity looked unconvinced. "I mean… they arrested that chef guy, didn't they?"

"What, and I should just go off and enjoy my life and go to Tarquin's party and ignore it?"

"Is that what you want to do?"

"I dunno. It's Tarquin's business associates. I feel like I'm on parade a bit. And the police said Tarquin was at Arabella's dad's house last week when they visited to let them know someone had broken into her house in the village."

Verity let this sink in. "He's in business with Miles Sweet? The one you said was as crooked as they come?"

"I think he might be. I don't think his investment company is doing particularly well."

Verity took my hand. "Please be careful, Arden. This is more than you realise. I don't want you ending up dead in a field too."

There really isn't much further you can take lunch after someone says they worry you might get murdered, and I made my excuses not long after. Verity and I made plans to go for dinner the next night, where she could meet Tarquin properly, and we would discuss business.

I went back to Tarquin's flat in Fulham and began getting ready for the party. I had a long shower in his bathroom, which – unlike mine – you actually felt clean in afterwards and nothing brown ever spurted out of the taps when you were running a bath.

I got my penguin suit on and waited. I was ready far too early. I meandered around the house, trying not to crease my tuxedo, and after a few fitful minutes watching TV went on the prowl. Was there something up with Tarquin's business? If he was… what, taking money from Miles, a loan, maybe, did that bother me? Miles Sweet was a fraudster, possibly, a dodgy businessman, maybe an embezzler, but I knew none of the details. If my business was struggling and I happened to know an extremely rich man who moved in similar circles to me, would I not go looking for a lifeline?

I opened the door to Tarquin's office.

It was a fairly blank space. A small room with a glass desk in front of the floor-to-ceiling sash window. A black designer chair that looked all angles and directions rather than comfortable. On both walls were shelves painted white filled with papers and knick-knacks, pictures of Tarquin with his friends, with his rugby team from Oxford, with two people I assumed were his parents. One of Tarquin and Guy in tuxedos toasting champagne glasses at the camera caught my eye. Below the shelves to both sides were cupboards built into the wall the same glossy shade of white as the shelves. I opened one. Papers and documents. I opened another, a filing cabinet. Locked. I opened the next; it was empty. The cupboard closest to the window was locked.

I went to the other side. Tax documents, bank statements, receipts, invoices, it was all here. Pamphlets for housing developments with Sweet Homes's logo on them. Glossy literature for Tarquin's own business in huge bundles underneath them.

After reading through a few, I decided it all looked legitimate, but I had no idea what I was looking for. I photographed a few pages. Some company logos, any names I came across, to look up later. But truth be told it felt fruitless. I was not a forensic accountant and access to anything like this was useless if you didn't even know you were holding the smoking gun.

What did I want anyway? To find my boyfriend guilty of fraud? Because one boyfriend had cheated on me, I had to up the ante on the next one? I shook my head and placed everything back, as carefully as I could, making sure it looked as spotless as it had when I came in.

I closed the door, and as it clicked my phone vibrated.

We're all set up. First guests arriving in a mo. You on your way? x

I put my phone back in my pocket, straightened my crooked bowtie, and left for the party.

Through my number of years living in London I had been to a fair few swanky parties in my time. People in this city will use any function as an excuse to put on a suit or a frock and drink warm Asti Spumante in a pollen-filled park or an un-air-conditioned drawing room of a period building with wild abandon.

Lawyers are particularly bad for this habit, and within a year of being with Ollie, I had worn out my first cheap tuxedo and had to go out and buy a rather more expensive one in the hope of price equalling longevity. If that isn't a First World problem, then I don't know what is.

The venue that Tarquin had chosen for his event was a hotel ballroom near Trafalgar Square. It was underground, beneath a baroque foyer and dining room, down a staircase of modern white walls, lit by blue floor flights, with the trickle of a water feature somewhere inside. The dull throb of music that was probably a little too techno for the crowd reverberated.

I waltzed in feeling quite confident, and that lasted, oh, about thirteen seconds.

In front of me lay the main room, tennis court size, with half walls creating several intimate seating locations, and the DJ in the middle of the room. Two young waitresses stood at the entrance, one on each side with trays of bubbly. "Sir," one said, bringing her tray towards me.

"Thank you." I took a glass and was relieved that it was at least cool-ish.

I walked down a small flight of steps and began to do a tour of the party. Around the bar, groups mingled and chatted. Everywhere a posh accent and a braying laugh.

"I was just saying to Lucille that we should all try and get the same villa in Tuscany..."

"The au pair is useless. I've told her half a dozen times not to give the children sugar, but she does..."

"It was a steal at seven hundred K..."

"And so we had to slum it in premium economy all the way to Tokyo..."

I caught my reflection in the chrome top of the bar. For a moment I didn't recognise myself. All dressed up, with my hair slicked back and a glass of champers in hand. It wasn't so long ago I worked at events like this.

"Arden! There you are. We've been sent by His Lordship to round you up." Millie put her arm through mine and dragged me away from the DJ and the bar to what I assumed was the inner circle. A semi-private booth filled with the in-crowd.

Freddie gave me a tip of his glass, where he sat with a fidgeting Chiara. And there was Tarquin, standing beside Miles Sweet and his wife Noor.

"Fuck me," I said very, very quietly.

"There you are, darling." Tarquin took my hand and pulled me into the booth. "Arden, this is Miles Sweet and his wife."

Miles didn't even look at me, instead focused on the other men around him and Tarquin, who were laughing loudly. Noor gave me a thin hand to shake and then removed it as quickly as she could. She wore a white dress, and her hair was in an elaborate updo. Beside Miles was a huge Arab guy in a suit, with the dead eyes of a shark. Unlike everyone else, he wore a tie, not a bowtie. Clearly some kind of security. Beside Noor stood another bodyguard, slightly lighter skinned but just as huge, with the same outfit on and the same shark eyes.

"Darling, these are some business associates of Miles's from Turkey," Tarquin said, gesturing to a group of men behind him. There was a round of introductions, where I was studiously not introduced as anything gay-related at all, an upstanding heterosexual who'd never even seen another man's penis.

"And what do you do, Mr Forrest? Are you in finance too? It seems like no one in London has a job in anything else," one of the Turkish men asked me politely, as he sipped his elderflower cordial.

"I'm a novelist," I answered honestly. "I write sci-fi books for teenagers."

Millie almost managed to hide her eyeroll at this. Surprisingly, both the man I was talking to and Noor Sweet seemed to find this interesting. "How fabulous!" Noor said. "Anything we'd have heard of?"

I laughed. "I hope not, for your sake. Though an American TV production company is interested in adapting them into a series. We're getting near a contract being finalised." Truth be told, the production company and I had been introduced and had a few "exploratory" meetings, as Verity put it, but they didn't need to know that. What was good, though, was that Tarquin was beaming at this conversation topic. Deals and money, whether they were his or not, was clearly the way to go.

The Turk carried on talking to his other associates and Noor came to stand closer to me. "I understand you've moved to Lilbury," she said in her lilting transatlantic accent.

"Yes, about a month or so ago." *Don't mention Arabella*, I yelled internally.

"I thought, when I came to England, I would love the countryside. I did not," Noor said bluntly.

"Any reason in particular?" I asked, taking a large sip.

"The people. In Lebanon, city people are city people. On the farms, people are farmers, yes? But in England, city people are living in farms and act like it is a city, and farmers get angry. I do not like it. It seems, maybe, the two is not compa… what is the word I want?"

"Compatible?"

She flushed. "Sorry, my English. I am jetlagged, and the champagne is not helping."

"Don't worry, it's my second language as well. But I was young when I moved here, so it's my native language I make mistakes in." Noor was full of questions after that, and we spent a happy twenty minutes discussing the experience of migrant life.

We were carrying along nicely when Miles swept up beside us, and I found myself penned in with the Sweets and their bodyguards. "I know you," Miles said. "You were at the funeral." *The* funeral, not *my daughter's* funeral.

“Yes, sir. I live in Lilbury,” I explained.

“You knowed her?” Noor asked – her tenses were her biggest weakness in English

“Briefly. I met her a couple of times.” I saw Millie looking at me, listening to every word.

“I was the one who found her body,” I said.

Noor gasped. “That must have been terrible,” she said, and put her hand on my arm for just a second. “It’s been hell. The funeral. And then someone is broken into the house. No doubt some tabloid photographer.” Her voice was filled with venom.

Miles was saying nothing. “Yes, the police asked. They thought some of us in the village might know the person who did it, if they were local,” I said. Thin. Ice. Forrest.

“I don’t know why the police are still making a fuss of it. They caught the little cunt who did it,” he said.

I stiffened. Miles Sweet’s voice was somehow posh and mockney, gravelly and nasally all at the same time. Whilst Noor was not what I expected, his fat little face and glaring eyes were the exterior of exactly the man I thought he was.

“You-you believe they have the right man?” I asked. My palms were sweating.

This caught Miles off guard. “You don’t?”

“It’s just… t-there’s a lot of circumstantial evidence,” I stuttered. “They haven’t even found her phone.”

“And that’s important because?” Noor asked, genuinely.

“Because there might be evidence on it. Maybe the killer kept it. It might have messages on there, details. Maybe they even kept it as a memento.” I was chatting shit, and my heart was beating so fast I thought the whole room could hear it, even over the terrible techno music.

Millie was still listening to every word but had apparently had enough. The moment there was a silence, she grabbed Noor’s arm (to the bodyguard’s ire). “Tarq and Miles are about to make their speeches. Come with me, darling, and we'll get a good spot."

No invitation to me was made even though Noor stood to let me join them, but Millie pushed her onwards. Miles left too, brushing past me with the two giant Arab bodyguards without a goodbye. His bodyguard, the fairer of the two, made a path for Miles to make his way. "Watch your back," he said to Chiara as he not-so-gently pushed her out of the way. So I waited while the troupe of Turks all went past as well.

I grabbed Tarquin as he made his way to the DJ booth. "I didn't know you were making a speech." I was mostly worried, as Tarquin had been chucking back his champagne since I'd got there. I'd had two glasses in this time, he, at least four. His eyes were shiny too, in a way that was not just alcohol.

"It's just a few words."

"How much coke have you had?" I asked, surprising myself.

"Millie just gave me some to help with my confidence tonight. It's my big chance to impress. Why, don't you approve?"

"It doesn't matter if I do or not, I just don't want anyone to notice."

He slid his hand up my leg and over my arse for a brief second. "Relax, nothing bad is going to happen." He grinned and walked off.

"Ladies and gentlemen," the DJ said after the music cut out. "Please, your attention for a few moments for your host for this evening, Tarquin Scott."

There was a great round of applause from the crowd and even a wolf-whistle from Freddie to gales of laughter. Tarquin (and Miles) were on the raised platform alongside the DJ's decks and Tarquin began his short speech.

From this distance, he looked handsome and calm, the man in charge of the room, whilst Miles leaned at the side surveying it all.

"I'd just like to say thank you all for coming. It's been a challenging process getting this company off the ground," (short applause) "but we're here!" (Bigger applause.) "And each and every one of you has helped!" Out of the corner of my eye, I saw a familiar shape coming into the room and accept a glass of champagne. "And here's one of them now! This man here, Guy Frobisher, uncharacteristically late by the way," he said to polite laughter, "my best friend and business mentor, is the man who helped this all happen."

Guy looked deeply uncomfortable at being singled out, especially as he was on the steps standing above everyone. He glanced around the party but didn't catch my eye.

"And of course, this man by my side, Mr Miles Sweet. Ladies and gents, a round of applause for this legend!" The crowd enthusiastically cheered for him. But Guy remained stonily silent. "Thank you and have a great evening!" Tarquin finished and the music began again. He was surrounded by men in suits shaking his hand. I assumed I should make myself known and made my way onto the main floor to join in. But typical me, I couldn't do so without first walking into someone.

"I'm dreadfully sorry, wasn't looking where I was – Eleanor?"

"Hi, oh, wow, Arden. Yes, I heard you and Tarquin were a thing now. Should've expected to see you here." Eleanor said all this without looking at me. In fact, she seemed downright terrified of being near me. "I'm looking for someone so I must—"

"Would you like me to get you a drink? Here, let me help you find your friend—"

"No, it's quite all right. Thank you, anyway, Arden." And with that, she vanished into the crowd of people.

What on earth was she doing here? I looked up and saw Tarquin staring at me. He pointed at where Eleanor had just been standing and mouthed something, but I couldn't make it out.

"What?" I called rather pointlessly, but he'd already returned to his conversation, albeit with a brief second glance over his shoulder.

I knew the next person I had to go talk to, but frankly, I couldn't think of anything I wanted to do less, right now. I made my way to the excitable gaggle of women near the bar and found Guy in the middle of them, already batting away proposals of marriage. "That is a lovely offer, Madeline, I'd love to come visit your parents' house in Norfolk, but I think in August I'll be a bit busy – oh, Arden… thank fuck."

It was the first time I'd heard him swear. "Excuse me, ladies. Must go chat with this chap over here about the weather," he said as he made his way over.

We found a more secluded area of the room and grabbed drinks. I was about to start apologising for the awful dinner party when I saw another familiar face by the bar, one who'd probably just seen the entire scene with both Guy and Eleanor. "Sorry, Guy, I've just seen someone I never expected to clap eyes on in this place – I'll be two minutes." I shoved my glass at him, which he nearly dropped in surprise. I heard him call my name, but I had already stalked off to the other side of the party.

"Hello," Ollie said as I sidled up beside him. I grabbed his hand, which was nursing a whisky and soda as he leaned on the bar, and dragged him from the room. To the left was a long corridor, which eventually led you to the loos, but not before you passed a way back into the main foyer where you could make a glamorous entrance down the main stairs into the room again. It was too early for many people to have splintered off into the various rooms and nooks and crannies, so we were relatively hidden, except for a thin line of guests passing us on their way to the toilets.

"What the hell are you doing here?" I whispered through gritted teeth.

"Nice to see you too. I'm doing exactly what you asked."

"Crashing my boyfriend's party?"

"Boyfriend? No, what? No. I'm not crashing. I'm here with Tim, my colleague who used to do some work for Miles's company. Remember, I told you about him? I asked if he could swing us an invite, and lo and behold he could. He's over in the corner attempting to get the number of some Turkish businessman's daughter."

"Okay, so that's how you're here, but why are you here?" I darted a look over his shoulder to make sure no one was watching us.

"Because I promised you I'd keep looking into this. I had no idea you'd be here."

"Really?" I demanded.

"Yes, really," he said, giving me his best honest face. I faltered. I had asked him to help me, though I had assumed he wouldn't any longer after the disastrous dinner. I flushed red with annoyance and embarrassment.

"Thank you," I said as sincerely as I could.

He looked less than placated. "Boyfriend?" he said quietly.

There was a long pause between us. I had no idea what to say.

Ollie sighed. "You really don't want to get back together ever, do you?"

I scrunched up my face. Ollie waved a hand. "Don't answer that. It was a stupid question."

"Ollie, thank you for looking into this but I don't think it's the best idea to be here. These are all Miles's customers, his associates. No one here is going to drop a bombshell, and they'll be suspicious."

"I know, it was stupid. But I thought I might get a lead." He looked at me. "And if it's not a good idea for me to be here, then it's definitely not a good idea for you to be here."

"I have to be here."

"Arden, please, just listen to me. I don't know much about this, but I know there's already one dead body associated with the people in this room. Nothing in what I've read suggests these are nice people."

"That's why I'm here, Ollie. I know Pawel didn't kill Arabella. I just don't know who did."

Ollie began to say something else but was interrupted by someone calling my name. "I am very popular tonight."

I looked up, and at the entrance to the corridor was Tarquin, looking extremely pissed off, with Guy standing behind him.

"Is everything all right, Arden?" Guy asked.

"Ollie, go out the other way, get behind me," I whispered as discreetly as I could.

Before he could, Tarquin moved towards us and held out his hand to Ollie. "Tarquin Scott, I don't believe I've had the pleasure."

Ollie smiled in his best barrister way and took his proffered hand. "Oliver Ross." He rolled his R's in the most Scottish way. "Arden and I know each other vaguely through a mutual friend. My mate Gravz is married to Arden's friend Verity. We used to work together before he ditched us for Canary Wharf."

"Is that so?" Tarquin was so drunk he was swaying.

"Pleasure to meet you, Oliver," Guy said sticking out his hand. He gave me a look and then focused on Tarquin.

"I think I'd best be off," Ollie said.

"Yes, that would be wise," Tarquin snapped. I looked daggers at him, which Guy saw. He nodded in my direction. "All right, we know who he is now, so let's go get you a non-alcoholic drink, shall we?"

Ollie gave me a final pause before he made his way. "Call me if you need me. I'm around. Cheerio, gents," he called out to Guy and Tarquin.

The three of us were left in the corridor. We all looked at each other. Tarquin had a face like thunder. "Who was he?"

"A friend, like he said!" I snapped back.

I made to walk past, and Tarquin tried to grab my arm— "Babe!"

I wrenched my arm away. "Sober up, or I am leaving!" was my only answer.

"All right, all right, everyone calm down," Guy said. "Let's all go back inside the room and play nice… come on." He shepherded us back in to sat with Tarquin and me while he forced his friend to drink a pint of water. But Tarquin was still drunk and stayed so for the rest of the evening.

I didn't see Eleanor again either, despite looking out for her. Millie and the others were all completely wrecked by the time the bar shut at the end of the night. Only around twenty of us were left. Guy helped me carry a drunk, but now calmer, Tarquin outside for a taxi.

Before we left, Miles and Noor had to be farewelled. Noor gave me a kiss on the cheek. "It was a pleasure to meet you," I said.

"Likewise!" she said. "I enjoyed our conversation."

Miles gave me a look and did briefly hold his hand out for me to shake. He kept it by his side and broke off the contact after a second.

"Well, there you go," said Guy as they departed. The party was winding down, and few people were left. The Turkish businessmen had all departed off somewhere, with Freddie leading them – from what I could tell – straight to a Soho strip club.

We made our way outside into the cold night, after Guy and I politely thanked the staff. I caught Guy slipping a handful of £50 notes to the manager of the evening. "Please do let your staff know we appreciate their hard work," he said.

Tarquin was being loud, despite attempts at sobering him up. In fact, as soon as Miles left, all attempts at maintaining his standards were out the window. Guy and I took a shoulder each and half carried him upstairs.

"He gets a bit arsey when he has coke," Guy explained. "Never violent or anything, just an annoying little shit."

It was pouring with rain outside, and the gutters were overflowing. A night bus sped past, and if a line of taxis hadn't been between us and the road we'd have been soaked.

After spending a while getting everyone else sorted with taxis, Tarquin was slightly more stable than he had been. "I'm sorry I've been a dick all night. Millie gave me a line and said it would help me relax and talk to Miles," he said to me. He was looking at me with his puppy dog eyes.

"I'm sure you'll get a proper apology in the morning," Guy said. He opened the door to a black cab for us, rain flattening his flyaway hair to his face. "Take this one and I'll get the next. Quick, before Millie tries to get you to go on to a different bar."

"Guy, you're wonderful as always," I said sincerely.

"Yeah, I know." He stood at the door as I pushed Tarquin in and waited for a second before I followed him in. Guy gave me a smile as he stood in the rain. Did he wish he was getting in here with me instead? Did I wish he was getting in here with me? Or was he just pleased to be shot of the pair of us? "Thank you for this evening," I said awkwardly before I hopped in.

"Where to, boss?" the taxi driver asked.

Tarquin lay back on the seat and closed his eyes. "Why is the room spinning?"

"Fulham, please," I said.

"If he needs to be sick, let me know. I ain't gonna be best pleased if he gets it on my upholstery."

"Don't worry, he can hold it in." I patted him on the leg with a bit more force than was necessary. Tarquin seemed to pull himself together after that and held my hand as we drove through Westminster and then on into Chelsea before I attempted to navigate us through Fulham and to the end of the mews.

Tarquin got out of the taxi and left me to pay for it, which I was glad of, as him attempting to pay right now would surely have been a long process. He was already at the front door when I caught up with him, my jacket over my head as an umbrella. "Come on, in you get." I helped him through the doorway. He stood at the base of the stairs and swayed as I closed the door to make my way in.

He grabbed my jacket. "I'm a dickhead," he said, and drew me in for a cuddle. "Sorry, I wanted tonight to be nice, and I ruined it."

"You didn't ruin anything." He was being sweet, and my temper had cooled down again. I'd yell at him in the morning, but contrition deserved respect. "The party went well, I think?"

"Who knows?" Tarquin said, taking off his wet jacket and then unbuttoning his shirt, which all ended up on the floor. He undid his trousers and turned to me with a cheeky look on his face. He came towards me and fumbled with the fastenings on my trousers. "We should go upstairs and wake the neighbours," he whispered into my ear.

I laughed. "A nice thought, dear, but you are so plastered" – I bonked him on the nose with my finger – "that it would be a miracle if it were physically possible."

I pulled him up the stairs by his hand.

"What are you on about, Forrest? I'm a rampaging beast of a man. I can get it up any time, any place," he replied as I led him to bed.

“Uh-huh, sweetie. Of course you can. What man in his mid-thirties can’t after all that booze?”

“Pfft,” he said as he crawled under the sheets. “Age is just a number.” And he was out cold.

I lay in bed thinking about the evening, listening to his steady breathing, looking at the curves of his body under the sheet. I looked at my phone. It was just after 1am. Hardly a late one, but we were all older now, so it was a respectable time to pass out drunk. I snuggled up beside him, my less than perfect, but still pretty goddamn good, man, and wondered what Guy was up to. Had he gone back to his flat in Mayfair to stew? Was Ollie still awake, in the bed that he and I used to share south of the river, wondering if I’d call asking him to rescue me?

It was an odd thought to fall asleep on.

Chapter 40

I had never awoken to the sound of a thief before.

My eyes opened and in a split second I knew what was happening. I rolled over as silently as I could and oh so delicately picked up my phone. It told me it was 3:24am.

Outside, the rain was still falling, absorbing some of the sound of my movements.

We'd been asleep for a couple of hours. I put my hand up to Tarquin's mouth and gently patted his shoulder. He jerked awake. I gestured for him to be quiet. I leaned in as far as I could to his ear without making the bed creak.

"There's someone in the house."

I saw the whites of his eyes widen as I pulled back to my lying position. We both lay still for a few moments and heard the creak of floorboards and a muffled noise as the intruder moved from room to room.

"Stay here," he whispered.

"You're drunk. Don't go down. I'll ring the police."

"I'm not having someone break into my house. I've won every fight I've been in when I'm drunk, anyway."

He stood up as silently as he could. Clad in his boxers, he reached behind the bed and pulled out a piece of lead pipe I hadn't noticed before. "What the fuck, Tarquin?" I said as quietly as I could.

"I got this."

I was frozen in terror. Before I knew what had happened, he was out the bedroom door. My heart was in my throat, and I fumbled for my phone and dialled 999.

"Whoever you are, you should leave," I heard Tarquin say clearly.

And with that, everything went tits up.

"Hello, emergency—"

"There's an intruder in my house, police, please, number four, Eel Brook Mews, Fulham."

"Okay, sir—"

The sound of a thud and then a scream.

"Tarquin!" I yelled. I flew out of bed, dropping the phone, and ran out of the room. Downstairs, I heard more crashing and sounds of glass breaking.

I made it to the stairs and paused. I took a deep breath and then crept further in so I could see them, but I hoped they couldn't see me. "I've called the police! And it's Fulham. They'll actually turn up!" I yelled.

In the living room, I saw devastation that will haunt me for years. Two masked men held Tarquin. Both had him by an arm and were dragging him across the floor on his knees. His face was battered and bloodied. The two men saw me, looked at each other and then threw Tarquin to the floor. They made their way to the door. One looked me in the eye. He had a balaclava on, but I could see his eyes clearly in the light from the street. "We'll be back," he said.

His mate kicked open the door and legged it into the night.

A strange thought popped into my head in that split second. Had his voice been familiar?

I gulped in terror. My hands were shaking. I looked at Tarquin's slumped form, and instead of running towards him I went back and picked up the phone, where the operator was still talking. "Sir? Sir, are you there?"

"I need the police and an ambulance. Now."

I charged back on to the landing and downstairs to Tarquin, who was lying on the floor in a pool of his blood. "Oh my God, what have they done to you?" I cradled him. For a few terrifying moments I thought he was dead. His breathing began to steady, though, and he tried to speak.

"Don't be silly, just stay still."

We sat in complete silence. I didn't know what to do. My mind was racing, but my body was frozen. After a few minutes, which felt like hours, I could hear sirens, and police officers rushed in, shining torches in my face.

"Please, help him," I said.

The ambulance crews rushed in after them. "What's his name?" one asked.

"Tarquin Scott," I said. "I'm his boyfriend. He went down. There was a burglar. Well, burglars. Well, I dunno if they were burglars, but they broke in."

"Have you been drinking tonight, sir?" a police officer asked me. I nodded.

"We've been at a party. We only got home an hour or two ago."

They looked at each other. Tarquin was put on a stretcher. "He needs to be assessed, but he'll live," one said to me as they left.

"We'll take you to the hospital. We'll need a statement too," the officer said.

I went upstairs and got dressed. I found the clothes I'd been wearing that day and pulled them on. A bit too late I realised Tarquin had been taken to hospital in nothing but a pair of boxers. I grabbed his gym bag from the corner of the room and stuffed a pair of jeans, underwear, socks, shoes, a T-shirt, and a jacket in there. Downstairs, as the police watched, I took his wallet, keys, and phone out of his tuxedo jacket and packed them in there too.

"Let's go," I said.

Luckily, Tarquin lived less than a ten minute drive from Chelsea and Westminster Hospital. In the car ride, which seemed to take only seconds, the police officer who wasn't driving – they were both men and white, so it was difficult to tell them apart in my current state of mind – asked me where we'd been that night.

"Sounds like a posh do," he said when I told him. "My fella never takes me anywhere nice like that." Great, I'd found the only woke gay police officers in the Met.

"That's because he's a maths teacher in Wimbledon," replied the one driving.

At the hospital I tried to see Tarquin. "He's being assessed right now," a Polish nurse told the gay copper, and instead they sat me down in a family waiting room with Tarquin's bag between my feet.

For the third time in less than a month, I had my statement taken from the police. "You had been out at a party organised by your boyfriend for the launch of his company this evening?" non-gay PC Plod said after I gave a vague explanation.

"Yes." I focused on his name badge. PC Bradshaw. I looked at the gay one. PC Duncan. They were both younger than me, which was horrifying.

"And you and… Tarquin… have been an item for?"

"Not long. A month?" I guessed. It was all a bit hazy. Why had men broken into his house?

They looked at each other. "And you normally live in Dorset, is that correct?"

I nodded.

"I know it's horrible, Mr Forrest, but sadly it looks like your boyfriend simply got up for a piss at the wrong time and disturbed these burglars, who, unfortunately, were armed."

My guts churned at the lie. I had no idea if the idea forming in my mind was correct, but something wasn't right. Those weren't normal burglars who'd cased out a house in a rich neighbourhood.

So, yes, I said to the coppers in my best I'm-a-good-citizen voice, wasn't it a pity that it was exactly that scenario they mentioned that must've happened.

I was sobering up and getting a headache. I was getting no more sleep tonight, I thought. It was nearly 5am and the police still had more questions. "We'll need you to sign a statement for all of this soon. We'll let you go and see Mr Scott, and we'll be waiting outside for you," PC Duncan said. "Watch yourself, eh?"

I was left on my own.

Watch myself. Watch my back.

It hit me who had been in Tarquin's house.

Chapter 41

A nice Spanish nurse came to get me. "He's sleeping now. There's no internal damage or broken bones, but he's going to be very sore for the next few days. He'll need to stay in for observation."

We entered the ward, and I saw Tarquin on a bed, wearing a hospital gown, his face and body already coming up with the dark marks. His face seemed to be one big bruise, it was so covered with shades of red and purple.

He was out cold, and I looked at him, sleeping, and felt sick. I could feel bile in my throat.

I put the bag I'd put together for him on the chair in the cubicle. The Polish nurse was there with me, filling in some of the endless forms that came with hospital stays.

"When he wakes up can you tell him that… tell him that… Actually, don't tell him anything."

The Polish nurse looked confused.

Outside his room, I saw PCs Duncan and Bradshaw waiting at the end of the corridor. I went the other way. The moment I got to the front of the hospital I got in a taxi and returned to his house.

My car was exactly where I'd left it two days earlier. I should just get in and drive…

There was police tape over the broken lock on the front door, so I pulled it aside and went in. The flat was a mess. In daylight, the living room floor was covered in blood and broken glass. *Oh well, I'd better add to it for consistency.* There was a utility room at the back, and just as I thought, Tarquin was masc4masc enough to have a toolbox beside his washing machine. I grabbed a hammer from it and went upstairs to his office.

I don't know exactly how much noise I must have made, but it was probably a lot. It was quicker than I thought to break the lock on the filing cabinet and rip it open. Inside were papers and documents. I shoved a handful into my coat pocket. I tipped it up and looked at all its contents, none of which was what I was looking for.

I returned to the shelves. The claw of the hammer made a satisfying sound as I tried with all my might to rip off the lock. It took a lot longer than the filing cabinet, but after about twenty minutes of hacking away at it, I managed to break some of the wood. Just like I did that night in Arabella's house.

A bit of MDF came off in my hand and I managed to reach in and turn the lock, though it was a tight fit - my fingers came out bloodied and sore from it.

The locked cupboard swung open and inside was exactly what I was looking for.

I grabbed my things and piled them all into the boot of my car. I went back inside and upstairs to his office. The glass desk made a cacophony of noise as I brought the hammer down on it.

I made sure I had everything before I slammed the door on Tarquin's house and got into my car. In the rear-view mirror, a dishevelled, unshaven, greasy-haired oik was looking back at me. He had big circles under his eyes and wore an odd mishmash of clothes.

The guy shrugged at me, and I started the engine. It was rush hour as I left, but everyone was trying to go into

London. I drove through the city in a daze. My driving was probably dangerous, and I was lucky not to be killed, especially considering I was still drunk from the previous night. I was lost in thought and didn't even realise where I was until all of a sudden I appeared above the rooftops on the elevated motorway going through Chiswick and into Ealing.

The sun was out for once, and there were fluffy clouds. My route was relatively traffic-free, and I floored it, not really caring if a speeding ticket made its way to me in a week or two.

Once I got out of London the traffic thinned some more. The oppressive nature of the city seemed less evident, and I began to sob. The enormity of the past twelve hours was beginning to hit me. The sight of the men beating Tarquin, cradling his limp body, it was all going through my head. I knew I should stop but I couldn't. Instead, I turned the radio up full blast and hurtled down the motorway as fast as I could. I needed to put some miles between me and London.

It took nearly three hours to get home, but I made it in the end. It was early afternoon and the mild sunshine that had followed me from London had receded. Thick black clouds were rolling in with a harsh wind from the east that promised a kick.

The cats were still with Sonia, which was for the best because I was in no fit state to look after any living creature. I brought in everything from the car and put it all in my living room before going and taking the longest shower of my life. I don't know how long I was under the water for, but by the time I departed, I began to feel slightly human again. I went into my bedroom and crashed. My head and my heart were hurting too much to play games with insomnia. When I woke up it was dark. I looked around my room and found my phone (one per cent battery life and a series of messages from Verity asking if we were having dinner still, becoming increasingly frantic as the afternoon wore on), which told me it was 8pm. I'd slept the longest I had in months. I plugged my phone into charge and went downstairs to search for food.

All there was to eat was toast, but I was happy for it, and I ate slowly at my kitchen counter, thinking about all the shit that was about to roll down my way.

After food, I retired to the living room and looked through the haul of things I'd taken from Tarquin's office. Everything was exactly what it seemed to be. With the end near, I felt free. I put my feet up and watched TV. I must have dozed again because I woke up to an old movie playing on the screen. I retrieved my now fully charged phone and saw more messages from Verity.

I'm fine. Will talk soon and explain everything, I wrote back.

It was just after midnight. I took up my spot on the bottom of the stairs and waited.

When it came, it was sudden. I thought there would have been more warning. He must have turned off his headlights.

It was raining again, but nowhere near as heavily as last night. I had my shoes and a big coat on. I was ready.

Footsteps on the stones outside. A pounding on the door.

I opened it, which I don't think he was expecting. Tarquin had a gun pointed in my face from the second the door swung inwards.

I walked backwards towards the stairs as he entered. He was wearing the clothes I'd put in the bag for him. He slammed the door behind him. It was not quite the same as that first night we'd been together.

"You found it then," he said.

I pulled out Arabella's burner phone from my pocket, the one she'd messaged Tarquin on all those weeks ago asking him to meet her at the pond, the one that had all the texts on it detailing what she knew about his work for her father.

"She begged you to come with her to the police, to help her bring him down."

"She didn't know what she was doing."

"How much money did Miles give you? Was your business entirely funded by him or did he just make the odd payment for his lackey to keep you on the leash?"

Tarquin cocked the gun. "Be quiet, Arden, and give me the phone."

I handed it over. "I'm guessing Miles is onto you as well. That's why he sent his goons around last night. He'd finally clicked and wanted to know if what I was saying was true."

"Yes, and now you can die being the cleverest guy in the room. Bully for you." He motioned towards the door with the gun.

I felt it press into the small of my back when we got outside. "If you'd just shut up, we could've been really good together. If you'd just let that stupid cook take the fall for it like everyone else was happy to do, we could have lived happily ever after," Tarquin whispered.

He motioned to my car. "Get in the driver's side."

He slipped the gun in his waistband and went over to his car. The Porsche, still looking like a tiny-dick replacement vehicle. Thank God I'd never have to ride in that thing ever again.

He opened the passenger door and pulled something out. *A package? No, wait.* "Oh my God, who is that?"

"Shut up and pop the boot," he said. I had no choice. There was a massive thump as whoever the person wrapped in the blanket was hit the boot of my car with a thud. He slammed the lid shut and got in. The gun was pointed at my face again,

"Drive," he said in a monotone voice. I was going to ask more, but he barked at me to shut up. "I'll direct you.

Away from the village, hang a right after we get to Parkinson's farm at the woods."

Hands shaking, I did as I was instructed.

"Who have you told?" he said when we were on the road.

"N-no one," I stammered.

"Don't lie to me, Arden," he said, now in a sing-songy voice. "I know when you're lying."

"I swear."

We proceeded in silence. "Who's in the boot?" I asked.

He shook his head. "Someone else who couldn't keep their fucking nose out of my business." He scoffed. "Do you know how hard I've worked? For ten fucking years I have built my own company, smarmed and smiled my way in because no one would give me a hand up. We lost everything in the financial crash, and no one would ever help. Guy would barely return my phone calls for months until I told him that I'd started my own business, and it was doing well."

"Miles gave you a lifeline?"

He laughed. "It was easy money, sign a few things, take a few hits now and again. He sent me out to Dubai and Beirut to do his dirty work occasionally and paid me. Always promising I'd get my reward, and just as he was coming through, just as he was about to pay me back for my loyal service, stupid fucking Arabella finally decided to investigate her own dad because she wants her inheritance, because she wants to fly off travelling with her roid-rage Polish boyfriend and fuck on a beach in Goa. 'Oh, Tarquin, what has my dad been up to?', 'Tarquin, why is your name on this statement?', 'Oh, Tarquin, help me or I'm going to the police!' I mean, Jesus-fucking-Christ, the girl was a moron."

"You killed her? For that?" If I swerved into one of the stone fences on the side of the lane, maybe I'd distract him, I was wearing a seatbelt, and he wasn't.

"I never meant to kill her, just to scare her. But she was an idiot, pulling at my arm, begging me to help her because her dad was evil, all those things he'd done to her mum. Yeah, everyone knows Miles is a piece of shit, but guess what, life's not fair, and he owed me, and if she took him down, I was going down as well."

"Sweetly Made Homes?" I asked.

He laughed. "All a crock of shit. Not one of them will ever be built. That money is sitting in the Caymans for that fat fuck to go get at his leisure. He'll write the whole thing off as a loss and make millions from it."

He tapped the windscreen. "Left here."

I slowed and pulled onto a track on the side of the road. It was too dark to see much. "What is this place?" Trees whizzed by as I drove, but I'd not been here before.

"This is Honningtons Wood. Yes, really. Guy even has his own fucking forest." Tarquin laughed. "God, that guy, huh?"

He pointed again. "There's a clearing up there, drive to it."

As I carried on driving, the potholed ground made the car jolt and woke whoever was in my boot. A muffled scream sounded, followed by banging.

"Shut up!" Tarquin yelled. The trees eventually stopped, and we made it to a clearing. There was a lot of moonlight, and I was able to see we were atop a small hill, with a clearance about forty or so metres across between these trees and the next part of the woods. The track then carried on through them.

"Stop here."

I parked up and tried to control my heartbeat.

"What are you going to do?"

Tarquin shrugged and then got out of the car. "It's obvious, isn't it? I'm going to kill you. And her." He pointed at the boot. "This is all part of your sick plan after you murdered Arabella, you deviant bastard. Come on now, up we get." Funnily enough, that was the same reasoning I'd had this afternoon that stopped me from calling Neuberger.

My legs were shaking as I got out of the car and walked towards him. "Closer, please."

I edged a bit nearer to him. His handsome face was still black and blue, and his lip was split. In this moment he was the ugliest thing I'd ever seen. He sighed dramatically. "Sorry about this. It's been fun shagging the past few weeks – no, really, I'm not just saying it – some of the best sex of my life, but you killed Arabella. And now you've come up here to burn yourself alive in your car after someone worked out your horrible secret."

Oh, God, this was actually happening. My knees were like jelly. I thought I was going to be sick. This all had to be a bizarre joke, even with everything I saw in his flat this morning, even with the phone and all the messages on it that I'd read while sitting on the floor in his office, I was hoping and praying this was all a dream. It couldn't be real.

He jabbed the gun into my ribs, and then kissed me. "Come on, just a little one. You've put your mouth everywhere else on me."

Feeling like I was about to be sick, I gave him a kiss. "Good lad," he said and started to smile.

I pulled the knife from my pocket and stabbed him.

It'd been in my jacket all evening and I was sure I wouldn't know when to use it, but this seemed as good a time as any. Except I missed. I'd been aiming for his stomach or side, something guaranteed to see him on the floor, but instead I misjudged the angle and got him on the outside of his thigh.

"Aaargh," he screamed and backhanded me with his gun-holding fist. I reeled and fell against the car, seeing stars. Blood spurted out of his leg, and I'd hoped even if

I'd missed an internal organ that I'd at least hit an artery or something.

I knocked him to the ground and kicked him in the wound. He fumbled for his gun but was hesitant to shoot – it couldn't be suicide if I'd been shot – and I kicked his hand. I jumped on top of him and punched him as hard as I could four or five times, hearing a bone crack under my hand. "You murderous cunt!"

That's where I made my second mistake. In the confusion, he dropped his gun, which I needed, and as he lay on the ground wheezing for breath, I stumbled around for it. "Where is it?" I yelled, dragging him up. I didn't have time. I kneed him as hard as I could and ran around to the boot of the car. The switch – mercifully – worked for once, and I opened the lid. Inside, the person wrapped in the blanket was screaming, and I pulled it down to expose their face.

Eleanor screamed again and spat in my face. "Ellie, Ellie, I'm not with him. Come on, we haven't got much time."

I dragged her still shrieking from the boot and dropped her on the ground. The knife was still in Tarquin's leg (that had probably been mistake number two, to be honest) but the bit of rope he'd bound her with was easy enough to pull off, and she spilled out of her binds. "Come on, run!" I yelled and took her hand. But she'd been bound up for hours and her legs were barely working. We'd only covered ten metres before she fell, and I had to half carry/half drag her. "Come on, Ellie."

Suddenly, the world went black.

I woke, probably a few seconds later, to see Ellie running off into the distance. My head was banging, and I could feel blood pouring from my forehead. I turned, which was insanely painful, and saw Tarquin standing over me clutching the tyre iron from the boot of my car. He dropped it on the ground, by my feet. "She won't get far," he said. Then he dragged me by my arm back to the car, limping only slightly. Every step must've been agony, as the knife was still in his leg. Dizzily, I tried to reach out and grab it, to twist it or pull it out so he might stop.

He opened the door and picked me up and deposited me in the seat. "You're going to die in this car if it's the last fucking thing I do."

He climbed around to the other side, but not before reclaiming his gun. What could I do? I had about two seconds before he came back in. We were parked on the slope. I looked down. Just as he opened the door, I did the only thing I could think of. He looked at me oddly as he sat in the passenger seat. "You're going to sit there nicely." He grabbed my hand in his. "Right, now if we angle it like this, then it'll look like you shot yourself, see? What's happening, why are we moving?" He appeared confused.

I jerked my head in front of his hand, so the gun was to the side of my head, and let instinct take over. With one hand I turned the ignition and floored it, with the other I bit down on Tarquin's wrist as hard as I could. Not glamorous, and not really effective, but it was all I had. The car surged forward, and we gained momentum. I bit down again as we started to go down the hill. At the bottom of it was a stone wall, a metre high, and at least half a metre in depth, and sure to create a bump in my shitty old car.

The gun was directly behind my head when it went off, and the sound nearly deafened me, as did the shattering of the window behind it as the bullet sailed out into the night. Tarquin looked at the view in front of him, his arm waving around as he hit me in the face again to make me stop. I'd expected that, reeled back, and grabbed my seatbelt.

"You little bastar—" But before he could finish, the car smacked into the wall with an almighty thump. His head made a cracking sound as it hit the windscreen.

I felt like my soul was trying to leave my body as I jolted forward. The seatbelt, however, gamely did its job, and I managed to avoid hitting the windscreen or crushing my chest on the steering wheel. I was stunned. I must've sat there for twenty or thirty seconds, probably longer. Actually, quite a lot longer. Between the near deafness from the gunshot, and the sensation that my sternum had just cracked, I was not feeling my best.

Eventually, the world came slowly back into focus. I undid the belt and fumbled for Tarquin's gun. He was alive, but unconscious; his forehead was a mess of blood and glass. "Good, I hope you're ugly for your murder trial."

I opened the door and fell out of my smoking wreck of a car. Ahead of me was the hill, which looked a lot fucking bigger from this side than it did going down. I staggered up it, weaving this way and that. My head was pounding, and my chest was on fire. The ringing in my ears was stubbornly refusing to subside.

It took me ages to reach the top of the hill, and when I did, I began to call out Ellie's name, softly at first, in case I woke Tarquin, but before long I was yelling at the top of my lungs. She was nowhere. "Ellie, Ellie, where are you? It's safe. He's in the car at the bottom of the hill. I promise, whatever he told you, I had nothing to do with Arabella's murder. This was all him. I promise."

I staggered on for a few more steps and then sank onto the ground, on all fours, and took huge shuddering breaths. The forest was pitch-black, I was covered in my own and Tarquin's blood, and what little I could see in the darkness was spinning. I heard rustling up ahead. "Ellie? Is that you?"

"Arden?" a voice called out.

"We have to get out of here and call the police… Ellie?"

There was no noise.

"Ellie, where are you, we have to go! He could wake up and… and…" There was a figure coming towards me. But it was too tall to be Ellie. "Tarquin?" I asked in a daze.

"Put the gun down, Arden," said a Scottish accent.

"Do what he says," said a posh male voice.

I got to my feet, which took, I'm not even going to pretend, a short amount of time. "Tarquin… he's at the bottom of the hill. In my car. He's knocked out. I have his gun."

"Yes, we know, Arden. Why don't you give me the gun?" said Simon.

Then a scream rang out.

"Yes, why don't you throw the gun away," said Tarquin from behind me. I spun around – ooh, such a bad idea. It took several seconds for the world to come into focus again and I stumbled to catch myself before ending up face down in the mud. He was holding Ellie by the throat, the knife now out of his leg and in his hand, up against her face.

"Or better yet, if you give the gun to me, I'll let Eleanor go. How about that? Do we have a deal, lover?"

"Arden—" Guy started.

"SHUT UP, GUY, YOU FUCKING PRICK!" Tarquin screamed. "You're always fucking talking! You never, for one minute, shut the fuck up. Ever since we were eighteen, I've had to listen to you bleat on about stock markets, and your inheritance, and boys who didn't love you because they were always in love with me, and your stupid dead fucking parents. For once in your bloody life, keep fucking quiet and let the adults talk, okay?"

For a long time after his outburst none of us said anything. Just the sound of my own ragged breathing filled my ears.

"Arden, don't give him the gun," Simon said.

"And you can shut it and all, you ginger cunt," was Tarquin's response to that – his accent suddenly switching to common.

"Shoot him, Arden!" was Ellie's input.

"He hasn't got the balls, has he," Tarquin said, smirking, dragging Ellie around as he smiled gleefully. "He's like all Poles, lazy and workshy. No cojones this one—"

"Arden, do it!"

"Don't, Arden!"

"He doesn't even know how!"

I pulled the trigger and fired. Tarquin screamed in pain as his kneecap shattered. Ellie screamed and sprang forward as he released his grip on her.

I dropped the gun onto the ground.

"Guy, call the police!" Simon yelled. He came up behind me and gingerly took the gun from the ground beside me. "Where did you learn to fire a gun… and with that accuracy?" he asked.

I ignored the question, and instead collapsed onto my knees. Tarquin was about ten metres in front of me in the foetal position, intermittently shrieking in pain and screaming every swear word he'd ever learned, his hands clutching his bloody knee.

Ellie was sobbing into Guy's arms. That's when an old farm truck arrived with John and Rita Parkinson. "We heard gunshots, what's happening? Oh my God!" Rita yelled.

A few minutes later, I heard sirens. All of a sudden there were a lot of people, and the forest was lit up like New Year's Eve.

I had a blanket put around me. A kindly paramedic came and gently escorted me to the ambulance.

As I sat there Neuberger and Wales turned up.

"Mr Forrest, you'll need to come to the station and make a full statement. And we really do mean a *full* statement," Wales said.

"I caught your fucking killer for you." They both stared at me. I was feeling belligerent. "You're welcome."

"We'll meet you at the hospital," was all I got in response.

Guy's face appeared at the door. He clambered up and embraced me. After a few seconds he let me go and sat in front of me, holding my hand.

"But how did you find me?" I asked.

"I got a phone call this morning saying Tarquin's house had been broken into and he was in hospital. I rushed over there and saw what had happened. One of his neighbours said he'd already been and gone. I knew something was up. Then I got a phone call from Ellie's mum telling me she hadn't heard from her since yesterday afternoon. Ellie says she went to his house to confront him and saw him standing in his office, which had been ransacked, and he flew into a rage. The next thing she knew she was in the boot of a car. She was Arabella's best friend. All this time she'd known a bit about what he'd been up to. Arabella had given her some of the story of his dealings, but not all. She knew he'd done something, but didn't know what, or how she could prove any of it.

"That's why she was at the party last night?"

"Exactly. Then I spent hours in London looking for him. Eventually I decided to come back to Lilbury. I couldn't sleep not knowing, so I went to Nigella's house and told her what had happened. She said Simon's good in a crisis, so she rang him and explained. The first thing he asked was where were you. We said we had no idea, and he said he'd go up and try and find you. I met him at your house. Your car was gone, but Tarquin's Porsche was there. We set off to find you both, thinking, well, God only knows what. That's when we heard the gunshot."

"And you came running to save me?" I asked.

He looked away. "Eleanor, mostly. We weren't sure what your deal was, but it's an added bonus, put it that way."

I wasn't going to be the hero of this story, was I?

"We're ready to get off," the paramedic said, the same spotty twink who'd helped the day Eleanor had been thrown from her horse. "Are you coming to the hospital?" he asked Guy, and seemed as disappointed as I was when, after giving me a long look, he said no.

"I'd best take my leave. My aunt needs to know what's happened."

The doors swung shut, but just before we left, I caught a glimpse of Simon. He was staring at me with cold fury. How had I learned to shoot like that, he was asking himself. Well, that's a story for another day.

Chapter 42

I spent the entire following day being questioned by Neuberger and Wales. They wanted to know every facet of my relationship with Tarquin. Every detail of our twenty-four hours together leading up to the shooting. The break-in, the party, my covert investigations into Miles Sweet and his dodgy business doings. They wanted to know what I knew about his business, what I knew about his family, how did I know where the phone would be?

It was about 6pm the following day when I was free to go. I hadn't slept. I hadn't showered. They were still convinced I was lying to them. Well, I was. They would never know about the break-in.

I'd barely taken a step outside when I was bombarded with reporters and cameras in my face, all of them demanding a question, screaming at me – answers, answers, we want answers.

A small Black woman swatted them out of the way. Verity was wearing her big sunglasses and had her most expensive Prada handbag on her arm, which meant she was in business mode. "Mr Forrest is not taking any questions at the moment, so do one, you pack of hyenas," she scolded, and dragged me to her car.

Before they would give chase, we were off in a cloud of dust. "I've been in that village of yours all day. I went to your house. Active crime scene, they told me. I said a few pairs of pants and a jumper aren't a crime scene, are they? Well, you're an unmarried man so maybe your pants are. I got them to let me in to get you a bag. It's probably for the best they still have your phone."

We sailed up into the country. Before I knew what was happening, we were going over the Second Severn Crossing. "Where are we going?" I asked.

"Shh, let Mamma Jones fix everything. Never should have let you move to the countryside in the first place – full of white people, and that's never a good thing."

"Can I use your phone?" I asked. She handed it over, looking dubious.

I logged into Facebook and tracked down Sonia – not like I remembered anyone's numbers. Can you keep the kittens for a while longer? I messaged.

She replied nearly instantly. Course. I'm so sorry about what's happened. I'll look after them as long as you need.

We made it to Tenby late in the evening.

A few years ago, Verity and Gravz had bought this place. Verity's mum and dad used to bring her and her siblings here as kids and everyone would stare at the Black family. Upon marrying a one per cent banker, the first thing she did was buy a holiday home in the most prime real estate the town had and redecorated it in pan-African colours and Caribbean themes until the whole place looked somewhere between a tacky tourist resort in Bridgetown mixed with the ANC headquarters.

I took the room at the back and slept.

Verity made me meals and talked through everything. I took long showers and walks on the beach. The cut on my head from the tyre iron was actually worse than it looked, and on the second day I had dizzy spells, prompting an all-day trip to the local A&E. A tough Welsh nurse accused the doctors who'd looked at it at the scene of being nothing better than butchers, and I was sent home with strict instructions to stay very still for a week or two. And I did. Verity's phone rang off the hook. Interview requests, enquiries, other work instead of me, but she was patient and calm (reader: she was not) and hid me from it. After a week like that, I dared to switch on the news. No word about the gay sex author West Country murder romp.

The next day I ventured down to the shop and looked at the papers. Tarquin was in a few, but I wasn't mentioned.

I had the gratifying sight of Miles Sweet in handcuffs instead.

"I think we can go back tomorrow," I said over dinner (plantain and jollof rice to piss off the neighbours). Verity looked unsure but nodded.

The next day we set off. On the way through I stopped and bought a new phone at a retail park outside of Bristol.

When we got to Lilbury, Tarquin's Porsche was gone, but the Parkinsons ancient Land Rover was sitting outside. *Thought you might need this until you can find a new car! R+Jx* read the note on the windscreen.

"That's sweet," Verity said.

"People in the countryside aren't all bad."

"I wouldn't go that far."

She helped me get the place in order after the police had searched it for evidence (or sheer spite). My laptop was waiting for me.

I stood on the doorstep and waved as she made to leave. I'd promised to call if anything went awry.

"I'll be fine," I assured her.

"Lies." She kissed her teeth before driving off in the enormous SUV she only drove once a month.

I messaged Sonia saying I'd get the kittens tomorrow. There was another instant response.

In my emails, there was a message from Ollie. *I'm so glad you're okay.*

I burst into tears. He really was a good man. He wasn't my soulmate, but he was my friend, and I wanted him in my life. I knew that now. You can love people with all your heart and not feel an ounce of romance towards them, even when you once did. And that's okay. That's what we would be.

I sent him a reply, saying I was glad of his friendship. If he chose to take it, it was there for him.

I looked around my half-finished kitchen.

"Right, better finish that book so I can pay to have this done."

So off to work I went.

Acknowledgements

Thank you to everyone who helped me to do this and listened to me for all those years go on about it. Every eye roll at my lack of progress was another kick up the arse to get it done. It took eight years, so maybe the next one will be a smidge quicker.

Thank you to Matthew R for being my first victim to read through the draft and complaining about my lack of understanding of semi-colons. I still think English grammar is taught differently in Canadian schools.

Thank you to Shayna C for the positive feedback/harsh criticisms/corrections in person and over various messenger apps over the many long years we've known each other and for reading previous manuscripts that will never leave the depths of my hard drive.

Thank you to Richard Sheehan for his excellent copyediting. All subsequent typos, timeline jumps, character mistakes, and general idiocy are mine and mine alone.

Thank you to Andy H for refusing to read it but giving feedback on what makes a good murder mystery. As well as offering the services of various people to help me including lovely Fleur and her draft cover designs.

Thank you to all my friends, family, colleagues, and random people at parties for your encouragement.

Last of all, thank you to my husband Alasdair for all of the above and more.

About the author

James Quentin is a self-published author.

He works as a journalist during the day and has a degree in English Literature.

Away from the world of work, he lives in London with his husband and an extremely needy cat that has multiple expensive health issues.

Published by Over It Publishing.

eBook ISBN: 978-1-0683290-1-2

Paperback ISBN: 978-1-0683290-0-5

Printed in Dunstable, United Kingdom

80345272R00231